REsolve

Book Two of the "Rain Experience" Series

Thomas W. Everson

This is a work of fiction which takes place on another world. Names, characters, businesses, places, events, and incidents are the products of the author's imagination or used in a fictitious manner. Any resemblance to real persons, living or dead, is purely coincidental.

ISBN-13: 978-0-9864120-5-9

DEDICATION

My wife and my son have been and always will be my greatest inspiration to keep going and fighting no matter the challenge. Brandi and Bubby, you hold the key my heart.

CONTENTS

ACKNOWLEDGMENTS

I've received a lot of support from encouraging readers and helpful authors in my journey so far. The list of people who have been great resources is too long to list, but you know who you are.

Special thanks goes to my artist, Jake Murray, for constantly exceeding my expectations in developing covers that astound.

My editor, Dean Fetzer, has also done an amazing job in editing my book. Like the first, he did what a good editor would do and went above and beyond.

Thank you all!

1 ISOLATION

Though the light emanating from whatever lies beyond our border is giving me a headache, I bring Eve to the edge of the property. Out into the vast, white nothingness, there is no horizon. There's no line of land other than the one which surrounds the house in a circle where the time vortex steals us away every month.

This is what the princess meant about my future being bleak?! Nothingness exists, and somehow we've found our way into it, but how? And why?

My attention is drawn away as I hear the horses neighing and thrashing about. A rope snaps. Still having to squint, I think I see one of the horses has broken free. Practically throwing Eve into Ami, I bolt toward the horse to catch it before it steps out into the white void. I am too late. I stop short of following it, right on our border, and watch. I expect it to fall at some point out in the white mass; I am surprised when it gallops out onto something solid, and doesn't collide with anything. The horse weaves about frantically, putting it far beyond our range.

Unwilling to follow, I watch and behold a strange sight: the farther it runs the slower it gets, but it is clearly still in full gallop with all four of its hooves off the ground.

Ami, Eve, and Agatha join me, but I can't tear my eyes away from the slow motion horse. Agatha soothes the other horse with soft whispers, but even she can't take her eyes off the escapee.

"How…?" I start a question, but fail to finish.

"This…this has never happened before," Agatha says quietly. Yet because of the deafening silence creeping around us, I hear her as clear as if she were yelling.

"This is impossible!" Eve can't contain herself. "First, you take me unwillingly from my people, and now you've trapped us all in some nowhere land!"

"Eve, shut up." Ami is quick to put her in her place.

The horse gets farther away, becoming just a blur and stretching farther and farther out. The image of it becomes elongated. I shake my head in disbelief, unable to find any words to accurately express my emotion.

"At least we know it's solid out there." It's the best I can come up with.

"It appears to be a time anomaly, slowing things down." Ami has noticed it too.

I point as if they weren't already watching. "Yes, but look."

The front end of the horse's elongated blur seems to have trailed over an invisible horizon, and slowly the tail begins to disappear. After what could be any length of time just standing here, any sign the horse existed at all completely dissipates. It's gone, and when there is no sign of it coming back, I feel I can finally break my stare from the white. Turning to my companions, I see the same shock and awe on their faces that I feel.

"We should go inside. Do we have any medication for headaches?" I close my eyes, and reach my arm out to steady myself against Ami.

"Don't worry, just hang onto me." Ami grabs my hand, comforting me.

"I can just carry you, Rain." Eve protests, likely out of rivalry rather than really wanting to lead me.

"Too bad, he reached for me," Ami sneers.

"Girls, not now please," I plead, my head throbbing.

"Mother, are you okay to find your way?" Ami looks over, concerned as Agatha continues to stare off in the distance.

Her mood shifts to sullen. "I'll be fine."

With my eyes shut, I am led to the house. Eve grabs my other hand despite Ami's snarky response, and proceeds to tug at me. At this point in time I don't care. I just want to get inside and rest a little.

Between the light and my physical exhaustion, I need to sit for a while.

Ami stops to open the back door, and leads me in. Eve is forced to relinquish my hand to follow, and Agatha trails behind. The door shuts. I slowly open my eyes. The white light is beaming in through the kitchen window, illuminating every nook and cranny. But the discomfort is manageable. While I sit at the table, Ami shuts the shades, allowing my eyes to relax.

Eve slouches in the chair next to me, while Ami gets into the pantry. She retrieves a small white bottle and makes her way back to me. From it she shakes out two pills and puts them on the table in front of me. I manage a weak smile, but she doesn't notice because she's already getting me a glass of water, and then comes back. I take the pills, one at a time, guzzling the water afterward.

"Any theories on where we are?" I close my eyes and hope the headache will subside.

"None. This place is impossible," Ami answers. "Light without a source, ground without ground. And I can't begin to comprehend what we saw happen with the horse."

"I have a confession," Evalyn's voice comes from Agatha. Peeking, I see her at the window, glued to the nothingness.

"Evalyn, you've been quiet since we got back. What is it?" I reply.

"I attempted something with my power as the vortex commenced. This appears to be the result," she states plainly.

"What were you thinking?!" My eyes snap open, my back rigid. "I thought you said you would kill Agatha if you attempted anything in her body."

"I wasn't *in* her body!" she retorts. "I was in my room! And I was doing it to break the power in place, so we might have peace at last!"

"Why would you attempt it without telling us?" Ami is calm, but her tone indicates she's upset.

"I thought I was doing what was best for everyone." Shame shows on Evalyn's face.

Back in a relaxed position, I sigh, and shake my head. "Can you undo it? Or is this something new we're going to have to deal with?"

"It should have worked. I just conjured my latent power to cancel it, but I guess I don't have enough energy in my spirit form. Since we shifted here, I can only assume in about a month we'll be shifted out, like normal."

"I hope so. We won't last if the vortex doesn't come," Ami states.

Eve sits with her arms crossed and head down. She is unnervingly quiet. As it's unlike her to not get upset, even at the little things, I prod her.

"Why are you being so quiet?"

"I'm..." she hesitates, shakes her head, and then continues. "I'm not sure how to convey my dissatisfaction, that's all. If Evalyn weren't a spirit I'd strangle her," Eve says with a frightful seriousness. Evalyn isn't amused.

"So, what do we do until the month passes?" I lean forward, and rest my elbows on the table.

"Stay busy. Tend the garden, if it will do any good. Rebuild your stable," Agatha regains her voice in this conversation.

My headache worsens, becoming unbearable. Tears form and blind me. The medicine isn't working fast enough, and this chair isn't as comfortable as I'd like right now.

Maybe if I go lie down.

Standing, I wobble and head for the kitchen door. Ami gets up to help me, but I hold out my hand to indicate I can handle myself. In my room I shut the shades, collapse face down on my bed, and focus on not letting the headache get the best of me.

~~~~~~

Rustling in the room directly next to mine causes me to wake. Groggy, it feels like I may have been asleep for days, if a day could be tracked in this timeless void. Though my headache is gone, and the silence around our plot of land is nice, I'm quite annoyed at being awoken by the rather loud shifting and rummaging.

A light-headed feeling rushes over me when I push myself up to go see what all the noise is about. It forces me to sit on the edge of my bed until it passes before continuing, or risk falling over. I stand and open the door. It swings hard, and unintentionally hits the wall, creating a bang. Under normal circumstances I would have winced, but I'm already at the door next to mine knocking. Eve's voice comes from within.

"What do you want?" She too sounds annoyed.

"What are you doing in there?" I ask, frustrated.

The door swings open, and Eve stands there sweaty and scantily clad in a ripped white t-shirt, and cutoff denim shorts.

"They're forcing me to clean this room in order to make it my own, but now you're awake I can focus on more important things!" She grabs my hand and pulls me into the room, slamming the door behind us.

Pressing me up against the wall with her brute strength, she leans in close. I can feel her breath on my neck. She snickers while I struggle to pull away. Her grip on my arms is tight, and with my back against the wall, I have little leverage to maneuver away.

"You're just a mixed bag of emotions, aren't you?"

"I am." She attempts to kiss my neck, but I block her by tilting my head against my shoulder. "But what I'm pulling from the bag right now is passion."

"I don't think you can make up your mind about me."

Her grip relaxes, and I manage to push her away.

"You simply can't control yourself, can you?" I ask.

"We've had some problems. I was too harsh with you, but it's nothing we can't work out." Her hand caresses my arm, and she advances, seduction in her eyes.

I raise my hand between us, but she repurposes it. She grabs it, and presses my palm to her chest: her heart is thumping heavily. Her cheeks turn rosy. Closing her eyes, and stepping in closer, she tries to make her move. I pull my hand away, and turn to leave. She feels the retreat, and slams her palm against the door to hold it shut, leaving my only option to get by as going through her.

"Why won't you give us a chance?" Her green eyes glimmer, hopeful for a positive response.

"Do you really want that answer, Eve?"

"Is it really Ami? Does she really hold your heart as you two pretended when we first met?"

"It's complicated. I feel a very strong connection to her..." I look away, embarrassed to be talking about it.

"But?" she prompts.

"I just don't think it's a good idea to pursue anything right now.

We're living a complicated life. If we had a relationship, and it turned sour, we'd still be stuck with each other. It would just cause an awkward situation." I shrug and sigh.

"What about a physical relationship? It would just be between us." She bites her lower lip, and runs a finger down my chest, her eyes following her tracing.

"Eve, I'm done with this conversation," I huff exasperatedly, and twist the knob to show I'm leaving.

She lets me go, but I know it won't be long before she is trying to bed me again. The floorboards creak on the stairs while taking them slowly. I reflect on her, and the current predicament.

Though she is physically attractive, her brash personality is off-putting. However, if I had been born in her era, and was a part of her clan, no doubt I would have given into her desires by now.

Despite our precarious situation, and not knowing if we're going to live past this month, I might not have been wrong to say it's not a good idea to pursue anything right now.

The white light pours in from underneath and through the cracks of the closed curtains in the living room. Though it's mostly blocked, it seems to find a way to illuminate in ways the sun normally doesn't. It makes things appear as if they're losing their color, dulling. I peek out through the division in the curtains and see the same as I had before: there's nothing but white beyond our yard. An idea forms in my head and I grow curious about beyond the border.

If it's solid, it must have mass. If it has mass, perhaps I can chip it and examine the fragment.

The idea takes root, and before I can second-guess myself I'm outside at the wrecked stable. Of all the tools available, a wood axe seems the best tool for the job. With the wooden handle gripped firmly in my hand, I walk to where the grass meets the white ground. Though the horse galloped onto whatever's out there, I'm still cautious. Extending my leg slowly beyond the green, I tap my foot down gently to test it. It feels solid underneath my shoe. Shifting my weight against the white mass, there is no give. But the moment I fully step out, Ami cries out in protest.

"Rain! What are you doing?"

"Don't worry." I smile warmly over my shoulder. "I'm not going far. I just want to know more about it."

She rushes over, long yellow skirt flowing, but she stays on the grass while I bend down and touch the white. It's strangely warm, as if heated from something underneath, and completely smooth. While on my knees I raise the axe up and heave it down. Upon impact my arm shudders in pain as the sudden stop sends reverberations through the handle. Groaning in pain, I grab my wrist, but even in my distracted state two things are not lost on me. The first, no sound was emitted when the metal axe connected. The second is that there isn't a scratch on the white ground. Looking at the axe, the immovable ground has left a dull spot where I struck.

"Strange." Ami's voice seems to ring in my ear.

"Indeed."

I look up to the white above us as well.

Is that really a sky, or perhaps just a ceiling? If it's a ceiling, how far up is it to the top?

"Stand back." I wave my hand so she'll move away.

She does, and I swing my arm back and forth, gauging the weight and trying to get an optimal upward throw. As it gains momentum, I time my release and let it fly upward. Not wanting to be hit when it falls, I run to the grass. By the time I turn around, it is already back on the "ground", making no sound at all.

"Did it hit something?" I furrow my brows.

"No, it went up and came back down."

"I'm going to try something else." I shake my head, perplexed.

Returning to the white ground, I pick up the axe and throw it skyward again, except this time aiming a hand, and unleashing a shockwave to carry it away. The shockwave connects, splintering the wooden handle. The head of the axe shoots upward at an angle away from me. I watch it fail to connect with anything above us. The farther it gets, the slower it falls to the ground. My eyes meet Ami's, and she shakes her head because she knows what I'm going to do next.

"Rain, don't! We don't know what will happen!" She rushes to the edge of the void's boundary to try and grab me.

"I'm just going to retrieve it." I shrug and grin.

"Just chalk it up as lost, and come back in here." She's panicked.

"The time distortion can't be *that* great." I look back to the axe head and point. "See, it's almost at the ground now."

She huffs and crosses her arms, pleading with worried eyes for me not to go. But my curiosity has taken control. Walking backwards allows me to keep an eye on the house, on Ami, and so I might figure out just what it looks like to be out of sync with normal time.

Several feet away I begin to notice subtle differences. Ami paces at what appears to be a brisk walk, and the horse shakes its mane like it's riddled with flies. Moving another dozen feet away, the distortion becomes greater, and Ami appears to be urgently motioning for me to return, her arms flailing. I ignore her request, and continue walking backwards.

At least a hundred yards from the border of our house, the time distortion grows so everything blurs, moving almost too quickly for my eyes to track properly. Eve speed walks out, and a half second later Agatha follows. They all wave, jump around, and appear to be yelling at me. I can't hear them, deafened by the barrier between us. They blur more, nearly creating a visual similar to the horse when it ran off, except their figures intertwine, and catch up at a much faster rate.

Such a strange sight to behold.

They, and the blurring effect, disappear completely as I reach the axe head. It frightens me. My heart thumps in my chest as I grab the tool, and begin running back. On the way back they reappear occasionally when they stop moving. Closer, I see all of the previous effects in reverse. Time begins to slow back down within the confines of the house's perimeter. Their blurs begin moving toward me, in the white, and the three bodies become normal again.

Before we reach each other, I am hit with a wave of sound. It's garbled. First is Ami's voice, then the others. The sound produced within the green border catches up to me, and I have to plug my ears when it turns to a loud chatter. The sound effect dissipates. Removing my fingers, they reach me and I can hear normally. We're synced in the same time stream again.

"Rain! Are you okay?" Ami asks.

"I'm fine. Why?"

"You've been out here for a long time. Enough to miss two meals." Agatha replies with worry.

"When you had stopped at the axe we feared you were stuck. We decided to come out and get you!" Ami's gentle arms wrap around me.

"Hey!" Eve tries to wrench Ami from me, but she's pushed off.

"That would explain everything I saw. I must have slowed down. But I'm unharmed; let's head back before we lose any more time," I suggest.

We return to the house in what feels like just a few minutes of walking. Because they say I appeared stuck in time for a prolonged period, I wonder how much time actually passed just moving back.

Agatha pulls the kitchen door open. I smell fresh baked bread. Hungry, my stomach gurgles. I grab some butter from the refrigerator.

"This *was* warm when we left," Agatha states while cutting it, and hands me a slice. "I had just pulled it out."

"My stomach doesn't discriminate." I smile at her, and spread butter all over it.

"We better not be stuck here." Eve grumbles under her breath, but her mood lightens when our eyes meet. "I suppose if it's with Rain, at least I have someone to cuddle up to at night."

"Not on your life," Ami protests. She glares while spreading peanut butter on a slice of bread.

Peanut butter seems like a good idea.

I grab a second slice and create a peanut butter and butter half-sandwich. I sit at the table, devouring it as if I'd been starved for days. The three women sit as well, and silence ensues for a few moments. My mind is filled with questions, but I anticipate I won't receive any answers.

Time is a strange thing. Despite appearing linear, it certainly isn't here. Or rather, it's possible to be in a linear time separate from another, out of sync.

"If we stayed out there, could we just get to the end of this month faster?" I think out loud.

"Seems plausible," Ami answers.

"Since this was Evalyn's doing with her power, there's no telling if the curse is still in effect," Agatha replies. "It could have been cancelled when we landed."

I nod and let a grumble escape my throat, but it doesn't keep me from thinking. Another thought comes to mind and I share it out loud.

"I wonder, if we venture out farther perhaps we can find where the other horse went. It's likely stuck in time out there."

Ami shakes her head at me. "It isn't a good idea. What if you can't make it back before the house shifts? You'd be pulled and likely injured."

"She's right," Eve chimes in. "It would be dumb to go out there not knowing what will happen."

"Because of the phenomenon, there's really no telling what would happen if you were out there past the shift," Agatha adds.

"With rope we could eliminate that to some extent," I offer up to appease their sense of security. "If it was becoming close to time, assuming there is any way to actually tell time here, I could be pulled back.

"I still don't think it's a good idea," Ami says.

I lean back and sigh, closing my eyes to focus my thoughts.

I'm sure there are things I could do to bide my time. I do have to rebuild the stable anyway. If the other horse doesn't come back it will be pulled back, and killed on impact, so I will only need one stall this time.

Standing up, I retrieve more bread and a glass of water. After eating and drinking both quickly, I turn back to them and nod in defeat.

"Okay. I'm just going out to start rebuilding the stable Eve wrecked with her stubborn attempt to stay in the past," I jab, knowing it will rile her up.

"Hey!" she protests.

"Do you need a hand?" Ami stands up, and walks toward me.

"Sure," I reply.

"Not without me!" Eve thrusts herself up, and places her palms on the table.

Back outside, I coordinate taking down the broken pieces of wood with Ami and Eve. Despite the force of the impact, Eve came out with minor abrasions, but the stable needs complete reconstruction. The four corner posts are the only things still fully intact. Using the claw of a hammer, I strip the frame down to just the bare essentials, allowing us to begin repairs. Separating out the broken pieces from the salvageable ones gives me a better idea of what could be used to reconstruct. It isn't enough.

The frame, with its supports and crossbeams can be rebuilt, but there won't be enough material for a roof or walls.

I remove the nails from the wood which are too bent to reuse, and begin putting the pieces back together while Ami and Eve help.

After what feels like several hours of steady work on the stable, we've completed as much of it as we can, the rest of the wood little more than scrap. Feelings of disappointment intrude on the accomplishment, knowing I won't be able to finish it. And now I have nothing else to bide my time. Ami smiles at me, lessening the blow, before heading to the garden. Eve hangs around, leaning against the house. When I attempt to walk away she grabs at my hand.

"Since we have little to do, and nowhere to go, I have an idea for a way we could kill some time." She winks and pulls me in.

"Me too." I lean in close, pressing my shoulder into hers, and craning my head around her neck to whisper. "More work."

Eve scowls, disappointed. I pull away, and walk toward the garden to see if I can assist Agatha with harvesting. She already has several baskets filled. Saving her the strain, I bring the heavier ones inside.

Fruits and vegetables will take us only so far. With no direct sunlight, as far as we know, the plants will likely stop producing. The stores under the house should last us the month. If we run out and the house doesn't shift through time, we will find ourselves dead soon after they're exhausted.

I set the baskets on the counter, and head back out for more. On my way out I bump into Ami who is also carrying baskets. Holding out my hands I offer to take them.

"It will be easier if you bring them to me," I suggest.

She willingly hands them over. Turning it into something of a game, we move back and forth, and each time we do we seem to increase in speed. Because she has to move farther away from the house to pick up the baskets, I reach the door before her.

While she's on her way back with another load I joke, "You're so slow. Hurry up!" I grin.

She sticks her tongue out, and hands the baskets to me, but before I can turn back into the house she has already run back to grab the last. Running into the house I toss them down, and return to the door just as she arrives. I reach for them, but she plays coy and pushes me out of the way. Agatha follows Ami in, smiling.

Her sunny attitude during a crisis is amazing, though I suppose we have to keep our spirits up, and not let worry take over.

Taking the food to the basement storeroom, we sort it and check the current supply across the shelves for any which may be going bad. The moisture in the room is low, assisting in keeping the food as fresh as possible. We find a little produce which has gone bad. It seems like a waste to dump it. I take it outside and throw it near the horse so it's not a complete loss.

We could use a compost container at some point in the future. We just need some more lumber for it, and then this food could be repurposed.

After several hours, I'm drained. Back in the kitchen my stomach grumbles. I open the refrigerator, and stand there with the door ajar. There are some leftovers, but nothing looks satisfying right now. I force myself to eat a pork chop. Shutting the door, I tear into it.

My sense of taste seems heightened. Whether it's due to my hunger, or some strange effect of where we are, there's satisfaction from the texture and flavor I didn't think my body was interested in. While I grab a plate and head for the table, Ami and Agatha come up from the basement, and they too pick at leftovers. The three of us sit at the table together. It's quiet and calm, until Eve finds her way in and complains.

"You guys are eating without me?"

I look back and shush her with the bone from the pork chop, instead of my index finger. She lets out a 'humph' and pulls out her own leftovers. She joins us at the table, but because Ami is on my right and Agatha is on my left, she doesn't get to sit next to me. She mutters under her breath, irritated about it.

I finish my food. Instead of letting the remains sit around, I open the back door and head out. When I'm close enough to the white land, I lob the bone as hard as I can. Satisfied with my success of disposing it in the void, I return inside. At the table, I stand with my hands rested against the back of my chair.

"You know, we could probably dump any garbage out in the time distortion," I chuckle. "I don't know where you've been putting it Agatha, but it has to be piling up somewhere."

"You're right. It's in the basement, in the tool area until we reach a time that has waste management, but it's been a couple months," she replies.

"Well, I could take care of it later if you'd like," I offer, giving myself something to do for at least a few minutes.

"Can we do that?" Ami asks. "I mean, I know out there doesn't seem like our planet, but if we put it there will it stay?"

"Why not? There's nothing there." I grin at her. "I'll take care of it after I take a nap." I push off the chair and straighten my back, stretching hard and letting out a groan.

"Sleep well," Agatha's sweet voice comes from behind a cup of tea.

"I'll see you up there," Eve chimes in and winks.

Looking back at Ami, I comment, "I need a lock on my door as soon as possible."

Ami giggles and nods. Eve scowls. When I enter my room, I close my door, undress, and climb under the covers. Tossing and turning for a few minutes I realize I'm too warm, and stick one foot out. It seems to appease my body. While I try to slip into a restful state, my mind still has things it wants to pester me with.

I was the king of Asta at some point previously. Why did Drake attempt to kill me? Who is he? Could he be a fellow ruler of another land, and just wanted mine? I went out to the woods with him, likely willingly. Why? I couldn't have suspected foul play, or else I think I'd have had the foresight to realize something was amiss because of the feeling he gives me now. Perhaps I was just blinded by trust under my previous persona.

Was I a good king? Just? Kind? Friendly? Strong? I suppose I'd like to think who I am now is similar to who I was then. Though I may be a little violent at times, it is out of necessity, or to help people.

What is my name?

My mind finally becomes as heavy as my body feels. The thoughts fade as if they had never existed in the first place. Sleep finds me.

~~~~~~

The horse neighs and whinnies, waking me from my slumber. Though I'm drawn unwillingly to consciousness, I feel well rested. I hope the quiet void had all been a bad dream. But even without drawing the curtains back, its permeating light is flooding the room, illuminating nearly everything. It crushes my wishful thinking.

I stand, and dress in clean clothes, a white t-shirt and blue jeans, before I make my way downstairs. My throat is a little dry. Rather than get a glass, I'm feeling nostalgic for drawing up a bucket, some remnant of my past creeping in. At the well it appears it's still quite full, and there are no traces of sand left from Eve's time only two months ago, both good things for us. After taking a large drink for myself, I unhook the bucket and bring it to the horse.

While he drinks, I look up at the apple tree. Though ravaged by the sandstorm, it has already begun to recover with new leaves and blossoms growing. Unable to offer an apple to the horse, I leave the bucket on the ground momentarily, and pull a small bale of hay over so he has more to eat than the bits I threw out earlier.

Sitting on the end of the bale, I stare at the two saddles sitting against the other side of the tree. Curiosity takes hold again, and I want to venture farther out into the nothingness. I contemplate both for and against going out there, battling it out in my head. The allure of adventure gets the better of me.

Hoisting the saddle onto the horse, I tighten the girth, undo the lead rope, and vault up on him. I loop the rope around the saddle's horn, slip my feet into the stirrups, and press gently to get him to trot. We circle the house a few times so I don't spook him before wandering out onto the white.

When the horse makes his first few steps out onto the whiteness, the silence of not being able to hear his hooves clop against it is a little unnerving. It's the same as the axe. I try to shrug the feeling off. Just outside the grassy boundary, we again circle the house and stop at the side with the half built stable.

It all looks normal. It's crazy. Out here time is passing slower. Or at least appears that way. I wonder what this place is. It has physical properties, but I doubt anyone has ever seen such a place in the whole of time.

I turn the horse and gallop past where I had previously walked, glancing over my shoulder every few moments in order to keep an eye on the house. Letting a few minutes elapse, I turn back around and see the house is a speck in the distance. Looking back in front of me I think I see something; another speck, smaller than the house. I have to squint to see if my eyes are playing a trick on me, but it seems there is clearly something there. It is a black dot against a white backdrop. My heart beats quickly, and I spin the horse back to the house. I put him to a full gallop. On my approach to the house I see no one at first. But like last time, blurs become visible, and finally I see Ami, Agatha, and Eve standing there, all frowning at me. The moment I've breached the boundary, I am scolded.

"Rain! What were you thinking?!" Ami asks frantically.

"You really should have told us what you were doing." Agatha keeps her calm, but her furrowed brow tells me she's unhappy.

Eve swings her arm back and launches it at me. I can't escape fast enough, and she catches me in the shin. "What if you'd died out there? Who would I make beautiful babies with?" Eve yells, gathering a spiteful glare from Ami.

"I'll go mad being cooped up," I tell them, grinning from ear to ear and rubbing my leg. "No one was outside to tell me 'no' so I went for a ride. More importantly, there's something out there. You can't see it from here, but it's there, and I want to know what it is."

"That's stupid! If you can't see it from here it means from there you wouldn't be able to see the house, and you could get lost trying to find your way back!" Eve says sensibly.

Ami quirks her eyebrows at Eve, glancing out of the side of her eye, surprised. But her attention is back on me and I can see she agrees. Their collective attempt to dissuade me isn't working. I'm set to go, and I trot around them, facing the horse back to the white.

"We had to take shifts watching for you to come back. We think you were out there for two days," Agatha mentions. "We didn't want to venture out that far on foot, so we waited here."

"We can't miss the opportunity to find out what's over there." I'm still excited at the prospect of potential life beyond our bastion. "Maybe it's the horse. Maybe it's other people who need help."

"Or maybe it was a mirage, or hallucination," Ami says.

"Maybe, but I can't take the chance it's a person and didn't try to help." I shrug.

"So you'll risk yourself? Can you survive an impact from that distance if the vortex pulls you back in?" Ami tries to reason.

"I'll survive. How much rope do we have?"

They all sigh at different intervals, and Agatha responds.

"Several ropes, including the one you have. Not enough to keep a handle on you all the way out there."

"That's fine. I'll use them as directional markers so I can find my way back." I'm confident.

No further arguments against my plan arise. Hopping down, I grab the lead rope and hand it to Eve. She tries to hand it off to Ami, but Ami refuses, and she's stuck holding the horse. Agatha heads to the house, but before I can follow she motions for me to wait here. Ami pulls me aside by the arm, beyond the apple tree. Eve watches with suspicion in her eyes but stays put.

She pulls in close to, and whispers with a serious tone, "I'm going with you."

"I'd like that, actually," I whisper back and smile. She blushes. I take it she probably expected me to deny her.

Agatha returns with a couple coils of rope wrapped on each arm. It seems there's enough to leave a path for a fair distance if used at the point of the house becoming a speck on the horizon. She hands them to me, and I hoist the rope up on the horse, hooking them on the horn. While I do, Ami yanks the rope from Eve's hand, and jumps up into the saddle, garnering a brash and loud protest.

"What do you think you're doing?" Eve asks, her arms thrown to the side while stepping up to the horse.

"A good question," Agatha's soft voice counterbalances Eve.

"He's going to need someone to keep him company, and he said he'd enjoy it if it were me," Ami says to antagonize Eve.

"If you're going, then I'm going!" Eve tries to climb up on the horse, but Ami kicks her in the chest.

"Get off!" Ami breaks her normally calm demeanor, and yells.

"How dare you! You little…" Eve tries to grab Ami but I intervene, blocking her.

"All right, enough!" I command. "Eve, you're staying here. There's not enough room on the horse for three."

The hurt on her face is apparent, but I feel no remorse. Eve storms off into the house. I mount the horse, sitting in front of Ami.

"Rain, keep her safe," Agatha says with worry.

I smile. "I will."

Ami wraps her arms around my chest, and my heart skips a beat. Though I know we're just going out for a ride, and to explore, I can't help but think of her holding me for the duration. My face flushes red, and I am glad she can't see me. Before Agatha notices, I wheel the horse around and head out onto the white plain.

Pressing my heels into the horse again, I push him into a quick trot and then a gallop, heading in the direction I had seen the speck. I periodically glance over my shoulder, checking my distance from the house. Every time I do, I see Ami smiling uncontrollably.

When the house is nearly gone from our vision, I slow and begin laying down the first rope in a line to lead us back. Looking forward again, I'm certain I see the spot I'd identified earlier. Farther from the house, I only trot the horse to advance. I keep the end of the first rope in sight, its dull color clashing against the white. The house has become invisible. When that rope becomes difficult to see, I lay another rope down pointing to the first one, all the while the speck on the horizon grows larger.

Ami tugs on my shirt and I look back. Her smile has dissipated, and fear is in its place. I grasp her hand against my chest, and smile to reassure her. She presses her face into my back as I continue.

The speck is becoming larger, and I can make out the shape. It's a house. I try to talk to Ami but nothing comes from my throat. I'm transfixed with fear, but to keep her calm I put on a brave face. I tap her hand. She looks up, and I point. While the horse trots along, a strange sensation falls over me as I recognize the house. It's ours. More importantly, it's the other side of the house we left from, as if we went full circle in this void.

Well that's highly disappointing. I wonder how long it's been to them since we left. Here I was hoping for something a little more exciting than our own house. So much for adventure.

There being no point now to lay down any more rope, I put the horse to a full gallop. We near the grass boundary, but something is off. The grass is brown, not green, and the color of everything else is more faded than the white light was making it previously. As we enter the safe zone Ami cries out.

"We've been gone too long! The house is still here!"

We jump down, and I tie the horse off at the well while Ami runs inside. With the time distortion outside the perimeter running at an unknown rate, the length of time here may be as she fears; I begin to worry when Ami calls out and no reply is heard.

"Mother? Mother where are you?!"

Running inside, Ami is already moving through the swinging door to the kitchen and I call out as well.

"Eve? We're back!" I shout. It seems the sound is dull here also.

Just like outside, the colors are off; it's degraded, as if the house has been sitting for a long time. Hearing Ami stomping up from the basement, it's only a moment before she bursts from the kitchen and runs down the hall toward her mother's room. Her eyes are teary. Though I know she needs me right now, I feel the need to search too.

At the top of the stairs, I walk to Eve's room. I push the door open and it creaks. In the bed lies a skeleton about the size and build of Eve, uncovered and dusty.

The house didn't shift through time, but why? How long have we been gone? If only a skeleton remains, what hope do we have?

It sinks in. An overwhelming despair falls over me as I come to the realization it's now just Ami and I, alone and stuck. Ami wails from downstairs, and I sprint to get to her. Speeding around the wall separating the stairs from the main hallway, we collide. She sobs, and I pull her into me, wrapping my arms around her like a shield while her tears soak my shirt. It's moments before I notice my own tears falling down my cheeks. Collapsing to the floor we both cry. My thoughts burn at me for an endless amount of time.

Now I understand what the princess meant. My future is bleak. Not only are Agatha and Eve gone, but they must have died of starvation, or perhaps dehydration. Now Ami and I will have the same fate. Time for us has literally run out.

I scoot us toward the wall, my back aching for support, and Ami climbs into my lap. She coils her body into me, her face pressed into my collarbone, and I rock her gently. The sobbing stops, and the tears no longer fall, allowing an uneasy silence to consume us.

I'm surprised when Ami wraps her arms around my neck, cranes her head up, and presses her delicate lips into mine. I kiss her back, and we become lost in an act of desperation. She turns into me, and we kiss with passion which lasts until we need to breathe. Even after catching our breath, several more soft kisses are exchanged.

"I'm sorry," Ami apologizes. "I…"

"Shh, it's okay." I pull her in tight and we rest.

Ami breaks into sobs again once in a while, and I soothe her by rocking, and stroking her hair. With the realization we are going to die here at the forefront of my mind, I'm struggling to just be at peace with it because I'm with her. But my mind still wants to escape, to find a way to survive.

What about Evalyn? She would still be here right?

"Ami, get up!" I tell her with enough urgency to shock her out of crying mid sob.

"What?" She hiccups and looks up at me scared.

She jumps up off of me, and helps me stand. My legs have fallen asleep, but I push through the pins and needles. I take the stairs two at a time, and by the time I've reached the top the feeling has faded, and I'm able to run without falling face first. Sprinting to the back of the second story hall, to Evalyn's room, I bang heavily on the door and yell.

"Evalyn! Evalyn, are you there? Can you answer me?" I shout.

"It would make sense she'd be here," Ami states, taking up a spot next to me. "But what can she do for us?"

"*She* got us into this, maybe she can come up with something to break us out of this time! Maybe she can reactivate the time vortex!" I continue to bang on the door. "Evalyn, if you can, inhabit my body! Tell Ami what to do!"

There's no response.

"She's never possessed anyone but Mother. I'm not sure if she can," Ami tugs on my arm. "Let's go check for food, see if there's anything left for us. Maybe if we give Aunt Evalyn a little time, she might make her presence known."

I huff, not wanting to give up on Evalyn, but nod in reluctant agreement. Back downstairs we head into the kitchen, and check for supplies. The apple tree and garden are dead. The pantry, the refrigerator and, downstairs are all completely barren, but a lack of jars or cans strikes me as a bit weird.

What now?

Moving back to the living room, our attention is redirected to the yard outside, and the lack of empty containers becomes the least strange thing to behold. Beyond the window, beyond the yard, the forest has reappeared, though much more dull in color than the last time we had seen it.

"What?!" I blurt.

"How?" Ami exclaims running over to the window, placing her hands on it.

"Did she fix the vortex without us knowing?" I ask.

"There was no quake, no shift. But I don't see any white!" Ami stares in shock.

Bursting out the door, I look all around us, and there is nothing but woods. Looking at the horse he seems calm, not like he would be if we had shifted through time, but we are no longer in the void. Both sadness and happiness fight within me, struggling for control. The tears begin to well up again.

It's just Ami and me now, but are we still condemned to traveling through time, or is this our fixed point?

Walking swiftly to the edge of the woods, I peer out into the dull brown forest line, and something is wrong about it. The colors are still faded. A sense of dread falls over me just looking out into it. When a glimmer near a tree catches my attention, my heart jumps. I become anxious and breathe heavily.

"Rain? What's wrong?" She grabs my arm gently.

"This…this isn't right. We shouldn't be here!"

Before I can tell her about the metallic object I see, an ear piercing yell echoes through the forest. A darkness from deep within the trees begins racing toward us, traversing the ground at a high speed. The 'shadow' yells and wails again. My throat closes up. Grabbing Ami's hand I turn to run, and she follows my lead.

"Rain?! What is it?"

We race toward the door. Looking over my shoulder I see *him*. His ominous and malicious presence hurtles toward us. I can't do anything but choke back the terror coursing through me right now as Drake barrels through the forest.

He's going to kill me!

When we reach the porch, I shove Ami inside first, and then slam the door behind us. My hands tremble while I lock it to stop his advance. Drawing the drapes closed, I no longer see him. But his dark armor, deep red hair, and cold eyes burn my thoughts.

"The other door! Go lock it!" I tell her.

Ami leaves me, and I look from left to right, trying to catch any glimpse of him I can, to know where he might be attacking from. He's nowhere to be seen. My heart is pounding and I can't stop my rapid breathing. A hand touches my side, causing me to nearly jump out of my skin from fright, but it's only Ami. She looks at me with great concern.

"Shh, calm down." She pulls me into a hug.

"I can't. Drake is…out there. It's Drake!" I try to explain through my hyperventilation.

"We're in here, he's out there. You have your sword, and I can get a tool from the basement." She caresses my chest to calm me.

Nodding, I pull away from her hug to retrieve my sword, but it's missing. I turn the bed over and trash the room, but it's nowhere to be found. Down in the basement we're a little luckier in finding two hammers, a rake, and some tree trimming shears. Though we are now crudely armed, I feel no better. There's no sound except for our breathing. With a hammer in each hand, I creep to the door separating us from the food store, and peer through to make sure it's safe. The barren shelves allow me to see there is no one waiting for us. A wall blocks the stairway up. It's a blind spot.

I wave for Ami to come forward. When she reaches my back, I run across the stairway opening to the wall, and peek around to see if Drake is waiting for us. He's not there. I slowly climb the stairs one by one. With the hammers ready to strike, I sneak to the top. There is no sign of him. Ami follows, and I slide my back against the wall to follow it over to the door in order to look out into the yard. Still nothing.

"I have a feeling there's no way he would give up just because of some locked doors," I whisper while looking over at Ami, who is right by my side.

"Then why hasn't he tried to get in?" Ami asks. "There's something very wrong here."

"I think you're right. Something is wrong, but I can't put my finger on it." I grab her hand and pull her back to the living room. I peer out the window, finding only the horse in the yard.

"Rain, I'm feeling extremely tired all of a sudden. Let's rest upstairs – the stairs will act as an alarm." Ami tugs on my arm, trying to tear me from the scenery.

A few moments pass before I nod at her. In my room again, I have to put the mattress and pillows back in place. We set our tools down on the floor. I shake the blanket, laying it across Ami who has already fluffed the pillow and found her way under the sheet. Closing the door, I bring the heavy dresser over to block it, and climb into bed with her. She draws in close, her warm breath seeping through my shirt and onto my chest. I place my arm around her waist, and rest my head just above hers on the pillow.

Though such a situation had been awkward before, I feel only sadness now as her tears once again wet my clothing. My attempt to console her is futile, but I run my fingers through her hair anyway. Soon enough I'm drifting to sleep. Despite great efforts to stay awake to keep an ear out for Drake, I come to the point of no return.

~~~~~~

When I awake there's just as much light flooding in as before we went to sleep, despite the feeling we've been asleep for hours. Looking down, Ami is still curled into me. I rest my chin against the top of her head and squeeze her in tighter.

What can be done now? We have to venture out to see if we can find food, but Drake could still be out there. Why he hasn't attempted to enter, or do something to the horse is beyond me, but he seems likely to have some sort of nefarious scheme thought up. Maybe he's trying to starve us out.

We will have to make a break for the horse at some point, maybe find our way to Asta and pick up some food and supplies. Perhaps we can draw Drake that way too, and lose him there.

"Rain?" Ami speaks, startling me and causing my body to jerk.

"Yeah?"

"Sorry, I didn't mean to scare you." She hugs me.

"It's okay. I was awake, just doing some thinking," I reply.

"About what we're going to do?"

"Exactly that. We need to grab the horse and leave. We're going to die otherwise."

She sits up and hovers over me for a moment while we stare into each other's eyes. Her brown, curly locks dangle down over my face, and it seems for a few moments she is going to lean down and kiss me again. Instead she climbs over my legs and stretches. Looking back and forth from the window to me, she's confused. I sit up and nod at her.

"I noticed it too. The light hasn't changed." I comment.

"What is going on here?" There's fear in her voice.

"I wish I knew, but we shouldn't hang around." I stand and grab the hammers. "If he's here, I don't want to be."

She's upset. I reach my hand out for her to take. She pulls me in, and I wrap my arms around her as best I can with the hammers in hand. We move the dresser from the door and she picks up the clippers. I crack the door an inch, keeping my foot as a backstop while we peer out into the hallway. When I'm confident Drake isn't there, I move from the room with Ami in tow. Looking over my shoulder back down toward Evalyn's room, I wonder again if she's still here somewhere.

The stairs creak and groan under our feet. I wince with each step. Though I might have been relieved at the bottom under normal circumstances, my flight response is still at its peak. Around every corner I look, I expect Drake to be there, waiting for us. I'm surprised and relieved to not see him within the house. At the living room window I can still see the horse tied off to the well post, as calm as if there wasn't an imminent danger lurking beyond our border. I half-turn to Ami and she nods.

"When I open the door I want you to run and jump on the horse while I untie him," I instruct.

"Okay."

Managing the doorknob and a hammer is difficult, but when I'm ready I raise my other hand and count. When I hit three, I throw the door open and Ami sprints. Right behind her, I grab the rope, fumbling to untie it. Clearing it, I jump on and pull it up as a wailing echoes through the woods. A chill rolls down my spine. My eyes dart back and forth, looking for Drake.

Multiple dark shadows begin to swarm about from the direction of Asta. It races at us. Pacing the horse around this side of the yard, I note whatever the shadows are, there's no way through them. Kicking my heels into the horse's side and snapping the reins, I push him to pick his speed up. We head around to the other side of the house. The shadows near the forest boundary follow us. An opening appears out past the apple tree. I kick my heels again and push him into a gallop.

As he breaks into the unknown, we deftly maneuver and dodge through bushes, roots and downed trees. The shadows begin to close in, and the forsaken wailing continues. Approaching another opening in the woods, I urge the horse to beat the shadows, whatever they may be, from reaching us.

But where we break out is just as impossible as the white void, and shifting into the woods without a vortex to carry us. The massive buildings of Chas have sprung up before us. I pull the reins to stop the horse in his tracks. Looking back, the forest doesn't exist anymore. The shadows have disappeared, and instead the house sits visible in the middle of the park of Emma's time.

"What did Evalyn do?!" I exclaim.

"This is…I have no idea what's happening here." Her voice is meek.

Looking back to the streets provides a disturbing sight, one just as terrible as finding Agatha and Eve's remains. Skeletons litter the streets as far as the eye can see. Death surrounds us.

"This has to be a bad dream," Ami states.

"This just doesn't make any sense. There's no vortex, so we can't really be in Chas, right?" I try to reason, mostly with myself.

Trotting the horse into the nearest street, the one Ami and I first ventured down when we were in Chas, we look about. Everything here is like it was in the forest, and at the house. The colors are dull. Nothing seems right, as if the world is hollow. The air seems stale.

Venturing past familiar places, there appears to be no food at any of the vendors. That doesn't stop me from jumping down off the horse and slowly creeping past a few skeletons to look in the open window of a sandwich shop. Nothing but more skeletons lie beyond the counter. Not even the decaying remains of food exist in their display cabinets. It seems unlikely they starved to death. Turning, my eyes meet Ami's, and I shake my head.

"There's nothing. I don't think they just stood here and starved. This was something else," I tell her. "But that makes it worse. Were they attacked?"

"Maybe Mother and Eve didn't starve then?" Her question comes out more as a hopeful statement.

Moving back to the horse, I put my foot in the stirrup and hop back on. "Possibly, but is any of this real? Things aren't adding up."

"It seems real enough, despite the inconsistencies. Let's head over to Emma's shop," Ami suggests.

"I'm not sure I want to see her skeleton." A lump appears in my throat thinking of saving Emma only for her to have died in some horrific manner.

I bring the horse to a trot, and steer him to try to avoid the litter of bones, but there are too many. The horse crushes the bones under his powerful feet. Crunching sounds reach my ears, and I fight back bile from deep down. I'm glad when it only takes a few minutes to find Emma's shop. It's as I last saw it. Glass is shattered, the doorframe bent, and inside is a mess. A little girl's scream from inside triggers an instinct reaction. I jump down and burst through the broken windowpane of the door, but no one is inside. It's silent again.

"What was that screech?" she asks.

My voice falters, "I heard a scream. I think it was Emma." I look back before heading to the door in the back of the shop.

With my hammers brought up ready for attack, I kick the door open. But there's nothing but blackness. The light seeping in from outside dares not to enter the doorway, and I am hesitant. Unable to see anything inside, I listen intently for the scream again, but it doesn't come. Reaching into the room, I attempt to feel for a light switch. I feel nothing at all; no solid mass, no structure. A sense of deep sorrow and regret starts to creep in and overwhelm me. I pull my arm out, but the shadow has latched onto my skin. It draws up my arm, attempting to consume me.

"Let go! Let go!" I drop the hammer, watching the shadow work its way up my arm, and now out toward my feet on the ground.

Backing up, I shake my hand frantically and free myself from it. It pursues as I run from Emma's shop. Scrambling onto the horse, the shadow floods out after me. I put the horse to a quick gallop to distance us from the darkness, but it follows.

"What's going on?" Ami asks frantically.

"I don't know. That shadow tried to grab me!"

Looking back over my shoulder, it, the darkness, rolls over the street and across the skeletons. My mind has a hard time processing what begins happening. The skeletons stand. Not only the ones which have been touched by the darkness, but the ones all around us. Climbing to their feet, they attempt to grab us as we race by.

"Rain!"

"I know!"

With only one hammer, I swing on one side and kick at the other. Ami jabs at them with her shears. Their bones scatter to the ground, but the waves are endless. They fall at us from the windows above in the skyscraping buildings.

"Keep going!" I focus on maneuvering the horse through the city streets, trying to escape from the horde of skeletons.

The only place there were minimal skeletons was at the house, but do we risk going back there? Will Agatha and Eve's skeletons attack us?

I turn the horse down a street and head back toward the park. More skeletons block our way. I mow them down with the horse. His legs shatter their forms just as easily as one of mine or Ami's blows. Fear grips my mind as they all try to grab us, to tear us down from the horse. I keep my emotions in check until we can find our way back to the house.

At the park, past the border of trees, everything around us changes again. The horse is barreling through the woods once more, and the house cannot be seen, but we continue on in its direction. Shadows swirl around us, forming silhouettes of people in all directions. Their moaning and wailing reverberates as if it's directly in our ears. The clearing comes into view and the house is there waiting for us.

In the yard I dismount, and begin tying the horse to one of the clothesline posts before remembering the door to the kitchen is locked. I throw the rope down, and we jog to the other side of the house, hugging its sides. I knot the horse's lead rope to the well post again. Our fear pushes us to run into the house, leaving him out there as bait, or a sacrifice, to buy a few more moments.

The skeleton army has been replaced by the shadows, and possibly Drake's ghost. I hustle Ami along, locking the door behind us. The curtains are open. I pull them shut.

"Rain, I'm scared." Ami throws her shears down and clings to me.

"I know. I don't know what to do. This…" I look out a crack in the curtains at the tree line. "I don't know what's going on. The dead coming to life, the shadows trying to cover me…"

The cries and moans from outside grow louder. I grab her hand and back away from the window. There's fright in her eyes, and I feel the way she looks. I focus on distancing ourselves from the noise. Back toward the stairs we collapse onto them and Ami hugs me tightly as we're terrorized by awful screams and deafening wails.

"I don't want to die," Ami's soft voice can still be heard clearly over *them*.

"I know." I kiss her forehead. It's all I have to offer her in these circumstances.

Lying there for what may be hours, or days, it's hard to tell when the sounds stop. Finally we are left alone in silence once again. Though I want to look outside to see if the shadows have gone, Ami has fallen asleep, and moving would disturb her. Still, my body is becoming restless, and my legs begin to twitch. Sliding out from under her arm I do my best not to wake her.

I move to the window. The moving shadows in the forest have disappeared, and Drake hasn't reappeared, but the tension in my muscles remains. A nagging feeling plagues my mind that whatever is there lurks just out of view. My eyes dart back and forth trying to see them, or Drake.

"Rain?"

Ami's voice in the quiet startles me. I jump, spinning around quickly to look at her. She stands, straightening her skirt and pulling down her blouse.

"There's a lull out there," I point out. "It might be a good time to try to leave again if we're going to have any hope of finding food."

"It's weird, but I haven't felt hungry at all."

"Same. I don't know what to make of it, but it doesn't matter does it? If we don't eat, we will die."

She walks to me and grabs my free hand with both of hers. Her soft smile and trusting eyes say she'll follow wherever I lead. Opening the door to the yard once again I notice the quiet covering everything. We cautiously make our way to the horse, and I help her up onto him. Untying his rope from the well, I toss it up over his neck and climb into the saddle.

Pushing him to the edge of the forest, I head the opposite direction from Chas, toward Asta's former location. The horse trots at a slow pace. I look left to right nervously for any sign of the shadows, or phantoms. Behind us still lies the house, a hundred feet back and nothing seems out of the ordinary now besides the silence and the faded colors. Several minutes pass and the house becomes indistinguishable beyond the forest's foliage.

Ami's breath resounds in my ear and amid the silence it sounds as if she's breathing heavily. When I look back her face isn't actually near me. The horse's hooves crush twigs and leaves. The crackling grows louder to the point it becomes hard to concentrate. But an opening in the woods refocuses my attention, and I push him a little bit faster to find out what it is.

My mind is destroyed when a familiar sight becomes visible. I have no explanation for it, like any of the other things we've seen recently. The house comes into view once more. Though I don't want to continue, screeching and wailing picks up from behind. When I look, the shadows have returned, larger and combining. They begin converging and racing toward us. It spooks the horse and sends him into a gallop.

It takes great effort to keep him from tripping and sending Ami and me flying. Back into the yard, we've come up on the other side of the house with the wilted garden and the clotheslines. Turning my head, I try to gauge Ami's reaction. I sense the shadows are no longer content to stay in the forest. They merge into a blob, like a tidal wave crashing onto the shore, to chase us through the yard. Steering the horse around the side of the house, the shadows are converging in from that side also.

"Get in the house!" I yell at Ami while pulling alongside the porch.

We both leap down, but she's inside before me while I stare at the shadows overtaking everything in sight. I step in and close the door on the horse. Turning, I expect to see Ami but she's nowhere in sight.

"Ami?!" I yell out.

"Up here!" her voice rings from upstairs.

Climbing the stairs quickly I fear something may have happened to her, but when I look into the sewing room she's looking out the window at the shadows surrounding the house. They're overtaking everything until it's pitch black outside.

"Rain," her voice quivers.

"I'm here." I wrap my arms around her from behind. "I'm here."

Ami looks at me, but her face turns a sickly pale when the direction of her gaze falls to the closet. She grips my hand tightly. She tries to speak; her voice chokes up in her throat for a moment.

"Rain!" She points. "It's inside!"

The black shadow swarms out of the closet, and reaches for Ami like long stretched out whips. She screams. Instinctively I raise my hand, and let loose a large shockwave at it. It isn't fazed. Ami runs from the room, and downstairs. Instead of following her, I run to Evalyn's room again.

"Evalyn! Evalyn, you need to help us *now!*" I kick the door open. Inside is nothing but blackness, and it swarms out at me from there also.

I run. As I reach the sewing room it reaches out of the door, and tries to grab me. Dropping to my calves, I slide under it and nearly fall down the stairs. I leap back up and bound down them, taking half the stairway with each stride. Behind me, it relentlessly follows as I run out the open door. The yard is clear of its dark mass and Ami's already on the horse waiting for me. I leap on from the porch and grab the reins.

"Hyah!" I crack the reins and put my heels hard into his side.

He gallops away from the house, deep into the woods. Loud moaning and wailing follows as the shadowy mass pursues.

I push the horse to his limit through the thicket. As the shadowy wave begins to overtake us, it consumes the forest behind and all around us. Though we have nowhere to go, I push the horse harder to try and escape. White light appears ahead of us. Though the shadow seems to be able to envelop everything, my mind hopes that within the direct light it will not follow. My heart sinks when I see what we are headed toward. We break out onto the white void and I can no longer hear the horse's footfall.

Expecting the shadow to stop, we both look back. Nothing but a black mass exists where we just were. Our hope is shattered when it continues forward, attempting to overtake us. The horse continues to gallop, now completely unhindered. I push him as hard as possible to stay ahead of the darkness. The white ground seems to tremble beneath us, and that too motivates the horse.

The time differential doesn't seem to be slowing it down! How are we supposed to gain any ground?

As the horse gallops, a strange sight catches my eye for a brief moment as we sail by it. One of the ropes we had laid out is there, leading us back in the direction we originally came from. For lack of better direction, I follow the course laid out. The ground continues to tremble violently. Though I had been unable to damage the white ground, it appears to develop black cracks in it, like veins shooting out from the shadows behind us. It tries to grab us, and I work the horse hard to avoid it.

Strangely, as we follow the ropes, we don't see the blackness in front of us as we would expect to if this was such a small circular world. Instead Ami points frantically, and I see what she's pointing toward. It's the house, not surrounded by the forest, not in the center of Chas, and not enveloped by this black shadow as we had seen only moments ago.

Looking back again the mountain of black now towers high above, and covers the landscape all around. I keep the horse at his limit.

He won't be able to do this for long.

The house grows in our vision, but the horse begins to slow, exhausted, until a large tremble shakes the ground again under us. It causes a renewed panic in him. The black has begun closing in on the sides, flanking us. The fear rises in me that it might cut us off.

To my surprise, I see blurs at the edge of the house. I can't help but feel a renewed hope, at least until I look back to see Ami focused on the darkness nipping at our heels. Agatha and Eve become clearly visible, and I aim the horse right for them. The poor thing begins to wheeze, and against my legs, his breathing labored. I feel bad, but I can't help think I'm going to have to let the darkness envelop him.

Maybe he won't suffer long. It might give Ami and I a few more seconds to retreat to the house. But then what?

He finds us one last burst of energy, and we make landfall into the green grass. Jumping down from the saddle I scream at the three of them, leaving the horse to die while I run and wave my arms frantically.

"Go! Go! In the house!"

They follow, but before we reach the doorway, yet another mystery confounds the entire experience: the black mass crashes like a wave against an invisible barrier right on the border of our land. We and the horse are safe from the darkness. The horse's knees buckle and give out.

We're protected from the black for now, but it begins to blanket everything beyond our border. It turns the pristine white void into a dark nothingness. Ami begins sobbing. She leaps into her mother's arms, rambling unintelligibly.

"Give the horse some water," I yell at Eve by accident, the stress of the situation putting me on edge.

Startled by my dominant command, she does as I request. The horse puts his mouth to the bucket, but it doesn't seem to have the will to drink.

My attention returns to the darkness just beyond them and it appears to be retreating, leaving white ground visible again, but not for long. It surges back, as if in a tidal pull, and then races forward again, crashing up the invisible boundary so the white backdrop starts disappearing. Instead of retreating this time, it climbs higher, and the white disappears, the black reaching far above us to snuff it out. I head back to the edge of the barrier and unleash another shockwave. Like before, nothing happens.

"Evalyn!" I turn back to Agatha but yell at the house. "Can you inhabit her? Can you tell us what's going on?"

"You're going to have to tell *me* what's going on, because I have no idea," Evalyn replies through Agatha. "What did you piss off out there?"

I head back to them, and Eve joins me, trying to draw my arm against her nearly bare torso. I pull away, having even less patience for her advances right now. She tries again, but when I glare at her she stops.

"We don't know what this is either." Ami continues to hug on Agatha's body while Evalyn inhabits it. "But the whole time I got a strange feeling, like it was sapping me of any happiness."

"We came to a house we thought was ours, and from our perspective we had only been gone for a few minutes. But the house was dead. Its colors were faded, the grass had died, and Agatha and Eve were skeletons," I explain. "And that's just the beginning. We saw the forest, Drake, Chas, and an army of undead trying to grab us. Then the shadows came, engulfing everything.

"I tried calling out to you for help in the house, Evalyn, tried to elicit a response but I had no idea if you could respond in spirit," I continue.

"I can control minor physical things in my spirit form. If I had been there I would have found a way to communicate," she replies while brushing Ami's hair with her fingers, staring at the darkness.

We all watch from the yard just outside the kitchen as the black now completely surrounds our house. The only light is a small circle of white left far above the house. Though the white void has been all but snuffed out its light continues to permeate the grounds inside our perimeter, illuminating everything just as it was previously.

Eve breaks the silence. "You've been gone for about two weeks by my count of eating and sleeping cycles. We weren't sure you were coming back."

"We almost didn't," I tell her. "Whatever it was out there causing us to hallucinate, I think it was trying to keep us there. We were chased back to one spot a few times."

I become entranced by the black wall climbing to extinguish the white above us, likely trying to enter our safe zone.

"Will this barrier hold?" I ask Evalyn.

"I have no idea. I didn't know one existed until now."

"Maybe it can't enter because of the time distortion between here and there," Eve suggests.

"I hope that's the case," I say.

Finally calming down, my stomach protests the lack of sustenance in my body. Hunger catches up quickly: intense cramps wrench my insides around, and I feel faint. "I need to eat or I'm going to pass out," I tell them.

Heading into the house, we prepare for a family meal. Eve sets the table, I slice bread, and Ami and Evalyn prepare rice, fried vegetables, and beef chunks. Our meal comes together, and we sit at the table to eat. With Ami to my right, Eve to my left, and Evalyn in the chair beyond Eve, I take my time to look at each one of them. My mind questions if any of this is real.

The smell of the food is real enough, and I can touch everything. I can feel the warmth from the plate, but everything there had a sense of realism too. Could this all just be a nightmare? Can I wake up from this?

I'm famished, but I stir the food about on the plate. A deep emptiness and doubts begin to overtake me. When Ami reaches over and places her hand on mine, I'm brought back to reality. Her caring smile reassures me that at least *she's* real. At last I move a bite of vegetables, rice and beef to my mouth. My tongue delights at the flavor, tasting like the most fantastic thing I've ever had.

My portion doesn't last long after the first bite. Wanting more I realize all the cooked food was divvied up between the four of us. And while there is more left in the house to eat, I know we must conserve our supplies until we – hopefully – make it out of here.

Ami eats slowly, continuing to hold my hand, while Evalyn and Eve are finished soon after me. I wait patiently for Evalyn to speak up, but after a few moments of her finishing she sits back, crosses her hands on her lap, and just stares at me. My anxiety begins to best me as I look out the window at the black. I break the silence.

"So you never encountered anything like this before?"

"I never tried to stop the vortex before, so no, we haven't encountered anything like this before. I suppose in a way we've known the barrier existed, but it was only thought of as the force of the vortex which pulls us back in. I guess there's a different application for it," Evalyn replies without sarcasm or malice.

Since we've spent time together, she's begun to soften toward me.

"Okay. So we wait it out and hope our barrier holds for another week and a half?" I ask.

"Seems about right. I guess it was a bad idea to explore wasn't it?" Evalyn states, giving me a playful glare.

"Yeah. I wish we could have found some native to this land, or maybe someone else stuck here. I can't help but wonder, since we went all that way and found our house which seems to have been long dead, if we'd have left from the other way would we have come across earlier versions of ourselves?"

She shrugs and I know it was a pointless question, but conversation is all we have at the moment. It distracts from the dread and despair I felt while in that fake world I presume was created by whatever the darkness is.

"What do we have for portable light?" Eve asks.

"Candles, a dozen torches, and some lanterns," Evalyn replies

"Maybe the shadow could be repelled by it. We should try to push it away," Eve wonders out loud.

"It doesn't appear to work like that. It seems to be able to completely consume light. Think about this; the white light from the void permeating everything right now can be snuffed out completely by it," I explain. "You can't see through the darkness. No hint of anything beyond it."

"The white light is part of this place though. We don't know what's causing it, and it's different than regular light," she retorts.

"We will prepare just in case." Evalyn nods at Eve in a rare moment of mutual agreement.

"There is another unanswered question: will the time shift still happen?" I ask.

"I think it's safe to say if there's a barrier out there holding the dark back, the power which draws us through time is still holding up. All we need to do is wait." Evalyn raps her fingers against the table in a rhythmic manner.

I nod and pick up the dishes, minus Ami's as she is still picking in silence.

It doesn't take long to clean and place them in the dish rack to dry. Out of the corner of my eye, I see Eve head for the living room. Ami seems to have come to a stop in her eating. Evalyn sits there, staring at the wall. I return to my spot at the table, and I reach my hand out for Ami. She looks drained. She half-smiles and returns the gesture. Our hands clasp together.

"So, what happens if the barrier doesn't hold?" Ami finally breaks her silence. "I don't want to see those things again."

"It will be okay Ami," I gently caress her hand to reassure her. "The vortex will carry us away from here, and we won't have to worry about that thing."

"Thank you for cleaning, Rain," Agatha's soothing voice rings out.

"Sure."

Agatha, now in control of her body again, stands and follows Eve to the living room. With just the two of us left, my mind becomes consumed by the embraces we shared earlier. A kiss of desperation, a need to feel comforted, but a kiss nonetheless.

Can I truly do this? It's like that time I overheard her. What if we try, and it doesn't work out? Then we'd be stuck together, and it might be awkward. I don't want to mess things up.

"I'm going to head into—" I start a sentence but am stopped by Ami gripping my hand firmly.

"Don't leave me. Please." She's clear in her wish to not be alone and I'm not going to disappoint her.

"No, of course not, Ami. I'm here." I settle back into my seat, scooting it around the corner of the table, closer to her.

She's clearly done with her food, despite not having eaten a lot of it, but continues to push it around the plate with her fork. We're both fatigued from the ordeal, and likely also due to being out in the distorted time. I help her stand, and grab her plate. We put it in the sink, and head into the living room.

The couch is empty, and I bring her over to it. She lays her head in my lap, curling her body into a ball closely to me. Pulling a blanket down from the back of the couch, I cover her up and lean my head back.

My eyes shut. I attempt to think of a solution, but my mind wants to rest. It's blank, and the dark void of sleep finds me instead.

~~~~~~

A deep, guttural moan wakes me from my dreamless slumber. It vibrates my eardrums and chest. It compels me to find out where it's coming from. Ami is asleep on my lap, and I have to maneuver slowly to move out from under her. It takes a gentle touch to lay her down comfortably without disturbing her, but I fear the sound I hear might wake her anyway.

It comes again, rumbling through the air. Listening intently I follow it to the living room window. The glass reverberates. Putting my hand up to it, I can feel the noise coming from outside.

Though hours before we had been terrorized by the imagery it portrayed to be real, the need for understanding causes me to act against the alarm going off in my mind. I open the door and step out into the yard.

The sound, the deep moaning, emanates from farther on. I move one step at a time closer to the edge. The grass all around is faded. The scenery begins to look like that of the dead house. Color is being drowned out by the light still beaming down from the void. Above, a single star-like dot exists in a sky of nothing but black, but it still has more energy than that of a hundred suns to illuminate so brightly.

Strange.

At the edge of the grass, the moaning strengthens, and I can now identify it's not a single voice. There are multiple voices in harmony creating a resonance, working to penetrate our haven.

"Shut up!" I speak harshly to whatever the voices are.

Silence falls for a brief moment, and then a single voice speaks out from the black mass. A man's. He sounds neither young nor old. He's terrified.

"Help me! Please! It's dark! I don't want to be here! I'm scared! Please bring me into the light!"

"Who are you?" I inquire.

"Please! Please let me in! Let me into the light and I'll be safe!"

Squinting to see past the impenetrable darkness reveals the outline of a face and hand. They press against the invisible barrier, squishing their dark, disfigured form as if it were a giant pane of glass restricting them.

My heart leaps into my throat, and swallowing hard doesn't push it back down. Unnerved, I remember it can play visual tricks. I take a step back.

It pushes harder on the barrier, and because it can't enter in, I know it's a trick. It's not really a man. Outlines of multiple bodies of all shapes and sizes come into view within the darkness. The pleading increases in intensity, this time a little girl.

"Please, mister! Let me in! I don't want to be in the darkness anymore!"

"No. You can't come in. You're not welcome here."

They moan and wail in unification at my rejection. Their volume increases to a deafening wail which causes my whole body to shake. It takes me a moment to quell the anxiety I'm feeling, but I muster the energy to shout over it.

"SHUT UP!"

The silence is nearly palpable when my voice dissipates into the black.

"Why did you try to kill us? What are you?" I ask it.

The voices cry out together and, though I can tell they're upset, the effect makes them sound ominous. "We are lonely. We have not seen anyone in a long time. We have only each other."

"What are you?"

"Despair! Despair! The darkness!" they lament.

My inquisitive mind seeks answers to the unknown.

"The house we saw, the copy of this one where two of my companions were dead, and where we found you. What was that?"

"Despair! Despair! It was a reflection! This is where despair finds its home! Let us into the light and out of the darkness!"

"What happens if I let you into the light?"

"We see the light! We find the light! Let us in! Reach into us!"

Though my mind vehemently tells me not to do what they request, the temptation to put my hand outside of our protective barrier becomes overwhelming. Recalling I had touched it in the illusion of Emma's shop, I begin wondering what the harm would be. When I reach my arm out toward our shield, the outlined bodies disappear.

Stepping forward, I reach for it, but my other hand is seized. Ami clings to me.

"Rain." She rubs her eyes with a free hand. "Who are you talking to?"

"They need help. They're trapped in there." I point to the darkness, my finger nearly ready to burst the bubble and let them in.

"It's another trick. They made us think Mother was dead, and that skeletons could come to life. Why should you believe anything it says?"

The voices wail again, louder than ever. They hiss at Ami, some spewing vitriol in the form of insults and curses.

"No! Don't listen to her! We need your help, Rain! Don't leave us out here!" The outlines of the bodies return again, and slam themselves up against the barrier. The bodies stack up as far as I can see, creating a pile of the dead.

Retreating to the house, something inside me wants to let them in. It feels like a separate part of me, another 'me' trying to control my actions. But Ami pulls me along. Back inside, she brings me into the kitchen where Agatha is entranced, staring out the window at the darkness.

It takes her a moment to acknowledge our presence, but Agatha looks at us and shakes her head. "I have a terrible feeling about it. After hearing about your encounter, I don't want to know what nightmares it would inflict if it found its way in here."

"The white sky is dwindling. It's only a dot now," Ami says. Her confidence has returned. "Perhaps the barrier will keep us protected, but if whatever *it* is finds a way to snuff out the light above we'll be overwhelmed. We need to keep all the lights on and collect our portable lighting."

Still in a bit of a trance, I nod while staring at the black. Agatha walks past and rests her hand on my shoulder for a moment before going into the living room.

Ami grips my hand, and our fingers intertwine. She pulls me to the basement, turning the light on and descending into the storage area. I look through the shelves, not at the food, but at the still shadows; there is nothing out of the ordinary about them. I watch them distrustfully anyway.

Heading into the tool storage, Ami follows the right side of the wall to where a few oil lanterns are hung from hooks. She retrieves four, placing two in my open palms, and we return to the kitchen area to start a collection.

"I'm going to grab Eve. We should probably all stay together if we think this thing might get in," I tell her with no emotion in my voice. I've been sapped of any positive feelings.

"Okay," Ami replies. "Just promise you're not going out there again."

"I promise. I'm just going upstairs."

The stairs creak and groan in the silence, and the floorboards to Eve's door do their best to alert her to my presence. It's cracked open a bit. I knock lightly, and it swings open a little more. When she doesn't respond I peek in. There, sprawled out and face down upon her bed in a lacy green bra and some loose pants, Eve is motionless. A lump forms in my throat. I swallow hard knowing she's not dressed properly, but the urgency of collecting ourselves in a central location overrides my sense of embarrassment. I attempt to wake her.

"Eve, get up." I call out softly so I don't startle her. "Put some clothes on and come downstairs."

She lies there lifelessly, and I watch her back, waiting for it to rise and fall under her breathing, but I see nothing.

"Eve! Wake up!" I bring my voice up a little bit.

Still nothing. An irrational fear that something has happened to her causes me to kneel down and touch the freckled skin of her bare shoulder. She's cold. When I attempt to feel for her pulse in her neck there's none. Shaking her, I whisper her name. It startles me when she does stir. She rolls over, grabs my neck, and pulls me down.

"Morning, babe." She twists her neck and kisses me on the lips abruptly.

Pulling away, I pick up one of her crumpled short tops from her floor, and throw it at her face. With my emotions in disarray because of the darkness beyond our border, I am confused.

Rather than being repulsed as I would have been before, I lick my lips. Despite being close to, and having an attraction to Ami, something in me longs to reach out to Eve.

Our eyes meet. Eve props herself up on her side, exposing her nearly bare torso. I fight against something deeper than my carnal instincts to not move back to her. I'm positive the darkness outside is trying to exhibit influence over me.

Could this be because I touched it? Has it somehow skewed my emotions that I'm losing the strength to resist her? Or is it just an overactive imagination, and pity for her, softening me?

With no power to abuse she's simply another person seeking acceptance in a strange and precarious situation. Should I allow myself to open up to her? Can we become friends?

This is not good, I tell myself. *If you don't keep yourself neutral to her she will take it as you weakening. Ami will be hurt. Don't make this awkward for everyone.*

Despite the long pause, I feign frustration. I stand and bark orders, "Get up. You need to join the rest of us downstairs. There's a chance the darkness will find its way in, and trust me, you don't want to see what it has to show you."

Before she can grab me, or dress herself, I turn and exit. I stomp down the stairs to keep up the ruse of irritation. Agatha is just emerging from the kitchen with several metal stemmed torches under her arms.

"Building a perimeter?" I say to make conversation.

"Yes. It seems like it would be smart to set up another 'boundary' to protect our house." She hands some to me. "Would you set up that half of the yard while Ami and I take the other?"

"Sure." I accept the task to keep me busy.

Pressing the torches into the ground isn't as difficult as I anticipated. The ground gives way as I stab the metal staves downward, planting them in a semi-circle a few feet out from the house to build my half of the perimeter. Ami meets me on the stable's side, and lights each one.

The circle around the house is small, but it will provide some light if the void's is drowned out. One by one the lights of the house are turned on, but it's barely noticeable.

Can this light hold the shadows back? It devoured the white void out there and not a bit of it is visible except for the speck in the 'sky' now. I hope it will last until the vortex sweeps us into a new time. But what happens if it finds its way in before that? Will it travel with us? What kind of danger does it pose?

The once star-sized white light above is now only as large as the head of a pin. It's nearly gone, and time is certainly running out. As I stare out at the black, the voices call to me again from the darkness. I'm thankful when Ami grabs my hand, giving me the strength to resist their siren-like call.

They wail again, obnoxiously hissing at her for holding me back. She cups our hands together again, and pulls me into the living room. Ami closes the door with her free hand. Eve scoffs from the couch, holding a lantern on her lap.

"Did you check with Agatha to see if there's anything you can do to help?" I ask.

"No, I only turned all the lights on in the house because I was scared of the dark," she replies rudely. Upon seeing Ami's hand in mine her agitation rises. "I *was* sleeping peacefully before you came in. I was having a wonderful dream where you were taking care of our gorgeous fiery-haired kids. Now, I have to listen to the racket coming from outside."

Distracting us, Agatha emerges from the hallway with a lantern in hand. Ami retrieves the other two from the kitchen, and lights their wicks. As if by fate, or perfect timing, I notice the permeating white light from the void disappear, and the yard becomes dark, all but for the ring of torches and light from the windows. Running outside, lantern in hand, I look up and confirm our fear. The darkness has finally enveloped the white ceiling, and the pillar of light, which was keeping us safe, is gone.

The barrier has fallen. Or maybe there was a top to it.

Our lights, lanterns and torches still provide a significant amount of light. But it doesn't seem to matter when the torches flicker, as if there were a wind, despite there being nothing of the sort. Darkness creeps in the shadows created by the flickering flame, and upon closer inspection they appear to be bodies. Arms, hands and heads creep along, and the wailing begins again, nearly beside me now. The flames flicker harder and before I can shield them, they are extinguished. Instincts drive my feet, and I run back inside the house, slamming the door as if it would stop shadows.

"It can affect the physical world!" I point to the corner of the room just beyond the couch. "Over there, now! Give me your lanterns!"

As we huddle, I set my lantern down a few feet in front of us and take theirs, placing them around us in a quarter-circle. Each of us keeps our backs to the wall, and we watch and wait for the bodies of darkness to creep into the house. Ami holds onto me fearfully. Tension rises in the room, charging it with a negative energy. The moaning seeps in from outside, low at first, but increasing in volume.

"It took the torches out with no effort. Let's hope the house lights and our lanterns can keep the shadows away." My confidence in the situation begins to fade, but I try to show some resolve that our plan might work.

The light wards off the shadows for now. But every shadow becomes suspect. I can't tell if it's my eyes playing a trick, or if it's all real, but shapes and forms creep along where shadows are cast. Hands and arms trying to reach to us continue to be held at bay. The crying becomes louder. They call out to me by name. The voices seem to come from the walls right behind me, prompting me to close my eyes and plug my ears so I can pretend not to hear them.

"Come, Rain. Let us into the light! Enter into the darkness! Let the darkness enter you!" My attempts to block out their pleas fail. Their tones reverberate through my hands.

"What will that accomplish?" I open my eyes and ask it.

"You can bring light to us, Rain. Share our despair, and bring us to the light!"

Dark shadowy hands hover wherever shadows lie, unable to penetrate the light yet. Still, it, they, are not deterred. A multitude of body outlines begin to cycle through. Different sizes, different shapes, but all appearing to be silhouettes of people.

"How long until we shift through time again?" Eve asks. "This is really creeping me out!"

"It might be as much as a week and a half, but tracking time has been difficult," Agatha responds but is taken over by Evalyn before she can finish her thought. "Not long. I can't usually tell but it's different in this place. I can sense it, feel it building like a pressure. Either more time has passed than we think, or it's happening early. We just need to last a bit longer and hope this thing isn't drawn with us."

"And if it is? What happens then? Won't we unleash it on whenever we end up?" I point out. "We should try to coerce it to leave."

"How do you coerce something like this? Whatever it is, it seems stuck on reaching us…" Ami starts.

"Me…" I interject.

"It wants *you* and doesn't like 'no' for an answer." Ami smiles softly. "I won't let it have you. Maybe we can push it back beyond the boundary again if we use the lanterns."

Eve growls in a low tone. "It does seem to be held back by the light. It might be worth exploring…"

"NO!" The voices wail from the walls and all the lights flicker.

"Okay, we're upsetting it." Their agitation becomes my own. "It has the ability to interact with physical things, and that's not a good omen for us. For now we move as a group, and only when we need to. Don't aggravate it."

"What about the bathroom?" Ami inquires.

"As weird as it's going to be, we need a buddy system. We'll have to watch out for each other." Evalyn chortles, apparently amused at the circumstances.

"Rain can be my buddy!" Eve exclaims.

"Not a chance." Ami glares at her.

"We're going to have to do it as a group." Evalyn grins playfully, getting more enjoyment out of torturing us than should be healthy. "Three will have to guard while one does what they need to."

"Eww, Auntie," is all Ami can muster as a response.

I shake my head and rest it against the wall. Ami leans on me, and Eve lets out a sigh of contempt.

With nothing to do but sit and listen to the moaning and wailing of the darkness, I try to think of different times. Once again I turn to the unknown of my past, despite having no more answers for the questions than I have previously. The princess pops into my mind, and I wonder if she could have told me more and simply didn't.

It would make sense for her to not tell me any more than she already did, for the same reason I didn't tell her about the future. The same reason I told her she would be better off not knowing. To avoid inadvertently altering things. Or maybe to avoid struggling against the inevitable.

I suppose we do that anyway by interacting at all with whatever time we're in. But perhaps this was all destined. Maybe my helping the slaves had, and was always, going to happen, in which case it isn't really altering things. If I knew more about my past I might be able to recall stories or historical facts learned when I was the king, to find out if anything had been changed.

Time is an interesting beast. By doing things in the past, it might be safe to assume it's always happened that way, and this temporal paradox we call our home will always exist on the planet, even when it isn't supposed to. And if Evalyn never used her power in death to start the process, what would the world be without the interactions we've had? Would it be a better place, or worse?

Trying to understand time hurts my head, and I cease thinking about it to save myself an endless loop of questions. It feels like hours pass, but without anything to keep our minds or bodies occupied it could just as easily be ten minutes. I eye the bookshelves on the other side of the living room, and the choice of reading a boring textbook or steamy romance novel do not appeal.

"Let us in," the darkness speaks anew in its unanimous cluster of voices. "Rain, you must let us into the light!"

"Silence!" I yell at it.

"Go away!" Eve chimes in after me. "You're not wanted here!"

"No!" The lights flicker again and a heavy humming from the house can be heard.

"Eve, stop badgering it!" Ami glares at her from across my chest.

"Let us in!" The humming increases, and the lights begin to flutter off and on.

It continues, a chatter so loud that it destroys any semblance of concentration I might find otherwise.

"I'll push you away with the light!" Eve yells.

The voices let out a screech, causing the hair on the back of my neck to stand on end. Something pops in the house, and the electrical lights die out. We are left with only our lanterns as protection.

"Good job, Eve!" Ami yells at her.

"Good job yourself! You guys pissed this thing off to begin with!" Eve points her finger in Ami's face. I grab it. "Gah! Why did I have to get tangled up in this mess?!" Eve rips her hand from me, glaring because I stopped her from doing anything.

"It probably just tripped the circuit breakers." Agatha is eerily calm in this chaos.

"What is a circuit breaker? Can we fix it?" I ask.

"They're special switches that automatically cut off power to prevent electrical damage," she responds.

"All we have to do is turn the switches back on, but if this thing can do it once, it will probably do it again," Ami adds.

"Is it even worth trying then?" I'm disheartened. Their silence is the answer I didn't want.

The shadows have closed in on us, held back only by the lanterns' light now. They whisper and yell at the same time. Nothing I do to ignore them helps. They whisper my name, calling for me to let them in, to reach into the darkness. The silhouettes of their bodies and hands all point toward me, reaching to grab me. It takes time, but eventually they become white noise. When I close my eyes I feel drained, like they're wearing me down. Wearing down my will to resist them.

~~~~~~

Cold, icy fingers grip my neck. They're strangling me. But there are too many fingers to count. It's not just my neck they're clasping, but every inch of my body is being crushed under their weight. Each one is trying to get at me, and they are uncountable. But, though they cannot be numbered, I feel them all. Each consciousness trying to impose itself on me in the hopes that I can help them.

It's overwhelming. When I try to scream, nothing comes out. My mouth won't even open. It's not there! My heart hammers my ribs like a woodsman chopping down a tree. The pressure from inside meets that outside. I can't bear it. My mind can't stay focused on a single thing while I wade through every cry of desperation.

A part of me wants to help them, but I can't decide if it's because I actually want to see their woes dissolve, or if I just want them to be quiet. It doesn't matter. They're taking over. Their depression is grinding away at my soul. I'm not here. I'm not there. I begin to not exist at all. I'm fading.

~~~~~~

My body jerks. My eyes snap open and I'm in the house.

Ami, who had also apparently fallen asleep, is startled and screams. I look around nervously, swiping at my arms to relieve an itching under the skin. The shadows are still being held at bay by our lanterns. I reach over and turn the wick up to increase the light a little more. The darkness hisses at me as it's pushed away, but becomes quiet again. My nightmare lingers, and a feeling of hopelessness has sunk in.

"Rain?" Ami rubs my arm.

"Sorry, I felt vulnerable." I keep it to myself.

I don't want to alarm them any more than they are.

"Maybe if you were in my lap you would feel safer?" Eve offers.

Again I'm not repulsed by her, but instead shake my head and give a weak smile.

Ami clings to me, and I feel a little relief. But as I sit there trying not to think of the darkness, or anything else at all, my body gives me something to make me physically uncomfortable. An urge I try to suppress pesters me. The more I try to ignore it, the more it persists: I have to use the bathroom.

Not wanting to risk our safety I fidget and cross my legs. The moans return from the darkness, breaking my concentration. I can't hold it for too much longer. I try taking deep breaths, but I've gained the attention of the women and know I have to divulge my situation.

"Rain?" Ami looks at me. "Is something wrong?"

"Yeah. We're going to need to move as a group." I blush.

"All right. Everyone grab a lantern." Agatha opens her eyes, and I jump because I was sure she was asleep.

We each grab one and form a tight diamond, facing outward from the person opposite to us. Holding the lanterns out to our front, our light barrier is secure against the shadows reaching out from the nooks and crannies.

One small step at a time, Agatha leads us down the hall. We're forced to cramp tighter together. While we move, the shadows are repelled but hearing my name from the hidden places doesn't become any less alarming. Fear sinks deep into my stomach.

Eve twitches, shadows making her jump. "I'm feeling claustrophobic. I'm going to freak out here."

"You're fine," Ami snaps at her.

"Can't we do just two at a time?" Eve questions. "I mean, I don't mind if Rain keeps me safe, but I don't want all three of you in there."

"You don't have a choice!" Ami's yell echoes off of the close walls. "We need to keep the barrier up, but if you'd like to go in alone, go for it."

"Forget that!" Eve shoves her shoulder into Ami. Ami pushes back and our grouping breaks up a little.

"Enough. I don't like it either, but we don't have a choice," I stop their fight before it turns into a brawl. "As much as I would like for none of you to be in there, and to not have to be there when you're relieving yourselves, we are our best defense against the shadows."

Agatha is silent, and I assume she feels no need to elaborate. Her light illuminates the knob and she hesitantly reaches for it. Her composure is nearly flawless, except for when she shoves the door open. It's a little too hard, and it slams against the counter behind it. I jump and Eve shrieks.

Light floods into the bathroom. It takes some squeezing to work our way inside and still keep our lanterns held up so we're safe. We huddle near the toilet, and without thinking about it, I put my lantern on the back of it to illuminate the little alcove it's tucked into. They face outward, but it's not enough to save me the embarrassment. I sit down to relieve myself and hide the noise.

To my surprise, Eve doesn't attempt to look at me, which garners her a little respect in my mind. When I'm done, I leave my lantern there and tap Eve's shoulder. She hands me hers, and we switch places leaving me on point, my back to all the women. I put the lantern handle in my mouth, biting down hard so as not to drop it, and plug my ears.

A few minutes pass and there's a tap on my shoulder to indicate they're all done. Having kept the lantern clenched in my teeth, my breathing has dried my mouth. I cough and suck on my cheeks to trick my body into salivating. We take turns washing our hands before moving back to the living room.

Since we had gained some experience in moving together, it's a little easier going back. Our pace is still quite slow though, so we do not let our guard down and lose our light barrier. Agatha leads us to the kitchen door, stopping only momentarily to let us know we're not returning to the corner yet. The darkness recedes in the kitchen, protesting the entire time while we move through the swinging door.

Agatha must have been preparing.

There is fruit laid out on the table for us to eat. Instead of sitting down in the chairs where the lanterns wouldn't be able to illuminate underneath, we climb one by one onto the tabletop and sit facing away from each other. The fruit is heavenly, more flavorful than I'd noticed before under normal circumstances.

Is it because I'm hungry, or the effects of this place?

The moans gain my attention again by raising their volume. Even against the light being produced by our lanterns, the room is noticeably darker. My lantern flickers briefly, creating an ebb and flow in the shadows reaching for us. It makes my heart skip a beat, and I adjust the wick a little more until it's burning brightly.

"Should we set up a sleep rotation?" I question with a mouth full of orange.

"A good idea. One person always awake to make sure the lanterns don't go out," Ami speaks.

"Does that mean I can sleep since you two just woke up?" Eve says cheerfully.

"Yes, you and Agatha sleep." I reach behind me and squeeze Ami's hand. "Ami and I will stay awake, and keep watch."

"Thank you, Rain," Agatha's voice sounds weary.

"We will need to communicate when we start getting drowsy. Since two of us have slept recently, I'm sure Ami and I can hold out." I try to appear confident. Their silence tells me nothing of their belief, or lack thereof, in my assertion.

Time, despite already seeming erratic in this void, drags on. With nothing to converse about we are forced to listen to the white noise generated by the frequently changing voices within the darkness. Their current mood has them speaking softly, trying to tempt me, to lure me into whatever their darkness is. When they fail, it dulls and quiets. Ami squeezes my hand and I squeeze back.

"Perhaps it's tiring?" I whisper.

"Can immaterial beings tire?" she whispers back.

"Doubtful," Eve states plainly. "It's likely trying to lull us into a false sense of security. It's what I'd do if I were it."

"You don't have the ability for subtlety, do you Eve?" I joke with her. "Aren't you supposed to be sleeping?"

"Believe me, I've tried, but it's too uncomfortable. How about you and I take our lanterns and go lay in my bed?"

"Does your vulgarity know no bounds?" Ami's voice is humorless.

"Are you such a prude you're telling me you wouldn't bed him if you could?" Eve retorts.

"Unlike you, I know how to act like a lady!" Ami's voice becomes elevated. "I can sleep in the same bed as Rain without trying to molest him!"

"It's not enough to act like a lady, when you can *be* a woman—"

"Girls, enough. This isn't the time or place," I interrupt.

The three of us become silent, but not for long as Eve doesn't seem content to just sit there and try to sleep.

"How long do you think it's been?" Eve asks at a normal volume.

"It could be minutes or hours. I'm becoming tired but it could just be from boredom," I bring my voice back down to a whisper, attempting to have Eve follow my lead.

"If you're tired Rain, go ahead and sleep some. I'll wake Mother in a little while," Ami offers.

"Thanks." Being tired and wanting to sleep are two different things in my mind. The nightmare from before springs forward. My only comfort is when I squeeze Ami's hand just to feel that she's there.

Adjusting my body a bit, I use the three of them as my support. I droop my head forward, and cross my arms at my chest. It takes a few readjustments, but I find a position where my shoulder blade isn't being ground against another shoulder.

Closing my eyes, I try to rest. For a few minutes I can't help but open my eyes every now and again, out of fear the darkness will creep in when I'm not looking. Finally they are too heavy to open again.

~~~~~~

"Rain! We know you hear us! We feel you as you feel us! Come!"

It's them again. The fingers around me, but they're carrying me this time. Somewhere I can't see. I feel as though I'm adrift on the sea, the undertow pulling me further out. The shore, reality, becomes a faded vision, and their incessant calling my name is drowning me. Each one that says my name fills me with a deep sadness. Regrets, desperation, despair, sorrow. It rings in my ears like a cascade of bells. Each one is different, but I don't understand why, or what they want.

I want to cover my ears, but I can't move. I want to speak, but my mouth is gone. Their hold is making me one of them. Lost and seeking, aching to change the things I can't control. I'm forced to reflect on my failure in not helping others enough. Those that have died, and those I haven't saved, including Ami and Agatha. I'm wracked with angst.

Then it shows me the worst one: one that hasn't come to pass. Ami, Agatha, and Eve are overcome by the shadows. The dark fingers, arms, and legs grip the three tightly and I watch as the life is choked from them. The life leaves their eyes, and their bodies become husks within the shadows before being completely obscured.

~~~~~~

My eyelids flutter open, and I am roused from sleep by *them*.

Feeling more tired than before, I wonder if maybe I was stirred by one of the women. I look back to see which one of the three might have woken me. They're all asleep, including Agatha, whom Ami had said she would wake. My heart is already beating fast. I begin to panic. I yell, attempting to rouse them.

"Wake up! Everyone, wake up!"

They sit there, seemingly lifeless. Turning from my lantern, I shake each one of them individually, but I can't wake them. Fear overwhelms me, and I grab Eve by the face. I point her head toward me and pull at her eyelid, there's no resistance. Her pupil doesn't dilate at the lantern's light.

It's killing them! It wasn't a dream!

"Eve! Wake up!" I yell, but she still doesn't stir.

I place my hand under her nose, and near her mouth. I can feel her breath, but it's shallow. Remembering her deep sleep pattern from when I was in her room, I move to Ami. Squatting on my knees, I lean forward and pry her eyelid open too. Her eyes are rolled back, but at least hers are moving back and forth rhythmically.

"Ami, wake up!"

The dull moaning stops, and the united voices speak again in unison, their collective vibrations burning into the core of my essence.

"Rain. They will not wake, but you can end this. Save them! Save us!" Their tempting tone burns my ears.

"Shut up! Leave me alone!" I yell.

Louder now. "Rain! Save us! It can only be you!"

"What do you want?!" I spin around and stand up on the table to address them with anger. "How can I save you?"

"We want to be in the light! Bring us into the light!"

"You killed the light! You snuffed it out! How can I give you something you destroy?"

"We are in darkness, we are in despair! Save us from the darkness!"

"How?" Exasperation rings out in my voice. "How do I save you from what you are?"

"We *are not* the darkness! We are *in* the darkness, the despair we died in! We are souls who died with no hope! But you can change it! You can give us peace! We have seen it!"

"What do you want me to do?"

"Reach into the dark and bring us into the light, give us peace!"

What happens if I don't do what they want? Are they going to choke the women of their life until I give in? If they can do this, what would they do if they came with us? What kind of havoc would they bring on the unsuspecting world with their demented hallucinations, or power over the physical realm? Will they seek out another to 'bring them into the light,' or will they be content in causing the world misery? I can't let that happen, but what is the cost? Will I die if I let them in?

"Why do you need me to find peace?"

"You are strong enough to be the conduit for our despairs! Then we can be at peace!"

"I am a single person. How could I possibly take you on?"

"When you reached into the dark we assessed you. You are strong enough. You must!" they cry out together.

The options are not favorable at all.

I look over my shoulder at my companions who are being affected. The presence of the souls begins to exert a pressure in the room, and it feels like I am being pressed upon from all sides, despite the shadows still not being able to reach me.

I adjust Ami and Eve so they are placed against each other, and then move the lanterns so they are still protected by the ring of light. I ensure they are in no danger. I pick up my lantern and stand at the edge of the table, holding it out in front of me to watch the shadows dance to my flame. I slide off the table and exit from the safety of our circle to stand near the island counter. Hands reach out for me from the darkness, but my lantern holds them.

"Let us in!" they yell.

"On my terms. I am going to exit the house, and then I will allow you to do what you need to. You are not to harm the other three."

They fall to silence, my words having appeased them for a brief moment. Out in the yard on a small visible patch of grass near the garden, the blackness surrounds me. Everything else is engulfed except for the kitchen window, where dull rays of light emanate. My breathing is heavy and quickened. I'm terrified. Setting the lantern at my feet, I look around. The bodies surround me.

"I just reach into the darkness? How does this let you into the light?" I ask wearily.

"Come, into the darkness," they chant. "You will understand."

"Once I 'let you into the light,' what happens?"

"Come!"

Hesitant at their lack of clarity, I cannot begin to fathom what they intend to do. But I take some comfort in knowing I am doing this to protect the ones I care about, and to keep it contained from being unleashed whenever we land next.

Their luring melody of whispers pulls me away from the house. At the edge of the light being created by my lantern, hands reach out for me. They grab my wrists. More light appears behind me, three distinct glows.

"Rain! Stop!" Ami yells out.

But I can't. Gripped by the darkness oozing into my skin, my body moves by itself, and I step from my safety zone. Ami yells again, but they're too slow to stop me.

In the darkness, hands grasp me, clutching, and I am drawn in, pulled away from the light. Their fingers, hands, and arms surround me as they had in the dream. Fear, grief, sadness, and despair begin to overwhelm me. I scream in the madness of a million voices crying out in my head all at once.

My senses are overloaded. I collapse to my knees, and my body goes numb and tingly, like I've been deprived of oxygen. I scream out again in agony; it's as though there is a storm tearing me apart. The voice which comes from my throat is no longer my own. It is the cries of the countless people who have become stuck in this void, sending reverberations through my body and the air, creating a horrifying sound. The collective souls lost in the dark become absorbed, transferring their entire essence into me. I fall onto my hands. Scream cut off, my body convulses, seizing, and I grunt and groan. I lose my mind to their voices.

There are so many of them!

Through blurred vision I see light in the darkness, but it's not the lanterns now at my side. Instead it's the white void returning as it once was. Everything lights up again with the white light penetrating every nook and cranny. But not my soul. It becomes laden with terrible images; some too much to bear.

I see my companions beyond the haze. They appear to be yelling, but I cannot hear them over all of the voices now inside of me. Their words fall on my deaf ears.

As the last of the darkness slithers into me like a serpent, I feel as though I will explode. My mind burns with the thoughts of so many. I yell, but my voice fails to form anything coherent. Waving my arms, something builds inside. It's different than my innate power.

Trying to push the women away, they fail to heed my unspoken warning, and they advance. I muster the strength to stand, and run from them. They're startled, but I manage to run as far as the edge of the grass. When I convulse again, the darkness spews from my body. A storm of black whips and tendrils swirl through the air, but it doesn't leave me. It has anchored itself deep within. It takes sheer force of will, but I pull it back.

Collapsing, the darkness has been contained, but not without affecting me. With my hands pressed into the grass in front of me, I see I have been consumed. My skin has turned as black as the shadowy, formless despair. I am now its permanent host, if only to save everyone else from it. I can already sense it's going to ravage everything about me.

Finally, my hearing returns, and I hear Ami call from a distance.

Looking at the grass I can understand why she doesn't approach – it's dead. Everywhere I let the darkness unleash its storm is dead.

"Rain! What is going on? What did you do?" Ami calls out through sobs.

I muster enough energy to stand. My muscles quiver underneath my own weight, just as my mind shudders under the weight of the burden I now carry. I turn to them and hear her gasp. Dejection runs through my mind.

"You must bring us to the light! You must change the despair which grips us! Change our fate!"

To my surprise, despite the devastation the darkness has caused in my vicinity, they run to me. I hold up my hands to stop them from advancing. They do, just before the decaying grass.

"Rain? Why?" Ami cries, tears streaming down her face.

"I had to. They had a hold on the three of you, and weren't going to let me go. They were going to kill you. I couldn't let them, and I couldn't let it roam free when we shift through time again."

"You're an idiot!" Eve yells while throwing her arms to her sides, her lantern clattering to the ground. "You could have died!"

Despite my insistence that they stay back, Agatha takes a step forward. I take one back.

"Don't. I don't want to see you hurt," I tell her while reasserting my hand's position to stop her.

"You have it under control now, right, dear?" Agatha asks in her soft and sweet tone.

"I think so. For the moment."

Boldly she reaches her hand up and places it on my cheek. I flinch, not wanting to hurt her. But she insists, pressing her palm onto my skin. It's cool to the touch. Drenched in sweat, it seems more likely that I'm burning with a fever, and she's a normal temperature.

She looks into my eyes and smiles. "At some point you're going to have to stop sacrificing yourself for us."

"I will never stop sacrificing myself if it's to make sure you are all safe. You are my family, and I would die for you." I close my eyes for a moment, tears beginning to stream down. Agatha strokes my cheek. Her palm is soft.

Seeing it is safe to approach, Ami and Eve join us, and I'm engulfed by a hug. Though despair courses through my veins, and the deaths of innumerable people haunt me, I'm comforted by the warmth. I weep. Tears flow as freely as a river does toward the ocean.

Overwhelmed by the despair again, it's a struggle to focus and stay conscious. But it's all in vain as the voices push to the forefront of my mind, and I am pulled into their world.

~~~~~~

I'm surrounded by a world of black, much as the void had been after the darkness enveloped everything. The same as my dreams. There is no light, but I can somehow see my body, see myself as I was before *they* infected me, and turned my skin the color of night. In this nothingness, I drift with a sense of weightlessness.

Their voices call out to me, asking for my help. They appear, no longer as shadowy outlines, but as their true forms, or what they were before they died. They are all different, all shapes and forms, all walks of life, from across the world. When I try to speak to them, nothing escapes my lips. The only sound is them.

I'm forced to listen while I float, carried in between souls. The voices take turns in trying to tell me their despairs. Though they all speak at once, causing an undiscernible roar, I can sense their meaning. I understand what they want.

Each wants me to solve their problem, to break them free of the despair they died in. The reasons vary, and while some have similar problems, some are completely different, each one urgent to its owner. Without understanding how they expect me to solve their problems, I try to convey that to them, but my voice continues to elude me. Their pleas become more and more urgent, as if I could do something at this very moment to alleviate their woes, but I am powerless. I am at their mercy within my own body.

Time, if a conscious concept of it could exist while unconscious, seems to be completely stopped as they plead. Unlike dreams, following what could be considered a linear flow, this has nothing of the sort.

Stuck in this dark void, it occurs to me an endless amount of time could pass in the real world, and I would never know.

Spinning aimlessly through this weightless space amongst the sea of souls, there are countless requests made. In an instant, for no reason apparent to me, my mind jolts. I think I understand what needs to be done, why I was chosen, and how to accomplish the impossible task of appeasing the souls.

Can I alter time to save these people from whatever despair has gripped them? They can't do it themselves. I am their conduit. Maybe while traveling through time I can identify events which would alter the course of their lives. Maybe I can save them. Is time not set? Is that why they reached out to me?

But how much damage will I do if I take this impossible mission on? Can I offset the bad which might occur due to my actions with the good I intend to do? What will the consequences be?

Trying to grasp a better understanding of time, and changing set events, is almost as painful as the voices constantly intruding. With my mind full of ideas for changing the past, present, and future, thoughts of paradoxes arise.

If I change something in the past which prevents Evalyn from using her power in death, will all of this not have happened? And then start again because none of this would have happened, and I wouldn't have changed the event...I suppose this wouldn't be happening now if that were the case, because the event would...

I have to stop myself, stop thinking about the complexities beyond my reasoning capabilities, and refocus on just accomplishing my new task.

Okay, Rain, ground rules. If we're in the decisive past from where Evalyn died, maybe I need to watch my interactions. I don't want to upset the balance.

A light appears in the bodies, and they separate, not unlike the way the darkness shied away from the light of my lantern. They allow me passage through. I'm pulled in. The light grows larger. Warmth blankets me. I close my eyes to the brightness.

When I reopen them, a familiar view comes into focus, in a familiar place, with a familiar face hovering over me. I'm on the couch in the living room I know so well, and Eve is sitting next to me placing a wet and cool washcloth on my forehead. It's soothing, and I shut my eyes again.

"Hey now, don't you pass out again," her voice is soothing, nowhere close to her normally harsh or sarcastic tones. It's a little surprising.

"I'm not. I'm just waking up," my voice is hoarse.

She looks over her shoulder and yells at the swinging kitchen door, "Ami! Agatha! He's awake!" My heart leaps.

I hear them enter, and when I reopen my eyes Ami has kneeled by me. She smiles, and a tear falls across her cheek. Weakly, I smile back.

"How long was I out?"

"It's hard to tell. We're still in the void," Ami answers. "A day or so?"

"I thought Evalyn said the energy was building." I rub my face with both my hands which provides a sense of satisfaction.

"It's still building," Evalyn responds. "However, at a slower rate than I had originally thought. Imagine my disappointment."

"Indeed," I agree.

"Still, it's close. Could be any time," Evalyn continues.

I take it slow and try to sit up, only to be aided by both Ami and Eve. They set me upright with my shoulders and neck against the back of the couch. My body is stiff, as if I had been unconscious for months. I stretch my arms and legs to try and loosen them, but when I arch my back the scar on my abdomen aches. I rub it to try and soothe it, but it doesn't work.

Even fully awake I recall the time spent in the darkness of my own mind, amongst the souls, and my mission to help them. I choose not to share it with the women for the time being, their worry for me already high. Instead, I focus on forgetting the fatigued feeling.

"Are you thirsty?" Ami asks.

"Not at the moment, but I am going to head to the bathroom and wash my face," I scratch my head.

"Before you do, we should tell you…" Eve frowns and stops when Ami shoots her a disapproving glance. "What? He's going to see anyway."

"Rain," Ami places her hand on my leg. "The blackness receded after a while. Your skin is normal again, but your eyes are still completely black."

"Well then, I guess you'll never know if I'm staring at you will you?" I joke, trying to lighten the mood, but I'm actually terrified to look. It makes Evalyn laugh. Ami blushes and smiles, embarrassed.

"Anytime you're facing me, then I'll assume you're staring at me." Eve runs her hand across my collarbone, but is immediately smacked by Ami.

"Be serious," Ami retorts. "You're likely going to receive a lot of attention regardless which time we end up in. It might even cause problems."

"You're right." She's right, more than she knows because I fully intend to interfere with time more than I have, and I'll be noticed for it. "Maybe I'll become lore."

She frowns, clearly not finding it funny.

I grab the towel and stand. I stretch hard again to push through the aches of my body. Grunting in satisfaction, I let out a huge sigh, and move past Evalyn to the bathroom.

At the sink, I stare in the mirror, at the darkness of my eyes. Black, with a sheen; a dreadful look. Unable to break away, I begin to fear myself, and the darkness inside. The sheer power of their presence threatens to overwhelm me if I don't maintain a grip on my emotions.

I'm able to finally break the stare with my reflection, and proceed to wash my face with warm water from the faucet, and the towel. As I exit, I'm tossed into the doorjamb by a tremor underneath us. The house jostles. I know full well it's not an earthquake, and rush to the living room in time to see the women run out the door.

The blue swirl starts around the house's boundary. It spins, kicking up loose dirt at the edge, and blurring the bright white void. Colors begin to appear as it rips us from the empty world. The quake becomes heavier under foot. To my surprise, our horse whinnies while galloping through the yard. It's hard to believe it is still alive after pushing it as hard as I had to, and after being in the darkness.

The trembling stops, the swirls dissipate, and I'm left in awe of where, or rather when, we are. Following them out, I stand next to the women. There's a spark of recognition in Ami and Agatha's faces. Towers rise far above our heads. Eve screams out in terror.

"Get down! They're going to fall!" She yells.

~~~~~~

2 ESCALATION

The scenery is familiar, but significantly different than before. Things are run down, decrepit and falling apart since last we were here. A part of me wants to laugh at Eve's response, but her fears may be real.

Chas, the city which thrived once before, appears to be dead now. The buildings are husks, windows are broken out, and chunks of material are scattered below along the street. No day walkers are in the park or streets as before. The railways across the skyline are destroyed, no longer connecting the buildings. The trees in the park, and the ones in a border between us and the skyscrapers are fewer, and dead or dying. The dark, overcast sky, looms as if to just make everything appear more desolate.

How long has it been? A city like this would have had to see terrible times to become this.

"What is this?!" Eve yells. "Those things are too tall to be stable!"

"Even in their disrepair, they still look pretty sturdy," I lie.

"You may not be noticed after all, Rain. I don't see anyone." Ami glances at me when I step up next to her.

"Me either, but it is daytime. It might be livelier after dark, if anyone still lives here, that is."

"I guess we'll find out." Agatha tries to smile, but it's more a dismayed half-smile.

"You've been here, in this time?" Eve asks.

"No. We've been in this city, but it's not the same. It used to be cleaner, nicer. As it is now, it's possible it's been a hundred years since then," I mention.

"*Save us!*" a collective voice calls out to me, echoing through the air, and into my ears.

"Did you hear that?" I ask, my eyes darting around to find the origin.

"Hear what?" Ami scowls, concerned.

It doesn't persist, so I drop it. "Nothing. Never mind."

Our horse has come to stop on the side of the house. He isn't doing anything but standing there.

"Where's the other horse?" I ask.

"I…I don't know," Ami replies. "Mother?"

"Maybe the time was so slow out there that it was being pulled back and never made it," Agatha suggests.

A moment of silence passes, either for the horse or just shock that it could have been any one of us stuck out there, and never making it back. The thought of dying alone scares me.

"I think you should still stay here while we scout." Ami slips her hand in mine to give it a little squeeze. "You might need more time to recover."

"I don't think letting you go off without me would be a good idea – especially because of the trouble we had before." I stubbornly refuse the request to stay put. "I can't protect you if I'm not with you."

"It's fine. I'll go with her." Eve winks, and smiles maliciously. "You could *barely* beat me before, so you might get into trouble in your weakened state."

Grumbling and discontent, I have to bend to their will for the time being. As we all head back inside, the women begin preparing. I head upstairs. In my room I see my brown cloak and heirloom sword hanging on the wall. They're tempting me. Lying down on my bed, arms rested under my head, I fully intend to feign staying put. My cunning mind has other plans once they're gone.

If I put my cloak on and flip the hood up, I could easily conceal myself in order to stalk them, hiding amongst the shadows. Stalking should be easy enough. If I get into trouble, I'll have the sword.

Ami appears in my doorway in a soft and simple dress, holding a woven basket. I smile innocently at her, but she frowns.

"I already know what you're thinking. So, I'm going to tell Mother to stay to make sure you don't sneak out."

"What? No!" I sit straight up in bed. "You need me!"

"No, I don't." She smiles playfully. "I'll have Eve. Despite our differences, she's not going to let anything happen to me because she knows she'd have to answer to you."

I cross my arms and turn my head away like I were a child not getting his way. Ami sits next to me, placing her hand on my leg. I avoid her eye contact for a few moments, but I can only play coy for so long with her. Finally when I look, I'm forced to admit defeat.

"Okay. I'll stay here, but only this time."

"Deal." She hugs me.

Pulling away just a little provides us a different moment of closeness. She rests her forehead against mine, and I remember her lips. The look in her eyes tells me she's thinking about it too. We smile and draw close, but not fast enough. Eve appears in my doorway, and the moment passes.

With no warning, she reaches in, pounds a closed fist on my door, and startles Ami. She stomps hard, and the sound echoes off of the walls. She grimaces. "Hey! We're supposed to be leaving, and you're in bed with him?" she yells.

"We're not in bed, we're on it," Ami corrects her.

"Oh, I'll remember that the next time I'm in here," she hits right back.

Before I can do anything to resolve the immediate danger of conflict, Eve yanks Ami's free hand, and hauls her out. Before she gets beyond my doorframe, Ami looks back at me with a conniving grin.

She's enjoying this. Not just what we might have, but tormenting Eve.

I can't help but wonder; is Eve acting this way simply for the attention she used to receive from her clan? Is she actually attracted to me, or just playing a game of dominance as before?

Does Ami worry about her? I've tried to stop Eve, but with every rebuke she seems to only strengthen her resolve to win.

Thinking only gets me so far. Boredom sets in after only a few minutes of sitting in my room. The door below opens and shuts. I don my brown cloak, hood flipped up over my head, and strap my sword to my waist. I watch them out my window, giving them a little head start.

There's time for a quick snack. It should be easy to find them in the commercial district.

There's nothing in the fridge which I want, so I head into the storeroom, and flip the light switch. At the back of the room on a top shelf I discover sealed packages of smoked fish. Ripping one open, the heavy scent fills my nostrils, and my mouth waters in anticipation.

While devouring large chunks at a time, a noise near the stairs startles me. I look over. Agatha is standing there. Caught red-handed eating something I'm not sure if I should have been, and dressed to leave, I grin sheepishly with a mouth full of fish.

"Help! A bum has broken into the house and is eating our food! Rain, come quick!" she jokes while yelling up the stairs at no one.

I chuckle, and she comes over to take a piece of fish from the plastic bag. Eating it, she stands there with me in awkward silence. I hold the bag out to her for more. As she reaches for it I place it in her hand, and speed walk past her up the stairs. Before I make it to the back door she's already at the top of the stairs and clearing her throat.

I turn around and put my hands on my hips. "You look familiar. Are you following me?" I point at her and squint.

She's onto me.

"Me? Never." She waves her hand playfully.

The fishy aftertaste in my mouth requires washing out, and I do so with a glass of water. Guzzling it down, I place the glass on the counter and let out a sigh of satisfaction. Agatha watches me.

"You're creeping me out, Agatha. Don't make me call Evalyn," I grin.

"Evalyn's preoccupied, and you aren't getting rid of me." She crosses her arms and gives me her motherly look.

"What makes you think I was trying to do such a thing?" I reach for the doorknob, and lean a bit on my feet.

She puts her finger up and points at me in a warning. Her face is saying 'don't you dare,' and I can't help but tempt her to find out what she'll do if I actually step outside. The doorknob twists with my wrist, and there is an audible click when the latch is free of its strike plate. Agatha takes a step forward. I open the door.

Did my parents mind me this closely? I suppose not as they were likely king and queen of Asta before me. They probably had to attend to duties and act properly. Did I have a nanny then?

"Don't." She waggles her finger.

"Don't what? Do this?" I fling the door open, jump outside and slam it shut.

With both hands gripping the doorknob, holding it from being opened, I play a game of 'who is stronger' with her. She tries to overpower my grip by twisting back and forth and pulling, but fails. I laugh at her disapproving scowl.

Agatha becomes serious, speaking through the window in the door. "You can't go. Not yet. You need to rest, and we don't know if the darkness is stable within you. If you have an outburst again it might hurt someone!"

I know she's right. Glancing over my shoulder, I see the patch of dead grass where the darkness exploded from my body. That alone convinces me to release the knob.

Reality slaps me in the face. As she opens the door, my own despair breaks the feelings I had been fighting to hold in. An overwhelming urge to sob crashes through my fragile barrier. While I realize though I may have saved the women, and this time, from the darkness, it may well be at the cost of my own existence.

I fall to my knees on the steps. Agatha steps forward, hugging me to her bosom as my strength is sapped away. My farce of acting strong has gotten me into trouble, and I'm unsure of how to cope. For a few moments, between fits of sobs, she helps me up and brings me back inside. I sit at the table, cross my arms on the hard wood, and put my face down into it to subject myself to darkness. Her hand on my head, she stays with me, silently comforting me.

She's right. I am a danger to people. I'm a danger to the house, but I can't leave. I'll constantly have to be on guard with all of them. I don't want to hurt them. Is the idea I had of having a relationship with Ami forever tainted by my decision?

Consumed by my own despair brings the despairs of some lost souls within me to light. They cry out for help, they cry about oppression and poverty. They wail about injustices committed against them. I ignore them for now. Regret fills me. I wish I hadn't listened to the darkness.

With nothing better to do, I sit still until my back starts to ache and I become restless. When I look up Agatha is still with me, despite knowing I could be dangerous.

"Why did you save me?" my voice is meek.

"We couldn't just let you die, dear."

"I was a stranger. Perhaps I'd been someone bad."

"We took a risk. And you've looked after us at every opportunity – I'd say it paid off."

"I feel defeated," I sigh heavily. "I feel useless. I haven't been able to do what I said I would for you."

"That's okay. As long as you know in your heart you aren't either of those. We're here for you, and I know when the time is right you'll come through."

I give a weak smile, and she smiles back. Standing, I stretch, and then head to the sink. I stick my head under the faucet for a gulp, and then splash myself. Agatha joins me, but I don't feel hounded. Rather, it feels like she's still the guardian who saved my life, and she's just looking out for me.

She's been here with her daughter so long, in her motherly role, it only makes sense she'd be this way with everyone. Maybe not so much with Eve, but she's still the head of this household.

If I could remember my own mother, would I feel closer to Agatha, or her?

Outside, the sun has set beyond the horizon of Chas's towers, and the sky begins to darken. While I watch for Ami and Eve, I wonder how long they will be out there. They're nowhere in sight, and it's becoming harder to see things clearly at ground level. Some streetlights, and sporadic lights in windows, have begun to come on – the city isn't as dead as we thought it might be.

My attention is called to a particular street to the left. Instead of seeing a brunette and red head heading home, long blond hair flails in the wind as a girl runs through the park, hurtling toward us. Her distance to the house decreases rapidly. She seems to have a sense of urgency, and I open the door anticipating something terrible.

Why is she running so fast? Are Ami and Eve okay?

Behind her, at the entrance to the park, the two figures I was expecting run toward the house as well. I'm puzzled.

Are they chasing her?

Stepping down into the grass, I quirk my eyebrows, and cross my arms. The blonde is nearing the boundary while Ami and Eve try desperately to overtake her. Though she's likely only five feet tall, her legs carry her with power and speed, even in overalls. She's built athletically.

She shows no sign of slowing, aiming directly for me. I plant my feet and drop my arms defensively. She's familiar in many ways. A wide smile; her small nose; that long blonde hair; her skin is fair and pale and her face is filled with a childlike youth. Before I can say anything, Emma preempts me.

"RAIN!"

Despite trying to brace myself, she tackles me at the waist, and my arms flail upward. As I collapse to the ground, the hilt of my sword shifts behind me. Our combined weight falling on top of it jams it into my lower back. I yell in pain. She cries and calls my name again.

"Rain! I thought I'd never see you again!" She bear hugs me.

"Emma!" I writhe in pain, gasping for air. "I need you to get off of me. Argh, my back!"

"Sorry!" She leaps up, allowing me to roll off the sword's pommel.

I lie there for a moment before returning to my feet. I'm given no time to regain my composure before she clasps her arms around my waist, and digs her chin into my sternum, grinning from ear to ear. Planting my feet, I do my best to not fall over.

With a glimmer in her eyes, she looks up at me with the same innocence she had when we saw her last. "You've changed! What happened to your eyes?! Does it hurt?! I bet you didn't recognize me, huh!"

Rambunctious and full of energy, her mouth spews words faster than I can comprehend them. Not given a chance to answer, she nestles the side of her head against me and I gently hug her. And then Ami and Eve catch up. The looks on their faces could kill; I throw my arms out to the side in an attempt to defend myself, but it's no use. Fury burns hot in

Ami's eyes, and contempt in Eve's.

"*She* tackled *me*!" I exclaim.

With grumbling and protests, it takes both Ami and Eve to pry Emma's arms free, detaching her. No sooner having separated us, Emma wrenches free of their grasp and clings to my arm like the little girl I remember. She sticks her tongue out at Ami and Eve.

"You little whelp." Eve tries to grab her overall straps, but Emma ducks behind me. "Get off of him before I swing you from that hair of yours!"

"Who are *you*?" Emma taunts. "I don't know you, and I don't have to listen to you!"

"Eve, calm down. Emma's fine." I hold my hand up to stop her from reaching around my back.

"She's fine, is she?" Ami crosses her arms and glares at me. In response I sheepishly smile, recalling Emma's crush on me.

"You know what I meant." I wink.

Seeing Emma on my arm, and my wink at Ami, frustrates Eve further. She huffs heavily and swiftly grabs my other arm so Ami can't, clenching it to the point I fear it will break. Like children, Eve and Emma glare at each other. Ami's eyes are on me, burning my soul with her stare as if it's my fault because I'm unable to reconcile the situation.

Ami pushes past us in a flurry, slamming the kitchen door. Agatha opens it again and her eyes are wide, likely rattled by having the door slammed. Emma looks over to finally take notice of Agatha.

"Aggy!" She releases her strong grip from me, and runs to give Agatha a hug. I hear Agatha let out a wheeze as Emma nearly crushes her ribs. "It's been so long for me, but it's like you guys haven't aged! How?! Where did you go? Why did you leave me behind?!"

"All in good time dear." Agatha smiles. "I'll cook us a meal, and you can stay for dinner."

"You mean breakfast." Emma giggles. "And no you won't! I'll cook for you!"

I shake my arm from Eve's grasp. She protests, and follows me into the kitchen. Before I can escape Eve to find Ami, Emma reattaches herself onto my left side. A sigh escapes my lips.

It's useless to fight right now.

"Rain, you're going to have to tell me everything. Like who *she* is!" Emma points at Eve.

Eve raises her fist to strike Emma, but I intervene and glare.

"Enough. You two need to calm down and make nice. Eve, take a breath. Emma, please refrain from antagonizing Eve." I sternly speak to them.

"Okay," they speak in unison unintentionally, and glare at each other.

Emma releases her grasp on me and moves as if she were in her own home, surveying the contents of the cupboards, pantry and refrigerator. She looks back at us still speaking with fervor.

"Where is all your food? This can't be it! How could you survive on this?"

"We have a store room downstairs," Agatha replies.

"You have a downstairs?!" She spins around and notices the door in the corner and proceeds to disappear through it. Agatha follows her. Her excitement and enthusiasm makes me laugh.

She has just as much energy now as she did when she was younger. What is she now? Sixteen? Seventeen?

Taking this opportunity, I try to slip away, but Eve heads me off at the white swinging door. When I attempt to bypass her and go upstairs, she blocks my path. Glaring, I try to show her I'm not amused but she's serious too. A scowl and frown show her disapproval of Emma.

"She's not coming with us," Eve whispers harshly. "I got stuck here by accident, but I'm making the best of it – I'm not competing with some child too."

"Eve, you're overreacting," I whisper, while looking toward the door to downstairs, preparing to cover myself for when Emma returns. "Emma's not a threat. We turned her down once. I'm pretty sure the only one with any intention of her coming with us, is her."

"I'll push her out if she's here when it starts, when the vortex comes to take us," she raises her voice a little.

"If you hurt her, you'll have to answer to me." I become defensive and plant my finger very firmly in Eve's sternum, moving past the embarrassment I would normally feel touching her in such a manner. "I understand your motives and I agree with not taking her along. But don't even think about harming her."

Thoroughly irritated, I push past her, and head upstairs. At the top, I hear the sewing machine going, and stop to think about checking in on Ami. Standing at the door for a few moments, I knock lightly, but no response is given. The sewing machine continues to run, and I hear shuffling. Knocking again, a little harder this time elicits a response.

"Go away. I'm busy," Ami answers sharply.

With Eve feeling the way she does, no doubt Ami feels more so. Imagine her surprise seeing Emma again. Do I intrude and reassure her, or give her space and let her calm down?

The former wins after another minute of quiet contemplation, and I twist the doorknob. With the door cracked, I poke my head in.

Ami is working furiously, tossing things about as she seems to be trying to piece something together. She looks up at me briefly, angrily, before returning to her work. Taking her silence as permission, I enter the room and shut the door behind me. She continues to shovel things around and sew something together.

"Hey," I open dialogue.

"What, Rain?" she answers with contempt.

"What's got you so upset?"

"Nothing." It's that tone which tells me it's *something*, but she is hesitant to talk about it.

"Why lie to me? It's not like you're going to fool me." I move closer to her, consciously keeping my tone light and playful.

She stops her machine, and looks at me. I can see it in her face, she's hurt and jealous. No doubt she sees Emma as another person to compete against for my attention. Now within reach, I extend my arm and grab her hand, pulling her to stand up. She resists. I tilt my head, and refuse to let go of her hand until she complies. Reluctantly she does and I switch places with her, sitting down and pulling her onto my lap.

"Emma's just excited to see us, that's all Ami."

"She's infatuated with you, like she was before." She crosses her arms and looks away from me.

"Last time we saw her she was a little girl. Just because she's grown up a little doesn't mean her status has changed. I still see her as a little sister."

"You didn't see the way she reacted when she saw me." She finally looks back at me. Anger has been replaced with sadness.

"So tell me about it," I speak soothingly.

"As soon as I looked into her shop window, she nearly knocked me down asking if you were here too. Before I could answer, she stuck her tongue out at me and ran off."

"So, she's like *your* little sister too?"

She frowns, but her cheek muscles can't take too much more. Her face softens. I wrap my arms around her. Placing her hands on my forearms she reciprocates the gesture. We sit in silence for a bit.

"Frankly, I'm not sure I'm safe to be around *you*, let alone anyone else," I say.

"Well you're not going anywhere. Even if you could." She raps her fingers on my arm gently.

"What if you and I happen," I start. "What happens if things don't work out? Won't it be awkward?"

"Isn't it too late? Us happening, that is." She turns around and straddles me, placing her arms around my neck but leaning back. "It's only been a few months, but it feels like a lifetime. Like I've known you forever."

"I know, and I feel the same way, but I want to make sure you're safe, and we're stable. Wouldn't it be better if we found a way to stop spiraling through time before we go any further?"

She's silent, and I can tell she doesn't like the idea of our relationship not progressing. I'm unsure of it myself, but my resolve to ensure her safety first is solid.

"Fine, then we wait before we become more serious than we already are. But it doesn't mean I'm letting Eve near you. She can go jump off a cliff. And Emma stays in this time."

I chuckle at Ami's aggressiveness.

"And you better make good on your promise to help break this curse quickly," she continues while staring me directly in the eyes. "Then Eve can find someone else to pester. You, my Mother, and I can just stay together."

"We'll need to approach with caution. Look at what happened when Evalyn tried." I point to my eyes. "I haven't forgotten my promise, but I want to do research."

Sitting for a few more minutes, just being with each other, I finally tap the side of her calf to tell her I'd like to leave. When she stands up she turns and grabs both of my arms, helping me to my feet. My legs tingle, and moments after trying to take my first step, my leg spasms. My balance falters. Ami catches me, and I laugh while struggling to not hit the floor face first.

"Always there to catch me," I joke.

"Always. Legs asleep?"

"Mmhmm."

The wait for my legs to reawaken isn't long, and we make our way back downstairs.

Eve is neither within the living room nor the kitchen, and I am thankful to not have to worry about confronting her again so soon. Emma bustles about the kitchen while Agatha sits at the table, watching a human storm blow through. Emma has taken Agatha's place preparing the food, and she is clearly displeased about it.

Emma sees me and stops briefly. "You're going to have to come to my shop, and help bring my food here tomorrow. You have a good amount of fruits and vegetables, but you're running low on meat."

"I thought you just sold produce."

"I did! That was seven years ago! Can you believe it?! After things got bad I had to take up additional products in order to keep going." She frowns but resumes her cooking. "I'm one of a few left in my district, and not for long."

"Wait, why are you bringing your food here? Shouldn't you be selling it?" I'm not liking where she's headed with this. "Especially because you're one of the few that's left."

"Rain, you have no idea how long it felt waiting for you to return!" She stops dead in her tracks, and turns to me with a bright smile. "You guys aren't leaving without me!"

"Why?" I quirk an eyebrow.

"What do you mean 'why'? Don't you remember what you did for me?"

"Of course I do."

"Well, now I'm old enough to repay the debt!"

"There's no debt," I try to explain, but Ami jumps in.

"It's too dangerous," Ami tells her. "You can't go with us."

Emma's innocence is lost in an instant. She slams a wooden spoon down on the counter, spattering a creamy white sauce all over the counter and her overalls. In a rush she shoves her way between us, and faces Ami in an act of defiance. Ami crosses her arms, and I anticipate a breakdown of the calm we just created.

"He's under my protection, and I'm protecting him from you!" Emma glares.

Agatha chuckles, and Ami fights back a laugh. Eve slams the back door open. With the ferocity of a wild animal Eve is upon Emma, towering over her short frame, nearly foaming at the mouth.

"You're not coming. End of story!" Eve yells at her.

"I'm pretty sure that's not your call!" Emma yells right back, and looks her up and down in a snooty manner. "Someone needs to protect him from *your* grubby hands."

"Let me tell you something, *child.*" Eve reaches out to grab her by her overalls, but is eluded. Emma bounces away behind me.

"You can't have Rain, you vagrant! Who dressed you?!"

A teenager is now deciding my love life? What is the world coming to?

"Vagrant?!"

Eve is infuriated. Her face has turned completely red, her eyes water, and she grinds her teeth. She's had it and pushes me out of the way, lunging at Emma. Emma dives between her legs, evading the long arm grasp. A chase around the kitchen ensues. Ami and I move out of the way to watch. While amusing for a moment, it soon becomes tiresome. I step in.

Jumping in front of Emma as she rounds the island, I place both of my hands out in front of me, and plant them firmly on her shoulders. Swiftly, I swing around Emma to block Eve.

"All right. Enough you two," I tell them with force.

"You're going to let this little girl talk to me like that Rain?!" Eve exclaims.

"Let her? What control could I possibly exert over someone this rambunctious?" Dropping my arms, I turn to face Ami, neutral to both of them.

"Yeah, he's not going to defend you because you are a tramp!" Emma doesn't want to let it drop. "Who dresses like that?"

"At least I don't dress like a man!" Eve reaches to smack her, but I grab her hand, and then look at Emma sternly.

Emma looks away, and I place my hand on her head. Eve lowers her hand, and I release it when I feel she's no longer a threat.

"You two, behave. Eve, Emma's only going to see us for a month. Emma, I'm sorry but it's too dangerous for you to go with us," I try to explain, yet again.

"But she gets to go?!" Her finger points accusingly at Eve, tears beginning to stream down her face.

"The four of us don't have a choice," I explain. "In the few months I've lived in this house, we've seen quite a bit of danger. Slavers, marauders, and a black mass trying to consume everything."

Emma isn't buying it. That hurt and angry look appears on her face while tears stream down her rosy cheeks. She raises her voice. "You don't know what it's been like! It broke my heart watching you disappear! You just left me! All I wanted to do was to stay here! Things only got worse after you left!"

I let her breathe before I try and explain, but Ami moves toward her and, in a surprise move, hugs her. Emma sobs into Ami's shirt, and the darkness tugs inside me. I feel something rising, and it compels me to caress her soft, golden locks in an attempt to quell the anguish.

"Emma, the four of us are stuck. There's nothing we can do until we break the curse on this house. We're forced into dangerous situations," Ami explains, trying to help me out. "It was good you didn't come with us because you'd be stuck here forever, or at least until Rain makes good on his promise."

"I don't care! It would have been better for me! Denis became a problem again and his father couldn't handle him! The city is like this because of *him*! He destroyed everything!"

I hug her tightly, squishing her between Ami and myself. But though times had been bad for her, I'm not sorry we didn't take her.

"Let's eat and you can tell us about it. Okay?" my tone is soft, and I smile sympathetically.

Emma calms down after a few minutes, and pulls away to finish cooking. The rest of us set the table. She's prepared pasta with a creamy, white sauce, and boiled beef chunks from our reserves on top. With the table set, and the glasses filled, Emma serves us, starting with me.

Sitting in my normal spot at the head of the table, Ami is to my right, and Eve to my left, leaving Agatha and Emma to sit toward the middle. But before we are completely situated, Emma drags her chair with one hand, her plate of food in the other, and interjects herself between Eve and me. Eve's furious expression tells me she's readying to verbally assault her again, but I catch her gaze with the shaking of my head. She backs down, with a loud and defeated sigh, and we begin our meal. With the first bite of creamy pasta in my mouth, Emma jumps right into her story since we last saw her.

"After you left, Denis disappeared for a while – a couple years, actually. But when he returned, it went back to the way it was before. Some of the fighters stayed loyal to him even after Mister Lindali put an end to it. He recruited his own personal army of mobsters to do his bidding. His father became ill when he took over, and he started punishing everyone, trashing things even if they had paid their 'protection' money."

Emma takes a breath and a bite of her food, but continues talking while she chews.

"When people couldn't afford either the repairs, or the protection money, they just started abandoning the city. I tried leaving, but Denis won't let me. He said if I did, he would burn the city down and anyone left in it."

"Has no one tried stopping him?" Ami asks.

"There was resistance at first. From whole neighborhoods. But Denis wore them down by destroying their lives, conversion, or death. The resistance was quelled within six months.

"He said if I marry him, I wouldn't have to pay protection money, and my shop wouldn't be ransacked anymore. Of course I refused. He's a pig!" Emma looks up at me, the glimmer having returned to her eyes.

Looking in Ami's direction, I stare blankly, taking bites of my own meal, thinking while Emma continues on with her story. Their voices become background noise to my own thoughts.

What happens to these souls trapped in despair, now inside of me, if I change things? If I remove Denis from his throne of power over the city, will things change? Am I supposed to stop him? Will some of these souls be put to rest?

"Yes. You must," despair calls to me again, and I realize it's coming from within me. It's no longer their collective voices, but their collective thoughts protruding in on my consciousness.

"Rain? Rain what's wrong?" Emma asks putting the back of her hand to my cheek, scared. "Rain? Why is your face turning black?"

Her hand is cool, and I flinch, startled. Standing, I move quickly to the sink, and douse my head with cold water from the tap. Feeling them rise in me, I fight to suppress it, to hold it in. They call to me, and I can feel the anguish of the city. It pricks at my skin, and the hairs rise on the back of my neck. Despite the shock of cold water, my control is slipping. I fling the back door open and run out into the cool night air. Darkness spreads through my body once more, and it envelops me, covering me from head to toe in a wave.

Hearing Emma call out to me, I run faster. Over my shoulder I see Eve and Ami restraining her from following. Safe from harming them, I run a few more feet, past the apple tree and into the dying grass of the park. I collapse in a heap on my knees, my hands on my head. They pound against my soul. The heat rises. The voices begin screaming, and I cannot control the darkness.

"AUUUGGGHHHHH!" I let out a cry of despair. Darkness spews forth, swirling around me like a tornado once again. Even under the darkness provided by the clouds in the sky, I can see clearly the black seeping through the ground and billowing into the air like shadowy whips lashing at anything in reach. I am powerless to stop it.

"Rain, fight for us! We are lost in despair! Stop Denis!"

"You don't have to convince me!" I yell to the voices.

"Rain, stop Denis!" They repeat their desire. *"Stop him* before *he kills us!"*
"I will!"
"Stop him!" They persist despite my telling them I will do as they ask.
"I know!" I yell, aggravated.

Slowly, the dark storm around me begins to die and recede into my body.

When I feel it's safe, I remove my hands from my head and stand, but my knees cave. My face impacts first on the dead zone I have created. Having sapped my energy trying to contain the darkness, it's a struggle to keep my eyes open. I force myself back up. Emma runs at me, Ami and Eve hot on her tail.

I put my hand out to stop her, but Emma grabs it and throws it over her shoulder. The feeling of weakness increases as she takes some of my weight. She struggles to support me, but is quickly assisted by Ami and Eve. They are my crutches back to the house.

Upon arriving, Agatha places a wet rag on the top of my head, and I shiver; the water is too cold now because the hot flash has ended. Tilting my head down, I drop it back into her hand and we continue inside and to the table. They place me back in my chair, and I rest with my eyes closed. I hear them retake their seats and sit in silence, no doubt watching me. Emma is the one to break the silence.

"What is it? Why did your skin turn black? Why are your eyes like that? Are you sick?" The questions come out one after another, but each one is cautiously asked.

"I can't explain it fully. The short version is that it's a collection of souls from this world who died in despair."

"What do you mean?"

"In the last time we were in, we don't know where we were. It was a nothingness. In this nothingness was this shadow which came to life, a collection of despairing souls trying to overtake Ami and I. They wouldn't let up until I 'let them into the light' which basically meant inhabiting my body until I can change their fate. I did it so Ami, Eve, and Agatha wouldn't die, and so it wouldn't be unleashed on the world when we shifted through time."

"Why were you yelling at it?" Emma asks after a few moments of silence.

"They speak to me in my head. They want me to change events in time so they will not have died in despair. Apparently that's how I can save them."

Silence falls across the room again for a few moments. It's awkward, and I open my eyes to make sure they haven't left me.

"I don't know if changing time would have a significant impact on their despairs," Ami points out. "Even if you can save some of them, you can't save them all."

"You're probably right, but I would still rather it be me than you." I sigh. "The question is; how much do I change things before it's too much? Are we safe from paradox effects? Or if I change something which prevents us from ever meeting will we become caught in a loop?"

"We've never had that kind of question come up because our interaction was never very memorable." Agatha's voice is soothing, but her words are not. "Evalyn might know because of her previous travels before all of this, but this was much more of an accidental situation than her planning out every detail of what would happen when we change times."

"The despairing souls want me to be their hero. Their 'champion of light'. Despite their insistence, I'm not sure how well I can fulfill the role." I look at them.

It seems I keep trying to be the hero. But is it worth it?

"Why you?" Eve asks. I'm not sure if she wants an answer or if the question is rhetorical.

"What do they want you to do? Right now, I mean," Ami asks.

"They want Denis stopped," I answer. "I can sense a strong ill will toward him. They want me to—"

"Sounds like a good idea to me! I'll help you, Rain!" Emma insists.

With a shake of the head, I stand with my plate before she can persist. My intent is to wash the plate, but a headache begins to rage through my skull. My eyes water and I become light headed. Rubbing my neck, I crane my head in an attempt to alleviate the pain, but it continues. The women look at me with worry, but I ignore it and move to the living room door.

"I need to rest."

"Rain, I think it would be a good idea if we all kept an eye on you," Agatha mothers me.

Half way through the swinging door, I look back and nod. Climbing the stairs, I long for the soft mattress to take away the aching. I hang up my cloak and sword, and stare at them for a moment. I chuckle.

The adventure I was seeking has found me instead.

While my body craves rest, my mind starts going stir crazy as soon as I'm lying down.

I wish Agatha hadn't stopped me. I need to feel like I'm doing anything but sleeping. How much time have I spent sleeping lately? Between shifting through time, and this problem I have now, I feel like all I do is sleep, but there are things to be done.

As I lie there hoping the headache will be gone when I awake, I hear the women coming up the stairs. Ami is talking. Her voice seems hushed, and distant. She's laying down rules for watching over me, and the shifts they will take.

"There will be absolutely no climbing in bed with him, Eve," Ami states clearly and accusingly. "You can sit at his bedside."

"Would I take advantage of Rain while he's not feeling well?" I can hear the grin in Eve's voice.

"Yes, you would. I might just have to sit with you so I can keep an eye on you both at the same time," Ami grumbles.

"What about me?" Emma asks.

"Same rule. No one gets in bed with him!" Ami speaks with exasperation.

With my eyes growing heavy, I can't stay awake. Time itself seems to stop, and I enter into ominous darkness.

~~~~~~

I am fully aware in my dream, trapped in darkness. Unlike past times where I floated along, it feels as though I'm on something like ground. It reminds me of the white void, how there was nothing, but it was solid. It's pitch black, and again I am the only thing illuminated. I assume I'm inside the despair. For a while I'm alone, and I walk in a straight line, or perhaps a circle, or maybe not at all. My projection appears to be walking, but there's no sense of movement.

It's endless.

Finally something appears, a body. While darkness surrounds everything, I can clearly see the person, as if the light is coming directly from them, as it is from me. Expecting an unknown person from the city, I am a little stunned when it's someone I know. Eve's figure stands in the darkness with me. For a moment I begin to think that instead of the subconscious reality of the despair collective, that this is actually a bizarre dream. The notion dissipates when I find myself overwhelmed with despairs from Eve.

"I'm lost, bumbling through time with people who don't care about me."

"My people are without me as their leader. I abandoned them for Rain. Were they killed? Or taken as slaves by another faction?"

"Did Kohan lead them well? Did they make it to the mountains?"

"How many people died because of me? How many people have I killed?"

"Am I alone? Without love?"

"What does Ami have that I don't?"

I'm led to question whether these are being absorbed from Eve now, or if Eve died in despair at some point in the future, and through some means is a part of me now. As other despairs of hers crop up, I begin to understand her a little better. Despite her selfish and brash front, I can see that deep within her, she's no different than the rest of us.

"My friends, my family, my home. My parents, lost to the war when I was a child. Everything I knew is gone. I'll never see them again. What do I have to show for it?"

"Why did the cataclysm have to happen? If it hadn't, maybe my life would have been different."

Her body fades back into the darkness, and I'm left alone again for a time. Because it's unclear how long I will be here, I walk again. Other bodies crop up every once in a while but their voices are too muffled to understand. They disappear completely as I move steadily. A speck of light appears in the distance, and it gives me hope. Heading for it as I had last time, it grows larger. I begin to run. Another muffled voice can be heard, but it's not coming from the darkness. The closer I draw, the clearer the voice becomes. It's Emma's.

"Rain, you can't leave me here again. Don't you understand? I just found you again and it feels like we're going to have to say 'goodbye' all over." She's crying.

The white light surrounds me, and I jolt awake, my eyes open wide. I gasp for air, feeling like I have been holding my breath. Emma is next to my bed in the dark of night. She's startled at my sudden awakening, but while I see the sheen of tears streaming down her face, my mind is preoccupied with Eve.

Standing quickly, I stumble as my vision goes white. I'm light headed. Emma holds me up. I regain my composure, and move from her without a word. Exiting the room I look down the stairs and find all is dark down there.

Is she in her room?

The door is closed and I press my ear to it for a moment, listening intently for any sound of her presence. Emma moves next to me.

"Rain, what are you doing?" she whispers, confused.

I look at her, and gently shush her with a finger to my lips. Knocking lightly on the door, I twist the knob and open it a crack. Eve is lying motionless on her bed against the wall near her window. I listen for her breathing; it's quiet but it's there. She's fast asleep, but a nagging in my mind urges me to wake her. Despite knowing she'll be irritable, or more likely try to seduce me, I move into her room and kneel by her bed.

She's sprawled out, no covers on her, and one of her two pillows is on the floor. Her nighttime attire of a lacy bra and matching panties would normally embarrass me, but I focus on waking her. Lightly I place my hand on her shoulder and jostle her. She swats at my hand. I narrowly miss a smack. When she returns to her former position, I try again.

"Eve, wake up."

She groans and opens her eyes, staring blankly at me for a moment before reaching for my face. Grabbing her hand before she can pull me in, my mouth takes over.

"Eve, I understand what you're going through," I whisper.

She gives me a puzzled look, and grunts.

"I had a dream, or something, and you were in it. I know about the war, and that you lost your parents when you were a child. I'm sorry you lost everything important to you. I'm sorry you've felt alienated—" she cuts me off before I can finish.

She rips her arm from my hand and points to the door, barking angrily, "Out!"

I've provoked a negative response, though it had only been my intent to comfort her. I stand. She pulls her blanket up, and crosses her arms over her chest. She looks away. Unable to tell if she's angry or embarrassed, this midnight timing feels like a poor choice in wanting to talk about a sensitive subject. Moving to the door I look back. Her scowl is intimidating, and I step out. Emma has retreated to the stairway. I turn around to try again, but Eve moves swiftly to the door.

"Eve, I—"

She slams it in my face.

"I want you to know I'm here to talk about it if you need to," I tell her and sit down, my back against her door.

"Rain, go away. Go back to sleep," she grumbles.

"No, I'll stay here."

Emma looks behind her, and then heads down the stairs. I hear her at the bottom of the stairway talking with someone. Picking up the sound of Ami's voice, I try to listen in, but I'm unable to make out what they're saying.

What was the point of jumping out of bed at night and waking her up? I probably could have waited until morning. But why would I be shown Eve's despairs if not to act upon it right away? Why Eve's? Why not Emma, Ami, or Agatha? Could I just be absorbing from people near me, as well as what I already have. Or did Eve die in despair at some point in our future?

I have to try to make it right. Maybe I am strong enough like the despair said. And if I alter things for people while still alive, the despair will lessen, and perhaps I will regain some semblance of control of my body and mind.

Eve opens her door abruptly, and I fall backward, my arms flailing out in an attempt to catch myself. I'm unsuccessful. Thudding to the floor I look up at Eve, still in her undergarments. This time I blush heavily, and look away.

"You're breathing too loud." She glares at me while I lay there.

Trying to lighten her mood a little, I suck in air, hold it, and puff my cheeks out. Though she's staring at me, it's too dark to tell if her expression has changed. After a few moments she picks her foot up and places it on my chest. She pushes down, and I'm forced to exhale.

Returning to her bed, she sits down at the head of it, placing her back against the wall, covering up with her blanket. She hasn't closed the door, and I assume she's inviting me in so we can talk.

When I enter, she motions to close the door. I do, and she turns on a lamp. Her room is fairly empty, with a single wardrobe in the far back corner, a desk against the wall closest to the hall, and a table with the lamp. Her bed is built for a normal sized person, but is clearly too short for her height.

Moving to her bed, I sit on the opposite end from her, and following her lead, place my back against the wall.

"I don't keep a diary and I know you weren't there, so how do you know about my past?" She's hostile.

"The despair within me. I don't have a definitive answer, but while I was asleep a few minutes ago, I came across you in my dream. It was like I could hear your thoughts."

"What did you hear, exactly?"

"That you had terrible experiences as a child with losing your parents and friends to a war. You feel lost and not cared about. You're alone. Something about a cataclysm."

"Well that's a bit presumptuous of your dream isn't it? I don't know how you learned about my past, but I am just fine." Her face is pained while she tries to put on a strong front. The despair within urges me onward.

"Maybe on the surface, Eve, but I can sense from you what I was shown is true."

She scowls and yells, "Yeah? What do you know? I'd be better off without the lot of you."

Turning toward her, I reach forward and grab her hand which is outside the blanket to hold it in place. A sliver of empathy surfaces. "I'm sorry you're stuck here with us. I know you don't want to be here, and if I could take you back I would."

She snatches her hand from mine, pulls her knees up to her head, and hides her face. Were it not for some quick inhales and hiccups, I would simply think she was angry, but she's crying. I've hit a sensitive nerve. Scooting closer to her I can't help but feel the sorrow she is feeling as I put my arms around her. To my surprise she doesn't fight me.

"Eve, I'm sorry if…" I start but she sits up and puts her finger to my lips. She replaces her finger with her lips.

Pushing me over, she collapses onto me, and pins my arms while kissing me passionately. Before I have an opportunity to break away, she does it for me. Lying there, she hovers over me, and I stare into her green eyes while she examines me.

"It's okay, if you're here, Rain," she says quietly. "I'm okay with being here as long as you're here."

"Eve, I—" Before I can finish Eve's door bursts open.

Ami has kicked it open and Emma stands beside her with her hands covering her mouth in shock. Ami's eyes burn with fire as she raises a fist to threaten Eve. She notices, and all semblance of sorrow is gone. She grins antagonistically. Before I can explain what's happened, I see Ami's disapproving look as Eve quickly asserts herself.

"Rain and I have declared our love for each other!" Eve sneers. "Looks like you two are out of luck!"

"Whoa there, Eve. Not even close!" I state and look at Ami. "Ami she's lying! I was just talking with her, and she threw herself at me, like she normally does!"

Eve looks at me and plays sweet, "Don't tell me our kiss meant nothing, babe." She looks up at the other two and nods. "He was comforting me…with his lips."

My face flushes. Embarrassment, shame, and anxiety set in. Looking at shocked Emma, and angry Ami, I realize I'm in a 'no-win' situation. There's no room for further attempts to try and defend myself against the oncoming storm. Ami's in like lightning, and grabs me under the armpits, attempting to wrench me out of Eve's grasp. When Eve pushes her away, Emma jumps in to help.

"Get out of my room! Leave me and Rain in peace," Eve squawks.

"Shut up and let go of him!" Emma yells, wrapping both of her firm arms around one of mine to tug.

"Eve, you need to stop pretending he is going to cave in to your vile will," Ami snaps while pulling.

"Oh he will. He and I shared a very tender moment." She playfully keeps me pinned under her weight.

Amidst the battle, Ami and Emma finally pry me free from Eve's clutches and drag me down onto the hard, wood floor. My feet land with a thud, and Eve giggles as I'm dragged out of the room.

"Bye, lover," Eve jests.

Clear of Eve's room, I'm expecting to be hauled to mine, but instead the two women drag me down the stairs forcefully. I dare not attempt to stand, for fear of knocking us to the bottom in a heap. Ami motions for Emma to open the door, and I know what's coming next. Emma flings the door open, and Ami shoves me out.

Before I can respond, the door is closed behind me, and I hear the latch of the lock. I jiggle the handle and look in the small window, expecting to see Ami or Emma there. Instead they've retreated into the hallway, and they're gone. Sighing, I sit down on the last porch step and plant my bare feet in the grass. It's nice and cool.

What have I gotten myself into? I don't know what I was like in the past, but even as a king I can't imagine being fawned over this much. At least Emma has a reason. I still don't understand Eve's pursuit. Perhaps it's because she knows she can't have me? I don't know if that's how women work, but it's my only explanation.

Emma won't be staying with us, and she will be one less to worry about soon enough. But no matter how much I try to push her away, it's going to hurt. She will just have to live her own life after we're gone.

Eve though. I think even if Ami and I declared we were going to pursue something together, Eve would still interfere. She's too stubborn.

Lying back, I place my hands behind my head, and stare into the night sky. The stars can be seen, but not as powerfully as when there are no city lights to contend with. I let my mind go blank and drift like the gentle wind passing by.

~~~~~~

Whether I slept or not is a mystery, as I seem to have been somewhat aware while lying there. But there was no darkness, no dream. I'm called back to reality as the sun peeks over the horizon, beginning to illuminate the city, and beat on my eyelids. Were it a winter night, I'd have frozen to death, but the temperature stayed warm, and it wasn't uncomfortable.

The horse neighs, and I wonder about the one we lost in the void.

Strange it wasn't pulled back. Perhaps the darkness got to it. Maybe it died? Or maybe it was being pulled back, and just didn't make it in time. I would rather something dreadful have happened to it than it starve to death. A quick merciful death.

Would it be possible to get far enough away to stay in a specific time? If it couldn't pull us back fast enough, we might just break away. We'd have to find a way to land safely. I will need to ask Agatha and Evalyn if this would be a good idea.

The broken cityscape greets me beyond the boundary of the dead park when I open my eyes. Husks of their former glory, the buildings put me in a melancholy mood, and I think about their better times. It was crowded, but it was full of life.

I stretch my back, which aches from lying on something hard for too long, and let out a satisfactory grunt. A brief gust of wind makes me want to climb into my cozy bed and wrap up.

The door is still locked, and I anticipate the kitchen one to be also. I bide my time by drawing up a bucket of water to take to the horse. He drinks slowly, and I look up at a branch on the apple tree. New leaves and buds have begun to form.

Both the garden and tree are recovering nicely after the sandstorm, but it will be a while before anything is ripe.

Still I reach up and snatch an unripe apple to give the horse. He takes it willingly. Stroking his mane, I can't tell if he likes the attention or not. He doesn't protest or try to bite me, so I take it as a good sign. A noise from the house piques my interest, and Emma rushes around, looking left and right. In her arms are two sets of shoes, one of them mine.

"Put these on!" she whispers excitedly as she tosses them at me, and puts her own on.

Doing as I'm told, I slip them on. Once Emma sees I've finished, she grabs my hand and pulls me toward the city. It doesn't take her long to gain speed. While shorter than I, she manages a good pace while dragging me along for the ride. Nearing the edge of the park, Emma looks back. I copy her. The house is a dot in my vision, and no one is following. She slows a bit, but keeps up a brisk walk until we're inside the city's inner border. The house is no longer visible. Looking down at her as she grips my hand tightly, she looks back with a conniving smile.

Making our way through a section of the city I hadn't explored previously, she continues pulling me farther in, and farther away. It's quiet, the shops and apartments dormant. The streets are empty, and eerily silent, too, devoid of day walkers.

Emma tugs on my arm and looking down I see a smug and confident look on her face. Turning around the corner of one of the many tall buildings I can't easily tell apart, Emma breaks the silence.

"I missed you, Rain. I missed you a lot when you were gone. But you're back now, and I'm not a little girl anymore."

"No, you're not, but I know where you're going with this Emma and—"

"Good! I can protect you if I come with you!"

"Protect me?"

"From Ami, and that indecent tramp Eve! You need me to stop them from trying to take advantage of you! Seeing you in Eve's clutches last night, taking advantage of you, made me so angry. Denis tried the same thing, and I can't stand that behavior!"

I'm caught off guard. While I thought her infatuation with me was romantic, instead it seems she seeks to keep me 'safe' from other romantic relationships.

"I don't need protection. What you saw last night with Eve wasn't what you thought it was. I was just trying to console her..."

"Oh no. That may be what you think, but she's a devil in disguise, like Denis. You *need* me!" She stops, turns to face me, and grabs both of my hands. Her infectious smiling causes me to grin nervously. "I tried to come back to let you in, but Ami was watching me closely!"

"Emma..." *I need to find a way to dissuade her from coming with us. But how do I convince her if she thinks she needs to be my savior as I was hers?* "Emma, I really don't know what to say. Ami and Eve, they aren't the danger. I'm the one that's dangerous. You saw that. I don't know what will happen if anyone is near when I have another outburst."

"So? Then I'll help you find a way to fix that too. I owe you! I don't care if it's dangerous!"

"Really, you..." I don't know how to respond. Embarrassed, I look away and up toward the sky. The high towers of the city obscure my view of the open blue. After standing in silence for a few moments, Emma leads me. I can't tell if it's to a particular destination, or just walking.

She means well. Will I cause her despair when I leave again? Will I have to fight against her anguish in the darkness? I have to make sure that somehow, someway, she lives a full life without despair, but it can't be with the house. It is a relief that I won't be a lost love interest for her though. She is just like a little sister, and Ami will be glad to hear she feels the same.

Uneasy, the silence has gone on too long, and I break it. "So, do people still do their markets at night? It seemed like people were at least awake with all the lights I saw."

"It's mixed now. There are some people who open their shops during the daytime. It's weird to see, but I've found some nice places in a section of the city where the markets are open right now."

After a significant time walking empty streets, people finally begin trickling in around us as we twist and turn down several streets. We reach an area that, while still run down, seems a bit livelier. While nowhere near what it was the night I was first here, there are a fair number of people making their way to and fro. This class of people, whom were previously called day walkers, appear to be in poor health, spirits, and appearance. They look sick with hopelessness, and I wonder if this is who I'm going to be fighting for. The voices that called out to me from the dark world.

"This may not seem like the best place in town, but I have a baker friend over here who makes some delicious pastries," Emma still sounds cheery despite the gloom in the air.

"All this way for some pastries, hmm?" I ask.

"I thought I'd treat you to *your* breakfast, and my desert."

Growing closer to the larger group of people meandering about, I notice with every person we pass they stop and stare. Everyone who looks at me seems to be completely drawn into my black eyes. I can't help but try and look away, only to be caught in someone else's stare.

Thankfully, when we enter a small bakery, there are less people and they seem content to ignore us. Emma drops my arm, and rushes to the glass counter with dozens of different shaped and colored cookies and pastries. They all look delicious.

"Terrie! Where are you?" Emma shouts.

An older woman with tight curly white hair, comes from beyond the door past the display case. She brushes her powdery hands off on a towel tucked into the sash at her waist. She smiles and I can see the recognition in her eyes when she finds Emma at her counter.

"Terrie, I'd like you to meet someone."

"Who's that, dear?" She cocks her ear to the side to hear better.

Stepping forward, I reach my hand across the display for a handshake. She reaches instinctively, but halts abruptly when she sees my eyes. Pulling her hand back a bit, she's unsure of how to react. I turn the handshake into an uncomfortable wave and drop my hand to my side awkwardly.

"Is he a demon?" Terrie whispers quite loudly.

"No! He's Rain. He's going to help me with my problem," she says excitedly.

Terrie looks me over and then back at Emma. "If you say so, dear. What can I get for you today?"

"I'd like a fritter, and…" Emma looks at me, waiting for me to choose.

"I'll take that one," I point at a solid circular one covered in chocolate.

Terrie pulls them out for us, rings us up on her electronic PayPad, and Emma pulls a familiar plastic card from her pocket. She swipes it and returns it to her overalls. Terrie hands us our pastries, and Emma shovels hers into her mouth, taking a huge bite.

"Thanks, Terrie!" she says while chewing.

"Mind your manners," Terrie scolds.

Emma clears her mouth, "I will!"

Turning to leave, I take a bite of my soft, sweet, chocolaty pastry.

While we walk back down the street, I savor the delicious confection. Before I know it it's gone, and I'm licking my fingers wishing I had another. Emma has done the same, and then latches onto my arm.

"Thank you for breakfast. Not what I would typically eat, and it was a nice change."

"Of course. Anything for you, Rain." She smiles, staring down the street.

Heading back in the general direction we came from, it seems to take longer to find our way back. People fade away, left behind in the awake part of the city. While I focus on the road ahead of us, I notice Emma look to the left when we reach a four way crossing. She pulls on my arm, and we move a little faster. Only seeing a few people far off, I'm not sure what her hurry is, especially because going back to the house would mean having to deal with Eve and Ami.

She leads us faster, and every street we come across she looks down, both ways, and continues straight ahead. She's spooked when people appear in front of us. She stops dead in her tracks, turns right down a side street, and looks over her shoulder every once in a while.

Unsure of what's going on I ask. "Emma?"

"It's nothing, just keep walking."

The worried tone in her voice is less than convincing. I look over my shoulder. There are four people following us, though I can't make out much about them from this distance. Rounding the corner of a building to our left, our pace quickens again to a light jog.

"Emma, what's going on?"

"We're being surrounded," she points in front of us. There are more people advancing in our direction.

"Could this be a coincidence?" I ask.

"No." she clings tighter to my arm.

Finally, despite our jogging, we're intercepted by a gang. They surround us, forming a ring. One of them muscles through the rabble, and he's different. He's tall and skinny, his wild black hair a mess like a rat's nest. Adjusting the dark glasses he's wearing, and tugging on the collar of his odd pinstriped suit, he advances.

"Emma, Emma, Emma. Do you know how hard it is to find you

when you're not where you're supposed to be?" the man asks.

"Of course I do. I don't do it by accident," she replies with attitude.

"Aww, now don't hurt my feelings by avoiding me." He grins in a malicious manner and struts toward us. "Denis wants to see you, sweetcakes."

"Tell Denis to jump off his roof," she snidely responds.

"Now, that's not a very nice thing to say to your future husband."

"He's dreaming." She avoids looking at the thug, and grips my arm to the point I feel I'm losing circulation.

"Who's this loser?" The gangly man points at me with contempt on his face.

Before I can answer, Emma jumps in and yells, *"This* is the man who is going to stop Denis! Again!"

I'm not sure whether I look shocked or dumbfounded at Emma's declaration, but I remain silent while this man continues.

"Oh, is that so?" He pulls something out of his side pocket, and holds it out in front of him. On a small round disk Denis appears as a see through image, and I remember this technology. "Want to repeat that for Denis, honey?"

Emma sticks her tongue out at Denis's image.

"Hey, your old lady says she found someone who's going to stop you," he tells Denis in a sickeningly sweet manner. "Again, apparently."

"What is she talking about?" He yells. "No one has ever bested me. The resistance was crushed under my boot!"

"That's what she says boss. She has some freak-show with black eyes on her arm."

"Who does she think she is?! I offered her everything!" Denis yells.

"I know boss, I know, but she's insistent you jump off your roof," the man toys with Denis to rile him up.

Denis looks intently at me, and he recognizes me. "You! Chase, you kill him. I want him dead! Then bring her back to me. She's not to leave your sight, or I'm going to have you hung out by your ankles and beaten with rebar."

"You got it boss." Chase puts the device back in his pocket, grinning from ear to ear. He waves his hand for Emma to come to him. "You heard the man. I'm taking you with me little lady."

"Stop." I put my arms up as Chase tries to advance. "You don't have to listen to him."

"What? You think I have time for chit chat?" Chase's face turns stern. "If you think Denis was lying about having me strung up, think again. My life is on the line here."

The other men who've formed a circle close in on us to constrict our movements. My defensive instincts kick in. Placing myself between Chase and Emma, I act as a barrier.

"Stop now!" I warn them, putting my other arm out over Emma's shoulder.

"Or what? Do you see yourself right now? You're surrounded. Might as well give up, lie down, and take what's coming."

"Last warning: leave Emma alone." The tension in my voice rises; I surge with power.

"I'm done," Chase reaches out with his lengthy arms for my neck, but I react and place my hands in front of his face.

Unleashing a shockwave directly at his skull, he flies into, and then through a couple of the men. The boom causes Emma to scream, startled by my unique ability. Knowing I've just started a fight, I quickly spin behind Emma, and unleash another, clearing a path for her.

"Run!" I yell.

Emma doesn't hesitate, and runs through. They converge on me in an attempt to overwhelm. Multiple targets produce various weapons to bludgeon or stab me with. I defend myself as they near.

From the front.

I block a right hook with my forearm. I swing in, and as my fist connects with his ribcage, I let a shockwave fly. My target hurtles into a few others behind him. Dodging successive swings from a small club, I grab a thug's arm as he comes in again. Using his own weight against him, I flip and slam him to the ground.

Behind.

I spin around and lean back to dodge a blow to my face from spiked metal wrapped around a tall man's knuckles. Taking advantage of his blunder, I grab his shirt, lean back and crack my skull into his. He stumbles.

While I rub my forehead briefly, two obese and very familiar men slam me in between their bellies. I'm immobilized. Another thug cracks me in the ribs, and I groan at the pain. He wrenches me by the arm from the two fat men. With chain he attempts to bind me. I'm able to slip one of my hands free, and blast him.

Grabbing the chain, I swing it in an attempt to hit a few of them. The group backs up as a whole. I wait for one of them to step a little closer. Spinning around, I keep my eyes on them. It allows me to catch one moving when he thinks I'm distracted. Before he can stop himself, the chain connects with his legs. It wraps around him, and he yelps. While it's bound around him, the rest of the thugs quickly advance back on me, running full steam. Before I can react, I'm hit several times across my upper body.

On my toes, I try to dodge attacks but the close quarters stop me. After being hit a few times the pain throws me off further. I misstep and I'm bludgeoned in the face, stomach, and legs. I have to kneel after a few moments just to breathe and I struggle to push them all back with random shockwaves. I hit several, but they just keep coming.

They push in harder. I do my best to fight back. As one swings their foot in toward my ribs I jump up and in, too close for his blow to be effective. I then ram his chest with my shoulder. Two more replace him as he falls. Feeling my strength failing, I struggle to stay moving.

More converging. Too many to dodge. Need to take them all at once.

Instinct kicks in. I crouch, push my legs up as hard as I can, and let a shockwave loose at the ground with both palms. The force leaving from both of my hands at the same time propels me upward, much higher than I normally would be able to jump. Putting my legs together I rocket up and when I reach the pinnacle I fall straight down.

Once I have my bearing, I pull my legs up to a crouching position with my hands facing the ground. A moment before landing I let out a two-handed shockwave. It softens the impact, and shatters the paved street. It buckles and flows in a circular wave, sending everyone around me flying. My legs and palms ring with pain, despite my cushion. I look around and I've cleared a few yards around me.

Several of them struggle to return to their feet, while some crawl away. Others lie lifeless. Collapsing onto my tailbone, I rest and collect myself for a minute. Looking for any sign of Emma beyond the mass of the men, her figure eludes me.

Is that a good thing, or bad? I did tell her to run. Wait. Where's Chase?

Back on my feet, I look frantically for his downed body. He's nowhere in sight. Emma's scream echoes through the streets. It's faint, and I cannot tell where it came from. She yells my name. As I anxiously peer around, I see neither of them. I run in the direction I thought I heard her scream from. At every intersection, when I look down the streets, I see no one resembling either of them.

I become angry: the same rage I felt against the slavers courses through my mind. I return to the gang. There's a thug still conscious. I grab him by his shirt, and punch him in the face for good measure.

"Where have they gone?" I yell, pulling his bloody face up to mine.

"Don't kill me!" he whimpers.

"I won't, if you answer my question! Where did Chase take her?"

"I don't want to die! I don't want to die!"

Useless!

I throw him to the ground, and move to another. I pull him to his feet, only to bend him over and plant a knee into his ribcage. He coughs heavily and tries to fall, but I stand him back up. When he's regained his breath I question him.

"Where?"

"I can't! Denis will kill me!"

I shake him by his shirt, and grimace. "*I'm* going to kill you if you don't answer me!"

"Please, please!" he pleads. I drop him.

Either they have completely solid loyalty, or he'll really kill them if they say anything. I'm not getting anything out of them. It doesn't help there are a dozen or more potential witnesses to any confession.

I burst into a run, heading in the direction I believe the house to be in. Emma being in danger is at the forefront of my mind, thinking the worst as Chase carries her off to Denis. After only about ten minutes of running, jogging, and back to running again, I'm at the edge of the park.

Seeing home gives me a renewed endurance. Though my lungs burn from heavy breathing, my legs carry me forward. Overcompensating nearly sends me face first on the grass, but I manage to stay upright.

Agatha is in the yard, hanging towels. She sees me coming, and concern is on her face, but I fly past and into the kitchen. The door slams against the wall as I tear through the house. She calls after me, but I ignore her. Charging through, I also slam the swinging door, and leap up the stairs, three at a time.

When I reach my room, I grab my sword and strap the belt across my waist. Once it's secured, I waste no time in bounding back down the stairs. Pushing the swinging door back open, I am nearly through when I hear Ami behind me.

"Rain! Where have you been?" It's her worried tone.

Reeling about on my heels, I place my right hand on the hilt so the sword doesn't smack the door. Precious time is being wasted, but I give her the run down.

"I don't have time to explain: Chase has taken Emma to Denis. I have to go." I turn and try to leave.

"Who's Chase? What happened to you? You look awful!"

"Chase is some henchman of Denis's. I'm heading to where I might find him, and Emma."

Through the kitchen I head outside again, but Ami once more stops me. Grabbing my hand, she pulls. I turn around a little annoyed. But she doesn't see it because she leans in quickly, and hugs me tightly, burying her face in my neck. Feeling the warmth of her breath calms me. She releases me, and smiles.

"Come home safely." She brushes her hand gently across my cheek where I feel a bruise forming. I wince, but smile reassuringly.

"I will."

"Rain, what's going on?" Agatha asks with concern while her eyes move down to meet my sword.

"Emma's in danger. I'll explain later." I turn, and quickly head away from the house again, but in a significantly different direction than she was abducted.

The place to look would be the U.F.A. building. It's the logical conclusion for where I might find him. He had to have gained control of it after his father fell ill.

Across the dying grass, I run, and keep my hand on the pommel of the sword to stop it from swaying.

I look around at the tall buildings, attempting to discern direction. Unsure, I do my best and run onto a street which seems familiar. I'm following my gut. Every once in a while I stop and look for landmarks, but with the city in its crumbled state, it's hard to recognize anything.

It was a tall building. I know the buildings had arches in their architecture. I had to travel through the residential district, but I can't tell what's what anymore.

Continuing on at a brisk walk now instead of a full run, I look all around trying to catch glimpses of the enormous U.F.A. building. Finally, after losing track of time and direction, I'm positive I see it in the distance. It becomes more apparent when the familiar stairs leading up come into view. The building is a husk of what it once was, its glory days clearly in the past. Planks of wood cover the windows at ground level; the glass of the revolving door is busted out; the lights are off inside. It appears abandoned now, and looks as though it has been for a long time.

I guess Denis wouldn't be here in its current state. But I might be able to find some information about the people who were employed here. Maybe get them to help me find his whereabouts.

I duck through the broken glass in the revolving door, making sure not to catch my arms. Minimal light enters the building from the door, so I am forced to let my eyes adjust before continuing. Past the ticket seller's booths, I head for the double doors into the bottom floor fighting arena. They're propped open a crack. A light flickers inside. When I look, peeking through the crack, it appears to simply be a few resident homeless men and women strewn about the stands and fighting ring.

Pulling the doors open, I move through the stands and off to the right where the elevator room rests. The windows there are also broken out, both in the door and the main viewing area. I enter familiar settings.

Many pictures still hang on the wall, though they are dusty and would need a good cleaning just to know what their subjects are. Like the pictures, most things in the room have been undisturbed for some time now. Still, I move to the desk, open drawers, and thumb through paperwork for any clues to Denis's location.

In one drawer there are several small books bound with spiraling wire, and strewn about papers. There are no maps of the city as I had once seen, and had hoped I would find this time. Thumbing through one of the books, there are names listed, followed by what I assume is information about the person. Numbers and named streets lead me to believe they are locations within Chas. The book is incomplete. There are shreds of paper left behind from pages having been torn out, and they aren't in the desk. I take what I can hold in one hand.

They're old, but maybe I'll get lucky with a name. If nothing comes of these, I may have to return and make my way up to Mister Lindali's office. With the building in this much disarray though, would the elevators work? Is there electricity?

Taking it, and several of the other small wire bound books, I find my way back out of the building, into the open, yet musty air. Having spent a lot of energy, and working on a nearly empty stomach, I hope I'm able to find an open market on my return. With several more hours until dusk, it's not likely, but I try to be optimistic. I distract myself by thumbing through the pages of another address book. Despite my worry for Emma, my pace lessens while I study street names.

Working through the city, and the papers, I come across a name I recognize. Anthony Grada. Next to his name is his address, but because I'm unfamiliar with navigating the city by street name or location, I begin looking about for anyone I might be able to ask. Day walkers elude me, despite my fervent searching. I arc through the large streets separating the skyscraping buildings, and anticipate coming upon the commercial district soon.

Maybe with the assistance of someone from the market I'll be able to find him, or at least where he lives. If I can beat an answer out of anyone, Anthony would be it. I'm sure he would have aligned himself with Denis again.

In the commercial district, it's still quiet. I wander a while longer before people begin appearing. Late afternoon has arrived, and turning onto another street, I notice market stalls have started opening for business. Unlike before, when there were multiple places to shop and eat on one block, now there is only a handful. Like the small number of people, they're random and intermittently placed. But I've not walked the distance, on this mission, to be deterred by a few more feet.

While finding my way to the nearest open shop, I see different classes of people are intermixing. The destitute mingle with upper class.

Is it by choice? Or because it's one of the last market areas left?

All of them shy away, trying to avoid contact with me.

Is it my eyes, or the sword?

Instead of asking someone who can run from me, I aim for a food merchant. He is serving a few customers, handing them bowls of stringy looking pasta. Its buttery, peppery smell causes my mouth to water. My stomach grumbles. I fight the hunger because I have no money.

I approach and hold out the little book, my finger near Anthony's name and supposed location, placing it in front of the man handing out bowls. He waves me off, and I shake it at him.

"Do you know how I can get here?" I ask.

"Shoo, get out of here. If you aren't going to buy anything, I have nothing for you," he scoffs while returning to a large stove behind him.

Rather than push it with that shop, I move farther down the street and try again, but the next merchant refuses to acknowledge my presence also.

If they're all like this, I'm going to find myself out of luck. Maybe information has a price now too.

Wandering for some time longer, I have no luck finding anyone to help me locate Anthony. It's become dark, and some streetlights have come on. I reach an area which is familiar. It's where Emma's shop is located.

I nearly pass it by, but as light reflects off of one of the windows, I stop because it almost looks like there's movement. Unsure if my mind is playing tricks on me, I wait. I'm positive a light flickers from the back of her shop. Cautiously, I investigate, moving in closer to peek in the window. Nearing, I find the door propped open a crack by a small wedge of wood.

With Emma having been taken, it's likely a thief trying to ransack her shop. Or maybe one of Denis's underlings.

I draw my sword. Pulling on the door with my free hand, I enter quietly to avoid alerting whomever is here. The skin on my knuckles taut, my grip is tight on the soft leather of the hilt. I draw it in close, ready to spear someone in this close environment. My eyes dart back and forth. There's no one in plain sight; however with an abundance of counters and shelves in the way, and food stacked up on them, I'm leery someone might be hiding.

Lifting my arm and moving around the first shelf, I ready my blade, but there is no one there. One by one I check behind the shelves and counters, clearing the room. It's empty. Dropping my guard a little, I let the point of my sword face the floor.

There is a trashcan filled with nothing but a bouquet of flowers. I kneel down to look closer, and attached is a card which reads "Love, Denis."

A good place for them.

A light clattering noise startles me, and I track it to the door back behind the farthest counter. I see the light which brought me in here, gleaming from the crack underneath the door. Moving to the side, I crouch and bring my sword up. I wait patiently for my moment to pounce.

The door opens, and light pours into the front of the shop. A very tall and muscular man steps through, and I give him no opportunity to see me and react. Jumping up and shoving him into the wall, my sword meets his neck. His hands fly up in surrender, and produce falls to the ground at our feet.

Lit only by the light coming through the back area, I see a scared look on a familiar face. Anthony Grada's other half. Driesen stands before me, mostly the same as I had last seen him, though now a long scar runs from his eyebrow down his cheek, and his hair has begun to gray on the sides.

"You!" we both exclaim at the same time.

"That's right, me!" I respond aggressively, and push the blade just a little bit more into his skin, drawing a bead of blood. "Where is she?"

"Wait!" he exclaims. "What are yous talkin' about?"

"Where. Is. Emma?!" I grind my teeth.

"I don't know!"

"Don't lie to me!"

"I haven't seen her since she said she was going to be gone for a little bit." He labors to speak calmly with my sword pressed to his flesh. "I fell on hard times, she took pity on me. I came'ta see if she was back, but saw she wasn't open."

"So you broke in to steal from her?"

"Are yous kidding? It's not like that." He reaches into the breast pocket of his shirt and pulls out a key, dangling it a moment before replacing it. "She lets me have some of her old produce that hasn't sold."

"So you wouldn't happen to know anything about Emma being kidnapped by Chase and taken to Denis, would you?"

"Chase did what?!" A genuine look of shock and irritation crosses his face.

"He snatched her while I was dealing with Denis's gang."

"I ain't had contact with Denis in a long whiles, and I sure don't trust Emma in his custody."

Hesitant, I keep him in check while I try to assess if he's telling the truth. Though we've had issues before, my gut is easing, and my grip loosens. Lowering the sword cautiously, I step back away from Driesen and wipe it off on my pants before sheathing it. He looks relieved to not be skewered. I cross my arms and glare at him, ready to pin him again if I need to.

"I need to know where Denis might be," I state plainly. "He needs to be stopped."

"There's a rumor floating around that he's on the outskirts somewheres. I'll investigate and we can get him together. I gots a score to settle, and if Emma's in danger it gives me incentive."

"That'll do nicely, but we better hustle. We're on a time crunch here since Denis seems insistent on marrying her against her will." I point my finger at him aggressively.

"It's gonna take me a bit, and I work better alone. Where can I find yous?"

"You remember the park?"

"Center of the city? Yeah." He quirks an eyebrow.

"The house has returned. You can find me there."

"Do I wants ta know how you get it in and out of there?" Driesen looks at me confused.

"No. Just come find me when you have the info, and be as quick as you can."

"Sure thing, boss." He's agitated, but it's not directed at me. He nods curtly.

Before I can make my way out, my stomach grumbles. Positive Emma wouldn't mind, I grab an orange. It takes me only moments to peel and devour it, then toss the peel in the garbage can. Driesen looks at me as if I had just committed a heinous crime, and I'm becoming more comfortable he's telling the truth.

Finished with my snack, I turn my back to him, leaving the store. My shoulders are tense as I expect Driesen to take advantage of my generous opening. To my surprise, as I reach the door and look over my shoulder, he's in the same place. He wipes his neck and watches me.

The street is fairly empty except for a few people in either direction. From Emma's shop, it's not hard to make my way back to the park. I have a few moments to think.

He acted convincingly, and he didn't attack. Was it real? I suppose he'd have probably put up more of a fight if he was still working for Denis, but I did have a sword to his throat.

I just wish I didn't have to leave Emma in the hands of some power-tripped narcissist while I wait for a gamble to pay off. I don't have much of a choice though. If Driesen doesn't come by tomorrow I might just go out and see if I can pressure more people into telling me anything useful.

Would it be ethical to use my abilities to scare people into talking if it's for a greater good? Would the ends justify the means if harm came to someone with information that would lead me to Denis?

The lights of the house guide like a beacon as I reach the border around the park. It's only a few minutes longer before I see the difference in grass at our boundary. Agatha's in the yard, illuminated by the light from the kitchen window and when I approach she puts out her hand and I stop.

"Hey, where've you been all day?" It's Evalyn, and by her tone she doesn't seem to be in a bad mood.

"Long story. Trying to track down Emma." I sit on the steps to the back door.

"What happened? You lose her in the city?" She sits next to me and jabs me with her elbow playfully.

"If only it was that simple." I sigh heavily. "I worry for her safety. For everyone's. I don't feel like I'm able to keep everyone safe."

"You know if I was younger, and not dead, I wouldn't mind if you kept *me* safe…" she trails off, and I catch her joke.

I shake my head and crack a smile for the first time in hours. She cackles and pushes me. Losing my balance, I hit the grass and it actually feels all right. It's springy, soft, and cool to the touch.

"Are you all right?" she asks.

Just lying there on my side, I can feel the heat being absorbed from my body, the ground drinking it in thirstily. It's comfortable, and I don't want to move. Evalyn prods me with her foot, and I'm forced to look at her.

"I'm just worn out. The effects of the despair, my own helplessness to do anything while Emma is in danger, and a lack of food is taking its toll on me. I'm stuck waiting for any information about where Emma might have been taken."

"Looking for a lost little girl as if she were your wife." Evalyn smirks.

I can only glance up at her and give her a dirty look before laying my head back down in the grass. She taps my hip with her foot, to be annoying and to gain my attention. I swat at her foot softly.

"Little sister," I correct her. "And it appears she sees it that way too."

"So what about Ami and Eve then? Have you decided?"

I close my eyes. "Unlike when you put that insane idea into Tamiell's head, I'm not sure how I got tangled in between."

"It's your essence. Something about you draws people. You're a leader. Maybe it's the power you wield, or something else, but it's strong."

"I guess that makes sense regarding who I was. Some things can't be lost to amnesia, it seems."

"Who you were? Did you remember something?"

"Remember? No. I found out from the princess I used to be king of Asta, in the future from her perspective. And Drake and I were cordial once. He must have been in my trusted circle to be that way. My leadership might be why he was with me."

"A king? That does shed a little light. We could do some historical research, see if there is anything out there about a king gone missing."

"Looking in the history books? Are you sure it's a good idea? I wouldn't mind knowing, but what if we inadvertently come across information about ourselves? Events which haven't happened for us yet."

"We could take a calculated risk. We know what era you're from, and could search for that timeframe only," she suggests.

"All right. But only after I've made sure Emma is safe."

I muster the energy to push myself up off the ground, and eventually stand. I make sure I have all of the books and paper before moving into the kitchen. The door to the living room swings back and forth.

Was someone listening in, or was it just from the pressure of the room changing when I opened the door?

Evalyn follows, and offers me a bowl of mixed rice and diced vegetables by waving it about in my face. She grins as I snatch it from her, consuming it with haste. Dishing myself up a second bowl from the pot on the stove, I eat a little slower than the first. My stomach is satisfied, for now at least. I clean up after myself and find my way to my room without any further conversation.

Collapsing on my comfortable bed, I nearly pass out, but the books and the belt buckle of the sheath dig into my body. I'm forced to flop around, pulling on the end of the belt to unlatch it. When it is free I shove it and the books to the floor. There's peace in my pillow.

~~~~~~

The morning sun begins to light my room, gently waking me. My sleep was deep and uneventful, without dream or interference from the despair within. I have a renewed drive to find Emma. From my dresser I pick out a tan, long sleeved shirt with Ami's signature orange chrysanthemum, and a pair of airy brown pants. I hang them over my arm, and sneak out of my room.

I tiptoe to avoid the creaky stairs. Eve is sprawled out on the couch, staring at the ceiling. When I reach the bottom step she looks over. She blushes heavily, making her already tan skin darker. Unconcerned with why, I head toward the bathroom, grabbing a towel from the closet on my way. Knocking lightly on the door, no answer comes from within, letting me know it's safe. Inside, I set my armload of items down on the counter.

I flip the light switch on and close both of the doors. Undressed, I kick my dirty clothes and shoes to the side, pull back the shower curtain, and start the water. After finding the right temperature, my body rejoices at the heat, and my aching muscles relax. Hands pressed against the wall, I let my head hang, and the water streams from my hair like a waterfall.

It might be time for a trim.

The click of the door's latch startles me. A brief gust of cold air flows through and I yell out.

"Hey! Taking a shower here!" I cover myself, despite the closed curtain preventing me from being seen.

"Shh! It's just me, Rain," Eve says softly.

"*Just* you?! Knowing you, you're going to try to peek, or climb in, or something!" My voice is still elevated.

"No, not this time." The level of her voice changes. She's quieter, gentler. "I couldn't do this face to face. This is perfect because I don't want you to see me."

"You've confused me. I'm not sure this is the right time for anything. I'm sure we can discuss this later."

"Would you quiet down? You're going to draw attention and ruin this," she whispers right against the curtain. "The other night I was tired. What I did was a moment of weakness, and it's embarrassing."

"It's fine. I'm becoming accustomed to you throwing yourself at me. That's not to say I condone it."

"Not that. You saw me cry," she says meekly. "It's been so long since I had, I didn't think I could anymore. And no one in the camp ever saw it. You're the only one, and that means something."

That stops me. "Eve, I can be your friend. If you want to talk, I'll listen."

"What if I want more?"

"I'll tell you the same thing I told Ami. I don't think it's a good idea to start a relationship while we're all permanently stuck with each other. It would become more awkward than it is."

"So what you're saying is, you aren't tied to Ami."

"Eve…" I struggle for words with her prodding me to give a wrong answer. One I know will cause a rift between Ami and I, and allow her to jump in. "You know Ami and I are very close, but I've told her I plan on ensuring her safety before I advance our relationship."

"It's okay, sire." the tone of her whisper lifts in spirit a little bit.

"What did you say?" I spin around and face her, despite the shower curtain being in the way.

"Nothing!" she replies in a singsong manner.

The water grows cold and I shut it off, but I can't step out of the shower while Eve is still here. Cold air begins to seep into my steamy closed off area, and I shiver.

"Eve, could you leave? I need to dry off."

"Do I have to?" she whines while putting her fingers through the curtain, and begins to pull. "You saw me in my underwear. I think it'd only be fair if I got to take a peek too!"

"Out!" I slap her hand, and point my hand toward the door.

"Fine." She sighs playfully, and it's only a moment before the door opens and closes.

Knowing she's cunning, I poke my head out first to see if she's still in the room. She's respected my wish, and is no longer here. I push back the curtain and step out of the tub, making my way over to the sink for my towel.

After I dry and dress, I wipe off the mirror and look at myself beyond the foggy haze left behind. Scratching at my face, my beard has become a little scruffy.

Though taking time now to shave feels unproductive, Driesen hasn't shown up yet. The razor nicks me, and I wash the blood away, but the cut immediately forms a bead again. I finish, clean my face off, and clear up any spots I missed.

I stare again deeply into my pitch black eyes. While it's still unknown who exactly I was, I try to define who I am right now, and it's difficult.

Am I strong enough to be their protector?

Am I strong enough to control this power without becoming consumed by it? I don't know how strong I am against corruption, especially knowing I used to be a king.

How did I become king? Did I take it from someone, or inherit it?

Who am I? Or who do I want to be?

I want to be their protector, their savior from this curse. I want to be a good man, and to lead a simple life after this.

I slick my hair back, and clean up my mess. Back in my room, I don my sword and cloak, and grab my dirty laundry basket. Agatha, or Evalyn, is cooking as I pass through to drop my clothes into the washbasin outside. Breakfast is the few eggs we have left, and toast.

When I open the door, a breeze hits my still wet hair, and I shiver. Though the sun is peeking above the skyline to shine its rays down onto me, there's no warming feeling.

Is autumn coming?

Out across the grass, I see no sign of Driesen. I roll my sleeves up and wash my clothing to keep from wondering if he's going to betray me, or worrying about Emma's safety.

The distraction fails. I'm plagued with thoughts of Denis doing unspeakable things. Anxiety and rage fuel an overactive imagination, all leading me to one thought: *Denis is going to die by my hands.* I wring my clothes as if they are his neck. Try as I might to will it away, the urge for violence has set in.

Most of the water has been removed, and I hang my clothes to dry before I destroy them. Inside the warm house again, I'm temporarily distracted by the delicious smells of breakfast. Agatha is finishing up and dishing scrambled eggs out on plates set out on the table.

I sit in my spot. "Thanks Agatha, it smells good."

"Of course." She smiles and pats me on the shoulder.

Ami pushes in from the living room while rubbing the sleep from her eyes, still in a pair of light blue fleece pajamas. She sits in her normal spot, yawning wide, and lazily covering it. While slathering butter across my piece of toast, I smile at her and she smiles back. Eve joins us, grinning from ear to ear, and giving me a wink. Ignoring it, I do my best to forget she intruded.

I really hope she doesn't try to stir things up with Ami by telling her she came into the bathroom while I showered just to have a heart-to-heart with me. It's not like I had control of the situation, but I know Ami wouldn't approve.

I lean back after I've finished the meal, placing my hands on my stomach, and resting to let it settle. The women sit and eat in silence, but they're all looking at me, smiling playfully as if they're keeping something from me. I raise an eyebrow in silent question, but it only causes them to intensify their strange behavior by grinning wider.

"What are you doing?" I ask, cautiously.

Ami covers her mouth to snicker a little. Agatha just continues to eat and smile. Eve however, I can see in her face she wants to say something, but she keeps it bottled up. Taking my plate to the sink, I look over my shoulder at them suspiciously. Their staring continues. Turning back, I cross my arms and stare back at them. Ami stands up, finished with her breakfast and moves past me to put her plate in the sink.

"All right, spill it," I demand, poking her in the side.

"Nothing. Nothing at all *m'lord*." She giggles.

"Mmmm. I see. So I did hear Eve correctly earlier."

"You did indeed, *King* Rain," Eve says seductively. "I knew there was a reason you and I belonged together."

"So which one of you overheard us last night?"

"No one. Aunt Evalyn told us after you went to bed." Ami spins toward me and grins harder.

There's a knock at the back door. I grab the hilt of my sword instinctively. Looking through the door's window cautiously, Driesen is there with an expectant look on his face. Opening the door, I allow him in. Though his frame is almost too large to fit through our doorway, he manages to with taking off his familiar round, wide brimmed hat. He turns to face me.

"Wait! Isn't that...?" Ami exclaims.

I look back at her, and nod.

"I knows where he is, and he's got Emma with him," Driesen states plainly.

"Okay, so what are we waiting for?"

"Just yous," he answers.

Looking over at the women, I flash an unsure smile. "Wish me luck. I'm probably going to need it."

"Should we go with you?" Ami asks.

"No, it's going to be dangerous. It's safer if you stay here."

I already kept it from Ami about the slavers. It's probably best I keep it that way for this too.

Am I actually going to go through with it? Am I going to kill Denis?

"I should come anyway. I can hold my own, and you know it," Eve protests.

She smirks when I shoot her a disapproving glance. I shake my head, and she stays sitting. Holding my arm out toward the door, I wait for Driesen to lead. He squeezes back out, and I follow, closing the door behind me. Around the house, he leads me parallel to the commercial district, the opposite way from the U.F.A. building.

Walking side by side, he's silent, and it's a bit uncomfortable. Deep into the city, through decaying unfamiliar towers and buildings which were once homes and businesses, I wonder if it could ever be repaired. Twisting and turning further in, after an hour I've lost my way.

I'm now relying on someone I am still not sure I can fully trust.

The eerily quiet streets bother me, and I speak up.

"Why do you have a score with Denis?" I prod, hoping to ease my tensions about him.

Driesen cracks his knuckles one by one. A pained look crosses his face. He's silent a moment longer before answering.

"My wife died because'a him."

"I'm so sorry." I feel terrible for asking. "He killed her?"

"In a round'bout way. She got sick. He wouldn't allow the hospital ta treat her because I opposed him in the resistance."

Nodding my head, I let the subject drop, and we continue to wind our way through the broken city, avoiding heavy chunks of its walls strewn about on the ground. Around us there are no day walkers, save for Driesen and me.

It almost feels like we could go on forever in this vast city.

Although I know people do in fact still live here, one couldn't tell by looking. It's as desolate as the desert. The sun travels through the sky and warms the street we are on; warm enough for me to shift my cloak off my shoulders. I regret the decision when we pass a cross street, and a gust of cold wind blasts us.

Several hours pass, and finally there is a change in the scenery farther ahead. It appears we're nearing the edge of the city when some green beyond the buildings enters our view. But before we close in, Driesen motions for us to hug the side of the skyscrapers while we walk. Ducking into an alcove, we peek out at our destination.

There, beyond the boundary of the city, is a hill of grass. Atop it is a luxurious stone mansion. It has properties one might find in a castle, nestled amongst a complex of smaller stone buildings. A paved road leads from the city streets up to it, blocked by a tall stone wall which surrounds the miniature city. A lone, silver colored gate and a couple guards block our immediate path, but inside there are many others bustling about.

No doubt they will be an obstacle as well.

"This is apparently it," Driesen's tone is low.

"Seems like the kind of place I'd set up if I were a control freak," Eve whispers in my ear, startling me. "I actually kind of like this place!"

Looking back at her angrily I push her back a bit. "What are you doing?" I whisper harshly.

"You know I can handle myself in a fight. From the look of it, you're going to need my help." Her smirk is smug.

"You stubborn…" I trail off, glaring at her.

Driesen looks at me, questioning. I shake my head in disapproval. Surveying again I see guns in the guard's hands.

If I rush them, will they fire or choke?

"Look." I point the guns out to Driesen and Eve. "This isn't safe for either of you. Let me handle this."

Driesen shrugs pulling out a gun of his own from his waistband. "Danger don't matter ta me. I want Emma safe, and Denis in a hole in the ground."

"Fine. We're all going to walk out at once, but I need you two to spread out to my sides. I want them to work to keep their eyes on us." I point at the gun in Driesen's hand. "Put that away, and let me take the lead. And don't step in front of me."

Turning, we begin walking toward the gate on the hill. Looking left and then right, Driesen and Eve have followed my lead. They've put some distance between us, but are still keeping pace. The scruffy looking guards see us coming, and raise their guns. Driesen and Eve move farther apart. The guards shift back and forth, trying to keep all three of us in their sights at once. When both of them shift away from me, I break into a full sprint. They see me, and aim back in my direction. But they're too late.

I release a shockwave. Though their guns fire, the bullets fail to clear the barrels. Leaping up into the air with a gentle push from a two-handed shockwave, I swing my hands up and together, and release another to hammer the two guards against the gate. The force of it leaving my palms while mid-flight sends me flying back a little. I stay steady, landing on my feet. I give them no time to recover, and blow the gate doors open. The force nearly tears them from their hinges as they swing and slam against the stone wall. A loud blaring from a horn rips through the air.

Unsheathing my sword, I glance to make sure Driesen and Eve kept up before I move inside the complex. As we jog in, a pack of vicious looking guard dogs come running, snarling and barking. Their teeth drip with saliva. My uncompromising resolve to find Emma, and bring Denis to justice dissolves my moral restraints. My sword finds home in one of them when it leaps for my throat. Then another one as it tries to latch onto my arm. I'm merciless.

The familiar and startling boom from a gun kicks off behind me, twice. Yelps follow, and it takes me a moment to realize it was Driesen's weapon: he wounded two dogs. He snatches them up, and bangs their heads together to put them out of their misery.

Like a child playing roughly with dolls.

A dog leaps for me, and Eve swings a lengthy leg upward through my peripheral vision, nailing it in the jaw. As it falls to the ground in a heap, I nod my approval, but point out a multitude of men and women running in our direction from the complexes on either side, and from the main house. They're all armed.

My distraction leaves me vulnerable when a dying dog leaps and snags my outstretched arm, biting hard and drawing blood. I lay the pommel of my sword into its skull. It lets go, hits the ground, and I put my foot into its ribs. Blood drips down my palm and onto the ground, staining the gray path as I move forward.

My arm again? Really? Dogmeat. That's what I should have been renamed.

Despite the approaching army, the adrenaline is making me feel invincible. I let out a bestial roar at the few remaining dogs, and gain their attention; Eve takes the opportunity to crush one underfoot. Despite the ferocity the animals showed on arrival, those not dead retreat into the oncoming men and women. I sheathe my sword and put my hands to the pavement to unleash a large shockwave. The surge of energy causes my arm to contract, and blood drains faster.

There's a small quake in the hillside. The ground cracks, the dirt and grass roll around the impact site. Some in the group falter and fall, but others keep coming. Guns are raised as they take to their knees for stability. Before they can fire, I unleash my power on them. Several are knocked over, and the mob stops in their tracks. Driesen takes a place next to me, gun raised, while Eve stands in front of me as my shield.

"I have no quarrel with you! I'm here for Denis!" I yell at them, gritting my teeth at the pain in my arm.

"You have a problem with us if you have a problem with Denis!" A man yells out from within the group. The voice is familiar.

"Denis is a tyrant! He will not cause anyone despair any longer! You don't have to die for his selfishness!" I yell again.

Chase emerges, his arms outstretched and a cheeky smile on his oblong face. "They won't listen to you because they know what will happen if they desert Denis's army."

"You're probably right. They're here because they fear what would happen if they weren't. But I will alleviate their fear for them." That inner wave of energy bubbles. My anger is ready to pour from my hands. "Get out of my way, Chase."

"Or what?" he taunts.

Raising my bloody hand, I aim in his direction, and the crowd around him spreads. Before I can unleash a blast, I'm impacted in my side. I fly sideways into Driesen. Both he and I fall, and tumble down the hill.

"Rain!" Eve calls after me.

She too is thrown in our direction by a blur. Her tumble is a bit heavier, and I jump in her path to stop her rolling down the hill.

There's no recovery time. Chase is already on top of me.

How did he do that? Does he have an ability like me?

He watches while Driesen and I return to our feet. Before we can gain our bearings, I'm on the ground again, with a punch, or maybe a kick to the ribs. It's too fast to see. Once again Chase looms over me. Driesen swings at him from behind, and Chase evaporates from sight. He stumbles forward and collapses to one knee near my feet.

Eve has recovered, and reaches her hand to pull me up. An unseen force slams our heads together as she lifts me, and we both cry out in pain. My vision goes dark, and I hunch so I don't stumble and fall.

"What…" I mumble but can't finish my sentence.

What is going on here?! Is he becoming invisible, or moving faster than we can see?

"You're not the only one with talents," Chase taunts, his voice only a few feet away.

Unsheathing and raising my sword to defend, I attempt to block another incoming attack, but Chase disappears again. Before I know what's happening my sword is gone, and I'm face down in the dirt. Chase is standing on my back. The edge of my sword is pressed against my neck. He is ready to make the killing blow.

Driesen grunts and yells. Eve stumbles for a moment before regaining her composure. They attempt to tackle Chase, colliding instead, and landing on me. Chase is nowhere in the mixture of body parts. I wheeze, out of breath from being crushed.

Pushing up, I force Eve and Driesen to roll off. My strength wanes. With the blood loss, and being hit heavily, I'm drained. My head spins. Driesen too begins to stand up and at that moment my eyes catches a blur of colors racing through the air. Driesen is down on his stomach again from a kick to the ribs.

With the chance to see exactly how fast Chase is moving, I throw up my arms in a guarding stance. Feeling a slight bit of wind to my right, I react without thinking and grab. Snatching Chase's hand, I swing hard and use his own speed against him. When I release, he goes flying, and impacts the ground. My sword flies out of his hand, and I realize I was a split second from death.

He tumbles down past Driesen and Eve, in a wild display of somersaults and rolls. I run up on him. He finds his feet once more, and vanishes from sight. A foot is pressed into my back. The momentum from running down the hill combined with his kick sends me tumbling and spinning.

I reach the flat ground at the bottom, and come to a stop. Leaping back up, I look for him. I feel the wind again. I duck and swing my leg out. It catches him and he falls, smashing his face into the pavement, but rather than halting, he grinds against it.

Chase stands back up, his face torn and bloody. He pulls out two small knives from behind his back and runs at me. His injuries slow his speed, and I successfully track and dodge him while he thrusts and lunges at me. Blood trickles down his forehead and eyebrow, blinding his right eye. The advantage is now mine, and I land several blows on him while he tries desperately to do the same to me.

His left hand comes in for a jab. When I deflect, I put my palm into his chest and blast him up the hill. He lands and lays motionless, arms outstretched lifelessly. Huffing, I climb the hill to him. Driesen and Eve have been taken down by the group, their arms pinned behind their backs. Barrels of guns are pointed at their heads. But though my comrades have been captured, the army is motionless while they watch me.

"Unless there's another of you with abilities like Chase, you don't stand a chance against me!" I yell at them, catching my breath when I can. "Go home. Forget about—"

Chase springs to life once more. He flashes out of sight. He hits me from behind, and kneels on my back. My head is yanked backward by my hair. The edge of Chase's knife finds my throat, the sharp edge cutting into my flesh. But before he can pull it across to end my life, the darkness breaks free.

"This cannot happen!" Despair cries out from my mouth.

Losing control, my teeth clench and I watch as my skin turns completely black. My hands tremble with fear, despair, and rage. I clench them to try and stop it, but I can't. Despair bellows in my mind, and I in turn cry out loud for them. Bursting forth from my body, a black storm rages out, shadowy veins sprouting through the air.

Chase is lifted off of me, and I can feel the terror inside of him, his despair welling up when he realizes he is no longer in control. I watch as if I'm out of my body. Eve's yelling, but I can't hear her. She's broken free, and is waving people to safety from the oncoming destruction. They scatter.

The darkness grows, spreading through the ground and air. When I look up, Chase is suspended, caught by one of the dark tendrils. The color is draining from his body.

Chase pleads for his life with his eyes, and I can hear his cry within my mind, but I am helpless to stop the darkness from taking him. I can't even avert my gaze while his body withers, and becomes lifeless. When Chase is gone, the darkness recedes, dropping his corpse to the ground. I collapse to my knees, exhausted.

My hearing returns, and people are screaming: they run past me through the gate of the complex. I stay motionless, trying to regain myself. The black shadow disappears from my skin, and I assume it's returned to just my eyes. A hand appears on my shoulder and looking behind me, it's Eve.

"Rain, are you okay now?" Her concern is clear.

I look at her emotionlessly. "I am fine. You can't tell Ami, though."

"You know a secret about me, and I know a secret about you. We're even." She smiles and helps me up.

Holding my bitten and bloody arm out, I move slowly to Chase's body. Using one of his knives to cut up his shirt, make a bandage. I wrap the cloth tightly around my arm a few times and then tuck it into itself. Staring at his corpse, I'm at a loss for words.

I strengthen my will, and push down the pain. "We need to find Emma."

"Are yous in any condition to keep goin'?" Driesen asks, having made his to us.

"I'll be fine," I tell him, and motion for us to move toward the mansion at the top of the hill. "We can't abandon Emma."

Moving through the faux kingdom Denis has set up, I understand why so many have rallied behind him. The living conditions within these walls are better than outside.

It would be the rational choice, even if you didn't agree with the leader's motives or actions.

At the front of the mansion, tall, heavy wooden doors greet us. The sight might cause others to retreat, but I am undeterred. Placing my hands on it, I muster up the energy to blast it open. One door swings fast, and slams against the entrance hallway. The other is completely unhinged, flying into the open area past an entry hallway. The fatigue of exerting so much energy, and the loss of blood, disorients me. I hesitate.

"Don't stop! He must not be allowed to continue, for our sake!"

The despairing souls drive me forward. Placing my good arm around Eve's neck, she assists me as the three of us find our way in. The hallway passes quickly, and we find ourselves in the middle of a very large, well-decorated grand hall. Solid pillars support the tall ceiling symmetrically throughout, as well as several smaller ones supporting a dual staircase leading to a second floor and balcony near the back of the room. Statues, busts, models, and paintings litter the walls to the point of clutter on both floors, leaving only room for doors leading elsewhere. The middle of the room has assorted seating arrangements. Tables, chairs and couches are meticulously placed to maximize the number of people able to be fit inside.

Eve breaks the silence. "Someone's a hoarder."

Without concern for safety, I shockwave a pillar. It cracks and buckles, causing the mansion to shudder.

"Denis!" I yell hoarsely.

"Hey, don't do that while we're in heres," Driesen scolds.

There is no sign of Denis.

"Denis! If you don't come out here I'm going to level this place!" I yell again.

Finally a response comes, but rather than from a person, a voice booms as if coming from the walls themselves. I look at Driesen, confused. He points out small black boxes hung from the ceiling around the room.

"Leave, or Emma dies," the bass in the voice rattles my bones. I look around for him.

"If she dies, I will torture you until you *wish* you were dead!"

"You can barely hold yourself up," he laughs and the echo bounces from wall to wall.

Driesen looks at me and whispers, "He can probably see everything within the house too."

"I have enough strength to finish this. Chase is dead. Your army has abandoned you. You're done in this city," I yell again.

"As soon as you three are dead they will fall back in line. Anyone who doesn't, I'll just kill them too." He laughs again.

"Be a man, Denis, and come face me," I goad him.

"No, I think not. Let's play a game. Come looking for me instead. Maybe you find me. Maybe I escape before you do."

"He would definitely have a way out or two built in here." Driesen grumbles.

"Driesen, why help this worm? If you kill him now I might take you back and make you my lieutenant, since the position has recently re-opened," Denis attempts to persuade Driesen.

"Not going ta happen. I want no part of your trash."

"Not for Emma's safety?" Denis taunts. "I know she's been like the daughter you never had."

"If Miss Emma isn't safe, neither are yous. If Rain doesn't get ya, I will, and I promise you'll meet a painful end," Driesen's calm finally breaks.

"Okay." I pull them into a huddle and whisper. "Eve, I want you outside patrolling the perimeter. Driesen, clear the first floor. I'm going to blow this house apart room by room until I find him. He's not to leave, even if Emma's not with him."

They nod and I release them. Eve swiftly disappears while Driesen moves toward a side door. Making my way to the dual staircase, I slowly climb one side, my body protesting the entire time. Bruises are forming already, and each one protests with every step I take.

"You can barely move – give up." Denis scoffs.

By staying silent, I give him no satisfaction. On the next level there are stairs leading up to a third story off to the left and right, as well as several hallways leading off into different portions of the mansion. While the front of the building definitely looked big, I hadn't thought much about the interior.

With so many choices on where to start, I walk back toward the front side of the house where there are large windows. Out in the courtyard of Denis's complex I see Eve. She's doing as I asked. Battle scars on the land streak in a few directions, and in the midst of them lies Chase's body.

Left from the windows, there's a hallway. With each window I pass, I send shockwaves to tear out large sections of the mansion's side, sending it to the grass below. When I reach the first room, and kick the door open, it's an empty barracks like room. There's no sign of Emma or Denis, so I blow the walls out. Instead of moving through the hallway, I make my own path through the enormous house by destroying walls connecting to adjacent rooms.

"I'm going to make you pay for the damage with your blood." Denis's voice reverberates through the openings.

"I'm going to keep wrecking this place until Emma's safely away from you," I speak plainly, unsure if he can hear me.

Moving from room to room, they vary from living quarters, to galleries of art, to storage. None of it interests me. Despite possible historic or monetary value, I trash it all with what energy I can muster. I'm tired, but the darkness pushes me to exhaust myself. The walls and ceiling feel my wrath. With every piece, every chunk of building which falls to my power, I become more irritated because I have to hunt him.

Irritation turns to anger, and my shockwaves become more devastating. When I reach the edge of the house I tear the wall and windows out, and watch it rain down like I had with the front of the building.

While I've only checked a fraction of the rooms on this floor, the time seems right to move up. I raise my arms up at an angle to destroy the ceiling of the hallway. It takes a couple blasts to break through the thick structure, but when a way is clear I jump up to the third floor with a little push with a shockwave. The house rocks.

"You're an idiot! You're going to kill us all if the building collapses."

"Maybe you should just release Emma, and this will all end." I grit my teeth, lying because both the despairing souls, and my own anger wants his blood.

With my body weak, and my energy level falling, I'm running out of time. Still, I blow a gaping hole in the roof, and leap up there. Fueled by rage, and the drive to see Emma safe, I tear apart the roof. Ceramic tiles and wood collapse inward. Little by little the building falls apart. I hear it begin to creak under my footsteps, but I press forward toward the center. Taking out large sections at a time causes the roof to buckle. A chunk shifts, and I lose my balance.

I fall to my chest on the roof, and begin to slide down the slope. I try desperately to grab onto anything, but all my hands find are smooth ceramic tiles. Twisting onto my back, I unleash a shockwave just before the edge. Instead of flying off the roof of the three-story mansion, I'm propelled upward a little bit, enough to tear a hole through, and fall back inside.

Lying there on the debris with the wind knocked out of me, I can't move. I *feel* movement though. A swaying motion. I quite nearly vomit on myself, but I'm able to hold it back long enough for the feeling to subside.

This corner of the building has begun to push and pull like the waves of water. With nothing else to listen to, I hear this story of the building begin to buckle. Some of the noises are loud, some faint, but it seems I've taken out enough to make it structurally unsound.

Unable to move from my position, I lie there, helpless to save myself from the destruction I've wrought on the building. Emma appears in the hallway to my far left, led as a captive by her wrist. She struggles against a clean cut man with slicked back, dyed black hair, in a white suit. He's muscular, appearing as though he may have trained with the fighters his father once employed. He drags her toward the set of stairs on this level. She sees me.

"Rain!" she cries out.

I can't stand to help her, my muscles unwilling to respond.

Denis sees me also and rather than leaving, he lets her go. Pointing a gun at me, he storms over. Anger burns his red face. With ease he stands me up to shove me against a wall I haven't destroyed. I nearly collapse on him. I'm whipped across the face several times with the gun, and he bares his teeth like a mad dog.

"You! You meddled before, but I was a boy. Now I'll have my revenge – this will be the last time!" he yells at me, pointing the gun at my temple. "You had to interfere with my life again didn't you?"

With the last ounces of my energy I grab his arm and struggle against the gun, doing what I can to stop him. Emma is too shocked to move. I mouth "run" to her, and lean back toward one of the large windows along the hallway. The floor rolls and buckles under us. Denis is caught off guard. I grab his shirt and lunge forward, smashing through the glass of an already broken window.

From the third story, we plummet toward the ground. Air rushes past us as we struggle in midair. He pulls the trigger on his gun, and the deafening sound near my right ear makes me think for a split second I am hit. But I am alive, and he's missed. We each try to gain the upper hand, but in the end I'm on top when we impact the ground.

His ribcage shatters beneath me. Denis coughs up blood, spattering my face. Between the blood, and the forceful removal of air from my lungs, I struggle to breathe. But I can't take my eyes off him. The look of shock and pain contorts his face. I'm sure he's been mortally wounded when he can't stop coughing, and wheezes with every breath.

"All…I…ever…wanted…" he chokes through his blood, "was for Emma…"

"Selfish…you did this…because you wanted Emma?" I struggle to speak against breathlessness and fighting to stay conscious.

"No…you idiot." He coughs violently. "I wanted…her to rule…with me."

"Rain!" Eve yells out, but it sounds so distant.

"Your life is forfeit to the darkness." I tell Denis harshly.

The earth rumbles, and the corner section of the mansion crumbles under its own weight. Looking back, the wall of the building has begun to lean toward us.

As large stones fall, thudding to the ground and threatening to crush our bodies, Denis and I are pulled away by our arms down the grassy slope. Driesen, Eve, and Emma have hold of us. Closing my eyes, for a few moments all I can hear is the destruction happening nearby, and then nothing but a steady ringing in my right ear.

My eyes are too heavy to open, but I still sense the presence of my companions. I'm rolled off of Denis. I lie on my back, my vision cloaked in the darkness of my eyelids.

I try to focus my attention, but I'm redirected when something changes within. The darkness, the shadowy collection of despairing souls is changed. I cannot discern how much, or in what way, but it's different. It feels lighter, I think. In Denis's last moments, I can feel the sadness within him; the despair he has for not being loved back; the despair of not living up to his father's expectations. All being drawn into me, into that endless black.

Had we not interfered in the past, would he have turned out different if he had won Emma over as a child?

Tortured by the thought that perhaps I was inadvertently the cause of his development into this person, tears stream down my face, and I cannot control them. Quickly turning into a breathless sob, the darkness overwhelms me, and I can't control my body as it convulses. I try to open my eyes, to let the light in, but my eyelids won't respond. Into darkness I tumble. Eve tries to snap me out of it, but to no avail.

It's creeping through my skin. I can feel it. It's going to break loose.

Once more I am at the mercy of this entity I know so little about. It consumes my body, and I become lost in the dark as I had previously.

I can hear Eve yell at Emma and Driesen in the living world, but I can't understand what she is saying. Emma continues to cry out to me, but they become more and more distant.

Finally there is silence, and I am left alone to wallow in misery with those lost in despair. Time is endless here within the darkness. Lying there, or perhaps floating on my back, I can't help but be overwhelmed by everything.

This is my fault. If I had died this wouldn't have happened.

Why did Ami and Agatha have to save me? I should have just left when I was healed, and they wouldn't have been subjected to these dangers. What reason did I really have to impose myself on their life?

Where do I go from here? How can I save them? How can I save myself?

Voices call out to me. I ignore them for a while, but they are insistent, becoming louder. Plugging my ears does no good because their voices are resonating against my soul. They cry out about their despairs, and I know now, no matter how many of them I try to help, my effort to save the women by letting the darkness in was futile. I will never fix them all. Chase and Denis are here within the despairing collective. With Denis's death, I'm unsure how much of the despair within the city has been alleviated.

If I succeeded, I would likely be unaware because it would have never happened. Time would be changed already.

What good is it to help, then? How will I ever feel like I am making a difference in this plight?

How do I make the despair go away?

~~~~~~

It's quiet and finally, the light appears again. I hear Emma whispering. Not wanting to face reality just yet, I try to stay here where I know I won't be able to hurt anyone else, but I fail. I am dragged along unwillingly into the light.

"I knew you'd save me again."

The light grows brighter despite my not moving in its direction.

"Rain, you have to be okay," she chokes through soft sobbing. "You're like the brother I didn't get to have. Please don't die…"

Reaching the light, I return to the conscious world. I keep my eyes shut. By the sounds I hear, and where I lie, I can tell I'm not in the grass of Denis's yard. I'm not outside. Light creeps in through my eyelids, and curiosity compels me to open them. I'm in the living room on the couch. Emma is sobbing against my chest. I'm home again. I'm safe.

Driesen or Eve must have carried me.

"Rain, please be okay…"

"H-how…long…?" I try to talk, but find my throat swollen and dry.

With a surprised look, Emma jerks her head up. But instead of a happy greeting she yells at me.

"Were you awake this whole time?" She hits me in the chest, and I groan in pain. Realizing she's hurt me further she begins crying again. "I'm so sorry!"

Ami appears in my peripheral vision, and offers me a glass of water. Emma tilts my head, and Ami presses the glass to my lips. I sip it slowly and carefully. After my throat is wet I clear it by coughing. It's painful, but necessary to talk.

"How long have I been out?" my voice comes out hoarsely.

"A week. You spent a few days at the hospital, and it was…" She chokes up a little. "It was touch and go until Evalyn came. You seemed to get better after that."

That's weird. I wonder why.

"Ami, I'm sorry…" I apologize.

She sits next to me on the couch, smiling weakly. Tears well up in her eyes also. Fighting it, she wipes her eyes before letting the tears fall, but she sniffles.

"I don't mind taking care of you. But you need to be more careful. If you die, how are you supposed to keep your promise?" She puts her hand on my leg, still smiling.

Seeing Ami's intimacy toward me, Emma swats at her, and clings to my chest. I have to pry her arm and grunt to let her know she's hurting me. Even breathing hurts. My ribs are damaged, possibly fractured. However, I'm alive. The thought that I was near death on a number of occasions hits me, and I'm not sure if it's worth it to continue being the hero.

"How bad do I look?" I ask Ami, smiling a bit. My mouth feels a bit crooked.

"Pretty bad." She frowns. "Your face is swollen and you have bruises all over."

"You didn't strip me and peek at me again did you?" I joke with her which attracts Emma's attention.

"You've seen him naked?!" Emma sits straight up, glaring at Ami.

"I didn't look!" Ami exclaims. "Mother had to, but I made sure my eyes were closed!"

"Aggy's okay, because she's the mother around here, and she has to do motherly things. But he's off limits to you and the poorly dressed homeless woman you took in!" Emma is furious.

I laugh despite it hurting to do so. Emma's overzealous attitude to protect me from Ami and Eve is near comical. Feeling phlegm building, I sip on the water and clear my throat again.

Likely having heard the commotion, Eve makes her way in from the kitchen, holding the door open for Driesen who has to duck and squeeze through. Agatha trails behind, and they move to just beyond the small table. They stare at me, concerned.

Do they fear the power within me like I do? Their proximity says no, but their true feelings could be hidden.

"Good to see yous alive and awake," Driesen says. "The city has been buzzin' about yous."

"Oh? And what are they saying?"

"That because yous did away with Denis and Chase, the city can be rebuilt," he responds. "Everyone gets a chance ta starts over regardless of what may have been done."

I look away. Though they were terrible people, remorse sets in for having to take their lives.

"I wish it hadn't come to that. I didn't want to kill them, but it was either me or them." I look at Agatha. "And I still have a promise to fulfill."

"Don't worry about it, Rain," Eve chimes in. "Seems like they had it coming."

I look at her angrily and bite my tongue, knowing full well those two were on the same level of power corruption when she was in her own time. She's taken aback. Everyone sees the displeasure in my eyes and they look at Eve as well. She looks away, and it seems she understands what I'm thinking without saying a word.

It could have just as easily been her if we'd have landed in her time after the void, or after I quenched a blade in the blood of the slavers. Who does she think she is to pass judgment on them? Entitled, self-absorbed, Eve.

"People have been gatherin' here in the park for the past couple days, just hoverin' around the house and holdin' a vigil for you," Driesen mentions, looking back at me.

"What do they want?" I ask.

"I think they're lookin' for yous. Without Denis to hold 'em down, they needs a leader."

I shake my head. "If I could stay, I'm certainly not the right person. You didn't fall to Denis's corruption though. You fought against him. I think that makes you a good choice."

"I think so too," Emma chimes in cheerfully.

"Just because I stood up ta Denis doesn't mean I know anythin' 'bout leadin'." He shrugs.

"It's your choice, but I think if anyone is going to do it, you should be at the front of the rebirth of Chas." My voice cracks under the rawness. "I can endorse you to the people if you'd like."

"I'll think 'bout it." Driesen nods, and heads for the living room door. Before he steps out, he turns back. "I'll check in on yous again later."

"I need help up," I state. Ami and Emma bring me to a sitting position, and then standing.

Finding my body weak, I rely on them to hold most of my weight, and I point down the hallway. At the bathroom, I push the door open, and let go of Emma while Ami leads me in. Shooing Ami out with my hand, she joins Emma, and closes the door. I tend to my business, and wash up. In the mirror, I see I'm as they said, worse for wear.

Would it have been better for them in the long run if I'd died this time? They would have been sad for a time, but they would have moved on. I don't know if they'd see less trouble or not, but I'm sure they would worry less.

Self-loathing does me no good, and I break my self-pity before it goes too far. I exit the bathroom, and Ami and Emma are still there, waiting for me. They assist me back to the couch, and I sit with my back pressed against the cushions rather than lay down again. They sit on either side of me, while Eve sits on the table cross-legged.

"You really do get hurt too often, Rain," Ami says. "We need to keep you away from dangerous situations."

"Hmm. Well, you'll just have to stay home all the time." I smile at her.

"Fine by me, but you eat a lot and our garden can't support you," she jests.

"If he hadn't come to save me, I'd have been forced to marry Denis," Emma says with a disgusted expression.

"I suppose that wouldn't have been very good," Ami responds, then pats my leg smiling. "What would you do without me?"

"Die," I joke.

"True. At least you weren't stabbed this time," she grins.

"Or shot. I mean, Kohan only pretended to shoot me, but it was still pretty intense."

"What?!" Emma and Eve both exclaim.

"You got stabbed? When?" Emma asks anxiously. and clasps onto my arm.

"Kohan told me he thought you were dead until we saw you again! I knew it! That rat!" Eve yells.

"Yeah," I lift my shirt to show Emma the scar running down my abdomen. She gasps, and Eve becomes more agitated.

"I'll kill him!" Eve barks.

"He's dead. He was in my time, before I met Ami or Agatha. He's the reason I can't remember who I was before they found me."

"If we hadn't saved him, he wouldn't be here today, and bad things would have happened to us for sure." Ami rests her head on my shoulder and I see Emma and Eve glare.

"At least things should be calm now Denis isn't around. I might be able to finish some projects. Like the stable, and a compost bin," I state, leaning my head against the back of the couch and looking at the ceiling. "I just need some wood."

"Don't worry, I'll get you some," Emma says cheerfully. "I can help too."

"And me," Eve says.

I nod, returning my head to its resting position, and relax, trying to forget about the pain.

The days pass, and I begin to recover. I watch out the window, at the crowd of Chas's citizens growing ever larger. They act in groups and seem to take shifts. It has become a bit ridiculous. I watch Emma bringing wood by the cartload, she has a hard time getting through due to the group being so thick. It feels like it is about time to send them on their way.

While their good wishes are appreciated, they can't be around here when the house goes to shift through time again.

Limping my way outside from the living room, I step down into the grass. Though I am in a disheveled state, I hear them murmur in an excited manner. It soon becomes a roar of cheering. They become silent when I raise my hand. Something about this is familiar. I chalk it up to being a king in my past. Having no speech prepared, I improvise.

"People of this once fine city; with Denis dead you can let your despairs dissolve, and return to a normal life. It will take time, but you will be able to repair this city to its former glory. You will need a leader for the city," I pause for a moment as they talk amongst themselves. "You should hold an election to determine who should be your leader. I nominate the man named Driesen as a candidate."

"You were the one who stopped Denis, you should lead us!" A random voice calls from the crowd.

"I cannot, and Driesen was a vital part of ending Denis's reign. I am only passing through."

"It's true!" Emma calls out. "I know Driesen, and he would be an excellent leader!"

The voices from within the group begin to overtake one another, asking questions, and giving me no time to respond.

"Does Driesen have abilities like you?"

"Can you show us?"

"Who are you?"

The crowd begins yelling. It turns into a frenzy of questions I can't, or won't answer. When I raise my hand again to silence them they do so and I'm able to speak.

"I am unable to appease you in your questions and requests. Just think of me as a drifter who was in the right place at the right time to help. That's all. Please, I must ask you to disperse from around the house, and return to your lives."

Without engaging them further, I turn to go back inside, waving for Emma to follow. Closing the door, I stand in the window for a minute before drawing the curtains shut. Emma stands by, smiling, and it's apparent in her face she wants to talk.

"You know the last time this house was here, not many people noticed it. When it disappears again, it will be noticed," she says.

"It can't be helped, I suppose." Shrugging, I make my way to the kitchen where Agatha is baking fresh bread. "Maybe we can convince the city to keep our secret."

The sweet smell of fresh baked bread fills my nose when I enter. Agatha hands me an already cut and buttered slice. As I devour it, the savory butter mixes with the sweet honey taste of the hot bread.

"That was delicious."

"Thank you. It's nice having a full stock of things again. Last month was difficult." Agatha smiles at Emma.

"I'm glad I could provide you guys with supplies. There will be more coming. I know you guys need to keep stocked," Emma says cheerfully.

I place my hand on her shoulder, and look her in the eyes. "Emma, we appreciate it, but I hope you're not giving us everything. You still need things to sell."

"No way. I still have plenty. I just want to help you out as much as I can."

She smiles. I quirk my eyebrows at her, unsure if I believe her, but I'm in no state to be walking to her shop to make sure she's telling the truth. Ami and Eve enter from the yard carrying a couple baskets of clothes freshly washed and dried.

"I haven't been able to wash my underwear since these people gathered! I hope your little speech makes them go away, Rain!" Ami proclaims.

"I'm used to being watched and waited on, but they're becoming a bit creepy. Always staring at the house," Eve chimes in.

With my arms extended to help Ami by taking her basket, she quickly turns away from me, swatting my hands. I put my hands on my hips, and sigh loudly. They're not going to let me do anything around here for a while. Going a bit stir crazy already, I itch for something to do, even if it would cause me pain.

"You know you aren't up to physical work yet," she scolds.

"I need to do *something*," I whine.

"You can model clothes for me," Ami says. "I'm going to trade them for more cloth with Anselmo."

"He's still around?" I ask.

"Oh yeah," Emma says. "He stuck it out. His broad range of clothing lines helped make ends meet."

"I'll go with you again. It'll be like last time," I offer to Ami.

"Last time?" Emma asks.

"Yeah, Rain and I went out on a date." She grins wildly, knowing it's going to cause a ruckus. I flinch at the oncoming storm.

"You went on a date?" Emma exclaims.

"Yes, we did. Rain had his first ice cream. He had his first brain freeze with me too."

"I don't think so. It's my turn!" Eve declares.

"I forbid it!" Emma turns to me. "How am I supposed to keep you safe from these two if you won't help yourself!?"

"Whoa. Hold on there. Let's not go making decisions for me now," I tell them all sternly.

"Too bad. Rain is my model, and I'm taking him." Ami becomes defensive.

Agatha laughs. I sigh. Stuck in a no-win situation, I remove myself from the debate. Returning to the living room, I can still hear them squabbling over what I get to do.

I get several sheets of paper, and a pencil from the bookshelf against the wall, left for me by Ami out of her supplies. I sit on the floor, legs stretched out under the table, and begin planning the rebuilt stable. Thoughts of constructing a compost bin cross my mind also. The cushion of the couch is comfortable against my back, and it takes me a few minutes to become motivated. Putting pencil to paper, I estimate the wood brought to us, and sketch. If what I want to build works, I will have enough for a nice stable and a decent size compost bin.

We will need some good fertilizer if we're going to grow a garden large enough to support the four of us. The compost bin will be a good way to create that with the horse's waste, and unused food.

The house quiets down as hours pass. The women walk through several times, occasionally stopping to look at my efforts. After I have several pages of ideas and sketches, I want to begin building. But I know evading their strict watch over me will be difficult. Reviewing my work, I find that I can make the stable larger than I had previously constructed. I play with different ideas. I draw a water trough and a hay bin, as well as an attached shed for all of the horse's supplies. It leaves me feeling accomplished.

Finding myself staring at the paper, I realize I'm not making any more progress, possibly because there's nothing else to be done. A knock at the door gives me an excuse to set my work aside and stretch. Answering the door, I stand to the side and let Driesen in. Removing his dome shaped hat, and his long brown coat, he hangs them on the coat rack and extends his hand in greeting.

"Hey, how are things going?" I ask, shaking his hand firmly.

"Well, since yous decided to put me up for bein' in charge I was bombarded. I'm now committed." Despite his reluctance in wanting to take control, he smiles.

"I know you can do it."

"It's not goin' ta be up ta just me here soon. We're going ta have an election for a city committee. Each sector of the city will have a representative, and no one person will hold the power. Everyone seems to be rallyin' behind that idea."

"Seems like a good plan."

"I was just passin' through, and wanted to let you know what was goin' on. I also wanted ta check in on Miss Emma."

"She might be in the kitchen, or maybe the other side of the yard." I pause for a moment. "She's not going to like having to stay here when we leave again. I'm going to need you to be there for her."

"Where will yous be goin'?"

"It's a very long and complicated story. You want the truth, or a lie?" I smirk.

"Eh, gimme the truth." Driesen shrugs.

As I explain our precarious situation, a curious look crosses his face. I'm not sure if he believes me. However, he stands there quietly after I've finished, as if pondering his next question.

"So, yous have no controls over it?"

"We all wish we did. The last time we were in got me these eyes." I point to my pitch black eyes.

"I was wonderin' 'bout that."

"That's a longer story. Come by tomorrow, and maybe I'll share it with you. But you should go find Emma. She'll be glad to see you."

"Sounds good." Driesen takes his leave through the kitchen door, and I'm left to myself again.

Finding I have some time, I venture outside, looking over my shoulder to see if I'm going to be scolded. It's late in the afternoon and I pine for something to do which won't land me in trouble. The groups have all but dispersed. There are still a few people wandering, but it's quite empty now.

Remembering that Ami said previously they usually pick up non-historical books from different times, thoughts of searching for a library pop into my head.

Was Evalyn serious about helping me search for my past? I might just want to do it alone.

Emma or Driesen would know where to find a library. I better ask Driesen though. I don't want to stir up any trouble by asking Emma to take me.

Walking around the outside of the house, I pass the piles of new building supplies gifted to us for the destroyed stable. As I reach the other side of the yard, Driesen is still talking with Emma. They're huddled together suspiciously, and she has him pulled down to whisper in his ear. Upon seeing me, she lets go of him and he simply nods.

"Driesen, I need help with something," I interrupt them. I squint at Emma and frown, wondering what she is being secretive about.

Driesen makes his way over. Playing the same game, I turn away from Emma so it's harder for her to hear.

"What's up?" he asks.

"I'm feeling a bit constrained. I need to leave the house. Is there a library of information around here?" I glance over my shoulder, and watch Emma, but she hasn't moved.

"Yeah. There's a library 'round heres. It's in bad shape though." He drops his voice to conceal my own secret.

"If you're not too busy, could you take me there? I need to do a little research."

"I can dos that." He claps me on the back and looks over his shoulder. "You don't want them ta know, right?"

I nod.

"All right. Here's what we're going ta do. I'll conceal yous in my coat as I'm leavin'," he whispers. "My feet are big enough for yous ta stand on. I'll do all the walkin' until we are out of their sight."

"Okay, I want out of the house pretty bad, but that sounds a bit awkward."

"Nah, it'll be fine. Yous will face outward, and I'll just cross my arms ta hold yous in place." Driesen peers over his shoulder again to make sure Emma hasn't snuck up on us.

This plan might work. It'll give me an opportunity to step away, and with good luck it will be a while before anyone notices I'm gone.

"Let's do it then," I tell him. "I'll head into the house first, and upstairs to turn my light on and close the door. It might fool them into thinking I'm still home."

Back around the other side of the house we enter the living room. No one is there. I make my way upstairs, stepping soft to avoid the creaky areas. Grabbing my dark brown cloak, I throw it over my shoulders, and return to the doorway. With the light on, and the door shut, I creep down the stairs to find Driesen waiting. He opens the door, and we are out onto the lawn, readying to go.

He pulls the long flowing flaps of his coat open. I move to step onto his enormous feet, but he stops me and spins me around to face outward from him.

Stepping backward onto his feet, he closes the flaps of his coat, and crosses his heavy arms to hold me in place. He moves his first foot forward, and then the next, but rather than walking he's waddling.

"Move your legs with me," he whispers loudly.

I do as I'm told, bending my knees as he bends his, and we begin a slow trek across the park. Unable to see because of the coat covering my face, I can only guess at which way we're going. Stifled by my own hot breath being reflected back at me by the fabric, I maneuver to the seam for fresh air. It opens a little, and I can see part of the city in front of us, but because it all looks similar, I still can't tell too much about the direction.

It seems like forever, but we arrive at the edge of the park, and he opens the flaps of his coat for me to step out from. Though we are away from the house, we are still in visual range, and I use his bulk to hide me. He looks over his shoulder before leading us into the city at an increased pace. When we feel we are safe, our pace slows.

"Let's never do that again." He chuckles.

"Agreed. Next time you can put me in a barrel and just carry me out." I laugh.

We travel down the street several blocks before he turns right, down a new one. I feel a sadness looking at the decrepit buildings left as a reminder of better times.

Such amazing architecture destroyed. I hope they can return the city to what it once was.

The silence between us is awkward, and I'm not sure if it's because I still have the idea of him thrashing Emma's shop in my head, or if there's something else. Still, I'm compelled to speak.

"Tell me about your wife," I say, my voice hesitant.

"I met her when I was fightin' in the ring." He sighs, but smiles. "She was a fan girl, and she attended every one of my fights. She followed me after them just to ask me out. It took a few months, but I finally gave in."

"Sounds a bit obsessive." I look up at him to gauge his reaction.

"Oh, she was. But we hit it off pretty well, and we gots married after a year."

"Did she know about the bad times with Denis?"

"Nah, she thought I was still fightin'. Never knew the difference because I was still gettin' paid. Even after yous showed up, I didn't have the heart ta break it ta her." His face turns sour.

"You said she got sick?"

"Yeah. I don't have any proof, but I think Denis was behind it. A lot'a people got sick back then, and those that fell in line with him got better at the hospital."

"I'm sorry you lost your wife."

Is she in here? Is she in the despair? Or did she die peacefully?

"It wasn't your fault." He looks down at me, and I can see there's no malice in his eyes.

"I feel like it's my fault, because I intervened when he was a kid." I struggle against a feeling of responsibility. "I've been thinking that if I hadn't interfered, he might've turned out differently."

"Yous can't think like that. Denis was an entitled brat. I've a feeling it would have been the same even if yous hadn't." He places his hand on my shoulder briefly to reassure me.

Deep in the city, we find our way to an open concrete area, a lone building in the center. It's four stories tall, and its stone structure has weathered Denis's storm a little better than the rest of the city. But though it's structurally intact, its exterior is rundown. Painted with lettering all across its sides, different colors and styles appear to write out names. I ponder the significance. Its large, wide staircase up to the massive double doors is uninviting. There are a number of ragged looking people strewn about both it, and the lawn.

"So, why the library?" Driesen asks.

"I have to find out about the history of this area. I don't know who I am, and I'm hoping to find some clues to the past."

"Well, I wish yous luck. I have some business I need ta see ta."

"Thanks, Driesen. Take care." I extend my hand and he shakes it firmly.

Parting ways, I look up at broken windows of the building once again. While I'm uncertain if I will find anything worthwhile, I must check.

I was king of Asta at some point, but how many were there before and after me? I will have to see if I can find any mention of a 'Drake' in the history books as a reference.

Moving up the large staircase to the front doors, I pull them open, and they creak loudly. Continuing inside, the state of disarray in here matches the rest of the city. It's spacious inside, all four levels visible from the ground floor with stairs leading upward to the next floor on the left side of the room.

Lit only by a few random lights, I see toppled shelves. Books are strewn about, and any semblance of organization it might have held once is no more. Along with the books, there are scattered people loitering about. People have made a home in the building. Their makeshift beds are made of destroyed chairs, tables, and piles of books littering the room.

Making my way around the first floor, I stay quiet so I don't disturb the inhabitants. I search for any sections pertaining to history, but after walking the entire floor, none of the labeled sections are what I need.

If I find the right section, I'm still going to have to look through all the books around it to hopefully find what I want. I could probably spend days here searching, which wouldn't be a terrible way to pass the time I suppose.

Up on the second floor, it's more of the same while I hunt for the historical section. Though I pass many vagrants, most of them barely look up at me. Despite the fervor of those who surrounded the house after Denis's reign had come to the end, none of these people seem to either notice who I am, or care.

Finally, on the second floor near the back of the building, I come to the section pertaining to local historical facts, but books are strewn about in piles. While trying to figure out where to start, I see a grey bearded man burrow into a pile of books, creating a blanket out of them, and I'm not sure what to think.

I'm left with the task of trying to find books not being used which might pertain to me. I start with what remains on the last standing shelf in the area. Picking up a couple I read their titles, and they are in no particular order. Thumbing through them one by one, I search for anything about kingdoms, castles, kings, and queens. Something to lead me in the right direction.

Hours pass as I flip through many books, but most are about the past few hundred years, some not even pertaining to history. Setting them down in a pile on a nearby table, I eliminate them from my search. When I pick up another and flip the pages, it's fictional. I become disheartened.

With books from other areas of the library mixed into the history section, this just got harder. If one exists which has any information about me in it, it could be anywhere. I'll end up having to search the whole building just to find something! Maybe I'll have better results tomorrow.

I let out a huge sigh, and return to the staircase. Leaving the heap of books I had looked through on the table, I hope no one mixes them back into the mess before I return. Being unable to find anything useful is disappointing, and I'm mentally spent.

Outside, the dark sky meets me, and it seems I've spent more time in there than intended. Wandering home through the darkened streets, it's quiet, despite a decent amount of people milling about. The stroll is casual, and though the city has only begun to recover from Denis's reign of terror, it appears things are becoming livelier.

The air is cold, and I pull the cloak's edges up over my shoulders, thankful I had grabbed it. Examining what I already know during my solitary walk home brings no new answers. By the time I reach the park, I've let my mind go blank.

Lights beam from the windows on both sides of the house. Around the side of the kitchen, shadows move in the light. At the door, I peer in and all four women are bustling about. Eve sees me and gestures in an animated manner.

I open the back door slowly, anticipating a berating for disappearing all day. I poke my face in. The door swings open, ripped from my hand. I fall forward, nearly face first to the floor. Agatha catches me, and Eve grabs me, leading me to the table. Instead of being scolded for leaving, and not telling them where I had gone, I'm sat down at the table where several dishes of food are placed near my spot. Ami, Emma, and Eve stand to the sides, I presume in front of their respective dishes.

"What is all this?" I ask, suspicious of any answer they're about to give me.

"Oh nothing, we just wanted to make you different foods," Ami says innocently.

I raise an eyebrow, cross my arms, and eye the three of them.

"Okay. I'll play." I sit up in my chair, and rest my forearms on the edge of the table. "Whose is first?"

"Mine!" Emma jumps up and down with her arm raised. "This is a chicken and rice dish, with a spicy peanut sauce!"

She pushes it in front of me, and I pick up the fork to take a bite. Chewing, I notice the sauce coats the chicken and rice thoroughly, and it's quite delicious. But despite her claim of spiciness, it is mild compared to what I assumed it would be. I put two more bites into my mouth, and the spiciness from the first bite kicks in, burning my tongue and throat. I cough and cover my mouth so I don't spew food all over. Choking the mouthful of food down only makes it worse, and it becomes difficult to breathe. Eve and Ami laugh while Agatha hands me a glass of milk. Guzzling it down doesn't seem to help, but after a few moments of panting and fanning my tongue with my hand, the fire in my mouth dies down.

"It wasn't *that* bad, was it?!" Emma looks sad.

"No, I just was expecting it to be spicy right away. I wouldn't have stuck those other two bites in my mouth if I knew it was a delayed reaction." I cough again, while pounding my chest a couple times.

"My turn." Eve hastily pulls Emma's dish away, and shoves a bowl of soup in front of me.

As it sloshes back and forth, vegetables float up, and settle to the bottom again. When I pick up the spoon in the bowl, I stir up the chunks.

"It's only vegetables and seasonings. Living in the desert, you make do with what you have, and this was what I came up with," Eve offers her insight.

Picking up a big spoonful with chunks of celery, potatoes, carrots, and onions, I blow on it to cool, and then put it in my mouth. As it moves about in my mouth, the power of the pepper and salt is too much for me to take. I can't force myself to swallow the spoonful. My eyes water, and I'm forced to spit it back into the bowl. Emma laughs, bending over in hysterics.

"What are you doing?" Eve cries out, offended.

"I can't eat this!" I exclaim. "Were your first ingredients water, salt, and pepper?"

Ami joins Emma, and Agatha is there to offer me another glass of milk, which I guzzle. Eve shoots the other women a dirty look, crosses her arms, and looks out the window.

"Rude!" she huffs.

"All right. I'm up!" Ami pulls the bowl away, and places a plate of pasta in front of me.

Long, flat noodles spiral the plate with a white creamy sauce drizzled over it, and green herbs sprinkled on top. It looks appetizing, and I've had Ami's cooking for the past couple months, so I'm unafraid to eat it. Picking up the fork, I stab it into the pasta and twirl. I put the bite into my mouth and chew.

The creamy texture and bold flavors of the sauce intermingle with the taste of the thick pasta. It's enjoyable, but for the sake of the other two, I pretend to have a hard time chewing it, over-exaggerating the movement of my jaw. Making an awkward face, I swallow hard, and grab for the glass of milk. I can see Ami's look of disgust at my reaction. Before anything is said, she snatches up the plate from in front of me, grabs my fork and shoves a large bite into her mouth.

"There's nothing wrong with this, Rain!" she yells through a mouthful of pasta, and scowls while chewing.

"Eww! You ate off his fork!" Emma sticks her tongue out, and makes a disgusted face.

"You're so juvenile," Eve laughs. "Rain and I have intertwined our tongues in a passionate kiss."

"What?" Emma yells and readies to punch Eve. "Try it again, and you'll have to go through me!"

"Shut up, Eve. No one wants to hear how you forced yourself on him." Ami slams the plate down and waves the fork menacingly.

I shrug. Agatha giggles from behind me.

"Okay. Now you have to choose the best one!" Emma smiles brightly.

"Wait, what?" I ask. "Why do I have to choose?"

"You have to be honest!" Ami tosses the fork on the plate, hard, and crosses her arms.

I can't do this. Ami's clearly the winner. Emma's was a good runner up, so I'll pretend and tell Ami later it was hers all along.

"Hold on now," Agatha intervenes. "It's not fair to bombard him like this."

"Thank you, Agatha." I look over my shoulder.

"Not when there's one more submission to this little contest!" She snorts through a laugh, and I'm not sure what's coming.

"That's not fair! You can't do that, Mother!" Ami shakes her head.

"You can't enter!" Emma squeals.

"Yeah, you're not in this!" Eve adds.

Agatha sets a plate down in front of me with a piece of pie on it. The crust is golden brown and flaky, while the center is a rich dark chocolate filling. I pick the whole piece up from the plate, and bite into it. It's delicious. It's sweet, with a hint of saltiness from the crust. I savor the bite, over-playing the bliss on my face. Without hesitation, I continue to devour the piece while the girls protest. When I'm done I lick my fingers for any crumbs.

"This settles it. Agatha is clearly the winner here," I declare, then turn and wink at her as a 'thank you'.

"You can't do that! She isn't a valid choice!" Ami cries.

"You have to pick another!" Emma slams her hands down on the table.

Shaking my head, I stand up. "No, I'm afraid Agatha has clearly won this contest. Thank you ladies for all of the food."

Agatha laughs hysterically, and the protests continue. I exit through the kitchen door. Running up the stairs to my room, I look over my shoulder to make sure I'm not being chased. No one is following, and I slow a bit.

"What's next?" I ask myself aloud.

Closing my door, I undress and slip into bed. I'm exhausted. Slowly drifting, I know I'm about to fall asleep, and my mind begins to throw random things into the forefront of my thoughts.

Hopefully none of the vagrants mess with the pile of books I've already gone through. I'm not sure I could handle having to go through them again.

It's a relief that Emma doesn't think of me romantically, but she still seems to be fighting pretty hard for my attention. Is that what sisters do? Did I have a sister in my past life?

We can't let Emma come with us. Convincing her is going to be difficult, but she's so innocent she might find danger, and not be able to get out of it. I'll play that angle.

The others have to back me up.

Finally, my mind shuts off and there is peace.

~~~~~~

Waking, I lie in bed for a few minutes before sitting up to let the grogginess fall away. My feet hit the cool wood floor, and it's a shock. It's dawn, but the sun hasn't risen above the skyline yet. Down in the park, only a few people mill about, as opposed to just a couple days ago when there was a sea of them.

It's good the group has dispersed. Working outside with them there would have been awkward. Maybe we will fade into history yet again mostly unnoticed. Or maybe we can get the city to hide our existence.

Heading to the dresser, I pick out fresh clothing. Taking my dirty ones downstairs, I find the living room and kitchen empty. It seems likely that no one is awake yet.

Setting my laundry down on the island counter, I pull an egg carton from the refrigerator. My stomach grumbles, and hard boiled eggs sound good. I put a dozen in a pot full of water and turn the dial on the stove. While it heats up I dump my clothes into the wash basin, and check on the horse. He lies huddled against the tree, a blanket draped over him. Though his eyes are shut, and he's likely asleep, I pat his nose anyway.

It's a good thing someone else thought to cover him. I wasn't thinking about it last night.

Returning to the kitchen, the water has begun boiling. Leaving the eggs in for a few more minutes, I retrieve my drawings from the table in the living room, and set them on the island counter. Turning the stove off, I drain the water from the pan, depositing the pan back on a cool burner of the stove.

While I wait, I review my plans, making some minor alterations. After considering the changes, I erase them and draw the original lines back.

I pick up a still warm egg, and crack it against the counter. It peels with ease. I devour it, and four more. I take my papers and pencil outside, and the sun has risen enough to see it. The light gleams through the city streets and it arcs into the park.

Around the side of the house, I set my papers on a pile of wood. Organization comes first, and though my body protests with aches and pains, I push through it. Sizing up what I have, I organize by type of wood as well as what its application could be. The amount of wood provided is substantial, and after organizing three separate piles they still stand at least a body length across, and come up to my shins.

I head back inside, and downstairs, stepping softly. In the tool area, I gather an armful of things which might be useful, and return outside just in time to see Emma running toward the house.

With all the time she's spent here, her business must be suffering. I'd be surprised if she's working at night. Probably sleeping then so she can spend the day awake.

I need to find a way to have Driesen keep her busy so it won't be as bad when we leave again.

Expecting she will stop to say "hello," I wait for her. As she approaches, she smiles from ear to ear. But she bolts past me into the house, a heavy bag on her back swinging back and forth. I'm left confused at her secretive actions lately.

Is she trying to stay here?

I shrug it off and return to my task. Setting down the tools, I look at my drawings again. Measuring, sawing and stacking, I prepare to reinforce the stable. Mid-morning rolls by, and now seems like the best time to begin making noise.

While putting cross beams up, I swing the hammer, and hit my finger. It takes everything in me not to shout. Instead I bite my lower lip, and cradle my hand for a moment. When the pain dulls, I return to hammering the nail. I flinch, fearful I will hit it again.

Morning turns to early afternoon, and the frame is nearly complete. Arms outstretched, I spin around inside the stall to make sure there's enough room, and to see what else needs work. Eve appears from the well with a big grin on her face, arms behind her back. She struts slowly, swinging her legs out far, and her knees high with each stride, making her look weird. She goosesteps toward me. I can't help but laugh at how awkward she looks, and it encourages her. She salutes me in an over exaggerated manner.

"Permission to enter the stall!" she barks.

"Permission denied." I smile at her. "What do you want? Other than to distract me."

"Oh, nothing. Just thought I'd come out here and help you." She grins and leans her shoulder on the frame's doorway.

"And what would I need help with?"

She points at a structural beam behind me. "If you put two angled pieces up at the top of that beam attached to the top frame it'll provide better support."

"Is that so? A technique you picked up in the desert?" I lean up against the beam next to her.

"As a matter of fact, it is." She shoves me playfully.

Turning, I look again, and move to make the changes she has suggested. She leaves me to my work, and disappears around the other side of the house. While I am cutting the supports, she returns with a glass of lemon water, and when I have a moment I drink it down.

What are her motives?

"Thanks." I hand the glass back to her and continue working.

She hangs around for a while, silently observing, but disappears again. The afternoon rolls on. The sun beams down on me, beginning its descent to the other side of the sky.

My stomach grumbles, and I take a break. In the kitchen, Ami and Emma are cooking together. They both look up and smile at me playfully. Smiling back, I shake my head, not sure I want to know what they're up to.

They're up to something for sure.

I head to the bathroom to relieve myself and wash up. Back in the kitchen, my stomach grumbles to remind me why I came in here in the first place. I pick up an orange from a newly placed fruit basket on the island counter, and peel it. It's juicy, quenching both thirst and hunger at the same time. I toss the peel in the waste bin below the sink.

Soon enough I'll be able to just recycle things like that with the compost bin. I need to find out where Agatha wants me to build it.

One thing at a time, though. I need to finish the stable.

Outside again, I continue my work. With the frame fully set up, and the water and food troughs built in, it appears to be nearing completion. With only the walls left to put up, I decide to put the final touches on tomorrow. I bring the horse to his new stable, closing the frame of the door, and removing his headpiece. While I stroke his nose gently, there are footsteps behind me. Turning, I see Driesen.

"Thought I'd come by again and see if yous were still here. Looks like yous are."

"Indeed we are. I was just about to head inside, care to join me?"

"Sure." He nods and sticks his hands in the pockets of his long brown coat.

Entering the kitchen, I notice two deep pots on the stove. The first holds a large batch of noodles, and in the second is a deep red sauce with chunks of meat. Emma is alone in the kitchen, and busy setting the table. When she sees Driesen she waves and runs to give him a quick hug before returning to her task.

"Are you staying for dinner?" she asks.

"If yous'll have me. I've been missin' your cooking," Driesen responds.

"It's a collaboration. Ami, Agatha, and I made it."

"Go ahead and have a seat." I put my arm out toward the table.

I wash up and sit in my spot. Driesen sits at the opposite end from me. His face is emotionless, and he appears to be lost in thought for a moment. Emma bustles about, and Ami comes in from the living room to help.

"So, how are things going out there?" I ask.

"Things'r good. Several people have stepped forward wanting ta help reestablish a functionin' government."

"Which sectors have candidates?"

"Most. Agriculture and commodities, which will be broken up ta import, export, and then the merchants. Public security, which is fire, law enforcement, and health. Then public development which will provide representation for the living quarters, the people of the city, and growth."

"The city seems much larger than just three sectors."

"It's bein' consolidated while we rebuild. No doubt it will branch out again. Each person elected will have a minimum of five sub-committee members whose'll will be delegated tasks and responsibilities by the main committee member. No one person will have all the power again."

"That seems like a wise course of action." I rest my elbows on the table, placing my chin on closed fists.

"Here you go, Driesen!" Emma says cheerfully and sets a large plate of pasta down in front of him.

"Thanks, Em." He smiles at her.

Ami brings a plate for me, and I lift my arms up so she can set it down. She winks at me, and I'm unsure how to respond.

"Thank you." I smile.

She returns to setting out plates for the others before sitting down at my right side.

"Mother! Dinner's ready!" Ami yells.

Emma jumps into the seat to the left of me, and grins wickedly, no doubt in an attempt to antagonize Eve. Agatha and Eve enter from the living room. When Eve sees where Emma is sitting, she scowls and slams her hands down on the spot next to Ami.

"You're in my seat, you little whelp!" Eve barks.

Emma's response is to stick her tongue out, and I chuckle. Eve glares in my direction, her fiery eyes threatening to burn a hole in me. But from this angle, the expression makes her look more attractive than normal. Her flushed face brings out her many freckles. Leaned over the table with her hands pressed on it, her bright red hair dangles dangerously close to the pasta. She keeps staring, even after sitting down near Driesen. Devouring her meal like a savage, she sticks a few strings of the pasta in her mouth and slurps it up.

The meal is mostly peaceful, free from any more disruptions by Eve. While the others converse about mundane things, I let my mind go blank while I eat. Though there is little I home in on, I do notice when the food on my plate is gone. Coming out of my daze, I realize I've been staring at Eve the whole time. She seems to have noticed, because in between talking, she looks over at me multiple times. Averting my eyes, I lean back in my chair and stare up at the ceiling.

I hope the other girls didn't notice. Emma might jump over the table to 'protect' me, and Ami would certainly take it the wrong way.

I wash my own dishes. Driesen starts to do the same, but Emma jumps up and takes his plate to wash it herself. I steal it from her, and wash it too.

"Thank you for cooking." I look over my shoulder and smile.

"Indeed. Thank yous for the delicious meal," Driesen follows my lead. "But I should really gets goin'."

"It was a pleasure having you," Agatha smiles at him.

Drying my hands, I extend a hand for a shake. "Check back again later," I offer.

"See yous." He shakes my hand with a firm and vigorous grasp. "If yous are still here, I'll update ya."

Driesen and Agatha exchange pleasantries while she sees him out. I watch them talking through the window while washing the dishes. When I've finished, I head toward the swinging door. The three girls huddled where Driesen was sitting catches my eye. Passing the table, they look at me suspiciously. I quirk an eyebrow in silent question, but all it does is make them turn back to each other and whisper.

Not knowing what they're up to makes me curious. I push through the door, and move to the stairs. Feigning walking up, I step hard on the first few to make them creak, and then creep back to the door. Pressing my ear to the crack. I hear nothing but heated whispers, and only catch every tenth word. With those bits, I can't make out what the conversation is about.

A few minutes pass, and it seems like a waste of time. A shower sounds good, and I grab a towel from the hall closet. I make it a quick one.

When I wipe the mirror down, the black in my eyes catches my attention. I stare. Their black emptiness is unnerving, regardless of how many times I look at them and try to find myself. Before the despair consumes me, I distract myself with shaving. Despite being careful, I still nick myself. It takes a few minutes, but I stop the bleeding, and feel for any spots I missed. I comb my hair, and it takes some work to break through the knots.

I'm going to have to ask Ami to cut it for me. Maybe tomorrow.

Towel wrapped around my waist, I peek out into the hall. There is no one in sight, and no voices coming from the living room. I jog through the house, up to my room, and practically slam the door behind me.

With clean undershorts on, I get into bed, the cool and soft sheets welcoming me. At the onset of sleep, I place my hands behind my head and let the abyss take me.

~~~~~~

Another week is gone, and the time in which the vortex will take us grows closer. In anticipation, my senses are heightened, and like Evalyn had felt it in the void, I'm positive I can feel the pressure building.

I wish I could have found something at the library. I can't say I didn't try, but it would probably take me years to sort through all the mess. And it didn't help that my piles had been disturbed.

I suppose I could have stuck it out a couple more days, but looking at so many books without any results is demoralizing.

Maybe it's okay if I don't know any more about my past self.

On the side of the house, I stand back and admire my handiwork on the stable. After adding some retractable shades over the open areas, I feel my work is complete. The horse drinks from his water trough, paying no attention to me. From the small shed I added, I retrieve a brush and give him a once-over with it.

There is enough lumber for the compost container I want to build. I dig into the ground near the edge of the property past the well, where Agatha indicated she wanted it. Creating a rectangular ditch in the ground provides an outline for a floor and walls. As a final touch, I use a sheet of wood with a couple leather straps as the lid.

It's crude, but it will work. Between the horse droppings and the other things which can be composted, we should be able to renew the soil decently around the house. All I'm missing are some earthworms.

As the sun is beginning to set behind some very dark clouds rolling in, it seems time to go inside. I draw the horse's shades shut, and enter through the living room. Agatha is just coming through the kitchen door, a stack of books tucked under her arm. She sees me, but before I can ask about them, she avoids me by climbing the stairs. Her actions tell me it was Evalyn. She, and the secretive conversations which have been going on around the house, make me suspicious.

She's done nothing but stay quiet around me. I don't remember seeing her leave or come back, but she got those books from somewhere.

Is she searching for information about me as we discussed? Maybe it's why she hasn't said anything. She might not want to give me false hope.

Sitting on the couch, I put my feet up on the table and relax from the preparations for time travel. The women have also been busy. Ami has been making additional clothing to barter with, Eve was tasked with reorganizing the basement, and Emma has been stocking the house with so much food I fear it will spoil before we can eat it all.

Emma has been here every day, and I know she hasn't been taking care of her shop. She's intending to go with us. Driesen's subtle attempts have failed, and I don't know how effective I'm going to be when I tell her she needs to stay in her own time.

Lightning flashes, and thunder cracks loudly outside. Out the window, I watch as a downpour begins. The clouds swept in fast, and the park becomes drenched within a matter of moments. Through the heavy rain I can't see the city. My attention is consumed by the storm while I reflect upon Ami and Agatha saving me, and my promise.

What can I do to stop this vortex? My destructive, innate ability doesn't help any. But I need to try harder to find a solution. I have a debt to pay. Evalyn might have some ideas, but though she's softened up a bit, would she be willing to help?

What about that idea of getting far enough away? We'd have to make sure there are no obstacles to crash against. But would it work?

Emma enters the room and sits next to me, hugging my side. I wrap an arm around her for a quick embrace, and then let go.

"You looked lost in thought. Figured maybe you needed guiding back to reality." She smiles innocently.

Smiling back, I nod and look out the window again. "I was indeed lost. Then again, it's no different from me being in reality. Most of the time I have no idea what I'm doing. I just bumble around doing what I think is right."

"Well, it's the good intentions that count, right?" She pokes my side.

I let out a small chuckle. "Not really. It usually lands me in a load of trouble and hurt."

"But you risked your life to save me from Denis. That's what counts in my book."

"I suppose so." I let silence fall then speak again. "Did Driesen stop by today?"

"No. He stopped by the shop when I was there last night though. Told me how well things are going. Seems like they have a solid plan for Chas's recovery."

"Good. If he doesn't stop by here again soon though, I'm afraid you'll have to tell him goodbye for me." I slyly broach the idea of her staying.

"What do you mean?"

"If he doesn't stop by here before the house shifts through time, you'll likely see him at your shop, and you'll have the chance to tell him."

"I'm going with you!" she proclaims.

"Emma, I…"

"No!" She crosses her arms and pulls away from me. "Am I such a burden that you wouldn't want me along? I already talked to Aggy! I have my room picked out! It's going to be down the hall from you, across from Evalyn!"

"It's dangerous, Emma. I don't know if I'll be able to protect you."

"I know you'll be able to!"

This isn't how it was supposed to go. She already talked to Agatha? Is that what the women have been whispering about?

It might make sense Ami would allow it, since Emma doesn't have those kinds of feelings for me. But it's dangerous. I can't just allow them to put her in danger, can I? Maybe I need to talk to Ami.

Standing up, I frown disapprovingly at her, and climb the stairs to the sewing room. Thinking about Ami, it comes to mind we haven't been able to see Anselmo yet, and it's something I want to do for her, the weather permitting.

Upstairs, light beams from under the door. I rap lightly with my knuckles against the wood. Waiting and listening for a moment, I receive no response. I open the door and peek in only to find her not there. I flip the light switch off, and close the door.

Down the hall there is a commotion in Eve's room, followed by a thud against the wall. I fear Eve might be assaulting Ami, but pressing my ear to the door, I hear snoring instead.

In my room, I turn on the light, and am surprised to find Ami. She's curled up with my pillow, asleep on my bed. Knowing full well if the other girls saw this, trouble would start. I shut the door quietly.

I bet she got tired while sewing, and just wandered in here instead of stumbling down the stairs. But did she do it to cause trouble too?

Not unfamiliar with sharing sleeping space with Ami, I take care not to wake her while I scoot her over. Readjusting the pillow I lay down, turning my back to her.

I just hope I don't roll over in my sleep and cling onto her. That would be a little awkward.

The rain drums against the roof and window rhythmically, and I drift off. But instead of sleeping and dreaming, I fall into the darkness. Though it appears I am alone, it's less unnerving this time around than previous times. In the midst of floating, I'm met with waves and visions of despair. Due to my proximity to Ami, they're hers. Things I already know come to the surface.

"Why can't I have a normal life? Why must I be stuck drifting through time?

"What isn't mother telling me about her health? It's Evalyn's fault by taking over her body. It's making her weaker."

But while listening, it becomes more personal.

"I want Rain to myself, but what do I do if Eve wins his affection? I've seen the way he looks at her. How long will he rebuke her advances?

"What am I supposed to do if he doesn't want to be with me?

"I thought we were becoming closer. I don't know what happened. Why is he pushing me away?"

It hurts to hear her pain.

She is *the one who saved me. She cared for me, taught me, took me out on adventures. Of course I like her, but she knows how dangerous it is.*

How can I ignore Eve when she's begun to grow on me? She's a friend, but I know she wants a lot more. It's impossible to ignore that, and the more I'm around her the more difficult it's becoming.

Ami is the one to whom I felt attraction to first.
I have to put a stop to their competing.

Ami's despairs become silent. I float along, and the distant speck of light appears. No sense of urgency compels me toward it, but I creep closer. It feels like there is a warm gentle breeze blowing by me. When I awake, I am face to face with Ami, and her warm breath is caressing my skin. Her eyes are not open, but in the darkness I can see a hint of a smile. When I move my hand to scratch an itch, I find our fingers intertwined together.

She must have woken at some point and taken advantage of me choosing to lie in the same bed as her.

The rain continues to pour, creating a gentle ambient noise. Lying here with Ami, I'm comforted from her despairs by having seen her smile, and holding her hand. I drift off.

~~~~~~

My eyes slowly open on their own to light pouring in through the window. Ami is still here. As I come to, I see she's awake, smiling and blushing at me. My heart skips a beat, and I smile back. No words are exchanged for several minutes as we just stare into each other's eyes. But our silence is broken by two distinct voices yelling downstairs. The yelling quickly turns into stomping, and then heavy footsteps up the stairs.

Before I can react and jump out of the bed, it's too late. My door slams open. Both Emma and Eve are there, and there's fury in their eyes. Eve shakes a clenched fist.

I begin to sit up, but I'm halted mid-way as Ami clasps my chest, burying her face into my neck. Looking sideways at them, she wastes no time in seizing this opportunity.

"Oh don't worry, this is *exactly* what you think it is. And this isn't the first time Rain and I have shared a bed! You remember, right, Eve? You gave us that tent."

Ami! What have you done?!

Eve and Emma storm over and grab me under the arms. Ami tries to resist, but they forcefully haul me down the stairs and toss me out onto a soaking wet lawn. I'm drenched. A click of the lock follows and I take my time, knowing I'll have to walk around the house, and hope either Agatha or Evalyn is in the kitchen.

In the middle of hoisting myself up, a familiar large palm reaches to my aide. Driesen pulls me to my feet. I nod in thanks.

"What was that 'bout?"

"Women problems." I shoot him a glance, and he smirks with understanding.

"We just gots done with a council session. I wanted ta see if you were still around."

"Not for long. That reminds me though. I wanted to ask you to keep our time traveling a secret. We've already interfered a lot, and I'm afraid if people learn about this, it might be a bad thing."

"That'll be no problem. Your secret's safe with me."

I shake his hand again.

"We scraped together a few more resources for yous. Mostly food. It'll be dropped off later."

"Thanks, but you really didn't have to. We've been pulling things together quite nicely to last us another couple months."

"Eh, it's no problem. Anyways, I gotta get some sleep before the next meeting."

"Keep an eye on this spot in the next few days. You might just see something amazing."

We wave to each other, and Driesen heads off toward the residential section. I make my way to the living room door. Looking in the window, there's no one inside. Rather than knocking to try for Ami or Agatha's attention, I move to the other side of the house. A perplexed Agatha stares at me through the kitchen window as I pass by. I smile sheepishly. She opens the door for me and before the question of "why?" I just close my eyes and shake my head.

Creeping through the kitchen, I listen for any sign of them. The coast is clear, and I push on the swinging door slowly. The girls are nowhere to be seen. I bolt up the stairs and close my door. Footsteps thud over, but I yell out while stripping.

"I have no clothes on!"

The door doesn't open, to my relief. They descend the stairs, and I'm left in peace to finish changing into dry clothes. Cautiously, I open my door to peek out, and no one is there. I avoid the creaky spots as I make my way down. Voices can be heard from beyond the kitchen door, and I can tell the three of them are going at it. Placing my ear against the crack, I eavesdrop again. I have better luck this time around in hearing them, as their voices are elevated.

"I'm going to make him choose!" Eve snarls.

"He's already picked me," Ami taunts her smugly.

"Neither of you can have him!" Emma bellows.

"Just because you have a little sister complex and don't want him doesn't mean you get to tell me I can't have him.

"I won't let him take forever. I'm going to push him along, and when he chooses to be my second, I'm going to take every opportunity to flaunt it," the confidence in Eve's voice is overwhelming.

"Don't be stupid," Ami retorts. "I've already won, but if you want to waste your efforts, you need guidelines as to what's appropriate."

"You *both* need them," Emma says. "And the first one is that under no circumstances should either of you get in bed with him!"

Silence from both Ami and Eve tell me they're going to have a hard time with that one, but they finally agree and move on.

"Okay. My turn. No initiating kissing with him, at all," Ami states, and Eve grunts loudly in disagreement.

"How else am I supposed to greet him when he comes to my room in the middle of the night? With a handshake?" she says sarcastically. "Fine, my turn: no seducing him."

I am taken aback, considering her previous actions.

"You're one to talk. You try every chance you get," Ami sneers.

"Oh no. The rule was for you, not me." I can hear the evil grin in her voice.

"That's not how it works, but since you said it, it applies to you too," Emma says.

I'm pretty sure I shouldn't be hearing any of this, but I can't pry myself away from the door. If they catch me, I'm going to get more than just thrown out on the lawn.

"And if he goes into one of your rooms, the door *has* to be open, and the lights on!" Emma adds.

Reluctant sighs come from both Ami and Eve and is followed by a synchronized 'fine'. I stifle a chuckle, but become silent when a new voice enters the fray.

"And there should be no reason any of you should go into the bathroom and talk to him while he's in the shower!" Evalyn cackles.

"What?!" Emma shouts.

"Who?!" Ami hollers. "Eve?!"

"Whoa, hey now! It was once, and it's none of your business! And you, I don't want to know how you know!" I imagine her pointing her finger accusingly at Evalyn.

"Off limits! If Rain is in the bathroom, and the door is closed, there is no reason for any of us to go in there," Ami scolds. "Aunt Evalyn, no going in there as a spirit!"

"I couldn't help it. When I saw Eve sneak in after Rain, I had to know what she was doing."

"You listened to my conversation? Gah!" Eve yells.

If they find me out here I'm a dead man. But I bet I can play a prank on them for throwing me outside.

Tiptoeing away, I move to the front door, slip my shoes on, and creep outside. Around the house, I find the kitchen window and peer in. Their voices are still audible, but I can only make out every other word. I slink under it.

I reach the door, put my face to one of the panes of glass, and breathe heavily to fog it up. I then proceed to press my face to it, grunt loudly, and bang on the door rapidly while jiggling the handle. All three girls scream, and I can hear Evalyn break into hysterical laughter. Angry stomping signals it's time to run.

The door swings open, but I'm already in full sprint away from the house. There is a person coming from the commercial district with a cart. Before I can pass him, I'm hit in the back of the head with something hard. I stumble and fall face first into the wet grass, soaking a second set of clothing today. A shoe lies next to me. It's one of Eve's boots. Behind me stands an unamused Eve, arms crossed, but before she can do anything else we're interrupted.

"Are you Rain?" the man asks.

"Yes," I groan and stand up, brushing my shirt off.

"This is from Driesen." He drops the handles of the pull cart, and dusts his hands off.

"Thank you. We'll unload it and you can take your cart with you." I nod at him.

"It's not mine."

"Oh, well thank you for delivering it," I offer my hand in a handshake, but when he sees my eyes, he declines.

"Well, I think we're going to be just fine for a few months," Ami blurts.

Eve retrieves her boot, putting it back on her bare foot. I haul the cart to the back door, and we spend a good portion of the day unloading and organizing the food. When we're finished, Evalyn prepares a chicken salad.

We sit to eat our meal, with Ami and Emma stealing the spots next to me again. We're silent, but there is a lot of eye contact between everyone. They seem to have no suspicion I overheard them, and I can't help but smile.

They all finish before me, including Evalyn, and stack their dishes. Ami points to me, and then to the stack. I chuckle and nod, accepting punishment for scaring them. It doesn't take me long to clean up.

In the living room, Ami is on the floor, hunched over the table with several sheets of paper and a pencil. She's sketching designs for clothing, but promptly crumples each sheet up, and tosses it to the side. Either Agatha, or Evalyn, is on the couch. From the musty tome she's reading, I assume it's Evalyn. When she looks up to see me, she hurriedly closes the book, and disappears upstairs, leaving just Ami and I.

"Coming up with anything interesting?" I ask, sitting on the couch.

"Not really." She sighs. "I'm having a creative block right now."

"Ah. It will pass."

"I know. It's just frustrating."

I lean forward.

"You know what'll take your mind off of it?" I whisper into her ear.

Looking at me puzzled, Ami asks without saying anything.

"How about we take off? Head into the city, maybe go check up on Anselmo?" I suggest.

A spark of excitement grows in her face, and she whispers back, "I'd like that!"

"But we have to sneak out." I look around cautiously.

"Got it!" She jumps up and puts her shoes on.

Holding my finger up to tell her to wait, I put it to my lips, and then point for her to head through the kitchen. She nods in agreement, and tiptoes. I exit from the living room door, the latch clicking. Around the side of the house, Ami is waiting.

Waving an arm, I work to gain her attention. Her eyes meet mine. I point rapidly with both fingers toward the city, hoping she understands I want her to run.

Breaking into a sprint, her long green skirt flows behind her. When she reaches the apple tree, I follow after as fast as I can. Once I've caught up to her, I grab her hand, and pull her along faster. Looking over my shoulder, I make sure we aren't being pursued. Ami stumbles a little, but quickly regains her footing.

Upon reaching the street surrounding the park, I feel we can slow, and we drop to a quick stride. I let go of her hand, and stick my arm out for her to take. She smiles, and hooks her arm on mine.

Safely away, we slow to a stroll, following the path we originally took when we were here previously.

It feels like years ago. It was years ago. But it was only months for us. Time travel can be so confusing.

Dusk begins to set in. Vendors and shops begin to open. Reminiscing about our first date, I look around at the somewhat barren street, and find it might be better with less people to dodge this time. But looking at the open stalls, I realize I don't have currency to purchase anything.

"I didn't grab any gold coins from our stash."

"No problem!" She slyly draws out the card she got the last time we were here, and waves it at me. "As long as they still take these, there's still some left on it from before. How about we buy some ice cream again."

"You sneaky girl. But you remember what happened the last time I had ice cream. Maybe we should try something a little less painful."

"No, I'd quite like to see you inflict that upon yourself again." She bumps her shoulder playfully into mine, and grasps my hand.

"I bet you would." I smile and tap her arm playfully.

We head over to the same shop we stopped at last time, and it's conveniently open. We place our orders. Hers is two scoops of 'chocolate cherry chunk' while I stick with what I know, peppermint. Eating in silence, we stare deeply into each other's eyes. Despite my best effort to savor the ice cream, I can't control myself. I devour it, only to cause myself a severe amount of pain. I stop eating only momentarily to rub my forehead. When it doesn't work, I hit my forehead a few times while squeezing my eyes shut. Ami laughs at my pain, and I can't help but laugh too.

"Stop laughing! It hurts!" I mock protest.

"You're laughing too! And you did that on purpose!" She pushes me by the shoulder, and I nearly drop what's left of my cone.

When I'm able to open my eyes again, there's delight in Ami's face, and it makes me smile wider. Finishing my ice cream, I take her by the arm again and lead her while she continues to eat hers. We take our time in reaching Anselmo's store, but we are there before too long. She finishes her ice cream just in time for us to enter, and I let her arm down to hold the door open for her. As she passes by, I bow and wave my arm for her to enter, like a gentleman. In response she curtsies.

His shop is duller than the last time, with very plain clothing throughout most of the store. Only a small section in the back corner has any real class to it, and they are familiar. They are Ami's design, right down to the flowers she puts on them as her signature.

Anselmo appears, and time has not been kind to him. Though he has a smile on his face, he appears fatigued. He has lost a significant amount of weight and his clothes are baggy. His receding hairline does nothing to help the wrinkles on his forehead and around his eyes.

"Welcome to…" he starts in, but stops and stares as if he's seen a spirit. "You! Let me look at you!"

He grabs Ami's shoulders and spins her around, then does the same to me. He's clearly in disbelief.

"You look like you haven't aged a bit! I heard you were back in town, but this is insane! You look almost the same as when I saw you all those years ago!" He points at me. "Well, except for you having black eyes. That I don't remember."

Ami laughs. "It's all a very long story."

"Well, here! Come, take a seat in my office missy! Oscar! Watch the front!" he yells at someone we can't see.

At the back of the store, he pushes his office door open, and allows us to enter first. Ami and I take seats in front of his desk while he moves around back of it and sits. His face has brightened up.

"How is this possible?" He swings his arms open, and then crosses them across his chest.

"Would you accept the answer that I take really good care of my skin?" she jests with him.

"You'll have to sell me whatever it is you use. I need it." Anselmo laughs while stroking his wrinkling face. "What are you? Immortal?"

I chuckle and shake my head. "I wish."

"So, how well did my clothing sell?" Ami leans on the table with her elbows.

"'How well?' she asks." He chuckles while looking at me, and pointing at her. "You did nothing short of create a fashion statement which lasted five years strong."

"That's amazing!" Ami squeals.

"I was the lead clothing store for both powerful and weak, the rich and poor! So much so I was able to put away a nice nest egg. It helped me through Denis's reign of terror. Now that he's gone, the economy will recover, and so will this shop."

"I noticed you have much simpler clothes out there right now," I observe.

"Yeah, well with Denis eating everyone's profits I had to make some cutbacks and make cheaper clothes. But it's over now. I can flourish again."

"You kept some clothes from the original designs though," Ami says, clearly pleased.

"I sure did. Made some alterations though to keep up with trends and styles as they changed. Kept them around not so much for sale, but for display. I'll have you pick one out for your own collection in return for all the money I made off of your original designs."

"Oh no, I couldn't. You already paid me." She puts her hands up, and shakes her head.

"I insist. The amount I paid was well below what you should have received. I can see that now. No arguing." He waves his finger at her, and grins.

Ami sighs, but she is smiling.

Anselmo stands up and motions for us to follow. Leading us back out to the sale floor, and into his special collection in the back corner, he opens his arms wide and smiles while turning around.

"Pick what you want. Doesn't matter what it is!"

He becomes rather excited, and makes his way through. Pulling out fancy dresses, he holds them up and looks at Ami questioningly before putting them back.

Anselmo looks beyond us, and waves someone over while Ami browses through the clothing. A small, stout man appears, and Anselmo whispers something to him. Then Anselmo moves to me, puts his arm around my shoulder, and leads me to the front of the shop.

"Here." He hands me one of the currency cards and points down the street. "Go buy some flowers about three blocks down. There's this little red headed girl who picks them and sells them to help her family make ends meet. Buy some flowers for your girl."

"But I—" I start to protest, but he interrupts.

"No. No buts. Go on now." He shoos me with waving hands.

I walk down the street, counting the lampposts as I do to keep me entertained. My feet carry me through the crowds, which have begun to swarm about in a 'business as usual' manner for this society. I look for the little girl with red hair and flowers. I have to scour the stalls to locate her as the population density increases. Someone matching Anselmo's description catches my attention, and I shuffle my way over to her. In her flower cart she has bundles of several types of flowers.

"Excuse me miss! Want to buy some flowers for the special one in your life?" She attempts to peddle to people passing by.

When I reach her, she throws her sales pitch at me. She crosses her arms in front of her dark blouse and bats her eyes. Catching my stare she lathers on the charm.

"You look like you want to help a little girl support her struggling family!" She dances cheerfully in place, her braided hair flopping around.

"I sure do. I'll take one bundle of your nicest flowers." I wink, and hand her the card.

"That'll be fifty thousand!" She snags the card from me before I can protest.

"Fifty thousand?! That's quite steep! Are they gold plated flowers?"

She looks at me out of the corner of her eye, a conniving smirk on her face. "All right, I'll give you a discount. Ten thousand. But you can't tell anyone I gave you such a great deal."

Knowing ten thousand is still a significant amount, I hesitate. She opens a sliding door and pulls out something different from the bundles of ordinary flowers sitting on top of her cart. They luminesce a light blue, and I'm astonished. Gently she carries the flowers, and hands them to me. They emit a sweet fragrance from their large glowing petals.

"Now, if you take care of these properly, you can make them last a whole month. In the daytime the petals are white, and they drink in sunlight. At night they release their stored light. Make sure you change their water frequently!"

She hands me back the card, and smiles wide, knowing she just made a large sale. Smelling the flowers, their scent is subtle, and somewhat fruity. I smile and nod at her before heading back toward Anselmo's with the flowers cradled safely in the crook of my arm. When I arrive, he is outside waiting. I can see a look of disbelief on his face.

"You bought *those*?! I was thinking you'd buy her something simple!" He whispers, but the shock in his voice is clear.

"I got swindled!" I whisper back. "Before I could respond she took the card, and whipped these out!"

"Cheeky little girl..." He chuckles. "I sure hope you didn't pay her full price for those!"

"Was ten thousand too much?"

He chokes, coughing violently. After he catches his breath he shakes his head and smiles.

"She sure has a way of hooking people. What did you talk her down from?"

"Fifty."

His eyes go wide. "I'm sure glad you *did* talk her down, but next time try to haggle lower. I don't mind helping her though. Her family and their shopping mart had it pretty tough under Denis."

"Anselmo, thank you." I return his card to him, and extend my hand to shake his.

"No problem, buddy." He grabs my hand, and shakes eagerly. "You just take good care of Ami, and we'll consider it even. She's about done with the alterations."

I nod and turn back to face the street while Anselmo returns inside. It's not too much longer before the door opens and shuts again. When I turn around, Ami is there, and I am stunned into silence.

She's wearing an ankle length, sleeveless, red dress. Slim in design, it hugs her body. When she spins, I admire its elegance. In a twist of modern-meets-classical, the shoulders have some fringe and pleats on them. The front dips down a fair amount. The back is nearly non-existent at the shoulder, simply cutting down to waist level where a red sash is tied off on her right side.

My jaw drops, and I blush heavily. She sees my reaction, and averts her eyes, blushing also. She looks down at her chest and plays with a small bow at the end of the collar, then looks back at me.

"Is it too much? I wasn't sure if it was appropriate for me to have this much showing…"

"I…I really couldn't say." I stammer. The invitation to actually look puts me in an uncomfortable position. When I look I make it only a glance.

Needing to take the tension off of the situation, I present her with the glowing blue flowers. Her eyes widen, and she looks at me with a puzzled look on her face, no doubt wondering where they came from. She takes them from me, and breathes deeply through her nose.

"They smell so wonderful! Where in the world did you find these?" she asks excitedly.

"A little girl down the street," I answer innocently.

She throws her arm around my neck. "These are amazing! Thank you, Rain."

I hug her back, my arms around her waist. The deep embrace makes me relax, and we both sigh. When she finally releases, I follow her lead, and she picks up a brown bag from the ground.

"Are your other clothes in here?" I ask, extending my hand out for the handles on the paper sack.

"Yeah." She hands it to me, and hooks her free arm on mine indicating she's ready to go.

Until the early hours of the morning, we walk slowly and silently through the city streets, sometimes through crowds, sometimes down empty areas. We stop for a bite to eat; meat and vegetables on a skewer, roasted over an open flame. When we continue on, she holds my arm and clutches the bouquet to her chest. Reaching the edge of the park, we stop. She turns to me, and I face her.

I don't want this to end. I'm sure she doesn't either.

She blushes. "I had a good time, Rain."

"I'm glad. I did too." I smile. "That dress really looks amazing on you."

She pushes her wavy brown locks out of her face, and looks up at me. Staring intently into one another's eyes, I can feel the urge to lean in and steal a kiss. Urges translate to actions, and I lean in a little. She closes her eyes, and pushes up on her tiptoes. Nervous, I also close mine. I feel her breath on my lips. Placing my hand on her cheek, I draw her in.

A whirring noise cuts through the air, breaking my concentration before I'm able to press my lips to hers. I'm hit in the temple with a hard and heavy object. Falling sideways, on my way to the ground, I hear Ami begin to yell. The assaulting object rolls off my face. It's Eve's boot once more.

"You were about to break your own rule, tramp!" Eve's scream pierces the air.

"Excuse me, but *he* was going to kiss *me!* Not the other way around! There's a difference! And I think ending a *date* with a kiss is acceptable, because it's clearly not random!"

"You don't get to go on dates with him!" Emma cries out. "Wait! Are those *Vibrant Iris* flowers?!"

Rolling onto my stomach, I slowly push myself up. While they are distracted by their argument, I make a break for the house, full speed ahead. Looking over my shoulder, I see they've noticed. Eve and Emma have begun pursuit. I reach the back door before they do, and as I charge through it, I slam it shut and flip the lock.

Without hesitation, I run through the house and up to my room. Shoving my bed up against the door, I barricade myself in. Their rules in mind, I strip down to just my undershorts and jump into bed.

Loud thuds reverberate through the room as they bang on my door, and I have to muffle my laughter with my pillow.

Taking a deep breath in, I yell at them, "You can't come in. I'm not dressed, and I'm in bed!"

The banging stops, and Ami laughs. The sewing room door opens.

"I've seen him without most of his clothes on anyway," Ami taunts.

She slams the sewing room door and Emma and Eve proceed to badger Ami through her door. They bicker in the hallway over the date and I just lie there until I'm tired. With the pillow over my head, I'm able to sleep with them still going at it.

Sleep, my reprieve!

~~~~~~

It feels like I only slept a few hours when I come around. I shove the pillow off my face, and take note of the silence outside the room, indicating it's probably safe for now.

Slowly I stand, put some light clothing on, and head down the wooden stairs, their cool touch somewhat soothing. Half way down the stairs the earth quakes beneath us, and Emma screams.

"Put me down!"

"Stop, Eve!"

No! Can I get there in time to push her out? I hoped I had another day to convince her to stay in her own time. Or that maybe she would be gone when it happened. I didn't even get to talk to Ami about it!

Continuing down as quickly as I can, I try to make it outside before the vortex finishes the transfer. I brace myself against the wall with my arms. By the time I reach the bottom the quaking has stopped, and I hear the horse whinny.

I'm too late.

I move to the living room window. The four of them are in the yard, and what I see doesn't surprise me. Eve has Emma slung over her shoulder. Ami appears to have been mid-struggle with her, while Agatha was trying to block her path. But they've stopped dead in their tracks to observe our new time.

I didn't think she'd take it that far after I warned her. I guess I only specified not to hurt her. Our motives for Emma not coming may have been different, but she knew it was the right choice.

But why were Ami and Agatha trying to stop her? Do they really think it's beneficial for her to be traveling with us, rather than reviving Chas?

We've come to rest on an open plain directly in the middle of a settlement. There is minimal vegetation. A multitude of animal skin tents surround us, and primitive looking people gather around. The house is being surrounded by men of all sizes, all shapes, all skin tones, wearing skirts of tall grass and leather, wielding spears. The women and children of the tribe scream and retreat back behind a line of warriors readying to wage war on the house. Eve practically drops Emma to the ground, ready to fight.

Apparently taking their advance as a personal challenge, she makes aggressive gestures at them.

No rest for the weary, or wicked?

~~~~~~

3 TRIBULATION

Rushing out of the house, I place my hands at chest level, palms open and outward to show them we're not hostile. I plant myself in front of the women as a barrier. The tribal people watch me with leery eyes.

One of them shouts at me in a language which almost sounds familiar in the way it is structured and flows, but I can't understand anything. To the left and right, they're forming a semi-circle around us in the yard. Another waves his spear, bellowing in their tongue. He is set apart from the rest with the headdress he wears, made from the head of a buck, its antlers still attached. He is likely someone of high importance. A leader.

"Rain, blast them!" Eve orders.

"I'm not going to harm these primitive people over your lust for battle," I bark.

I sigh, trying to think on my feet for a way to diffuse the situation.

"There's no way this is going to work," I mumble. With my attention on the man of importance, I speak in a soft and hopefully disarming tone. My arms are still raised in a surrendered position. "Do not attack. We are friends."

He looks at me puzzled, and yells a short phrase. Looking over my shoulder, I see Ami has joined me.

"Quick," I whisper. "Go fill a small basket with some food, and bring it to me."

Ami disappears into the house, and it catches the man's attention. Stepping into his vision, I redirect him, and force a smile. Moving forward, I place the palm of my hand on the tip of the spear in good faith.

"We are not going to hurt you." My voice calm, I push the tip of the spear down a bit, trying to point it to the ground. But he quickly asserts himself, and points it back at me.

Something catches my eye about the spear. The poles are formed metal, wrapped with leather. The tip appears to be forged, rather than a hammered out stone. It's out of place for their level of advancement, and I'm confused by it.

That's not as crude as it should be. Where did they get it?

The leader's eyes shift to look behind me. Ami returns with the basket, and holds it out to me. Taking it in hand, she has thrown an assortment of items in the basket, not necessarily stuff which fits with this primitive time. As I offer it to him, he looks down.

With speed and precision, he snatches a small loaf of bread out of the basket and sniffs it. He tosses it over his shoulder, and thrusts his spear menacingly at me. I hold a hand up in submission, and grab another small loaf of bread from the basket. Putting it to my mouth I take a bite and chew vigorously.

"Mmm!" I over-exaggerate my delight as I chew and swallow. I rub my belly in an attempt to indicate it is good to eat.

I offer it up. He looks with caution, and then grabs it. Sniffing it again, he turns to look behind him for a moment before returning his attention to me. Taking a slow bite, he chews it, and barks out something else, though not directed at me. Women dressed in animal skins pick up the other loaf, and begin to tear it apart and eat it.

Once more I offer the basket to him. This time he takes it, and passes it behind him to a tribe member. His eyes never leave me though. Taking a less aggressive stance, he uses his spear to point instead. He speaks slower in his language, and points behind me. All four of the women are standing at my back.

When I turn to him, he barks out orders, and his fellow tribesmen begin to move in on us. I fear he intends to take them. With their spears still being wielded against us, my choices to keep them safe dwindle. Surrounded now, the option of sending them back into the house is gone. Taking the only action which will save us, I point my hand into the air, and let out a small shockwave. The boom echoes across the land.

They scatter, yelling as the shockwave dissipates above us. It has had the desired effect, instilling fear into them. They chatter amongst themselves beyond our border while the leader holds his arms out to protect his tribe. I drop my hands back into a peaceful position in another attempt to show I'm not going to harm them.

Our eyes meet again, and I break away to turn and point at the women. Facing him again, I pat my chest a few times quickly to indicate they are with me. He then shouts a few times, and motions for some of his people to follow. A swath is cut in the crowd, and they disappear into a larger tent. The tribal people back away.

Turning to the women, I command them in a low tone. "Inside."

We retreat, and I lock the knob. Agatha closes the drapes on the window and my shoulders relax a bit.

"They look primitive enough that we could probably just scare them more and they won't bother us," Eve suggests.

"Maybe. But did you see their weapons? The metallurgy is similar to *my* time. And their language is far more complex than ours." I reply. "They may appear primitive, but something's not right here. Scaring might not be the right course of action."

"It certainly *seems* to be earlier on the timeline than we've ever seen before," Ami makes an observation. "I'm not sure what kind of records exist about tribal people, but if there was ever a time our actions would have serious consequences, this would probably be it."

"I vote we allow *our* alpha to use his powers more to scare *their* alpha into leaving us alone." Eve won't budge on her idea. "What big change in time will happen if we just scare them?"

"Wait. So if this is happening now, this has happened already, and it can't change the future?" Emma asks. "Or does this mean we could possibly be changing the future now just by being here?"

"Without some recording of this time it's difficult to tell," Agatha tells her. "It's possible to change things. Eventually we might make such a significant difference it shows up in a history book somewhere."

"We might want to start reading books to correlate our interactions. I have this despair wrapped up inside me, and I'm trying to drive it from my body by changing things as needed to make things better for people."

"What if doing that stops us ever meeting?" Ami frowns.

"I'm really not sure how I'd accomplish it, but I've come to the conclusion since I'm still here, and so are all of you, it's probably not likely." I try to sound confident, despite not knowing if it's true.

It becomes quiet, and I hope they've accepted it as a valid response. Our attention is diverted back outside when we hear several people shout, and then one loud bark from their leader. The horse begins to neigh in distress, and I peek out the window's drapes to see it being hauled off.

"This is not good," I state and pull back the curtains some so they can see as well. "So, what do we do?"

"Get out there and exert your dominance!" Eve shoves me to the door. "Make me swoon at your power to command."

I look at the other women for confirmation. Emma's eyes are wide, but she appears lost in all of this. Ami and Agatha nod reluctantly.

"Should I use my sword, or just shockwaves?"

"Sword. Weapon for weapon, maybe he will see yours is superior and back down." Eve becomes giddy.

"I'm not so sure." I shake my head. "But I will take it anyway."

Ami retrieves it for me. When she hands it over, I stall, fumbling with the belt and scabbard. Eve taps her foot impatiently.

"Quit stalling!" Eve calls me on it, unlocks the door, and shoves me out.

Walking forward a few steps, I look back at the window. All four of their faces are pressed in it. At the edge where our grass and their settlement meets, the chief steps forward a few feet from his gathered tribe, spear still in hand. Instead of pointing it at me, he points it up and raises it to the sky and shouts. In an effort to come to common ground, I draw my sword and copy him.

The leader raises and lowers his spear several times, and I continue to mimic him. His motions are still not hostile. After one last thrust into the air he shouts, and everyone in the tribe drops to their knees. Their hands are outstretched in front of them and they chant. The chief is the last to do so, but he sets his spear down in front of him in a neutral position and chants as well.

Sheathing my sword, I glance over my shoulder and shrug. The chanting stops, and when I look back, they're kneeling but copying me by looking over their shoulders and shrugging. I'm confused, as I'm now the one being copied. I watch and cross my arms, only to be copied again.

I realize this is going to escalate quickly, so I move to the chief and wave my hands for him to stand. Instead of standing, they all make the same motion.

"Up." I tell him, and they repeat me to the best of their ability.

I shake my head, and plant my hands firmly under his armpits in an attempt to pull him up. Understanding what I'm trying to do, he stands up and I repeat myself. "Up."

I have to wonder if it's worth the effort to try and communicate through speech. And if I teach them words, I might actually have an effect on their speech patterns. Who knows what it might cause.

I motion with my hand to the rest of the tribe by placing two fingers on the palm of my hand like legs and show them I want them to stand. They look around, seeming puzzled, but they understand. Picking up the chief's spear, I hold it out for him to take. As he does, I spin him around and raise his arm in a triumphant manner to show the tribal people their leader is still in charge. He hoots, and the village cheers for him. While they are preoccupied, I return to the house and head inside.

"What are you doing?!" Eve asks with exaggerated frustration. "You probably just empowered their leader over you, and over us!"

"No, I don't think so. I really think we are far back enough, if we do something drastic, we're at a higher risk of changing the timeline. I don't sense any despair here which would need intervention."

Agatha appears from upstairs with a musty tome. She flips through pages, and when she finds what she is looking for, she holds the book up for us to see. In it is a picture of a faded, crude drawing on the wall of a cave. Two lines straight up and down, connected by one straight one across the bottom, and two more angled up to meet each other, all surrounded by an oval. Five stick figure people exist in the crude depiction of a house, while a multitude of stick figures stand outside the oval. Snapping the book shut and putting it under her arm, she opens her mouth to speak.

"That's us, isn't it?" I ask, preempting her.

"This part of our journey seems to be already written," Evalyn's voice comes out. "I just happened to recall this while history hunting. It's definitely us. The only way to know if we're changing something is if we look at the history before and after. This isn't the only example I've come across recently. We are being noticed."

"Wait. I thought we weren't doing that!" Ami protests.

"Well, since Rain and I discussed finding out more about his past, I figured the rules were off. We both took turns sneaking off."

"That's where you were going?" Emma looks up at me with big eyes. "I could have helped you!"

"It was something I needed to do on my own, and I didn't find anything." I turn my attention back to Evalyn. "So then what do we do?"

"Do what you do best, Rain. Meddle in the affairs of time." She laughs heartily. "Just make the best of the situation. Maybe we can convince them to move away from here."

"Perhaps," I reply.

Commotion outside piques Ami's interest, and she returns to the window, then motions for us to come take a look. We do, and an odd sight is seen. The tribal leader is calling forth several women in a wide range from amidst the closest of his tribe. Lining them up at the edge of the property, he makes them kneel down and passes his spear over their heads while pacing back and forth.

"This doesn't look good," I state.

"Maybe he recognizes you as supreme, and is going to sacrifice one of them," Eve says in jest.

My eyes become wide when I realize her joke is plausible. Before they can react I've ripped the door open, and am running toward the chief. The women outside begin chanting with their hands out again and the chief raises his spear into the air. He too chants, but it is different than what they are saying. He speaks, they speak. He leads them in whatever it is they're doing.

When I reach him, he looks at me, and smiles with perfect teeth. He questions me with his eyes as he moves to the front of the line, and holds the spear over an older woman's head. I shake my head, and put my palms out in protest in hopes to tell him I don't want him to do this. But he takes it to mean I don't want that particular one, and moves to a child who is no more than six or seven, and holds the spear over her head.

I move to intercept him, my arms outstretched to take the spear from his hands, but he sees my movement and points the spear at me. He barks an order I can't understand.

"Hey!" I yell.

I am perplexed at what to do here. Shouting back, and waving my arm in a sharp manner, I hope it conveys that I want him to just go back to his tribe. I motion for the girls and women to stand up as I had before, and they do as I request.

"Go!" I point rapidly with both index fingers beyond where they all are. "Go!"

The chief looks at me with bewilderment, but they follow my command and return to the throng. Except for one. A young, dark-skinned girl, with straight black hair tied into two pigtails is left after the others have cleared. She is still kneeling, her palms out and eyes closed. I lower myself to her level, and take her hands. She opens her eyes, staring at me with eyes nearly as dark as my own.

I see in her an innocence I've never seen before. I hesitate, made unsure of myself, my violent nature to this point. Before I can stand her up and turn her away, the chief is standing over us. He slams the end of his spear into the ground, and lets out a great shout to the tribe. They respond with a synchronous cry back. He smiles, and grabs my hand, then places it on the spear. With a swift move he stands me up, and positions the spear to kill her.

No. This is worse than I expected!

I fight against him, snatching the spear, and pushing him away.

"What are you doing? Take it and use it on him!" Eve yells at me from afar, but I can tell she's closing fast.

"Rain, don't!" Ami barks at me from behind Eve.

I point the tip of the spear at their leader, and grimace. Shaking my head I try to tell him no, but he doesn't back down. Instead he puts the tip of the spear right to his sternum, and prepares for me to push it in.

Seeing his willingness to sacrifice, either one of his own or himself, angers me. I thrust the tip of the spear into the ground at my feet; I make sure it's embedded deep.

The tribe is silent, but they move with swiftness. I'm surrounded. They grab me, and I'm lifted up and carried away. Eve and Ami yell at them and try to break through, but they're not fast enough.

With so many hands on me, I struggle to break free. They keep me moving until I can roll from them, and drop to the ground. Hands grasp to stop me while I sprint in the direction I think the house is in. I'm hopelessly lost in a sea of bodies. With only one real way of escaping, I jump up and roar like an animal. Raising my arms up, I let a shockwave loose.

The boom causes them to back away in a circle. I can see the top of the house, and hear the women calling. I can't believe how far they carried me in such a short amount of time. The house is a fair distance away. I rush to return to them, but a wall of people pushes me back. They turn me around and send me back toward the middle of the ring.

"Rain!" I hear Emma yell.

"Stay there!" I shout back. "I'm heading to the house!"

Surrounded in a small circle, I have only one way out. They try to close in again. Another shockwave breaks the air above, and they widen the ring to give me room. They've given me enough space to boost my jump, and not hurt them.

At the far edge, I run at full speed toward the other wall of tribals, bend at the knees, and leap. With my palms pointed down I let a shockwave go, and launch high into the air, bounding over the crowd. I see Ami and Eve's wide eyes as I fly over their heads.

My upward velocity peaks, and I begin descending. Having not thought it through, I realize the impact at this angle is going to hurt. The ground comes up on me fast, and instinctively I place my arms out. On contact, I swing them under, and tuck into a somersault in the grass. I leave a skid mark behind, but come to rest on my back unharmed. I look up and see the leader a few feet away. He yells in fright, and the tribe scatters backward. Ami, Eve and Emma are with me momentarily, and scoop me up, dragging me to the house.

"Well, this is going worse than I expected, and we haven't even been here an hour yet," I joke, and am promptly smacked upside the head by Eve.

"You should have killed him. Assumed the command of their tribe."

At the steps to the living room door, they set me back on my feet, and Ami shoves me inside forcefully.

"Am I bad luck?" I ask a question out loud which was more meant to be in my head than anything.

"Well, we certainly didn't have these kinds of problems before you showed up. Now look at us: three tag-a-longs in what used to be two people and a spirit." Evalyn laughs and lets out a snort.

"This isn't funny," Ami says. "They were pretty adamant about you taking her life, or his."

"If you don't do anything, I'll kill them if they try to take you away again." Eve is serious.

"At least they didn't try to marry you to her. That could have been them hauling you away for a ceremony and consummation." Evalyn is having more fun with our situation than I'd like.

"Eww! That's gross!" Emma covers her mouth. "That'd be like *me* and Rain!"

Eve shoves Emma and points her finger at her. "Don't even think about it."

"You're sick!" Emma hits her in the stomach. "I bet you'd look at your own brother that way though, barbarian."

Eve nearly topples me to get to Emma. I chuckle, holding her back. Ami sighs and sits on the couch. When Eve calms, I join Ami. I sit on the end, thinking of leaving no room for Eve. She defies me and sits on the arm of the couch. Emma slumps down at the other end, and Evalyn stands in front of the table, crossing her arms, still smiling.

"Hopefully I've scared them enough with my power that they'll just leave us alone. If only there was a way to communicate with them."

"How did you come up with that?" Ami asks. "The jump, I mean."

"I just sort of made it up when I was trying to protect Emma before she was kidnapped."

"I'm telling you, just give me a few minutes out there and I'll scare them all off." Eve's boldness and brash attitude knows no bounds. "I'll make sure they'll never bother us again."

"You know that isn't…" Evalyn trails off. The luster is lost, and she's become pale. She's exhausted. Her condition is concerning, and I lean forward.

"Are you all right?" I ask her.

"Agatha will be fine."

"She doesn't look like it," I reply, standing up to help.

Evalyn looks at me angrily, and then her facial expression changes suddenly, indicating Agatha is in control now.

She is looking worse for wear. The frequent possession by Evalyn is taking a heavy toll.

"Before we do anything else, we should eat. We're going to need our energy if we're going to think of a way out of this." Ami changes the subject from her mother's health.

We file into the kitchen. Like a cohesive family, everyone begins to help. I head down to the storage and pick up a half dozen bananas, and a few oranges. On my ascent, a cupboard door slams. Ami is berating Agatha.

"Mother, you need to rest. She's taking over you too much lately. Let us handle this," she scolds.

"I'm the mother here, I should be taking care of you." Agatha tries to retain control.

"I'm old enough to take care of myself *and* you! Sit!"

I watch Agatha reluctantly sit at the table. Ami's concern is coming out as anger, and Agatha is hurt. Though I'm cutting up the fruit, I keep my eye on Agatha. It appears as though she hasn't had a decent night's rest in a while.

Breakfast is fruit, scrambled eggs, and toast. Eve gathers glasses, filling them one at a time at the sink. She stares out the window at the tribe on this side. Reaching over to bring her back to reality, I jab her in the side playfully. She jumps, letting out a little yelp.

"What are you thinking?" My eyes are fixed on the tribe also, but I glance at her from my peripheral vision.

"Just bad memories of large nomadic groups like this. Nothing I won't forget about soon enough," she says confidently.

We sit to eat. The book Evalyn had been looking through is on the table near Agatha, and I motion for her to push it to me. She does, and I eat while flipping through the pages. I turn my attention back to the cave drawing she had originally showed us, and notice something strange. There is another cave drawing I hadn't seen before underneath the first one.

In this new picture there is a depiction of a stick figure with its arms and legs spread out seeming to hover over many smaller figures. Spinning the book to Ami on my right, I point, and quirk an eyebrow.

"What is *that?*"

"What?"

"*That!*" I point at the new picture.

"I...was it there before?" she asks.

"I'm pretty sure it wasn't." I shake my head.

Turning the book to Emma and Eve on my left, they look at it and shrug. I stand up and bring it to Agatha, and a look on her face confirms my suspicion.

"This picture is proof that even minimal interaction has an effect."

"So what do we do then? Nothing? We've already started something. What is on the next page?" Eve asks, and reaches to grab the book from me.

Snapping the book shut before she can flip the page, I pick it up and hoist it under my arm. I shake my head while looking each one of them in the eyes.

"I think it's best if we limit the number of eyes on the way history is unfolding, or unfolds. If each of us sees what changes, we might each try to affect the way things happen, rather than just interacting normally."

"Up until now we've just done what we thought was right. It's probably best if no one looks at the book," Ami suggests. "If we make a mistake, and see its full effects on history, it could have negative effects on us."

Moving to the door to the living room, I turn and nod at Ami,

"You're probably right. I'll return this book to Evalyn's room."

Can I use it to rid myself of the despair? Or maybe lessen it?

I'm gone but a few moments while I return the book to Evalyn's room. Pushing the swinging door open to the kitchen, I catch Ami mid-sentence.

"...*can't* share any information about the future with the people we encounter."

"They can't understand us." Eve scoffs.

"I'm not just talking about these people. I'm talking about anyone in general," she snaps.

"Does it mean we shouldn't tell people we travel through time?" Emma asks.

I interject myself back into the conversation while taking a seat. "I agree with Ami. We should keep the information of our time travel limited. I already asked Driesen to conceal his knowledge of us."

"Set one ripple here, and it could become a tidal wave later. If we save or don't save someone, it will affect things. Because we're all here we can assume nothing we've done so far has caused time to fold in to a paradox. But because we can change time, it's very possible," Agatha says.

Her knowledge of time travel is greater than mine. I have to remind myself that she's been doing this a long time.

"Is it possible to meet ourselves in different times?" Emma asks.

"In our experiences so far, only one version of the house can exist in one set period, so we'll never meet ourselves," Ami explains.

"So, I've been meaning to bring up a couple things. What can we do to stop the cycle? Can we get far enough away like the horse in the void and just hope for the best?" I ask.

"That sounds dangerous. Not only would obstacles be a problem, but the speed we'd be traveling if we got too far away would likely kill us on impact." Agatha offers. "The horse was a unique situation."

"What about Evalyn's powers? Or something like it?" I scratch my chin.

"Well, Aunt Evalyn's true potential of power was brought out on her deathbed: an act of desperation. To be able to muster that kind of power when not in a desperate situation would likely be as rare as finding someone with powers similar to Auntie's," Ami responds.

"There have to be others out there. Evalyn, me, Chase. We can't be the only ones with some extraordinary ability." I look around.

"There may not be a solution. Or if there is, we may not find it. Even after we're dead and gone, the house will likely continue on with Evalyn, possibly drawing in new tenants," Agatha bleakly suggests.

"What if we found a way to set Evalyn's spirit to rest?" Eve asks.

"Hello. Have you met Evalyn?" I joke. "Putting her to rest would be like trying to stop the world from spinning."

"She heard that, Rain. Expect retaliation later," Agatha smiles weakly.

"Well since she can hear me," I start speaking directly to her. "Evalyn, when you are researching, let me know if you find anything of importance regarding powers. Maybe we can find someone like us to help stop the cycle." While there is no audible response, I assume she's heard me.

My body feels restless, knowing the tribe is out there, possibly closing in, or maybe planning war. Standing, I pace the room, occasionally stopping to look out the window. The room is silent as we all seem to think to ourselves.

"I hope that little girl is okay." Emma is the one to break the silence.

"He seemed serious. I'm hoping that he'll forget about it after my display." I run my fingers through my shaggy hair, and scratch nervously.

"What if we set up a fence?" Eve asks.

"What if we *invent* the fence, you mean?" Ami asks her in a condescending tone.

"We don't have the lumber," I tell them. "And Ami's right. Let's not give the tribal people any more new ideas. As it is, they've seen things far beyond their understanding and we might just be the inventors of stationary homes."

"So, we just stay inside and do nothing all month?" Emma asks.

"As much as we can, anyway. Tend the garden and do laundry, but keep our outside actions to a minimum," I reply.

"That's so boring!" Emma whines. "I hoped we could go on an adventure!"

Eve sighs. "Well, let's do the chores now then."

"Mother and I will take care of the laundry. Eve, Emma, you two can water the garden, and pick anything ripe," Ami commands and then looks at me. She speaks with a softer tone. "Rain, you clean out the stable."

We break away and set out to complete our tasks. At the horse's storage, I retrieve the shovel and move the waste to the compost bin. During my trips back and forth, I note that we're completely surrounded by the camp, seeming to have materialized in the center of it.

While refilling the water trough, I see their chief hasn't moved. He is keeping his distance, but watching me intently. Seeing he's staring, I avoid direct eye contact with him.

I wish I could communicate with them to tell them to just go about their daily lives and ignore us. I hope they don't starve themselves standing there watching us.

Finished with my job, I head into the kitchen. I wash up while watching the women from the window.

I really need to resolve this situation. As flattering as it is to have two beautiful women fawning over me, things between Ami and Eve are just going to escalate. If we can accomplish our goal of stopping the cycle, this will be easier.

Ami's been there for me since I was wounded, and I have grown extremely close to her. Is it wrong that Eve, as insane as she can be, is actually growing on me? I don't mind her company. But if I keep letting her in is my mind going to change?

I watch the yard for a few minutes. The tribals watch from their village with intensity, keenly studying the women's movement. Eve and Emma bicker in the garden, and they begin to fight, but I can't hear the conversation. Ami and Agatha ignore it to focus on the laundry.

Hmm. With another person, we're going to need another line to hang clothes.

Feeling useless, I retrieve a soup pot and fill it with water. I set it on the stove and turn on the heat to a low temperature. I go downstairs to collect a frozen chicken from the deep freezer and various vegetables from the shelves. I'm heading back up the stairs when the kitchen door slams, and Eve grumbles angrily.

Nearing the top of the stairs, the basement door has swung mostly shut. Before I can open it, Eve stomps through while taking her shirt off. She throws it into a wet mess on the floor with a grunt. I blush heavily. With her back to me I see her bare, freckled skin, covered only by her bra straps. I hold my breath, avert my eyes, and huddle against the wall.

Great. If she catches me, she will assume I was spying, and try to throw herself at me.

She huffs, and I hear her move through the swinging door to the living room. Her footsteps are heavy on the stairs. I breathe a sigh of relief and return to preparing soup, as innocently as I can. While I'm cutting up vegetables on the island counter, she reenters, grabs the shirt and lobs it outside.

"Little wench," she mumbles while glaring at Emma from the doorway.

I look over my shoulder, and through the open door. Emma sticks her tongue out. It provokes Eve more, and she slams the door. She stands next to me with her back against the counter, her arms crossed. Looking over she squints her eyes in a questioning manner.

"Where did you come from?" she asks abrasively.

"What?" I play ignorant.

"I mean, I was just here. Where were you?"

I hold up a potato and stalk of celery. "Bringing up supplies from the storeroom."

She looks at me for a moment longer, and I fear she won't believe me. But she returns to staring at the door. I'm off the hook. I try not to, but find myself looking at her more than I should. She notices. The wrinkles in her forehead disappear, and her bad mood lightens. My eyes are quickly redirected to the vegetables again, but it's too late. I've piqued her interest.

"What are you looking at?" she asks while scooting closer.

"Nothing. Just wondering why you're not out helping."

"Dirty little brat soaked me with the watering canister."

"Oh."

"It's too bad you were downstairs. I had my shirt off in here," she says seductively while sliding over a little more, bumping her hip into mine. "I could do it again if you want."

"No. Keep it on," I try to sound put off.

"With them out there, we have a chance to just be together." She moves from the counter to my back, and places her hands on my shoulders. "We don't get that often."

"Eve, this isn't right and you know it."

"Is it because of Ami? Why do you favor her? I am twice the woman she is, *and* better looking."

She bends over and breathes on my neck. Her lips press against my skin. My body fights my mind. A forbidden desire rises up, and I blush.

"This…isn't appropriate." I fight the biological urges. "Eve, I won't betray Ami."

"She understands this is a competition, and I don't play fair." Her whisper causes the hair on my neck to stand on end.

Her arms wrap around me, her hands slipping up under my shirt. Pressing herself to my back pushes me to a breaking point, and I fight to push away. She doesn't take 'no' for an answer, and pursues me as I put distance between us.

Finding my way to the other side of the table, I use it as a barrier. She grins, and firmly plants her hands on the table. She hoists herself up onto it, crawling across it like an animal hunting prey. I back away only to be met by the wall.

"Rain, it could be just you and me against the world. I want you to choose me over her."

"Eve, a relationship isn't possible right now." My words falter, and betray me, and I give her a glimmer of hope.

"Right now? You mean you would choose me if she wasn't here?"

"If it was just us, probably. But that's the problem. Ami's here, and I…"

"She wouldn't have to know. I could sneak into your room at night, and we could be together."

"No, Eve."

She climbs down off of the table. Her vibrant red curls fall down her shoulders. My mind tries to tell my body to run while she closes in. It fails. Pinning me with her hands, she brings her face close to mine, and we're a hair away from a kiss.

"Rain," she whispers and closes her eyes.

The back door flies open, and Emma lets out an ear-piercing scream. Before I can react, Eve spins to look. I'm hit in the face with something hard and heavy. My nose crunches. An onion meant for the back of Eve's head falls to the floor, and I bleed profusely. I do what I can to catch the blood with my hands cupped together. I fail miserably as it pours through the cracks of my fingers.

"Look what you did to him, you little brat!" Eve yells at her.

"Oh, Rain! I'm so sorry! I was trying to hit *her*!"

While moving to the sink, I become light headed and stumble. Emma rushes to my side while Eve holds me up. Though I'm hurt and bleeding, they continue to fight.

"Don't touch him! He's hurt because of you!" Eve yells.

"This wouldn't have happened if you weren't being such a tramp. There are rules!" Emma matches her loudness.

"I didn't do anything! I just provided him with the opportunity to kiss me! I wasn't breaking any of the rules!"

Ami bursts in the door. "What is going on in here?"

She sees me hovering over the sink, bleeding. Ami joins them at my side. She shoves both of them out of the way and grabs my nose. Pinching near the top, she tilts my head forward. I wince at the pain spreading through my face.

"What happened?" Ami asks me.

Emma and Eve try to tell their stories at the same time talking over each other. It's a garbled mess.

"Eve was trying to kiss him—"

"She threw an onion at Rain's face—"

"She was going to break a rule—"

"She's an overbearing brat—"

"Enough!" Ami yells.

Ami grabs a white towel, and plants it against my face. She places my hand on it and guides me over to the table. She makes me pinch my own nose while she disappears from my sight. I hear the freezer open and shut, and she returns with a bag of frozen vegetables. I move my hand out of the way so it can be placed on top.

"We established rules for a reason Eve, and I have no doubt you were pressuring Rain into something he didn't want to do!"

"Didn't want to do? He practically said when you were out of the picture he would pursue me openly."

"I doubt it!" Emma's voice is heated. "When I walked in, you were forcing him against the wall!"

They fight in a triangle around me, yelling in my ears, and pressing themselves into me, arms flailing in accusing motions. Their voices intertwine.

This hurts. How do I get this to stop?

I close my eyes. A headache has already set in. My face is cold because of the frozen bag of food, making it worse. Their yelling is becoming too much. Before I can speak up, it ends as quickly as it started. Eve huffs loudly in defeat, and stomps out of the room, slamming the swinging door against the other side of the wall. Quiet falls over the room. Ami and Emma tend to my injury. Ami removes the frozen bag while Emma removes the towel. Both gasp.

Must be pretty bad.

"So, big bruise? Crooked nose?" I ask in a nasal voice.

"This is going to hurt. A lot." Before I can react, Ami grabs my nose in between her hands and pulls hard to the left. It snaps loudly, and I can't help but yell, and reach for my face.

"Sorry, I had to reset it. Otherwise it would have healed crooked," she places her hand on my forehead.

"I was in the middle of making soup before all of this." I point toward the pot.

"Don't worry. I'll take care of it. I'm *so* sorry I hit you!" Emma clings to my arm.

"You couldn't have known Eve would move. Don't worry about it." I try to smile, but with the swelling it feels like my face is just stretching outward.

Emma takes over cooking while Ami continues to examine me. My nose has mostly stopped bleeding, and I can feel it caking. She wets the towel, and wipes my face gently. I wince, but when I open my eyes she's gone, throwing the towel outside. Ami returns and lifts me under the arms. Following her lead, I stand, and she helps me into the living room.

On the couch, she sits next to me, and looks at it again.

"The bleeding has stopped, but you need to take it easy. You lost quite a bit, and it's going to hurt for a while," she says in a gentle voice. "I'll bring you something for the pain."

"Is it going to make me loopy like before?" I ask.

I have my answer when she snickers, and heads for the kitchen. She's gone for only a moment before returning to my side, handing me a familiar pill, and some water. I take both, and struggle to sit up. Choking a little, I hold my mouth closed, and manage not to cough it back up.

"Rest, Rain. We'll take it from here." She rubs my chin gently, and leaves.

My head already feels light, and there's no one to embarrass myself in front of. For that I'm thankful. It makes me tired also. I drift in and out. Things blur together. At some times I am fully aware, while others there is only a sense of existence and nothing more. While I'm adrift in my mind, staring at the walls, Eve appears on the stairs.

How did she get up there? I don't remember seeing her.

She creeps down without making a noise, and finds her way over to me. Sitting on the edge of the couch she talks, but I don't understand. My hand acquires a mind of its own, and reaches up to stroke her arm. She tears up. Leaning over, she presses her lips against mine. But rather than one of her forceful, passionate kisses, it's gentle and quick. The tears which had streamed down her face ran from her lips to mine, and I taste the saltiness.

"I'm sorry," her voice comes into clarity and it's unlike her normal demeanor. The words are soft and it makes me feel strange. I try to keep my thoughts in line, but they're fragmented because of the medication.

Why? I don't feel angry with her. It wasn't her fault.

Why does she have to be nice? She's making things harder for me. I want to like Ami.

It was easier to not like her when she was violent and brash. No, Eve.

I can't.

Despite the numerous thoughts running through my head, not a single one slips out. We sit together silently, Eve caressing my arm. I fade out again.

Before I slip away into a restful state, Emma appears and picks a fight with Eve. At first everything is hazy like before, but I open my heavy eyelids and focus on the conversation.

"Don't you think you've done enough?" Emma berates her.

"I was just telling him I'm sorry you hit him. Something I bet *you* didn't do," Eve replies.

Eve leans over, and hugs me. I have no ability to react under the influence of the medicine. Emma glares as Eve heads back upstairs. When Eve is gone, Emma lies on the couch, resting her head on my leg and draping her arms backward across me.

"I can't stay for too long, the broth is cooking down, but I need to keep an eye on it." She pauses for a moment. "I'm sorry I hit you. I didn't mean to."

I need help. Maybe Aggy will help. I need advice.

Closing my eyes again, peace comes in the darkness. It doesn't seem like long before I am drifting further from consciousness.

~~~~~~

A light tapping on the front door awakens me. Sitting up, the smell of the soup has wafted into the room. My mouth waters. My senses are returning to normal.

The tapping comes again, but when I turn to look at the window there's no one there. Hoping it's not a member of the tribe, I fear I might have to confront them to turn them away. It takes a little effort to hoist myself up due to a pounding headache, but I manage to find my way over to the door.

The door creaks as I pull it open. When I see what lies beyond, I can't react fast enough. Drake is there in his black armor. The darkness of his stare burns into my soul. His malicious grin, full of rotted teeth and decaying breath makes me nauseated. I try to protest but my voice is caught in my throat when I see him brandish a familiar curved blade. Grabbing me by the shoulder, he pulls me in close and plunges it into my gut. Pain shoots through my body as it pierces all the way through. I struggle, but his grip is firm, keeping me in place while the blade does its job.

"I found you, *brother*," he whispers in my ear. "This time, you die!"

"Why?" I manage to choke out.

"You should not have inherited the throne. It was mine! You are not fit to rule any longer!"

Everything seems to move in slow motion as he dumps my body on the floor, retracting his blade. My sight becomes blurry, and when I refocus the four women are standing over me in a circle. My head is the last to hit, and when it does I black out.

~~~~~~

Waking abruptly, I sit straight up and nearly collide with Ami. Her hands are on my shoulders, and it appears she was shaking me. Bucking her grip, I scramble to lift my shirt and inspect my abdomen. The scar is there. No blood, no open wound. My eyes dart around the room, and Drake is not here. His evil presence lingers, though.

"You were having a nightmare. It was about Drake again." She attempts to console me with gentle caressing.

"I know." I pant heavily, trying to come down from the rush of fear. "He's my brother, and his attempt on my life was jealousy over my being king."

"It's okay. He's not here, and he can't get you. He isn't born at this point."

My body is hot and itchy. I scratch, and it moves, crawling through my skin. "I know, but I can't shake the feeling of dread."

Something is wrong. That wasn't like the previous dreams. Why were the four of them standing around me as I fell? He said 'I found you'. Was this a premonition?

Out of the corner of my eye, three heads poke out of the kitchen. Smiling weakly causes them to quickly disappear. I rub my face, and realize it's quite swollen.

"They're just worried about you. I told them you'd be all right," Ami says. "Dinner is ready."

"Was I out that long?" I ask while she assists me in standing up.

"It's only been a few hours. You're going to bed after you eat so your body can rest, and your broken nose can heal."

We enter the kitchen, and she sets me in my normal chair. My dinner is already in my spot, waiting. Steam from the chicken soup reaches my nostrils, but I'm only able to breathe through one as I inhale. My spoon shakes in my unsteady hand. I try to bring some soup to my mouth, and fail. The soup ends up back in the bowl. Fear lingers.

This is ridiculous! How can I be so afraid of him? He isn't here! He isn't born! And I'm powerful!

My nerves calm as Ami leans over my shoulder, and places her cheek against mine. She nuzzles me briefly. Taking the spoon from my hand, she feeds me, blowing on each bite. This garners a reaction from Eve and Emma. Angry stares beat at Ami, but she lets out a small scoff.

"You had *yours* earlier," Ami states. Their eyes widen, and I'm confused by the reaction. Eve continues to stare, but Emma drops her eyes to her bowl.

"What?" I mumble.

"Don't worry about it, Rain."

Eve finally returns her attention to her own bowl. Knowing they aren't staring anymore allows me to feel a little more at ease. Agatha smiles sympathetically.

"I think I can manage now," I tell Ami. "You need to eat too."

My jitters have subsided, and my hand is steadier when I bring the spoon to my mouth. Ami takes her seat, and our meal is quiet. When we're finished, we sit there exchanging glances for a few minutes. But sitting still doesn't feel right. I become restless, and begin to take my bowl to the sink. Agatha appears at my side, and taps my hand lightly while stealing the bowl away. She leaves me standing there, smiling over her shoulder in the motherly way I've become accustomed to.

"Do you want help?" I ask.

"No, I'll handle it," she says.

I thank her by giving her a quick kiss on the cheek.

Did I kiss my own mother's cheek? What kind of relationship did I have with her?

Returning to the living room, a faint glow seeps from between the cracks in the curtains. There are numerous fires spread out through the camp, and there's a lot of movement. But to my surprise, none of the indigenous people have crossed into our territory. It seems like for now they've gone back to their lives.

Backing away, my foot catches something against the wall, knocking it over. Instinct kicks in and I jerk my body down to catch it. I miss, and my sword hits the floor with a 'thud.'

Picking it up, I pull the sword from its sheath. In the open living room I brandish the sword. Testing its balance, I swing it in mock attacks and blocks. Though its wider base makes it heavier than a traditional sword, it's still easily managed.

Why would they have rounded the top edge though?

I stop for a moment and run my thumb over the top. It's sharp enough that with light pressure, it draws a trickle of blood. Sticking my thumb in my mouth, I suck on it until the bleeding stops.

Returning to my practice, it helps me relieve some built up anxiety. I become accustomed to the sword. I move faster and become more coordinated. Frustration replaces the anxiety as I dance with my blade. My body takes control, and things become hazy while rage builds. I imagine myself against Drake. I hear his voice in the back of my mind.

"You are not fit to rule any longer!" His voice lingers.

Block. Thrust. Parry.

What made me unfit to rule? Was he just blinded by jealousy? He was older than me. Why did I inherit the throne?

Swing. Dodge. Chop.

I no longer feel in control. I'm like an actor on a stage; I know what my next move is as it comes. My body reacts, as if I've gone through all of these motions already. Quick and decisive attacks, blocks, and a sweeping blow. I stare down in contempt at an empty floor, holding my sword as if it were to someone's throat. My mind begins to recall some of the lost information.

No longer within the house, I'm surrounded by the woods. I'm waiting alone for Drake, my brother.

That's right. He wanted to meet in private. I chose the place and time so I could arrive first.

I see him coming in the distance, riding his stallion. Within the shadows of the forest, his black armor is unmistakable. I wait upon my steed. Looking down briefly, my hand is gripping the hilt of a sheathed sword. My silver armor glimmers as a wind shifts the leaves above. I prepare to draw as he nears.

My vision blurs for a moment. When it returns, Drake and I are in the midst of fighting a grueling battle with one another. I attempt to stay on top of him, our weapons clashing loudly. The reverberations through the metal are strong, but I hold my grip.

Our movements are blinding fast. We each know the other's fighting style, and react accordingly to avoid being sliced or run through. Despite it feeling like a long battle, it only lasts minutes. I finally gain the upper hand when there's an opening to slam my shoulder into him and put my leg behind him. He stumbles on me, and trips over a root. I am upon him and the tip of my sword rests at his throat, threatening to puncture the main artery. We huff, exhausted.

"Our hands are dirty brother," he chuckles. "And your time is over."

"The throne is mine," I tell him.

"Not any longer."

"It would have been yours in the first place if you had not killed our parents." I yell. "You are an ungrateful brat. You were banished, and I brought you back! I gave you purpose! I see now I should have just killed you."

"You do not have it in you to kill me now! I am the one who carried out your assassinations! You had to have your servants kill for you because you are weak!"

I'm snapped back to reality as a cool hand touches my bare arm. It's Emma, and she's concerned. I'm left feeling unclean, and I wrench away from her. Returning the sword to its home, I take it with me as I head outside to the well.

Dropping it into the grass, I trade it for the handle to pull the bucket up. A full bucket of cool water dumped over my head brings my temperature down, and I let the water drip off of my face. Looking back, I'm alone for now, and I'm thankful.

Assassinations? I don't know how to deal with that. There's no reason he would have said what he did as a trick. I wasn't having memory problems then. Was I a bad person?

I can't be around them right now. If they knew I was involved in assassinations, what would they think of me then?

With my back against the well, I slide down into the grass. Tears stream down my face, and I can't control them. Clasping the sword against my chest, I cross my arms, and stare up into the night sky. My eyelids become heavy. I am too tired to hold them open. A deep sigh escapes my lips, and I let them close.

~~~~~~

The morning comes. The sun begins to illuminate everything. I push a blanket off of me, and I don't recall how it got there. As if the world were waiting for me, a cold breeze passes by as soon as the blanket is on the ground. I'm refreshed, despite the awkward sleeping position of sitting against the well, and an unknown quality of sleep.

I push to my feet. My legs wobble, and it feels as though I'm fighting vertigo. I strap the sword's belt on so I can carry the blanket unhindered. But when I bend over, I nearly lose my balance. I try to shake it off, but the unsteadiness worsens. One foot after another I struggle to make it to the house.

When screams come from inside, and a loud chatter arises from the tribe, I realize it's not me that's having the problem.

Earthquake!

I attempt to run to the door. The blanket trips me up. Hitting the ground, I can feel the intensity of the shaking increase. The house begins to sway on its foundation. I leave the blanket behind, crawling toward the steps. The quaking makes everything difficult, but I grip the doorknob for stability.

I shove the door open and yell. "Agatha!"

She appears in the kitchen door and motions for me to move around the outside of the house.

"Is this an early time shift?" I yell across the room.

Shaking her head, she yells back, "No, this quake is too heavy! And we would have seen the vortex by now! Go out to the garden! The girls are there!"

I leave the house, and make my way around the other side, using the building as a brace. The earthquake doesn't let up, instead it intensifies. The ground cracks nearby, and drowns out panicked screams and yelling from the tribe.

The women are huddled by the apple tree, gripping it tightly. When I reach them, my attention is diverted and I behold something terrifying. Outside our perimeter, to the right, the ground rolls like an ocean wave, tearing through a large section of the tribe's camp. But the horror really begins when a chasm opens up, swallowing people, tents, and animals alike.

Scattering, the people of the tribe try to escape, but the chasm grows larger. The plains buck and roll like a stormy sea, and the ground rips wide open. Watching as they are consumed, and seeing their distress, my instinctive need to help overpowers me. My legs work faster than my mind, already carrying me toward people in peril.

I ignore the cries from my family as I reach the edge of our yard. The chasm stops short of our boundary, but begins to circle around us, blocking my path. Taking a few steps back, I start running and upon reaching the edge, I leap and propel myself to the other side with a short burst shockwave.

Despair from these people screams in my head. The darkness begins welling up inside. Even though I can't understand their language, I know they want to be saved, they don't want to die. But between the despair within, and the people running all different directions it's hard to focus on who to save.

A woman slips into another chasm several yards ahead. I run to her aide. She has grabbed the edge of quickly collapsing dirt, and I dive to grab her arms. My arms interlock with hers, and I lie across the ground trying not to let her slip into the dark pit below. It takes all of the strength I can muster to wiggle backward, and pull her up. Some younger tribal men stop, and with a tug, she is freed from the hole. Pulled to safety, I point and shove them off in a direction away from the ever widening chasm, and its offshoots.

In the middle of the largest chasm stands a pillar of stone and dirt with people trapped on it. A little girl wails, and a woman appears next to me, pointing and yelling. The pillar begins to buckle as the dirt around it sloughs off, causing a couple to fall in. The little girl stands in the middle screaming as the ground quickly disintegrates around her.

This is going to hurt.

I leave the woman to gain some distance. With a good running start, I plant my feet at the edge of the chasm, squat, and leap. My hands release shockwaves, and I shoot skyward. My legs flail, and I try to position them in front of me as I reach the peak of my ascent. Coming in too fast, I'm forced to tuck and roll so my legs don't snap backward. But by some miracle, I'm back up on my feet, running with the girl under my left arm. The next edge comes up too quickly, and when I bound from it, I have only one hand to propel myself.

I veer to the left, out of control. Knowing it's impossible to land on my feet this time, I roll midair to save the girl. My back contacts with the ground. The thud shakes my body, and I exhale sharply. Skidding across the dusty plain, rocks and brush cut my skin. I come to a stop, the girl in my arms, safe.

It takes me a moment to recover, but the urgency of the chasms opening up across the land motivates me. Standing up, we are separated from her probable mother.

"Hey!" I yell at one of the tribe members a hundred yards off trying to help someone else.

I pick the girl back up, and begin running, trying to gain his attention. He looks back, and stops just long enough for me to catch him. I point at the woman now sprinting to safety, and thrust the little girl in his arms. Taking her, and another child, he runs, following the crowds.

I survey my surroundings. I'm trapped. People are being consumed by the ground left and right. The main chasm has wrapped around the house, and continued to splinter off like veins as far as the eye can see. Few people are left in the immediate area, either swallowed up or moved to a safe zone beyond the cracks. The quaking slows, and the bucking of the ground lessens, but the damage is heavy. Large chunks of ground continue to fall into the black depths.

A cry for help gains my attention. I track it to one of the larger openings, and over the ledge rests a chunk of land. A man clambers to find a way back up, but his digging causes another heavy shift. I drop to my stomach, and reach my arms out, but he's lost his balance. His arms flail outward. At the risk of falling in, I slide down enough to grab them. I lift him up enough to grab the ledge, but the ground has another jolt for us. We're both tossed in.

I hear a faint scream. A woman's.

Hitting the sloped opening, my hands claw at dirt, but it only kicks it loose. I'm distracted by dirt falling into my eyes and mouth, and I lose sight of the man as he falls into the dark abyss. I spit, and try not to fall, but it seems futile. I can't get my hands in far enough to keep from following him. The ground gives way, and my hand catches a sharp rock. It slices into my palm, but I grip on for my life.

Unable to see through my dirty, watery eyes I am left hanging there. Blood trickles down my arm. My mind races, and though I want to scream, the falling dirt threatens to choke me. The realization sets in.

I have no hope of climbing out of this hole.

My hand slips, and the rock cuts deeper. Though I try to hold on to the rock with sheer will, my body finally gives up. The muscles in my arm and hand release. I fall into the darkness below.

After everything, this is how I die?

My body meets the wall several times. I tumble, my arms and legs taking the brunt of the damage. The walls begin to close in on me, and daylight begins to fade. I'm struck with an epiphany, and my body reacts accordingly. Thrusting out both of my arms, and putting my legs out I try to slow my decent. The wall and debris batter me, causing me to fail, but I'm not deterred. I try again, and am able to dig my arms in up to the forearm, and plant my feet on either side. Rocks and dirt gouging my skin, I slow.

It takes a few minutes for everything to settle, but when it does I'm able to look up without catching a face full of foreign objects. Blood flows down my face from my nose, and it throbs. I'm only able to tilt my head up briefly or risk the blood flowing down my throat.

Above, there's only a sliver of light, and it illustrates just how far down I am. There is an opening several feet below me. From it I can see a faint glow which was previously invisible in what appears to be a cavern. I hear water. A shimmer confirms that's what's below, but I can't tell how far away, or how deep it is.

I don't really have a choice. To wish to be rescued would be hoping for the impossible. No, rescue isn't coming. I'm not climbing out either. Maybe if I go down I can find a way out. Caves usually have outlets somewhere, right?

I got myself into this. I'm sure I can find a way out. But why do I have this overwhelming drive to help people which always puts me in trouble?

That same drive pulls on my heartstrings when I hear distraught cries. I shimmy down, and reach the opening. My feet hit solid rock, and a chunk breaks off. It falls through, and I hear the plunking noise of it hitting the water.

If it's not deep enough, no matter how I fall I'm going to break something. Hands, legs, tailbone. I can't stay here though.

I prepare to drop. Pulling my arms out of the dirt, I support myself with my legs, and crouch. With my arms against the side once more, I stick my legs through. My sword becomes stuck, and trying to wiggle it free nearly causes me to lose my grip. I grasp the stone tightly, regaining my composure before slowly lowering myself into the cavern.

With my arms fully extended, I dangle above what I hope is deep waters. I let go and drop. Freefalling feet first, I wait for the impact, and when it comes, water breaks my fall. I'm fully submerged, and I paddle to pull myself up to the surface.

Gasping, I look around, and see the cavern walls sporadically lined with crystals, glowing a light pink-purple hue. Something bumps me in the water, and I startle. Flailing, I push whatever it is away. When there's distance, I see it's a body lifelessly floating, and there are dozens more.

There is solid ground a few yards away, and I swim to it. Climbing up reveals an open area with more bodies, and items, strewn about. Screaming and wailing ring out from a couple locations up ahead. An animalistic growling can be heard amongst the other noises. In a heightened sense of awareness, I catch a glimpse of a large muscular creature dragging off what appears to be one of the people from above. A massive tail whips through the air, and my hand immediately reaches for my sword.

What is that?!

The focus on my injuries recedes. Both my heart and body leap in fear. I'm on my feet, and closing in on a nearby wall. Blade drawn, I keep it close to my body as I follow the monster. Several more distinct growls echo through the cavern, and from passages my eyes can barely make out. I hear bones snap, and a shattering sound. My stomach sours.

A cry for help sounds from a nearby tunnel branching from the cave, and a man comes barreling out. Deep thudding against the ground tells me a creature isn't far behind him. The man turns toward me, screaming and waving his arms. The monster lunges out, and skids sideways to a stop. I can see it better, and it's more terrifying than the silhouette I saw a moment ago.

The creature appears to be a humanoid, bipedal lizard which I liken to an alligator. Its snout is long, and its jaw opens wide, letting out a guttural growl, then a hiss. The scales and bony spikes protruding from its arms and legs shimmer in the dim lighting provided by the crystals. Its massive spiked tail flails back and forth, and it appears to be readying to swing around and kill the fleeing man.

Not giving it a chance to attack, I break into a run past the frightened native. Using my sword as a lance, I barrel headlong into it. The sword's edge flays the beast from its belly up with little effort. It screeches in pain, and attempts to skewer me with its long claws. I am too close for it to get a good swipe. It struggles against me, and I retract the blade. I expect it to try again, but instead it collapses to its knees, screeching. Its deep yellow eyes squint at me, and it whimpers.

Though it's a beast, I feel bad letting it suffer. I swiftly behead it, and wipe my sword off on my torn, ragged pants. I kneel down for a better look. Its hands and feet are webbed, and it has a muscular and skeletal structure much like humans, but larger. I am perplexed.

What could this be? I may not have my memory back, but I certainly don't feel anything familiar about this creature. Is it some mutation?

Another scream resonates against the walls, this time feminine. It reminds me of the man whom I saved, but looking behind me, he's gone. I focus, and the scream comes again. I'm swift to track it, coming from a corridor up ahead, off to the right. I make my way deeper, hoping to intercept them before the tribal is killed. There's a patter of feet, followed by a growl. Turning a corner, I step light to keep myself hidden.

It's there, readying to pounce. With my sword ready, I jump, and dig it into the creature's spine. It wails and attempts to reach behind and grab me, but I hang on tight to the hilt. It hisses, and tries to back into the jagged crystals embedded in the wall. Dropping to the ground, I duck out of the way, and it only succeeds in pushing my blade in farther.

A few more moments in agony and it drops to its front. I pull my sword from its back and sever its spine at the neck with a few hacks. After cleaning my blade again, I sheathe it.

Collapsed nearby and crying, a girl threatens to draw more of the lizard creatures to us. I kneel and try to gain her attention, but when I reach to touch her she moves away and inhales sharply. She opens her mouth to scream, and I grab her face. Muffled, she kicks and screams while I pull us over to the crystals to show her I'm not one of them.

When the light hits her face, I recognize her as the one the chief tried to sacrifice. I'm baffled she survived the fall.

"Fate has apparently smiled on you, that I would save you a second time," I whisper.

She sees who I am, and stifles her sobs with a few hiccups. My grip relaxes, and I pull my hand from her mouth. I put my finger to my lips, and stroke one of her pigtails to soothe her, in the hope that she understands. Her sobs are now sniffles, and I'm able to listen to our surroundings.

Another noise catches my ear. I wave for her to follow, but when she just stares at me, I grab her hand and pull her back toward the larger cavern. More dirt and rocks collapse from the ceiling of the cave, raining down into the water as if someone else had fallen into the chasm above.

"Rain?!" Eve's voice echoes through the cavern. "Tell me you're alive, and I didn't jump in here for no reason!"

"Barely!" I yell back, wiping the blood from my nose on my sleeve, and my hand on my pants.

"Urgh! Good. I was going to be really pissed off with you if you'd died! Where are you? I can only see a glow from here."

I hear growling but it's faint. Still, I look over my shoulder every few moments just to make sure they're not creeping up on me.

"There's a huge underground cavern here, and it looks like there's a network of tunnels," I tell her.

"I'm stuck here in the dirt."

"Why did you come down here?" I ask.

"I couldn't let you have all the fun, now could I?" she playfully replies.

"Did you find enough rope to reach down here?"

"I wish. This was a one way trip, but I couldn't leave you alone down here."

"I'm not quite alone. There are tribal people, and something else."

"How do I get down there?"

"Just wiggle your way down to the opening until you hit solid rock, and then jump through. There's water below which will break your fall."

The growling intensifies, growing closer. I know I'm making far too much sound, and more 'lizard-men' are undoubtedly honing in on me.

"How far is it?"

"Just hurry up and drop!"

What follows is a scream, and then a splash, as Eve plummets and enters the water. Before she can surface and make it to solid ground, scratching and thudding alerts me they've found us. Growling and hissing fills the cavern. I spin on my heels, and brandish my sword, thrusting the tribal girl behind me. Several of the lizards approach, and I know I'm going to need Eve's help.

"Gross! Are these dead bodies?" Eve yells.

"Climb out and help me!" I yell.

"What are those?!" Eve shrieks.

Moving in a pack, there is no opportunity to go one on one with them. They close fast, and I let a shockwave loose. They anticipate its impact, and brace. It is ineffective against the creatures, only pushing them back a few inches. They resume, and I hear Eve splash out of the water.

"See if you can find one of the spears!" I yell.

"Where?"

"Anywhere!"

"I don't see any!"

I point to the crystals on the wall. "Try to dislodge one of those to use as a weapon!"

The lizard-men have begun a new charge. My shockwaves have been an integral part of my success in battle previously, and being unable to use them leaves me feeling helpless. I ready my sword and go on the offensive. I run headlong at them.

"Keep low! You might avoid some blows!" Eve advises while kicking at the wall.

When we meet, I drop to my knees, and slide across the smooth ground. They reach for me. I jump to the balls of my feet, and swing the sword in a wide arc. Some fingers are severed, and the blade catches one in the chest, dragging as I turn. They spread out, but show no sign of retreating.

Eve lets loose a battle cry, and she leaps onto the back of one to jam a pointed crystal into the lizard-man's neck. It reels about, and attempts to buck her, crying in pain. The others are momentarily distracted, and it gives me an opening.

I focus on the one farthest away from the group, and rush it. It sees me, and tries to filet me with its long claws when I near. Ducking, I run my sword up and through. Its knees buckle, and it falls forward. I withdraw, and bring the sword down on its skull.

Before I can turn to kill another, I'm tackled by two at once. They pin me to the ground. Claws and teeth tear into my arms, legs, and shoulder. Snarling in my face they both attempt to tear my head from my neck, but I fight, and put my legs between them and me.

Their weight is too much!

I shove with as much force as I can, lifting them enough to angle my sword upward. My legs give, and I roll while one falls on the blade. The other reaches its long snout in to rip my face up, but Eve clubs it from the side. In brutal fashion, she hammers it until the skull is concave, and my face is spattered with its blood. Lifeless, the two lizard-men are still pinning me.

I wiggle against the ground while Eve pulls on them, but she disappears from view, and her battle cries vibrate the air in the cavern. A body falls lifeless while I free myself. Two more close in. Eve grabs my hand, and pulls me to my feet with ease. Establishing a foothold, I use a shockwave to spread them apart.

With my sword inaccessible, I improvise. As the left lizard-man nears, I dive through its legs, past its tail. I leap to my feet, and jump on its tail, scaling the beast like a mountain. It swings about trying to throw me, but I hold fast until the shaking subsides, and continue up. I reach its head and place both hands on its face, unleashing a powerful shockwave into its eyes. It screams and reaches up. Grabbing me by my head, its claws tear into my cheeks, and I'm thrown across the cavern. It stumbles around, blinded, and Eve takes the opportunity to dispatch it.

When the air clears, there are more than half a dozen lizard-men dead or dying around us. Eve crushes one's skull to finish it off. I struggle to flip the creature my sword is stuck into, but I can't. My arms don't have the strength. Eve assists by putting her whole body into rolling it, and I'm able to wiggle my sword out. Pulling it free, I wipe it on my shirt, but just as I clean it, blood from my face drips onto it. Blood oozes down over the already caked layer from my nose. My arms and legs blare with pain. Coming down from the adrenaline rush, I begin to feel cold and weak.

Eve grunts. There's a heavy, sickening squish sound every time she lands a blow on a lifeless corpse. I shuffle toward her and reach for her hand, but I don't make it. My legs give, and I collapse to my knees. She looks at me with rage in her eyes, the same I had seen when we fought each other. But it subsides, and her muscles relax. Letting go of her crystal it clinks to the ground, and she jogs to me.

"You're hurt." She kneels and touches my cheek with concern.

"I...feel like I'm dying." I wince at her touch.

Soft, rapid steps pad toward us. The little tribal girl jumps from the shadows, and clings to my torso, bawling. With what little energy I have left, I try to console her by putting my arm around her. Instead I end up resting my weight on the child.

"How did this girl survive the fall?" Eve is stunned.

"Maybe she had a straight shot into the water. Others survived too."

"I came down here so you wouldn't die alone. I guess now the three of us will die down here." She pokes me in a playful manner, but her tone is serious.

"I am optimistic we can find a way out."

"I think it looks bleak." Eve smirks, and the glow from the crystals makes her look more devious than normal. "Since I'm the one who came after you, you should just give in to me. We could even have some alone time if *she* wasn't here."

Shaking my head in disbelief, I become dizzy. Blood drips onto the girl, and I try unsuccessfully to clean it off. The pain returns to the front of my mind, and my hand reaches for the wound on my cheek. My palm is coated with a fresh layer of blood. I feel sick.

"We should get you cleaned up," Eve suggests.

"I can't stop the bleeding."

"We have to wash it off in the water," she suggests.

"I don't trust that water. If it isn't already tainted, those dead bodies will do it."

The tribal girl sees I am in pain, and attempts to comfort me by touching the wounds. Shaking my head, I push her away, but she insists and forces her hands near my face. Eve protests, trying to take her away, but the tribal girl scolds her harshly in her language. Eve becomes oddly silent. The girl begins chanting with her eyes closed, and I'm startled when her hands glow green.

My eyes shift back and forth nervously, but I calm when the pain begins to subside. Her hands close on my face, and when they touch it tingles. She moves to my arms and legs, one at a time. When she's done, the wounds have closed, and the pain has all but gone. She opens her eyes and smiles at me, looking for approval. It takes me a second to break my shock and return the smile.

"Well, that is certainly handy and amazing," I blurt.

"Should have just let it heal on its own," Eve responds with a snarky tone. "You'd have looked more rugged with some scars across your face."

"I might have died from blood loss." I push her over, and she lands on her tailbone. She grins.

The little girl turns to Eve to heal her also, but Eve swats her away. The girl doesn't fight her.

The dizziness has passed, but my energy is still sapped. A survey of the cavern reveals we are no longer in immediate danger. We are still stuck in an underground world, with water which might kill us, no food, and giant lizard-men. I sigh.

"We're in a pretty bad situation here. We're dead if we don't find a way out." I stand and move to the edge of the underground lake.

"You're right," Eve says optimistically while wrapping her arms around my chest from behind. "But we're together."

I push her hands off, and turn around. "This isn't the time. Even if we find food and water, when the month ends, the house will still try and draw us back in. We're going to be crushed against the roof of this cave."

"All the more reason to finally be intimate." She steps closer, inching her face closer to mine.

"Eve," I whisper.

"Yes, my love?" She closes her eyes as if expecting me to kiss her.

I lean in close. "No," I whisper again.

Moving to the nearest wall, I kick at a long, thin crystal until it dislodges. Using it as a torch, I survey the area again. The dead lizard-men are haunting under the light. Beyond them, I note at least four exits.

Eve huffs behind me. Over my shoulder, I see the look of disappointment on her face that I've left her there. I smirk. She scowls and crosses her arms.

"There could still be more people alive down here. If there are, it's only a matter of time before the lizards find them. Maybe we can find them first, keep them safe, and figure out how to climb back up one of the openings?"

"And if we can't? Then what?"

"Then we make the best of what we have."

Her eyes light up, and it's obvious what she's thinking.

Though she's brash, pushy and conniving, I suppose it's okay being stuck down here with her. She's already saved my life.

I just need to keep from doing something hasty and irrational.

She grabs her crystal from the bludgeoned corpse, and holds it out, expecting me to lead the way. I motion for her and the tribal girl to follow me. The girl understands this time, and quietly we move toward the passages. Two on the right wall, several yards in between them; one straight ahead, on the back wall; one off to the left.

"I think our best bet in finding, and saving people would be in a radius from the house, so left or straight are our options," I whisper just loud enough for Eve to hear.

"Whatever you think is best, babe." Eve seems happy enough to let me lead.

More growling echoes through the cavern, but it's distant. The passage on the left seems quiet, and I cut across the cavern. Leading us into the unknown makes me nervous. My senses are still recovering, and little noises make me jump. The farther into the branch we move, the quieter it becomes. I draw my sword, readying to cut down any more of the lizard-men which might lurk in the shadows ahead.

"Eve, follow at the back – keep her in between us."

"Aye sir!" She's giddy.

We walk in a single file line, near to the right side of the passage wall. Every once in a while there's a speck of light from above where the chasm has ripped open the roof of the cave. There are many bodies scattered lifelessly, torn open not by the monsters down here, but the fall. There's a glimmer, and I see one of the spears underneath a dead warrior. I point it out to Eve and she retrieves it. The tribal girl whimpers, letting out a quiet chant. Eve hugs her head, and strokes her pigtails soothingly. I smile at Eve and she nods.

Who'd have thought that the ruthless Eve is actually a little soft on the inside?

The girl calms, and we move forward through the curvy corridor. Passing by a few openings, I peer down and listen for movement. There is only shifting dirt and rocks. I keep us on the main path, with the chasm opening above us. We hear something. The cry of a man is faint in the distance. It's soft, but he sounds like he's distressed.

Our pace quickens, and we nearly meet our demise. I stop suddenly, a foot from falling into a crevasse inside the cave. There are no crystals lining it, there is no light inside.

Holding up my crystal, it provides enough light to see the other side. A moan comes from a pile of bodies and large stones. The opening is only a few feet across, but the child's legs are too short to give her enough boost to make it. My sword slides into its sheath with ease, and I reach to pick her up. Eve grabs my hand and shoves the spear in it.

"I've got this." She winks while scooping up the girl, at the same time managing to keep hold of her crystal.

I nod, step a few feet back, and leap across. The fear of falling into another hole in the ground races through my mind midflight, but when I land I've cleared it by a few feet. The girls join me, and we find the man crying out in pain.

He lies on his back, one foot crushed by a large rock. Blood drips from the side of his head. Eve and I lift the stone, and the tribal girl tends to his wounds with her healing ability. They speak in their native tongue, and I can only guess at what they're saying. Their conversation is short, and so is the healing process. He attempts to stand, but can't put any weight on the healed leg. When I tap the girl's shoulder, I question her with an expression, and point to his leg. She shakes her head and frowns.

I turn to Eve. "Seems like she's not able to fix it all the way."

"We don't have anything to splint it." She points out the obvious.

"You'll have to support him. I'm not at full strength."

She sighs, but moves to help him. She throws his arm around her shoulder, and supports his side. Moving again, slowly, I notice the opening in the roof seems to be mostly following this passage, disappearing every so often down other corridors, only to return a few yards later. There are plenty more bodies in our path, but no life.

The way the lizard-men were eating the people, they must have had some sort of other meat to eat down here. Perhaps there are fish in that water, or maybe this isn't the first occurrence of people falling victim to these things.

The quake seemed localized right in the spot where the tribal camp was, and the chasm openings correspond with the tunnel system. Could this have been intentional? It seems a little farfetched for these beasts, but I don't know enough about them.

We wind around a corner and enter a chamber larger than the first cavern. We're at the top of a ledge where the ground slopes sharply downward. At the bottom are a few of the lizard-men, and a pile of human corpses. I force everyone down to the ground, and we observe their movements. Instead of devouring them, the lizard-men seem to be gathering the dead bodies.

"Curious," I whisper.

"Are they planning a feast or something?" Eve asks.

"This seems like something else – I have a bad feeling about it."

My gut proves correct when the creatures point their lengthy snouts into the air, and begin a synchronous barking from the back of their throats like I've never heard before. They finish their calling, and the cavern walls begin to quake heavily in a rhythmic pattern – like something walking.

The lizard-men scatter to the sides of the chamber and hide within corridor offshoots. A loud and deep growl comes from a large opening on the opposite side. I pull everyone back, scooting away from the ledge until we can barely see. An enormous claw swings outward and grips the wall, causing deep indentations in the rock foundation. Then another appears, and hangs on the opposite wall.

Pulling itself from the darkness, a monster emerges, its body nearly becoming stuck in the opening. But it wiggles through and enters the chamber. It stands upright, and it's at least three times the size of any of the other lizard-men. It lets loose a deafening roar, arcing its head from one side of the chamber to the other. The lizard-men hide from sight, no doubt cowering in the presence of this beast.

The girl begins to scream, and I have to clasp my hand over her mouth again in order to avoid detection. She looks at me, scared, but I can see in her eyes she isn't going to try and scream again. I release her.

We watch. I'm mortified by what the creature does next, and I presume the others are too. It bends down and begins gorging itself on human flesh, devouring entire limbs in single bites. It picks up a woman and puts half of her in its mouth. The girl buries her face in my chest, and I wrap my arm around her.

With my arms tied up, I'm powerless to stop the man when he steals the spear and begins to crawl forward. Not wanting to alert the lizard-beast, I'm forced to stay silent. Eve tries to grab him, but he's quick to pull away.

On the ledge, he cries out, weeping and yelling in their language, possibly distraught over the woman being devoured. I break away from the girl and try to grab him also, but he pulls away and tumbles down the steep slope, tearing his body up further.

The giant lizard stops feeding, disturbed by the commotion. The man brandishes the spear against the monster, trying to make strikes. He's like an ant against a human. With a swift stride forward, the lizard-beast sweeps the man up. He flails. It crushes his spine.

It looks up to where he came from, and locks eyes with me. Roaring, it bounds up the rock incline toward us. I jump up, pulling the girl with me. We dodge just before its claw comes down on where we had just been.

It pulls itself up, and I shove them toward the opening we came from. Buying time for Eve to lead the girl to safety, I put a hand up and blast it in the face with a shockwave. It is unfazed. It roars again. I can smell its decaying breath, and I'm sprayed with its spittle. It swipes at me. I leap back and head for the opening. It pursues. Once I'm inside I turn around, aim my hand at the roof, and unleash my power.

Rock and dirt begin to collapse, but the beast continues to reach through. I drop my crystal, and hit the ceiling again, this time with a shockwave from both hands. It buries the giant in rubble and sets off a chain reaction. The ceiling begins to collapse toward me.

I turn and run toward Eve and the girl. They are already far ahead. I push to catch up and avoid being buried. While rocks and dirt collapse into the passage, I manage to stay just ahead of it. My legs and lungs begin to burn, but the consequences of stopping greatly outweigh the increasing pain.

Eve and the girl reach one of the openings we passed, and I yell, "Left! Left!"

They duck in, and I follow shortly after. Though we continue to run, the destructive sounds fade away behind us. We are out of danger of being crushed, but our path back is blocked. No longer is the chasm above us, and I'm sure we're moving away from the house.

I stop.

"Hold on."

Using the wall as a prop, I heave and cough. Eve and the girl try to catch their breath as well, but the dust in the air makes it difficult.

When we've recovered, we move in the only direction we can. This tunnel's crystals are farther apart, making it harder to see. Eve takes it upon herself to scout ahead to avoid obstacles or pitfalls. Not far down this path, the girl perks up and grabs onto Eve's arm, causing her to stop. We listen.

Voices come from ahead. The girl is excited because they are in her language. She pulls on our arms, leading us hastily along. We reach a small room where two men and a woman are huddled in a corner. A dead body lies propped to their side. One of the tribals has a spear, and he is quick to assert it until he sees we aren't lizard-men.

The girl begins conversing while healing their light wounds. As she tends to them, I take a moment to recuperate, leaning against the wall and closing my eyes.

"Why would he do that?" Eve asks. "He just leapt right into the thing's grasp!"

"I don't know. Hysteria? Maybe he recognized the person being eaten." I shake my head and frown. "Or maybe he thought he stood a chance."

My eyes open a little when the girl's voice becomes a little more animated. She runs back over to me, and explains something to them. They look at me, and I see hope appear in their eyes. They band together near me, and I now have a group to look after. The girl has healed them, but they look like death.

Though we might be able to escape these creatures for now, there will no doubt be more. How can I keep them safe?

"If we're going to gather survivors, we need a base camp, and this looks good enough for now." I look directly at Eve. "I'm going to need you to stay here and protect them while I search."

"Okay." She complies too easily and leans forward.

I back up as she moves a little too close. It's awkward enough when she tries to kiss me under normal circumstances, but I'm embarrassed with the tribal people watching.

"Come with me," I tell her and move to one of the corridors.

The tribals try to follow, but I turn the child around and move her back to where we just were. I point my finger at her, and then to the ground in hopes to indicate I want her to stay there. I back up while facing her, and they stay while Eve follows me to the left tunnel. When we're out of sight I grab Eve's hand.

"I'm entrusting their lives to you." My tone is serious.

"I understand, Rain. I won't let you down." She smiles, and I believe she understands me.

"Thank you." I lean in to kiss her on the cheek.

She doesn't attempt to turn it in her favor by kissing me back, or taking advantage of the situation. Instead she accepts it, and I hope she sees it for what I mean it to be, an act of friendship and trust. I nod to show my appreciation.

She speaks up, her voice soft. "Be careful."

"I will." I begin to walk away, but I stop and point my finger at her. "By some miracle we live through this and see the others again, not a word about that to them."

"Of course not." She innocently bats her eyes at me. I suspect she will do otherwise and exaggerate it greatly in her favor.

I kick at one of the crystals to loosen it from its dirt and rock home. I pull it free, and use it to light the way while heading down into the passage alone. Continuing down the winding path, I keep my ears open for potential survivors or threats. Ahead, there is an opening in the roof where another chasm, or perhaps the same one, cracked all the way down into the tunnel network. A few dead bodies litter the ground, and I step carefully over them. Thoughts flood my mind, keeping me alert.

Dying on the way down versus dying down here. After everything that has happened, I'm going to be conquered by a hole in the ground and monsters.

The way these tunnels are carved out, it seems like these things have been down here for a long time, so maybe we'll find a way to survive until the end of the month. There has to be something edible in here.

But even then, Eve and I will die, and the survivors will be stuck. Their existence will be short without us here to fend off the beasts.

Cautiously, I enter a new tunnel branching off from the current one, and find another cavern. Water drops into puddles all around, but with the risk of potential parasites, I hesitate to drink any.

Looking up, it seems the rip in the earth flows up the wall, and then shoots across the ceiling. Doing so causes me to become dizzy, and fatigue hits me hard. I rest against the wall near my tunnel back to Eve. I want to rest for only a few moments, but I become too comfortable.

With my knees to my chest, I hold the crystal across them and rest my face on it. Not having had anything to eat, my stomach grumbles. I try to focus on that, but it too fades. The water creates a soft ambiance and I drift in and out. I try to stay alert, but I can't. My eyes close, and they're too heavy to open again.

~~~~~~

Something skitters across my skin and I startle awake. Looking around, afraid I might be in danger, there's a lone beetle crawling across my arm. Smacking it away angrily, I focus on my surroundings. I'm still alone, and alive.

Weary still, I pull myself up, and hold my crystal in front of me to light my way. I wiggle another crystal loose, and set it next to the opening I came from to direct me back.

The cavern is large with many puddles, which makes me thirsty, and a number of offshoots which could be taken to locate survivors. Not wanting to become lost, I locate the branch closest to straight in front of where I came from, and head the direction I hope leads back toward the house.

In the new tunnel, I put extra effort into listening. There are branches off from this corridor, and down one I hear noises, but it sounds like scratching. It gives me pause for a moment.

It could be another person. But there are no voices or human-like sounds.

I pass it by, not sure I have the energy to fight right now. Farther along, the tunnel arcs sharply to the left. I hug the wall and peer around the corner. Nothing but more tunnel and crystals, but I continue to follow it. I reach yet another cavern, smaller than the last. This one however has a distinct difference. In the middle of it there is a large, reflective metal cylinder stretching from the ground to the roof. It's unnatural.

Examining this 'room', the entrance is the only exit in here. I feel safe enough to focus my attention on the strange object. It appears to be made from a light colored metal. Imprinted are symbols and patterns I don't recognize. Swirls, sharp edges, and shapes appear to form a language. Putting my hand on it, it's cold. While my fingers move across these strange markings, I lose myself trying to understand something clearly beyond my level of comprehension. After touching several of these runes, it shocks me with a small blue arc, and I retract my arm with haste. Numbness sets into my hand, and I shake it frantically.

What was that?! Is this technology? How does this exist right now? This is a primitive time isn't it, both for the people and lizard-men?

If I had to make a bet, I'd say this had something to do with the quake. What other explanation would there be for such a large quake leading directly into this network?

My thoughts are somewhat erratic while I observe it from a distance for any further reaction. None comes as it sits idle once more.

I better not mess with this. If it did have any involvement in opening the chasms, I don't want to start the reaction again.

It feels like I've been gone from the group for too long.

I return to the tunnel, and head back to the cavern. Coming upon the opening into the cave, I am met with an obstacle. Noises bounce off of the walls and resound throughout. Before I enter, I stop and peer around the edge. There are a few lizard-men wandering around, crouching on all fours to drink from the small pools of water at the far side of the cavern. They move lethargically.

Can I sneak by them?

Looking directly across from me, I see the crystal I had placed as a marker, pointing my direction back to Eve. When I look again at the lizard-men, they are focused on drinking: my opportunity is now if I want to evade them. With a few hundred feet in front of me, I am anxious.

Hunching over and stooping in order to make myself as inconspicuous as possible, I jog across. My heart pumps and beats as if it is about to burst from my chest. About mid-way across, I feel discovery is imminent – they could look over at any time. My jog turns to a run.

I've made it across, and duck into the pathway. My sword slips from its sheath easily. I hold it up, lying in wait to ambush any of them that follow. My breathing steadies the longer I wait. Nothing comes for me. A quiet sigh of relief escapes my lips, but I dare not move. I stand still for another few minutes, just to make sure it's safe.

On my way back to where I left Eve, I can't help but constantly look over my shoulder. Paranoid, my mind thinks it hears noises, but every time I look, I'm alone. My swift strides carry me near to where I left them and I hear noises ahead. But it's not voices.

As I reach the area, several of the creatures are huddled around, gorging themselves on something, and I can't see who it is. My blood begins to boil and rage fills me. My grip tightens on the leather handle of my sword, and I bring my crystal up, ready to charge in there, but I'm grabbed from behind and pulled back.

It dawns on me only as I'm swinging around to bludgeon whatever has a hold on me, that it isn't claws on my face. It's Eve, and she grabs my wrist mid-swing. She puts her finger to her lips to shush me, and leads me quickly away.

Back a few hundred yards, we duck into a side tunnel, and she whispers, "We were discovered by one. It tried to feed on us, but when I hit it in the head, it retreated. I didn't want to risk chasing it and running into more without you as backup, so I moved us and left the already dead body there.

"Where have you been?" she scolds. "It feels like you've been gone for several hours. I was beginning to think you'd been eaten."

I put my sword away.

"I passed out. I don't know how long, but if I hadn't woken up when I did, I probably would have ended up a snack.

"I took a path away and, when I came back, there were a few of them milling about. I didn't find any survivors, but there are plenty more branches I didn't look in. I did find something strange that I'll have to show you later though."

"All right. Let's head to where I have the tribals hidden away." She motions for me to follow.

"Eve, I need to use you as a support. I'm still feeling pretty weak."

Coming in close, she grabs my arm and slings it over her shoulder. I don't put a lot of weight on her, but I am more secure. While we walk, Eve can't resist herself. With her arm around me, she pulls in tight.

"This is just your way of breaking the ice with me, isn't it?" she jokes.

I smile weakly, and she leads on into a side network of tunnels. There are many twists and turns and, surprisingly, a lack of dead bodies. All sense of direction and distance is gone. I'm lost. We reach a hole in the wall. A narrow nook which we have to hunch to climb into. Bending, I become dizzy due to hunger, and nearly collapse, but Eve holds me.

Devoid of crystals, and only leading back a little way, it seems barely large enough to fit our band of six. When Eve lets me down, I look at the tribal people and notice they are probably feeling terrible, like me. The little girl nears, and uses her green glow on where I was previously wounded. It relieves pain I didn't know was there. My mind is now focused only on the hunger fatigue. I smile at her, and she smiles back.

"Rain, I'm going to look around down this way. Rest up, and don't go dying on me," Eve whispers.

I nod. "Be careful."

She nods back and disappears. The light fades as she slides away, and I'm left with the others. They chatter quietly amongst themselves, and I wonder what they're talking about. With nothing really to use as references to begin attempting to communicate, I sit in silence. Though I keep my crystal at the ready, I begin to doze off. At the last moment before sleep, I'm pulled into that darkness of despair.

Not amused at being drawn into this entanglement of people's despairs at such a dire time, I cross my arms in defiance and stand on the invisible 'ground'. Hesitating to walk forward and confront the cries of those despairing around me, I stand there.

If I don't move forward, I'm unsure if I'll be able to come out of it. But do I have the strength to take on their sorrows right now? How far can they tax me before I break?

Unsure of the answers, I walk and find myself surrounded by the despair of innumerous people, first by those nearest to my body, then from others scattered underground and the world topside.

Even Eve's despairing reaches me. I sense her deep worry for my health, as well as dying down here. Seeing into the tribal girl's woes, she is thinking of an older man. She aches terribly thinking about him being swallowed by the chasm. I'm left to assume it's her father or grandfather, but her connection to him is strong. The others nearby worry for themselves and, I assume, their families.

While a language barrier exists, I understand how they are feeling at this situation. I move forward, and am confronted by a massive grouping of woes. It surprises me when they become clear, and they are my own. They are great in number. I can't avoid them, and they begin plaguing me, overwhelming me.

Why did Drake cross me?

What kind of person orders assassinations? What kind of king was I?

What kind of man am I now? I'm violent, irrational, and unpredictable.

I want to remember! Why won't things come back to me faster? I don't know who I really am!

Why can I not keep the women out of danger? What happens if I fail to save one of them? Will I be able to live with myself?

If I die, will they be better off?

Though I have no physical body here, I feel the sadness set in, and my soul weeps. Curling into a fetal position I try to block it all out, but I am unsuccessful. Time and despair rage at me.

I lose track of myself, but a soothing sound eases my anxiety. Humming. The despairs are drowned out by it, and the light signifying my way out appears. I move closer to my escape. The humming increases, and when I reach the exit, my eyes open.

Staring up, the little girl is over me, my head in her lap. Her hum is soft and calming, and she runs her fingers through my hair. My cheeks are wet and cool with tears.

I must have been crying here too.

She smiles at me, seeing I've awoken, and I muster a small one back. As I roll off her lap and face the entrance, I'm startled as Eve appears and whispers my name. My body jerks and I sit up, nearly smacking my head on the low roof in the alcove.

"Rain!"

"What?"

"Look!" She's excited for something in her hands and when I look I see what looks to be a mushroom the size of a mixing bowl. "Food!"

My eyes squint a bit and I question her, "You know some mushrooms are poisonous right? I've never seen anything like this."

Before she says anything else she takes a large bite out of it and my jaw drops while she chews.

"Eve! Spit it out!" I yell, forgetting to be quiet.

But she continues to chew, and then swallows the bite of fungus. Smirking, she offers it to me. I hesitate, but she shoves it into my lap. Her eyes go wide and she begins to seize. Falling over, she spasms on the ground, making gurgling noises.

"Eve! Eve!" I drop the mushroom and move to her aide. "What did you do?!"

I fear that she's stupidly eaten something that's made her sick, or worse, sentenced her to death. But she looks me dead in the eyes, and stops squirming. I realize I've been the victim of a joke, and punch her hard on the arm. She squeals with laughter. Fuming, I glare at her.

"That wasn't funny!" I whisper harshly.

"Oh come on. I was just kidding. You need to lighten up Rain, we have something to eat now and there's plenty more." She touches my bare arm, and her cool hand feels good.

"How did you know they were safe? You could have really died." I berate her.

"Are you kidding? I ate these as a kid. I used to live in caves. The same ones I was going to take you to. Do you think if I had any thought they might be bad, I would have put it in my mouth?"

By now, my mouth is salivating at the thought of eating, and I grab the mushroom cap. I bite into it. While bland, the meat is tender, and after a few bites it settles on my stomach. The hunger pains subside.

I offer it to the tribal people and show them it's edible by putting it to my mouth. They break it apart and eat until there is only a small portion left.

My body hasn't had time to digest the mushroom, but it seems willing to relinquish a little more energy from its reserves. The tribals also perk up a bit, and it seems we can continue surviving for now. The girl leaps and hugs Eve tightly. Not knowing what to do, Eve simply pats her on the head.

"Okay. Food, good. Now we need to know what water is safe to drink," I mention.

"Already solved," she says smugly.

"Well, it certainly seems you had a lot better luck than I did with searching."

"I did, and I think we should move to the area where I found the mushrooms. It's a secluded, natural room with only one opening," her excitement is infectious, and I am eager to move out of these cramped quarters.

Eve and I shuffle to the entrance of our little hideaway. We scout for any of the creatures. Upon seeing none, we motion for the others to follow. Eve leads us away from the direction in which we came. The tunnel slopes down, and farther in the chasm rejoins us overhead. It's a much smaller opening than the others we've seen.

We must be farther away from the house.

We move with stealth, Eve in the lead while I cover the rear. Random sounds keep me on edge, and my sword is ready. A growl comes from far behind, and I look to Eve for direction. She waves us on. Because our stomachs have been appeased, we are able to keep a good pace down the twisting corridor.

We reach an intersection, and Eve stops to listen. Growling comes from the right. Flagging me with hand gestures, she takes a left, and I guard the junction. The growling grows louder. Behind me, Eve waves her crystal from an opening on the left a few hundred yards down. I make haste to catch up, checking for lizard-men.

The new tunnel arcs around into a large room, and it appears to be the one she mentioned where there is plenty of food. Enormous mushrooms grow in patches all along the floor and wall line. Enough to feed us for a fair amount of time.

Hissing and barking echoes through the network, and I prepare to cut down any lizard-men that enter the chamber. Back out to the main tunnel, I hide at the edge of the opening, lying in wait. Eve joins me with her crystal. The scratching and stomping increases, and it sounds like a herd of them.

A dozen of them run by our opening, passing by without a second glance into our area. Hugging the wall, we do our best to blend in so we're not noticed, and it works. A few minutes pass after they've gone before I feel safe enough to move away from the opening. We return to the safety of our cave and find the tribal people haven't moved.

Crystals line this cave, as they had with the others, and it allows for fair visibility. Sounds of water droplets hitting puddles all along the floor indicate Eve might know something about the water I don't. In the far back, near a corner, something shuffles near a familiar object.

Sword pointed out in front of me, I move closer. I'm put at ease when I see a torn up little boy about the same age as the girl. He whimpers, but hope gleams in his eyes. Before I can call the girl over, she's already here, taking care of him. While she does, I examine the metal cylinder, this one halfway stuck in the wall.

Though I'm unable to circle this one, when I raise my crystal up to see better it appears to have similar, or even the same markings as the other one. Eve stands with me and I can sense she wants to say something.

"I have no idea what it is," I preempt her.

"Well, it's writing for sure."

"You don't say?" I ask sarcastically and smile.

Eve's hand lunges out to touch it, and before I can stop her she runs her whole palm over it. The same electrical discharge happens, arcing to her hand and into her fingers. She yelps and pulls back. Rapidly speaking in her language, the tribal girl springs up and heals Eve's hand. The girl points to the object, lets out a sentence, and looks at us in a questioning manner.

"We don't know what you're saying." I shrug and hope my tone conveys the lack of understanding.

For the first time, the girl looks a little annoyed. She begins using her hands to communicate, but she's moving them too rapidly, and I am at a loss if the gestures mean anything. I shrug again and shake my head. She snaps off a mushroom cap, and snatches the crystal from my hand.

Looking me dead in the eyes, she runs her hand across the top of the mushroom, and then points up to the ceiling. Not knowing what to do, I slowly make the same motions she did, causing her to nod excitedly.

She stuffs the mushroom in my hands, and then begins pointing to the metal cylinder, and then to the crystal. Moving my hands for me, she positions the mushroom above her. She shakes the mushroom and punctures a hole in the underside with the tip of the crystal.

"Is she saying what I think she's saying?" Eve asks.

"I have no idea. They're primitive: how could she have any understanding of this? Of technology?"

"I don't know. The others don't seem excited about it." Eve looks back at them, tending to themselves and eating casually.

Reaching out, I pretend to touch the cylinder and look at the girl. When I get close, she swats my hand away, convinced I was going to make contact. I shrug, and she kneels down while using my crystal to scratch lines on the smooth ground. I hover over her shoulder, but she pushes me away while looking up at it and back down to her scribbles.

Eve pulls me away, and though I keep my eye on the girl, I focus on Eve.

"So, while she does whatever it is she is doing, we should start filtering water," she says.

"How?"

Taking the mushroom cap from my hands she flips it over to expose the gills. She runs her finger along the soft, porous gills, and smiles cunningly.

"I told you, I have had these before, and I know a variety of uses. This type has a unique quality in that its gills can be used as a filtration system. If you put water in at the top of the gills, as it trickles through to the center of the cap. The gills will pick up potential parasites and heavy metals, leaving us with clean water."

"I would have died of thirst down here. You're smarter than you let on, Eve."

"Survival skills are just one of my specialties." She winks and pokes me playfully.

"We're still in dire circumstances and all you can think about is *that?*" I laugh. I don't feel as put off as I have been in her previous advances.

"Of course. I won't stop until you succumb." She grins.

"Eve, we need to clear that up," my tone becomes serious.

"What's there to clear up? I know you like Ami more than me, and I don't blame you. We got off on the wrong foot. But you have to admit I'm growing on you." She leans against a nearby wall, the crystals illuminating her red locks and wicked smile.

"Eve, we would never work."

"Give me an opening. If you still think that way when we break the curse, then I'll head out and leave you and Ami alone."

The urge to tell her 'no' again is there, but she's being obstinate, and it feels like she won't budge, no matter what I say. I sigh.

"Let's start filtering."

We proceed with her methods, and pop the caps off of several mushrooms. Lining them up with the water dripping down, we make sure it hits the gills as much as possible. Thinking of water makes me thirsty, and I do the only thing I can think of to alleviate it right now, eat. In order to collect enough water for all of us, we set up a dozen or so filtering mushrooms.

Thankfully the mushrooms are plentiful. We will have enough food and water to keep us going until the end of the month, or until the girl hopefully figures out if that thing can get us topside.

Sitting near the entrance on guard, Eve and I admire our handiwork and smile at each other. With the tribal people huddled together near the back, and the girl still scribbling away, I'm more at ease knowing we're doing everything we can to survive. Relaxed, with Eve by my side to protect me, I drift into a daze.

~~~~~~

Distant growling startles me. Eve is already up and ready with a spear in hand. Looking back, the man who had one previously is empty handed. The tribals hover back near the cylinder, hopefully difficult to distinguish for any lizard-men. I join her.

Eve motions for us to move forward through our branch back to the main tunnel. Claws scrape against the rock, and it sounds like one is nearby. It's sniffing the air. It picks up. Coming close to our opening, discovery is imminent.

I draw my blade, ready to kill the lone lizard-man, but it turns around and runs the other way. With a glance, Eve and I know what the other is thinking. I leap out after it, to the left of our opening. It's already disappearing into the darkness.

A scout seeking our location?

The more I feel they have some intelligence, the more dangerous they become in my mind. I'm after it with Eve at my side. It gallops on all four legs, giving it the advantage of speed. It nears a corner, and has to slow and shift its weight. We gain some ground, but not enough to catch it. It barks out. Intense growling resounds from ahead. Turning on its heels, it's joined by a few others in a wave. It barks and hisses. They barrel headlong into us while the scout disappears among them.

The narrow tunnel provides limited room to fight, but the lizard-men advance anyway. We collide and begin the inevitable. I quickly parry a claw swipe and dodge a lunge. The edge of my sword comes down hard to sever an arm. The beast wails, and I drive the tip up through its jaw and skull.

Eve jumps into the rest of them and spins the spear around. She lands blows left and right. They narrowly miss her, and I charge in to draw their attention before she's overwhelmed. In the middle I'm forced to duck and defend. An opening presents itself, and I put my shoulder into one. It doesn't budge so I put a shockwave to its chest. It reels backward to impale itself on the jagged crystals jutting from the wall.

Eve grunts as one picks her up by the head. She tries to jam the tip of the spear into its neck, but she's too close. It slams her down. Her pride keeps her from staying there, and she leaps back to her feet. She's slow to react and is clawed across her chest. Before I can get there she collapses, blood spurting.

The lizard-man leans down, opening its maw wide to take her head off. My heart beats hard in my chest, and I let my rage take over. A battle scream echoes off the walls, catching its attention for a split second. It's enough for me to jump in. I swing my sword hard, cutting clean through the lizard-man's gut. Like any wounded animal, it lashes out, and nearly catches me in its snapping jaws.

One remains. When it opens its mouth to bite me, I jam my arm down its throat and loose another shockwave before it can clamp on. It's ripped apart from the inside. Guts explode outward.

Eve moans in pain. I put my sword away and grab her up. She's heavy, but I run back to the safety of our cave. She's bleeding bad and has lost consciousness. Pressure builds in my eyes, but I fight my emotions back. When I'm there I bring her straight over to the tribal girl.

"Hey! I need you to heal her!" I yell, setting Eve down near her.

I rip Eve's shirt open to check the wounds. Without realizing it, I've begun putting pressure on to try and slow the bleeding. A normally awkward situation is replaced by the need to keep her alive. Eve's chest rises and falls, laboring to pull in the air she needs. The girl joins me, and her hands glow green. Eve winces at the touch, and the wounds begin to close, but she coughs up blood. I turn her head to clear her throat. I look at the tribal girl for signs of hope, but she's lost in her chant.

The green glow disappears and the girl pulls Eve's eyelids up to look at her. Her breathing is weak and she's unresponsive. Worry overcomes me.

"Eve! Come on. Wake up!" I shake her shoulders.

The girl slaps my hands away, and shakes her head. She turns to her tribesmen and speaks to them. They come over and pick Eve up to move her toward the wall. One retrieves a mushroom which has been filtering water, and they force Eve to drink. On my knees, I watch helplessly as they take care of her.

A few moments pass and it dawns on me that the scout escaped. The fear that more could be coming puts me back into action. It takes me only a few moments to run back out of our cave into the tunnels. At the bodies of lizard-men, I consider continuing to find the scout, but the idea of running into more is disheartening. Aiming my hands up I release a single shockwave, and it quakes the walls. The roof starts collapsing, and I have to retreat. Large rocks stack, and dirt fills in the holes until the tunnel is mostly blocked. Growling and hissing can be heard from the opening at the top, but the gap is too small for them to fit through.

If they start digging through, maybe I'll hear it. They'll be easy targets trying to crawl through.

Eager to return to Eve, I wait only another few moments to see if there's any movement. When it remains clear, I run. Back at her side, I wait and hope that she'll be all right. She's breathing normally now, but she's still not awake.

Next to her I sit, feeling impotent. The cave is quiet, except for random shuffling, or water droplets hitting puddles. It's possible that hours pass and I don't even know it.

~~~~~~

"Mmm. Rain."

My eyes open, and I'm face to face with Eve lying on the hard and uncomfortable ground. She's resting her chin on my chest, half her body on top of mine. There's a seductive look in her eyes.

"It's awful sweet of you to keep me warm. What happened?"

My normal instinct to push her off of me in these kinds of moments falters, and I let her lie there.

"You almost died. If it wasn't for the little girl, you would have."

"Liar." She grins mischievously and pulls herself up more on me. "You just wanted to tear my shirt off."

Though she's still wearing a bra, it's shredded. I can't see anything at this angle, but now that my attention has been called to her chest, that instinct kicks in. I'm on my feet and away from her before she can do anything. Turning away, I remove my tattered, but more intact shirt, and throw it over my shoulder at her.

She shuffles, and her arms wrap around my chest as she presses her chest into me. I blush heavily, and try desperately to keep my voice in check.

"Eve, please put the shirt on."

"Don't deny me this moment."

Every time Eve pushes herself at me, all I can think of is Ami. I can't hurt Ami. I won't.

Perhaps I was too hasty to tell her we needed to wait until I stopped the vortex before furthering our relationship. I need to try harder so we can all move forward.

There has to be someone who can help. Chase was fast. The girl can heal. Surely there's someone out there that can break the cycle besides Evalyn.

I step away from her grasp, leaving her to put the shirt on.

"I'm sorry, Eve. The most I can offer is friendship."

She's silent for a few moments. The feeling I've hurt her is almost tangible, and it nags at me. She shuffles back to the wall and there's some murmuring from the tribal people, but I don't have the fortitude to turn and face anyone at the moment. Instead, I move to the entrance of our cavern to guard.

Resting my shoulder on the wall, the cold rock is a shock to my system, and I stay alert for a while. I try to let my mind go blank, but end up thinking of the one person who might help me understand my violent nature better. The woman who jumped into a hole to die with me.

~~~~~~

Our only way to mark the time passing is through our sleep patterns, or trying to see the sky above. It's impossible to keep track of how long we've been below ground. Eve is sure it's only a couple days, while I am sure it's been at least a week.

The mushrooms grow fewer in numbers because of their dual purpose. What once was a plentiful stock has now dwindled to covering about half our chamber.

We may have to move and look for more if the girl can't figure out if that thing does what we hope.

I tread lightly, making my way back to the safe chamber from the one we've dubbed the 'bathroom chamber' down the opposite direction from the collapsed tunnel.

Nearing, I don't feel like going back in just yet. The tension between Eve and I is almost palpable, and waiting for something to happen makes me anxious. But because I have nowhere to go I enter anyway, staying just at the entrance of the tunnel. I duck to the side, not wanting to draw the attention of any lizard-men that might wander by.

Save for a few stragglers, it's been too quiet. We've had time to heal, but how much more can we take if there's another big wave?

Lonely and bored, I go into the cave and over to the young girl. Hovering over her latest scribbling, which has spiraled outward from where she originally started, I look on for a few moments before she shoos me away. I linger, looking at the others, huddled together. They seem content to talk, eat, and sleep. One of them calls out a word at the healer. 'Taki'. The girl looks over and she speaks with them. A woman nods and they all look at her with anticipation.

Is Taki her name?

Eve has moved to the wall near the exit and is lying down. I sit first, then lie down next to her to share body heat. There's no hesitation as she puts her arm over me to draw me close.

"Eve...I—"

"Stop. I don't want your pity. I'm just cold."

"I'm sorry I hurt your feelings."

"Rain, I knew I was in a losing battle back in my camp." Her voice waivers. "I'm used to getting what I want, and it sucks..."

I can't see her face well, but I know she's crying. It causes my chest to tighten, and I feel terrible. She makes an attempt to wipe away tears, but she can't stop them. Because she's taller than me, I am forced to scoot up in order to pull her into my bare chest. My fingers find her hair and I run them through her curls.

"What if we found you someone from another time and brought them along?" I suggest.

"It's not just about 'someone'. It's about getting what, or in this case who, I want."

This declaration shuts me up.

Why are you making this so difficult, Eve?

As if she senses my thoughts, she looks up at me. We stare at each other for a few moments before she breaks the silence.

"It's not what I want, but if we do die, at least I have this moment with you."

"I have hope we will see the light of day again. And you should too."

She nuzzles back into me for a moment. Before we can relax, a noise comes from down the tunnel. I'm quick to my feet, sword drawn. Eve is by my side with her crystal ready. We peer around the corner, but nothing has breached our boundary. The noises grow louder beyond the tunnel.

We pass through our short tunnel to the main junction. Low guttural growls, and the sound of claws scratching against stone becomes a frenzy of noise from down the corridor. It draws closer. I imagine hundreds of lizard-men passing through. There's distant rumbling from the other direction, and the distinct sound of rocks collapsing to the ground.

The blocked tunnel!

"Eve, go cover them. Maybe they'll pass over us." I want her out of harm's way, knowing there's only one place they could be going.

We retreat to the cave. She moves to the back, and I lie in wait at the mouth. My already shaky hopes that they would pass by our hideout are quickly nullified as the first one appears through the door. I swing up hard, sending its head into the next one behind it. A roar resounds, followed by a multitude, becoming deafening. A few rush in, claws extended to grab me. I dodge and lunge with a few more decisive strikes and two more fall.

This isn't going to work. If there are half as many out there as I think, we're dead no matter what I do.

Doing the only possible thing I can think of to spare our lives for the moment, I unleash shockwaves at the entrance. One after another connects. Large chunks of rock fall to block the way of the other lizard-men, and gives me an opportunity to kill the few which found their way in. I hit their legs, arms and chests to keep them from tearing me apart.

The rest scratch and tear at the debris, trying to break through. For good measure, and a few more minutes of safety, I unleash additional blasts to bring the roof down directly above the mouth. It cracks, and several chunks crash down, but not enough to keep them out for long.

Breaking any more might cause a cascade effect and bring down more ceiling across the cave. I'll have to pick them off like I planned at the other cave-in.

Patiently, I wait for the first one to dig through. I'm startled when something brushes my hand. The tribal girl tugs on my wrist and points to the metal object. Shaking my head at her does no good. She insists. I sheathe my sword, and she leads me forcefully over to the cylinder. Positioning herself in between my arms, she manipulates my hands. Moving my fingers across several symbols, it shocks me, and I pull away. The girl looks up and scowls, then places them back.

What feels like electricity sets my hands aflame for a few moments, but she runs her fingers over a few of the runes in a few different places, and my hands go numb. She moves my right hand down and repositions my fingers on new symbols, then returns to tapping on certain ones. With a triumphant final tap, she turns around and smiles, but only momentarily.

The cavern begins to quake heavily, and we're thrown from our feet. I let her land on me so she isn't hurt, but I hit my tailbone hard. I have no time for the pain, though, when the quaking begins tearing down my rock barrier. I'm ready to fight again, but my footing is unsteady. The lizard-men claw at the top of the pile. I step forward, but I'm yanked backward. A piece of the ceiling falling nearly crushes me. Eve smiles when I look over my shoulder, and she points up. The whole ceiling is fracturing.

I knew there was a reason I didn't hit it again. Now I can use it to my advantage.

Several shockwaves tear from my palms, aimed at the ceiling above the cave-in. More rock piles on, but they're digging through faster than I anticipated.

A cracking sound resounds over the noise the earthquake is causing. The cylinder has begun to drive itself upward by means I can't distinguish. It disappears, leaving a gaping cylindrical hole in its place.

"Taki?" I yell over the noise. She looks up at me with wide eyes. "What was that supposed to do?"

Rocks fall toward the group of tribals, and Eve. I quickly shock them away and they're safe for the moment.

We're dead.

The quaking stops and the sounds of the monsters finally breaking in alarms me. Their roaring echoes across the cavern and they're rushing toward us. They close in from a few hundred yards away. Looking back, I see the scared looks on everyone's faces.

If I kill the people now, they won't suffer being eaten alive.

The little girl begins yelling, and a literal ray of hope appears. A white, sparkling light beams down from inside the hole left by the cylinder. Too bright to be daylight, I am left to assume that it's the cylinder above. 'Taki' jumps and yells, pointing at it.

"Get in!" I yell and point at the doorway.

Eve jumps into the light and disappears in a barrage of bright particles emanating from the beam. The tribal people, clearly frightened, hesitate. But when I point to the girl and then toward the light, she leads them in. I am left alone with the beasts.

Lizard-men close in, and I begin shooting shockwave arcs across the ceiling, collapsing in huge portions of the weakened cavern. A lizard-man draws close, and I quickly grab up a loosed crystal. The point enters under its ribcage, causing it to hiss and growl in pain. It attempts to slash me anyway. Hoping to use it like a bullet, I unleash a shockwave on the crystal to push it all the way through.

The moment my shockwave touches the crystal, it reverberates. My power is amplified through it, knocking both me and the lizard-man away from each other. My body collides with the wall, and I narrowly miss impaling myself on another crystal. An idea is quick to assert itself.

I can't let them follow me through the door. I might be able to collapse the whole cavern!

Placing my hands on the crystal directly next to me, I muster as much energy as I can and unleash power into it. Crystals all around the room resonate, and the cavern buckles. The wall explodes outward directly in front of me. The earth splits, and a deep crack tears across the ceiling, causing the cave to collapse.

With little time to spare, I snatch up a dislodged crystal, and jump into the light.

A strange tingling sensation overwhelms my body. My vision goes completely white. Like in an elevator, I can feel myself being projected skyward, but at a much faster rate. A heavy sense of gravity pulls on me, but only for a moment. The stop is sudden, and I squint at the area around us: we're on the plains, lit by a setting sun. A bit dizzy, I step forward from the cylinder onto the soft dirt. Eve is there.

"This isn't good!" she yells, pointing behind her.

On the decimated plains, numerous cylinders have arisen from the ground, a couple hundred yards apart each. From each one come lizard-men in droves – dozens quickly become hundreds. Acting on impulse, I shove Eve out of the way and, before any appear from the one we just came through, I place my hand on the crystal and send a blast through it. The amplified shockwave propels me backward. I impact and roll a few times in the dirt. I recover. The back of the machine is blown out, and sparks shower outward. It fizzles, and the light disappears.

"Get them to safety! I don't care where it is!" I point at our survivors who are gathered nearby.

"Aye!" She nods, and rushes them along while I follow behind.

The house is a speck on the horizon. We've traveled much farther than originally thought. Returning to it seems a daunting task with the landscape littered with cylinders, and the lizard-men army. In numbers we hadn't seen down in the caves, they amass battalions around the individual cylinders they came from. It terrifies me.

Eve takes the group into an open area between cylinders while I head for the nearest one. The lizard-men are barely aware of my presence before I tear through the cylinder to keep more from pouring out.

Some are knocked aside. I have their attention, and they fixate. In the daylight I can see their harsh features better. Their dark scales, spikes, and sharp claws are glossy black. There's no soft spot I can pinpoint. While technically naked, they have no outward reproductive system. I'm left guessing where I might strike to quickly disable them, rather than having to tussle with each one.

A flawed plan to take them head on comes to mind, to keep the attention on me, and not the fleeing group. I run into them like a charging bull, yelling. I gore the first one with the crystal's sharp point. Feet planted and grip firm, I lean in and release a small shockwave through the crystal to send the creature flying into a few advancing. They aren't deterred. The fallen lizard-man is tossed to the side. Sharp claws swing wildly at me.

I dodge and roll, stabbing one from underneath. Before it can grab me, I leap away. I stand with my back to the cylinder.

This is going to be a nightmare to contain.

The lizard-men circle me. A shockwave-leap puts me over their heads, and out of their grasp. I hit the ground with a roll, and I'm back up on my feet, but they are already upon me. Another group from the next cylinder over has taken notice too, and are running to engage.

Not knowing how far the crystal will amplify my power, I wait until they are a few feet away. In a defensive stance, I unleash a powerful shockwave through the crystal. It engulfs the ground in front of me, and I'm sent flying backwards despite bracing myself. The last thing I see of the nearest group approaching is their insides becoming their outsides.

The landing from the kickback hurts tremendously as I land on my neck and shoulder blades. I skid to a stop in the dirt. Nearby roaring keeps me alert. I get back up to see more converging on me from multiple directions. The ground trembles with their stampeding.

Good. I have their attention. Eve and the tribals should have an opportunity to escape. I just need to draw these things away from the house and tribal people.

"Hey! Hey! Over here!" I yell at the top of my lungs at the creatures. "You want a fight? I'm right here!"

How do I do this?

Hundreds of lizard-men track and chase me. I run out of time. They close in from all sides. To defend myself, I draw my sword, wielding the crystal as a mace. When the first wave arrives they attempt to maim and maul. I duck and dodge under their arms, through their grasp, and between their muscular legs. In a flurry of swings, I club and slash at them anywhere I can, but I only land grazing hits because I am keeping out of their reach too.

One makes a grab at me. I pull away and feel the breeze as it barely misses my chest. Bringing the sword down, I cut its hand off; it lets out a screech and stumbles back. I turn around, swinging the crystal wildly. It meets with the arms of another, deflecting the blow. In a smooth follow through motion I bring the sword down on the ridge between its eyes. The efforts are useless against the wall of innumerous beasts. I am surrounded with no way out but up.

Blasting the dirt with a few shockwave bursts sends up a dust cloud to give me cover for a brief moment. I sheathe my sword, and jam the crystal as deep into the ground as I can. With the dirt cloud settling, they can see me again. They begin to advance.

"Come get me," I mutter, glaring at the ones directly in front of me.

I wait until the last possible moment before they attack. I squat, place my hands on the crystal and force the biggest shockwave I can produce into it. Launched skyward so rapidly, my heart nearly stops out of fear, and I choke on my own breath. Reaching this new height gives me a bird's eye view; but I focus on where I had just been.

The shockwave tears through the air across the ground like an explosion. A dirt-storm rolls across the land, and the lizard-men not obliterated by the initial blast, or tossed into chasms in the ground, are caught in the current of the wave and bounced around. The ground opens up and begins sucking everything down in a whirlpool of destruction a mile wide.

I freefall. My destination is the center of the crater, with the same fate as the creatures if I fail to act. Though I have nothing to push against, I point my arms out in front of me and let a shockwave go; my trajectory barely changes. The speed at which I am falling reaches terminal. I do everything I can to spin to face the ground. Coming up on the churning earth below me, I use another shockwave against the unsettled ground to put me back into the air. Because of my angle of attack, I'm not launched high enough. I fly straight at a cliff of level ground. The impact against it hurts. I clamber to grab the top of the ledge. My arms dig deep into the earth and the sinkhole underneath threatens to suck me in. I heave and cough while I try to pull myself up, but I don't seem to move. Loose dirt sends me sliding a bit.

A shockwave now would either cause the ground to collapse faster, or not give me enough energy to clear the crater.

The feeling of all being lost overwhelms me, and I nearly succumb to despair. But a glimmer of hope appears a few feet above my head at the cliff's edge: a hand reaches over and Eve's face appears.

"Don't just sit there, imbecile! Grab my arm!" she barks.

I struggle hard against the current pulling me to grab hold of my last lifeline. My hands and feet dig and grab at anything. The effort is nearly useless. I gain little ground. Exhaustion from using so much energy in so little time begins to set in. I'm weakening. I look into Eve's eyes, and she sees it.

"Don't you dare! Don't you dare give up on me, Rain!"

"I can't go on, Eve," I yell up at her.

"That's garbage, and you know it! Try harder!"

She arcs her head around, momentarily distracted. She yells, but I can't make out what she said. When her eyes meet mine again, she smiles and tosses a rope down at me. There is a faint whinny from a horse. Help has arrived. The rope reaches me, and I snatch at it. I wrap it around my arm several times, and grab firmly with both hands. She disappears, and I hear grunting from what sounds like a few people. They pull me up and over the ledge, and I scramble to move away for fear of it collapsing beneath me.

"I told you." Eve punches me in the shoulder.

Looking up, I see Eve, Taki, and the chief of the tribe there, along with our horse. I give them a weak smile and collapse on the solid ground with a sigh. But my rest is short.

"This isn't over, Rain. There are still lizard-men everywhere, and more are continuing to pour from the cylinders," Eve is blunt.

"Well, we can't just let them run amok, can we?" I sigh.

Standing up slowly, every muscle in my body aches. Knots have already formed in my hamstrings and calves. Behind me the crater has swallowed a large portion of land, taken out countless lizard-men, and destroyed several pillars.

The chief and girl mount the horse. He hands Eve a spear, and gallops off toward the tribe. Eve and I head for the next group of creatures. They appear to be massing in a group rather than just attacking.

Their actions indicate they have some intelligence, but how much? Could they be hive-minded?

"No rest for the wicked," I sigh.

"I'm going to sleep for a week after this nonsense." She laughs.

"Agreed."

Along the outside edge of the crater, Eve and I take out as many of the creatures as we can safely, and I decimate every cylinder within our reach. Within a few hundred yards from where the creatures are gathering, we stop.

"Can you do again what you did back there?" Eve asks.

"No, I don't have another crystal – it magnified my power." I groan. "We're going to have to try and lure them out of the larger group to pick them off."

Nearing a cylinder, we holler for their attention. It only takes a moment for them to see us. Several break away from the group and begin advancing on our position. We hold our weapons at the ready, but before we can engage, there's yelling from the other side of the grouping of lizard-men. I can hear the war cries of the tribal people while the creatures let out ear-piercing screeches and guttural growls.

I look at Eve and nod. She nods back, and we break into a sprint. We engage the creatures coming at us while listening to the same thing happening on the other side of the group. Battle ensues, and there's no time for thinking.

Clashing on the battlefield, I evade being skewered by claws and ripped by teeth. I leap and somersault underneath one. Back on my feet I wheel about, and run my sword into its spine. I draw it out and spin to counter an incoming attack. Holding a set of claws in place for a moment gives Eve the opportunity to run her spear into the beast's underarm. It drops its guard. I behead it, and engage more.

Roaring fills the air directly in front of me. One charges. I brace myself in a battle stance. It feigns attacking me with its claws. When I go to block, it switches tactics and swings around, using its tail to sweep me off of my feet. I hit the ground with force, and it tries to tackle me. I position the flat of my sword between us.

Battle tactics?

Snapping teeth approach my face. Its decaying breath makes me gag. I turn my head to breathe, and so it can't bite me. Propping my feet on its chest, I push up. It gives me room to position my sword, and I let my legs down a little. The lizard-man descends right onto the tip. It flails and struggles to kill me. I twist the sword and shimmy it upward, spilling its innards all over me. When it stops moving, I have to heave to shove it off of me.

Upright again, I leap onto the back of another one, thrusting my sword in. Hanging by the hilt, it attempts to buck me, scales scratching my bare skin. I wrap my legs around it the best I can, pull my sword free, and bring it back down into the scaly flesh. It collapses to its knees. A heavy set tribal comes to my aide to finish with a slit to its throat with a knife.

As quickly as he takes it down, another one tackles him and rips into his flesh. I leap at it, throwing my shoulder into its ribcage. I knock the monster free, but I am too late. The man is already beyond saving. The creature falls. Its arm swings around and catches my face with sharp claws, gashing my forehead. Blood runs into my vision, and I'm forced to close my eyes. I stumble. Eve shouts and I hear the cracking of a skull.

Wiping my face repeatedly does no good. Eve rips off a strip from my shirt she's wearing, and wraps it around my head. I can partially see again, and we rejoin the battle where numbers on both sides have begun to dwindle. In the heat of the battle, I head to the nearby cylinder.

"Eve! Here!" I yell.

She comes as requested, and I point up. Nodding, she puts her hands together and lifts me so I can climb on top of it. From there I have a good view. Despite the lizard-men's height, I'm able to stay out of harm's way for a moment.

The battle looks even in numbers, as far as I can tell. I start tipping the balance by sending out controlled shockwaves to distract the lizard-men. It works. The people gain opportunities to take the monsters down while the lizard-men are focused on me. Soon enough the lizard-men realize they are outnumbered and some attempt to flee. No mercy is shown as I blast at their feet. They stumble and are overtaken. Tribal people put them down for good.

Another shockwave, this time at my feet, disables this cylinder. I feel a sense of triumph. Tribals pick off smaller groups of lizard-men here and there across the shattered land.

When the earth begins to quake, and the cylinder tilts, I'm thrown to the ground.

"Again?!" I think out loud.

The quaking is localized to the crater nearby. I turn to look. Dust and dirt spew upward. A spine-chilling shriek bellows from inside. Everyone and everything has stopped to look. All attention is on the crater. What couldn't come up through the cylinders is breaking up through the ground. As its enormous head and shoulders appear, there comes frantic cries and weeping from around me.

The giant lizard-beast I collapsed the tunnel on arises from the hole. It pulls its whole body up onto the plain, and lets out another ear piercing shriek which turns into a roar. The air vibrates so heavily my bones quiver. Everyone falls silent. We stare in awe at the monstrosity, taller than our two story house. The tribal people begin to run away screaming. But it pays no attention to them. Its eyes fix directly on me, a beacon for it to focus on.

It recognizes me!

Looking around with haste, I find the chief is still on the horse. Heavy thudding against the ground brings my attention back to the sinkhole. The lizard-beast hurtles toward me on all fours. I'm its prey. The earth trembles at the weight in which the beast forces upon it with every bound. I have little time to act. I run to where the chief is.

Grabbing his crude reins, and hopping up, I commandeer it from him. He's startled, but jumps down when I yell and point at the lizard-beast. I turn the horse and gallop directly at the monster.

"Hyah!" I shout at the horse while digging my heels into his sides.

The horse's legs carry us on a collision course toward the beast, while it uses the ground as a springboard to reach me. A few hundred feet before we meet, I fire a shockwave at its head and turn the horse, leading him away from the people. It's obsessed with me – it changes course.

Spinning around on the horse while he gallops, I face the lizard-beast. It's closer than I'm comfortable with. The horse feels the ground rumbling behind him, doom on its heels. It runs hard, trying to escape.

The beast is determined to catch me. It snaps its jaw. Drool drips freely onto the dusty plain. Only my legs hold me on to the horse, but I'm ready to fight. I grab my sword from its home and ready to find it a new one. The lizard-beast nears, taking a swipe at us. I deflect it with a decisive slice to its hand. It roars, but doesn't falter.

Leading us wherever it pleases, my steed sees fit to arc around and run through a group of tribal people and lizard-men still waging war on each other. I swing my sword down to fell a couple foes while passing. Barreling through, the larger one takes out just as many tribal people, crushing them underfoot or sending them flying. The screams and the sounds of death makes me queasy, but I shake it off and focus.

Over my shoulder, I see where the horse is headed. My heart skips a beat. We are near a larger portion of the chasm in the ground – too big for him to clear. Turning around, I take the reins again. I barrel straight for the chasm, forcing the horse to do my will despite it wanting to turn away. At the last possible safe moment, I pull the horse sharply to the right. It makes the turn without sending me over the side, and gallops along the edge of the cliff. The beast behind us has too much momentum to stop. Just when I think I have the creature where I want it to be, it leaps the chasm with a powerful push off the ledge from its hind legs. The ground rumbles as it lands safely on the other side. It roars so loud it's all I can hear.

Having landed directly in the middle of an encampment of tents, it begins rampaging, tearing everything apart while staring me down. However, the area is empty of native people, and I breathe a sigh of relief.

Leading the horse along the main chasm, he leaps over smaller offshoots of the giant cracks in the ground. We reach a point where it becomes thin enough to get across. I spin the horse away and gain some distance. I slow him, and turn around to see the monster is still decimating the remnants of the encampment. It has lost its fixation on me.

Back into a gallop, I aim the horse directly for an area I know he can clear. Though I have confidence in his ability to make it across, my heart palpitates. Leaping into the air, he vaults the chasm with ease and we're now on the same side as the creature.

It sees me again. It throws its arms out to its sides and leans forward to screech again. It takes some effort, but I force the horse to gallop directly at it. The lizard-beast simply waits for me. Closer, I begin to position my legs on the horse's back, and shift my weight. Sword and reins still in hand, I crouch on the saddle.

Die!

My jaw clenches, my mind races, and my body tenses up when I leap off the horse as it passes the monster. It swipes at me and, as it connects with my torso, I bring the point of my sword to cut deep into its forearm. It screams in pain, and snatches at me with its other set of claws while I hang from the hilt.

I squirm and pull the sword, enlarging the gash while kicking its enormous scaly paw away. It finally grabs hold, and begins to squeeze the life from me. I wrench the sword free, and before it breaks my bones

I chop down on its thumb. Its grip loosens. Aiming the sword between my arm and body, I thrust and dig the sharp edge directly into the soft flesh of the monster's palm.

In protest, it screeches and spikes me into the ground, with only a tent to break my fall. All of the air leaves my lungs, and I nearly lose consciousness. I lie there recovering while leather collapses in on me, concealing me. I wheeze, trying to catch my breath and it begins rampaging again, tearing up the area to find me.

A few moments are all I need. I wiggle free and jump from the sheets of leather. The lizard-beast hovers directly over me on all fours, its armored underbelly directly in my face.

Gripping the sword tightly, I scramble toward its hind legs and tail. I arc back, and swing with all of my might. I hit it right in the crease where the front of its foot meets its leg. As I draw the sword across, black blood spurts out.

Its legs wobble. I leap out from under its tail just before it collapses to the ground. I jump on its back, and stab into its spinal column. It squeals and tries to dislodge me, but its arms aren't long enough to reach the middle of its back. It stands up on hind legs, bucking and spinning wildly to shake me off. One hand is gripping my firmly planted sword, and the other is digging under sharp scales. I hang on. When it slows, I pull the sword free, leap up and find a new home for it right underneath the armor plating. I flay it open, cutting a chunk of its armor off.

Furious it cannot reach or stop me, it acts in desperation. It stands straight up, and falls back trying to crush me. I jam the blade in as far as I can. It fails to kill me, and I find myself dangling over the edge of the chasm. I hang tightly onto the sword embedded deep into the lizard-beast's dense muscle. But the blade won't hold for long. My weight and the creature's writhing causes it to slip.

I swing back and forth, catching my feet on the ledge. Using my lower body strength, I pull myself to safety, sword in hand. I scoot away from the edge while the creature squirms.

Though I want to catch my breath, I seize the opportunity of the behemoth being on its back. I climb onto its belly.

It notices and tries to grab me, but I swat its arms away with a couple strong shockwaves. Sword ready, I aim where I think the thing's heart might be. Its scales peel off with a few swings. A fair sized opening now exists, and it's a perfect home for my blade. The beast continues to swipe at me.

Either the heart isn't in that location, or it's too far down to reach.

I duck, free my sword, and jam my whole arm into the bloody mess, into the beast's innards. It screeches and wails, but I do as I did with the smaller one below ground. I end its misery by unleashing a shockwave directly inside its body.

Gurgling for a moment, its muscles go limp and finally it lies lifeless.

I retract my drenched arm, and collapse in a heap on its stomach, sighing in relief. But the relaxation is short. Nausea rolls over me. My muscles ache, and my bones hurt. I become dizzy and vomit. I close my eyes, and curl into a ball.

~~~~~~

The sun has set, and a cool night breeze flows over my body. I don't want to move. But battle continues in the distance, urging me to rejoin the fight. Under the ever-darkening sky, I grab my sword and sheathe it.

Dismounting the beast, I find my horse a few hundred yards away, grazing. I pat him gently and slowly make my way onto his back.

How am I not dead?

The cylinders are easily pinpointed in the dark, as the light pouring from their doorways act like beacons. Trotting along between cylinders, the lizard-men have stopped coming through. I blast holes in each one, and veer off to stop at nearby fights to turn the tide of a battle in the favor of the tribal people. Bodies litter the ground as I circle wide around the house, which is not too far away now.

Cleaning up seems to take forever, and it continues on late into the night. The numbers of the lizard-men dwindle. It feels like we've won. I aim for the house, slumped onto the horse's neck, weary from blood loss and exhaustion.

I hold on, trying to stay atop the horse as he jumps the smaller gaps in the ground to get home. Midway through the yard I fall off, landing painfully in the soft grass. Moments later the kitchen door flies open, and worried chatter fills the air. With my eyes closed I wait.

"Rain! Are you okay? Speak to me!" Ami cries out, kneeling down beside me.

Oh, how I missed her.

I open my eyes momentarily to let her know I am still alive, but shut them again.

"Where are his clothes?!" Emma squeals in embarrassment, maybe for me, maybe for herself.

"Save it for later, he's hurt pretty badly, and we need to get him inside," Ami commands.

How familiar.

"Don't worry dear, we'll have you back on your feet in no time," Agatha's voice soothes me.

My dear adoptive mother. I can always count on you, can't I?

They lift me up, and I can only grunt in pain while they carry me in. They put me on the couch and rush off into the hall, returning momentarily to tend to my wounds. My temporary bandana is removed from my gashed forehead, and they dab and wipe me down all over with wet cloths. My muscles finally begin to relax under their tender care. After cleaning the blood away, mine and lizard-man, they start bandaging me up. I stop them as they pull out some gauze.

"I need to shower," I tell them weakly.

"You need to rest. You're badly wounded." Emma's stern in her caring nature.

"No, it's okay. Just find the little tribal girl. I think her name is Taki." I mumble while trying to stand up. "Please, I just need to shower."

Agatha helps me while Ami and Emma are left confused. She walks me to the bathroom, and sees me in. I adjust the temperature of the water, and nod to her, letting her know she can leave. She smiles with worry.

"If you need anything dear, I'll be right outside the door."

"Thanks, Aggy."

The door is closed, and I remove the ribbons of my tattered pants and underwear. I climb into the shower, but rather than standing, I sit on the floor and let the water wash over me. My muscles ache, my wounds sting, but worries and anxiety wash away.

The water feels so good. It's been too long since I've been able to relax. There are times when I'm not fighting, but there is no such thing as a calm life for me.

I suppose if I worked harder at finding a way to stop the vortex, things might calm down. I need to provide them a better life than this dangerous wandering. I can't let them continue to be drawn into danger.

My anxiety levels rise again as my body crashes. I can't help but feel that before I lost my memory, this was how it was for me, caught in the middle of trouble. I lose time, and realize the water has run cold. I jump to turn it off. A light knock on the door startles me, and I answer hastily.

"Y-yes? What is it?"

"Are you okay in there? You've been in there for a while now," Agatha's soothing voice comes from the other side.

"I...I need a towel, please."

Her footsteps are soft, but in the quiet I can hear her retrieve one from the closet. I crack the door so she can slip it in. When she does, I take it and close the door.

"Thank you."

"Of course."

My clothes are nothing more than rags, so putting them on would be pointless. I wrap the towel around my waist after drying off.

"Aggy, would you move the girls into the kitchen? I need to head upstairs, and I only have the towel."

"Sure. Give me a minute." By the tone of her voice, she's smiling.

I wait, my ear pressed to the door, and listen for them to enter the kitchen. There is protest from Ami about how it's not a big deal, but Agatha is insistent. When I hear the swinging door come to a stop, I grab my rags and enter the hallway. Before I can climb the stairs, the door swings open and Eve appears with Taki.

"Is this where you've been?! Wait, did you take a shower?!" Eve protests. "We've been looking everywhere for you!"

Emma and Ami burst through the kitchen door while Agatha tries to stop them, and fails.

"Yes. Sorry. After I took the giant lizard-beast down, I helped where I could and returned here. I got our horse back too," I respond.

The little girl sees my wounds, and shoves past Eve. I flinch and lean back as she reaches out for me, tightening my grip on the towel. Placing her hands on my chest, she whispers, and there is an audible protest from Ami and Emma. Eve cackles while Ami and Emma move to pull the girl away from me. Holding my palm up, telling them to wait, I receive a dirty look.

"It's not what you think," I tell them.

Taki chants, and her hands glow green. The wounds on my body begin to heal rapidly. The gash on my forehead stops stinging, and when I touch it I can feel it disappearing.

"How?!" Emma exclaims.

"She just does," I reply. "It's like mine or Evalyn's ability."

"That explains a lot..." Evalyn speaks through Agatha. "She might be one of the earliest people in history who has such abilities."

Finished healing my wounds, she removes her hands, looks up and smiles. I smile back and ruffle her hair to show approval and appreciation.

"Thank you, Taki."

Her eyes widen with confusion. She backs away and she's displeased.

Is that not her name?

I touch my chest. "Rain." I point at her. "Taki?"

She nods and runs outside. I don't know if she's scared, or embarrassed. I don't understand, but it doesn't matter. She's gone. I return my gaze to everyone else.

"I need to rest. I'm completely exhausted."

Without giving them a chance to respond, I turn and march up the stairs.

Just as I'm closing the door, Ami yells, "Why are you wearing Rain's shirt? What have you done to it?"

I chuckle and slip into some clean nightwear. The bed feels amazing. The soft texture of the pillow, the gentle hug of the sheets; modern comforts bring me peace. Within moments, sleep comes to whisk me away, and I let it.

~~~~~~

Despite my initial resolve to rest after the ordeal, I feel obligated to help the tribe relocate their encampment away from the house, and the larger branches of the chasm. Self-imposed duties keep me busy, and a week has already passed since returning topside.

With the bodies of the dead cast into the large chasm, the smell of death should pass soon. Still, I feel bad for the tribe. Of course they wouldn't understand the bodies would become a breeding ground for disease. A mass grave was the only answer. The task would have been impossible if they hadn't eventually followed my lead.

The lizard-beast, now that was messy. At least the whole tribe helped a little more willingly, even if with dismembering and rolling it into the chasm. I just hope I can find a way to bury that which hasn't fallen to the caves below.

Though burial is on my chore list, I focus on the living.

I help some men and women scavenge tents for possibly important items. Finding random things, we put them into a leather tarp strung to the horse's saddle. While some gather, the main body of the tribe has already begun to set up again; the landscape once again covered with their abodes and belongings.

Arriving at the encampment with another load, the chief nods at me with reverence in his expression. I nod back, causing him to motion for me to dismount. I do, and lead the horse to where he is. He grabs my arm forcefully, and raises it in the air, then turns to his people and shouts triumphantly, cheering in his language. The people let forth a resounding cheer. He releases my hand, letting it drop, and speaks to one of the tribe.

The man disappears into the chief's tent, and returns with a head garment. It is the skull of a lizard-man; pelt cut off at the nape, the bottom jaw ripped off, and the innards removed. Its black scales and spikes have been polished so they shimmer, and the teeth have been cleaned. The chief takes it and then turns to me. I lean over so he can place it on my head – I take it as an honor.

Straightening up, I smile at the chief and put my hand on his shoulder, then turn to mount the horse. Back toward the house, my stomach grumbles. I've forgotten to eat all day, and after the heavy work I've been doing, my body is protesting.

The horse trots along at a decent pace, but the road home is complicated due to the number of cracks and gaping holes we have to avoid and jump. Still, it doesn't take long to reach the yard. I stable the horse, and provide him with some hay and water for his hard work. With a quick pat to his mane I leave him. Around at the kitchen door, Emma sits, looking bored. She gives me a funny look and I ruffle her hair as I enter the house. After a quick wash, I rummage through the fridge.

A salad of assorted fruits and vegetables beckons, but my body wants more. I crave meat. Raw ground beef sits thawing in a bowl, and I assume it's for dinner later. Huffing while I close the fridge, I move to the basement. I sift through the shelves for a dried hunk of meat. I tear open a bag and retrieve a large piece of jerky, gnawing on it while replacing the bag. Biting off a chunk, I let it sit in my cheek for a few moments to soften. Back upstairs, I grab some buttered bread, and a glass of water, then sit in my spot to rest.

I take my time eating, letting my body relax from all of the bending, twisting, and lifting of the day. Though it is nearing late afternoon, it seems there is still much work to be done with salvaging belongings, or collapsing the chasm in. But my body, having got a taste of rest, resists me going back out there with a bout of fatigue. I finish eating, slouch in the chair, and rest my hands behind my head.

My eyes are closed but a moment before Emma stands up from the doorway. She sits at the table, and I peek momentarily with one eye to see her resting her head on her arms and looking at me.

"What's going on?" I ask.

"I'm bored," she complains. "This is not at all what I thought it would be like. I want to help you."

"It's too dangerous out there. Better to be bored than dead." I stroke one of the teeth on the upper jaw of my headdress.

"You look like you're having fun with that on your head." She giggles.

"Want to try it on?"

"Sure!" She becomes excited.

Removing it, I place it on her. It wobbles, clearly too large for her head. When I let go, it nearly falls off. She laughs. Holding it on with both hands, she stands up and pretends to charge me, stamping her foot against the floor.

I play along and jump up, shoving a chair between us, but she runs at me anyway, and I run around the table as she chases. Gaining ground away from her, she reverses and goes the other way. I do the same.

"I'm going to get you!" she roars.

"Not going to happen!" I veer off and head around the island counter.

Ami enters from the living room, and gives me the 'what-are-you-doing?' look. Letting Emma catch me, she pretends to chomp down on my back with the teeth, and I pretend to be wounded. But I grab the headpiece, and stick it back on my head. With a roar, and stomp of my foot, I grin and aim toward Ami. Her eyes widen, and I charge. She bolts through the swinging door. I push through to see she's already disappeared out the other side of the house.

Out the door after her, I look right in time to see her vanish around the side. I pursue, holding the bottom of the skull so it stays put. Tearing through the yard, I reach the other side, and Ami has hidden within the clotheslines. I maneuver through the freshly washed clothes.

She flips towels into my face in an attempt to tangle me up in them. I am adept at moving through the obstacles, only becoming caught once. However, it gives her enough time to make a break for the apple tree. Though I push to catch up with her, she's too agile and nimble. She reaches the tree and springs up into it.

Staring up at her, I hold the lizard-man's skull. She smiles at me, but I notice a tear roll down her cheek. I take the piece off, and set it on the ground. Climbing into the tree with her, I sit on the next branch over and take her hand in mine.

"I...was so worried. I didn't know if you had died." She sniffles and wipes away the tear, fighting to contain more.

"I know. But I'm alive, and I'm here."

"Hey! You aren't the only one who was worried!" Emma protests from the ground. "And take your hand out of his!"

I smile at Emma's protectiveness.

"When Eve jumped in after you, the only thing I could think of was how she was with you, and if you were alive, the advances she was making." Ami laughs a little, wiping her eye with her free hand.

"I was hoping Rain would come back up, and she wouldn't," Emma remarks snidely.

"Stop," I scold Emma.

"I hoped falling in wouldn't kill you, but knew that the house would if it shifted through time with you down there." Ami says.

"Well, a lot of people did die down there. The few of us who made it back up wouldn't have survived if it wasn't for Eve's survival knowledge, and the little healer girl who knew more about technology than she should have."

Ami and I sit in the tree, backs pressed to the trunk while Emma sits at the base. The afternoon turns into evening. Closing my eyes, the responsibility of caving in the mass grave chasm weighs on my mind; but I still can't find the motivation to do it just yet. A light breeze flows through the branches, and it cools my skin. Footsteps approach. Agatha stands at the base looking up.

"I'm going to start dinner. Rain, would you help me?" she asks.

"Sure, Aggy," I call her by the nickname she's stuck with, thanks to Emma. "What do you want me to do?"

"You can make patties for me." She smiles.

I jump down, retrieve the headdress, then walk with Agatha back to the house. Ami and Emma linger for a minute, but they follow. The headpiece finds a home on the back of my chair while I wash up and help prepare dinner.

She pulls the salad from the fridge while I take the bowl of meat. I make several balls, and squish them flat on a plate. Emma seasons them. Ami heats up a pan. It doesn't take long for the delicious smell to permeate the house. Eve stumbles through the door groggily, drawn in by the food.

"Well, good morning," I playfully comment.

"Shut it. My head is pounding," she snaps.

"Maybe you shouldn't have spent all night drinking with the tribal people," Ami says snidely.

"Maybe you should mind your own business, 'Miss Priss'." Eve rolls her eyes.

Though their banter puts a smirk on my face, I stop them before it escalates. "All right now. Let's play nice."

With only bread to serve as buns for the meat, we create sandwiches for everyone, and each puts their own condiments on. At first it's quiet while we eat, but Emma breaks the silence.

"So, what happened down there?"

With my mouth full of a bite, I look at Eve and chew slowly.

I guess we could only avoid the topic for so long. If Eve can keep quiet about her declaration, or that we slept next to each other for warmth, we might be in the clear. I'm sure Emma is just looking for the story.

Clearing my mouth of the bite allows me to speak. "Not much to tell really. We fell in, encountered lizard-men, saved a handful of people, and made it out."

"He's being modest." Eve snorts with contempt for my shortened version. "Despite being near death, he fought off a least a hundred of those things down there to keep us alive. And the big one he fought up here, he tangled with down there, too. I was sure he killed it when he collapsed a tunnel on its head."

"*You* found the food and water. I'm not the one being modest here. I just killed things. And it was Taki who kept us both alive, and mysteriously knew about the cylinders."

"Eh, so I knew a little bit about survival."

"I wonder then if fighting and death were my life before." I think out loud, testing their reaction. "It's all I seem to know."

"Don't say that, Rain," Ami scolds. "I'm sure it was nothing of the sort."

"You're a protector: sometimes you have to fight," Emma says.

Drake's accusation of assassinations pesters me. There's silence again as we continue to eat. I drink down a glass of juice, staring off at nothing in particular. But I'm aware that it may look to the others like I'm staring at Eve. My mind runs through the events again.

What could I have done different? There were so many paths I didn't take. I hope there aren't any more people still down there. With the cylinders destroyed, the only way to find out would be to jump back in.

I suppose I'll have to accept I can't save everyone, and if there are people down there, hope they find a way to avoid those creatures. No doubt there are more who never made it up; perhaps other larger ones too.

Ami clears her throat quite loudly, and I look over. She stares me down and then looks at Eve.

"Is there something we should know? You've been staring at Eve for more than a few minutes now." Her jealousy rears its head.

"I wasn't staring at Eve," I become defensive.

"Sure you were. Just gawking. Did she get too friendly with you down there?" Ami interrogates.

Eve smirks wide and seeks to egg Ami on. "What, he didn't tell you? We cuddled close to keep warm down there. And then when I was vulnerable he took advantage of me, ripping my shirt off, and putting his hands all over my chest!" She puts her hands over her face and turns away, feigning embarrassment. "It's why I had his shirt on."

I was hoping we were done with this. I guess when Ami's around, Eve can't just pass up the opportunity.

"Liar!" Emma yells out. "Rain is a gentleman and would never do that!"

"Then why did I have his shirt on when we came back, and he have none?" She grins evilly.

"Of course she's lying," Ami responds spitefully before I can interject. "Because no one would actually want someone as manly as she is."

"Who are you calling manly?" Eve stands up, and slams her fists on the table. Eve glares, and Ami doesn't back down.

"Why are you upset? Afraid it's true?" Ami goads her.

"I'm ten times the woman you are." Eve's anger turns to pain.

Eve storms from the room. Her stomps can be heard all the way up the stairs. Her door slams shut, causing the house to shudder. I look at Ami, disappointed, and a little frustrated. She stares back, annoyed.

"What? She started it with her lies, trying to put me into a tizzy," she defends herself.

"Ami—"

"What? Are you defending her lies? Or are they true?" Tears form in her eyes.

"I didn't take advantage of her. She was wearing my shirt because I gave it to her after she nearly died. One of the beasts ripped her chest open. I had to remove her shirt to put pressure on the bleeding. But she's not lying about having to sleep next to each other. We had to keep warm to stay alive."

Eve. Why do you have to antagonize her?

Whether she believes I'm innocent of wrongdoing or not, Ami abruptly leaves the kitchen. Her bedroom door slams as well, and somehow I'm left holding a bag of guilt I sought to avoid. Looking over at Emma, she is upset too. She plays with the food on her plate with a fork, her head down. I dare not say anything more. Instead, I simply cross my arms, and put my head on them.

After a long amount of time, I hear Emma begin cleaning her dishes. She leaves, and it's Agatha and I left. Agatha stirs and moves around the table to where I'm sitting, and rubs my shoulders. My muscles are tense, and she does a good job helping them release their tightness.

Elbows on the table, I rest my head in my hands. Turning my head to speak, I seek Agatha's guidance. "Why does it have to be *this* difficult? This can't be a normal rivalry, can it?"

"Rivalry is inevitable. I can try and offer some perspective," she says in her motherly voice.

"Please do, because women confuse me."

"You're Ami's first real friend since we started; the only semblance of a normal life she's had in a very long time. It's natural she would seek a relationship with the one person she knows she has a lasting future with. Being jealous comes with it, since she can't have you to herself."

"With Eve, well she's a woman who knows what she wants and takes it. It's her way of life. When you crossed her path, she fixated. Now she's stuck with the person she obsesses over, but because of how close you and Ami are, she can't get what she wants. It probably bugs her a lot, so she is antagonistic to drive a wedge between you and Ami."

"Makes sense, I guess." I sigh. "At least Emma can act as a barrier."

"True, but be careful not to dote on her too much. You were, and are, her hero. That means she's already protective of your relationship status and might just try to cut in." Agatha titters.

"Please don't say things like that." I tilt my head back and frown at her. "I know it's not fair to say I care for Ami and Eve, but I do, just in different ways. If I pursue Ami, it will hurt Eve, and she'll be stuck with us until we find a way to break the vortex cycle. I'm trying to fix problems, not make more," I explain.

"But sometimes indecision does more damage." She gently pats my shoulders.

"So you're saying I should make a decision?"

"It's up to you. I can't tell you if deciding or not will be the fix. You could be right to not make a decision until you and Evalyn find a way to stop our travels."

"I'm still just as confused."

My neck begins to hurt, and I bring it back down. While I don't know what to do, I take a little solace from talking about it with a neutral party.

"Thanks, Aggy. You're like the mother I can't remember," I chuckle.

She laughs and begins to clean up. I help, and together we're quickly done with the dishes, and kitchen. More time has passed than I thought, as the sky is dark and no trace of the sun shines across the land. A sliver of the moon provides very little light.

Agatha disappears into the living room, and I'm left alone. Fatigue sets in, and I make my way out too, shutting off the light as I pass through the swinging door to the living room.

Upstairs and into my room, there's comfort just knowing I'll be lying in bed soon. Into some warm nightwear, I slip into bed and the cool pillow feels great on my warm cheek. I sprawl out.

~~~~~~

I start the self-tasked job I couldn't yesterday.

After a hearty breakfast of eggs, bacon, and toast, I am energized enough to begin collapsing the chasms inward. Outside our border, I head to the largest part of the chasm, and when I reach the edge I look in at some bodies still visible. Without the tribal people surrounding us, my mind reflects on the quietness. It's the same as breakfast: not a whisper from anyone.

A breeze drifts by, and I breathe in deeply. Ready to go, I point my hands at the other edge of the chasm and begin by ripping at the opposite cliff with a continuous shockwave. Dirt and rock begins to collapse in, causing a cascade failure of the ground. It avalanches.

The once visible bodies at the bottom become invisible. I do my best to make the collapsing of the giant crack uniform. My feet carry me along, but the work is slow going. I rest after what feels like an hour of constant energy usage, sitting with my legs dangling over the ledge.

Footsteps approach. When I look, I see the little boy we found huddled near the cylinder. He's sad, by the look on his face. Sitting down next to me, I'm unsure of what he wants, except maybe comfort. Placing my hand on his head, I attempt to consciously use the ability the despair collective has cursed me with.

I concentrate, and close my eyes. Reaching into the darkness, wading through the despairs I'm not looking for, I have to dig deep before I can manifest anything. What I receive is a glimpse of a man, a bit younger than the chief, falling into the chasm. The boy tumbled down after trying to save him.

A new sorrow and image appear from him in my mind's eye. He stands away from the tribe, and a ghostly image of the man who fell in fades between. When the image fades, it leaves a gap between the boy and the tribe. I remove my hand and I feel his pain deep inside my soul.

He looks up at me, and holds a closed hand out, indicating he has something he wants to give me. I open my palm under his hand, and he places in it a round gem about the size of a horse's eye, with a leather strap through it. Upon closer inspection I see it's a chiseled, polished crystal from below with a crude hole punched through it. I smile and nod at him in appreciation.

"I know you can't understand me, but thank you. This will help me finish faster."

I stand up after my break and hold out my hand for him to stand too. He dusts himself off and points to the house, as if he wants to go inside. I shake my head, and watch his face turn sour. He begins to cry, and though I understand he feels separated, there's no way I can let him in the house. I ruffle his hair, and when he looks up I point back to the relocated tribe, and then to him. He sniffles hard, but runs off toward them and doesn't look back.

I wrap the leather strap around my hand, putting the crystal in my palm. Bracing my lower body, the crystal resonates, and I let forth a massive shockwave toward the middle of the chasm. An explosion of dirt fills the air. The chasm avalanches inward at great speed, and with a few more charged shockwaves, I am able to significantly fill in the ground.

When the dirt and dust settle, there is a large divot in the ground in front of me. Falling in is no longer treacherous, only requiring now a little assistance to climb out. Throughout the day, I make my way around, doing the same in order to bury the dead, and make the land safe again. Though I can't expect to fill it all in, I do my best with the time I have.

It feels like evening comes too quickly. Tired from the day's work, I hang the crystal around my neck and make my way back to the house. Agatha is outside taking clothes down from the lines, and I help her. We bring the baskets inside where Emma and Ami are working on dinner, but Agatha leads us to the living room to fold the clothes.

"This is the end of the cycle. Day thirty already," she states as matter of fact.

"Really? I didn't think we had been down there that long."

"It was a pretty scary time not knowing if you were alive or not," she says with concern.

"I was kind of hoping to be able to close more of the openings."

"There's only so much you can do, Rain. It's not up to you to fix everything." She smiles.

"I guess not. It will fill in over time anyway I suppose, as the openings don't exist in any other time we've seen."

We finish with the laundry and return to the kitchen for a meal where no one speaks. It's awkward, but there's nothing of great importance to talk about anyway. I simply sit until they are done, and then take their dishes. They disperse, each in their own directions, and Agatha squeezes my shoulder as thanks on her way out. Cleanup is quick, and I seek to relax. I shower and return to the confines of my room.

Disrobed and in bed, I close my eyes. Despite wanting to sleep, my mind is still active. I can't help but think about the days past, and the ones still yet to come.

I wish I could follow a roadmap to making things better. In the house and outside. With the history books as potential guides, it's more than likely the harder I try to fix something, the more it will become broken.

No sooner does my mind finally unwind, there's a quake. It's not the same as the one which opened the chasm, but rather the familiar one marking our hurtling through time yet again.

The windy vortex kicks up. Blue swirls illuminate my bedroom, and when they've gone the sun is beaming in. I turn over and groan, slamming the pillow down over my head. It does nothing to drown out the scream I hear a few moments later coming from outside the window. Emma begins frantically shouting, and soon Eve confronts her from her room, yelling out the window.

"Shut up! I'm trying to sleep!"

I do my best to ignore the commotion. But two sets of feet stomp up the stairs, and my door bursts open. Ami and Emma barge in.

"You are never going to guess what is outside the house right now!" Ami sounds a bit frightened.

"The view is amazing!" Emma shrieks with delight.

"It better be a future where the land is made of fluffy white pillows in which I can sleep." I sit up, taking the pillow off of my face, and revealing the near nakedness of my body.

Emma's eyes go wide, but Ami is unfazed. Surprisingly, Eve appears from her room and drags them both out. My door is slammed shut. Lying there for a moment, I want to sleep, but the three continue to chatter out in the hall. Their reaction makes me curious.

I suppose I can sleep later.

~~~~~~

4 REVELATION

"Leave him be!" Eve scolds Ami.

"Don't tell me what to do," Ami replies. "I think he's going to want to see this."

Eve sighs. Two sets of footsteps head downstairs, one fast and one slow. There are light raps on my door. I take my time getting dressed, more because of fatigue than trying to make whomever wait. I rub my face. I'm tired and want to curl up into a ball and sleep. They knock a little harder, and I pull the door open.

"Sorry." Ami looks down, embarrassed. "I just…"

"It's fine." I step out, but she doesn't give me room to pass.

Awkwardly we stand there for a moment, and she throws her arms around me. I hug her back. The hair on the back of my neck stands up, and I enjoy the embrace. My shoulder becomes wet, and I stroke her hair to soothe her.

"So, what's this all about?"

She pulls away, and I hold her waist while looking into her eyes. Wiping her face of the tears, she sniffles.

"Rain, I love you…" the words flow from her mouth, but she frowns. "But that's not what you were meaning, was it?"

"Ami…" I pull her in, and caress her hair again. "…I love you too. But I need to make good on my promise. To make sure you're safe."

"I know. I just don't like that you've gotten closer to Eve. I've just been a little jealous."

"I told her that all I can offer her is friendship."

I sigh. There's a moment of silence between us again, but the tension is gone. With neither Eve nor Emma to interject, I savor our embrace.

"I have no idea *when* we are. There are some large creatures outside. We're too high up for them to reach us, so you don't have to go kill them all." She taps my arm playfully.

"Well then, let's go take a look."

Releasing her, I follow downstairs. We make our way out the living room door, and the sight is breathtaking. A crystal blue sky expands before me, and beyond it I can see a definite edge to our plot of land. We walk to the boundary and look out. Our house is perched on a plateau atop a large pillar of rock which tapers out the farther it gets to the base.

Out as far as the eyes can see, there are many other columns of rock varying in height and girth, with green trees and vegetation scattered amongst the top of them.

Far below us lies a land covered in green. Many kinds of vegetation blanket the landscape. Enormous trees reach skyward, while rivers cut a swath through the jungle below to create a network of interconnecting ponds and lakes. Amongst the foliage, very large and lengthy reptilian creatures mill about casually.

"What are they?" I ask. "Those aren't the lizard-men from the chasm. They're too big, even to be the lizard-beast."

"I have no idea," Ami replies.

Our moment of peace is interrupted when Emma, Eve, and Agatha join us from the other side of the yard. Eve's face is pale, and it's apparent she's afraid to come near the edge. Emma strolls over and lies prostrate, head hung over the side. She squeals in wonder. Turning up to me, Emma smiles wide and giggles excitedly.

"This is so awesome! They don't look like the lizards you fought. These things are way bigger!" Emma says.

"I was just saying that same thing." I crane my neck and lean part way over the edge to get a better glance at the ones directly below.

"Rain! Get away from the edge!" Eve yells.

She grabs my hand, and pulls me back. Ami slaps our hands apart when we are away from the edge. Eve glares angrily at her.

"What has you so worked up?" I ask.

"Just…I don't know. I just don't want to hear Ami bawling if you fall over."

I raise an eyebrow, and there's a moment of silence.

"Well, if they're dangerous, we're safe up here. Finally, a quiet month." I grin.

"No danger. Stocked up on food. Quiet sounds nice," Agatha states.

"Good! I'm going to catch up on my sleep."

I begin walking back to the house.

"Wait! You're going to sleep?!" Ami protests my departure.

"I sure am." I laugh loudly without looking back.

In my room I breathe a sigh of relief. It doesn't take me long to become groggy once more. As my eyelids become heavy, I have my last thought before sleep.

Finally.

~~~~~~

My nose rouses me. While drifting back to consciousness, my stomach joins in waking me with a gurgle. A sweet, buttery, baked smell fills my room, and my body protests me continuing to lie here. My hunger isn't urgent, so I take my time swinging my legs over the side of the bed. The wood floor is cool to the touch, and I shiver. The air is also chilly, and a long-sleeved shirt feels warranted.

Today, I relax. If sunbathing doesn't warm me up, I'll just have to take a nice hot shower.

Downstairs, I push through the swinging door, and the smell intensifies. My mouth waters with delight. Agatha looks over with a smile, removing a waffle from the waffle iron. Next to her, a stack of them is already piled high, and she makes it taller.

"Good morning, Aggy." I yawn and stretch in the midst of greeting her.

"Good morning indeed. How are you feeling?" she replies cheerfully.

"Pretty good. My body is a little sore, but it will recover just fine with a nice quiet month ahead of us." I grin from ear to ear.

Emma appears from the basement with a heavy jug of syrup. Her face brightens with a smile when she sees me. Setting the jug down, she throws her arms around me for a quick hug.

"So, I assume I've been out for a couple days?" I ask.

"Only a full day," Emma replies, returning to her task. She begins heating up the syrup in a pan.

"Good. Nothing like wasting a bunch of time asleep!" I am playfully sarcastic about our predicament. "Where are Ami and Eve?"

"Ami's outside tending the garden, and we haven't seen Eve this morning," Agatha replies.

"Well, it looks like you've got enough help in here." I walk over and rub Emma's head, and kiss Agatha on the cheek. "I'll go keep Ami company."

Funny. A couple months ago I would have never thought of kissing her on the cheek. Now it's like she's my own mother.

Outside, a cool breeze moves the air. It's refreshing with the light mist being thrown up by Ami watering the garden. Her yellow summer dress and wavy brown hair waft in the wind. Seeing me, she smiles, and I smile in return. The grass is nice on my bare feet as I walk over. I rest my chin on the crook of her neck.

"You smell nice," I compliment her as the scent of her flowery shampoo enters my nostrils.

"Stop it." She giggles, and playfully elbows me while keeping control of the hose and nozzle.

"What? You don't want the compliment? I can go give it to Eve," I jest.

"You wouldn't!" She spins around, and nearly sprays me with the water, save for me jumping out of the way. "Oops!"

She turns the hose back to the garden. Moving beside her, I watch as she meticulously wets every patch of dirt. Looking at the crop, another harvest is only a few months away.

It's going to be time to replant soon. The resilience of these plants to produce multiple crops in a row is amazing. But if we land in winter, we can kiss it goodbye.

The apple tree is taking a lot longer to recover though. The leaves have barely begun to hide the scenery beyond it.

"So, is there anything you want me to help with?" I ask.

"Well, you can go brush *your* horse." She grins.

"I meant with you." I reach out and grab her waist, causing her to blush heavily.

"N-no, I'm okay!" she stammers. "There's nothing really for you to do here. After breakfast though, I'll help you with the horse."

"Sounds good to me. I'll brush while you shovel his waste into the compost bin." I wink and poke her lightly in the side.

"I think you have it backwards, mister." She elbows me again.

"Perhaps I do," I concede. "Well, if there's nothing I can do out here, I suppose I'll go bang on Eve's door and wake her up."

"Just stand back when you do. She's likely to grope you if you're too close!" Ami warns.

I nod at her, and head to Eve's room. Knocking lightly produces no response so I rap my knuckles on the door a little harder. The door opens swiftly and quietly. She's scantily clad in a white tank top and panties. I avert my eyes. Despite Ami's warning, I'm too close, and she pulls me in.

"Hey," she whispers as she pins me against the doorframe with her body. "I miss our cuddling."

"You remember it was only out of necessity, right?"

Eve pouts, her bottom lip sticking out while her bright red hair falls across her face. My face becomes hot, and I realize I'm blushing. She sees it, and her eyes twinkle with delight.

I can't stay here any longer. I can't let her think I'm indulging her fantasy.

"Breakfast is ready. Get dressed."

"I'd rather stay here and have you kiss me deeply." She leans forward for it.

I squirm away by ducking under her arm, and jump to the other side of the hallway. I point a finger at her and shake my head to indicate it won't happen. Putting her hands on her hips, she looks at me, frustrated, but stays put.

"I'll see you down there." I turn and leave.

So much for the 'friendship' talk.

In the kitchen again, the others are already seated, and I take my place at the head of the table. We wait until Agatha helps herself before digging into the stack of waffles. I pile two on my plate, slathering butter and syrup all over.

By the time I've savored every square of a single waffle, Eve finally makes an appearance, dressed less provocatively. She sits and mumbles, clearly displeased at something, but I can't make out what was said. With no snide remarks following from Ami or Emma, I assume they didn't either. I scan the table, and see my family. Four beautiful women who have made my life worth living.

What did I do to deserve being surrounded by these women who love me? We have our ups and downs, but I wouldn't want to be apart from any of them.

"Thank you for breakfast." I smile at Agatha.

"You're quite welcome," she responds.

I enjoy the quiet company. After I've had my fill of food, and quiet, I break the silence by getting up to clean.

The kitchen doesn't take long to tidy up. I head outside to be greeted by the amazing, vibrant blue sky. The magnificent view is only obstructed by the horizon of intermittent columns of rock with their greenery towering all around.

I inhale deeply at the crisp morning air, and exhale just as exuberantly. Away from the house, at the edge of the land, I look down and see the life of this prehistoric world going on far below.

Lost for a few moments, I stare at the giant beasts roaming the land at a slow pace, or perhaps not at all. They just seem to graze, like cattle, on giant trees. There are a couple different notable types. Some have really long legs and necks, while others are stout and compact. A flock of two-legged creatures come running around the plateau, darting in and out, and spooking a few of the more lethargic ones. But none attack and I'm left to assume they were simply playing.

Those fast ones have to be as tall as a small house. It's a wonderful feeling to not have to worry about them up here.

Lying on my stomach, I let the sun warm my back while I observe the world free from strife and suffering. The quiet, save for a few strange chirping and cawing noises from below, is calming. Though I've only been awake for a little bit, I could fall asleep again. My heart skips a beat when Ami plops down next to me, and I'm fully alert again.

"You scared me half to death." I look over my shoulder at her.

"You didn't hear me coming?"

"I sure didn't." I return my gaze to the world below.

Ami scoots close, sitting cross-legged, and looks out as well. The silence is awkward, so I fill the void.

"It's nice to be able to see what's below. At least if I fell, I'd be able to see what trouble awaits." I let out a small laugh.

"Don't joke like that." She frowns.

"Problem is, if you fell from here there is no other side to wedge yourself against to slow your speed," Eve says behind us.

Someone climbs on my back. When I look, I see Emma looking over my shoulder. In an un-ladylike manner, Emma spits over the side, and watches it disappear. She giggles while Ami and Eve make disgusted faces.

"You need to shave. You're looking kind of grungy!" Emma says.

"I agree. I need a haircut too," I tell them.

"I think I could manage that," Ami offers.

After lying there for a few more minutes I shift my weight. "I'm going to get up, Emma."

"Why? I'm comfortable!" she protests.

Ami and Eve abruptly lift Emma from my back. I chuckle and head to the stable to care for the horse. Ami joins me, and begins brushing while I shovel. She's finished before I am.

"Thanks, Ami."

"Of course," she says with a smile, and heads around the house.

I finish my chore soon after, and boredom begins to set in already.

Nearing the kitchen door, it's propped open a crack. There are low, but heated tones inside. I'm unable to make out anything being said, so I lean a little closer, and lose my balance. Instinctively, I reach up for the doorknob, but all that does is swing the door open. I'm caught. The door is ripped away from me before I can shut it.

"What do you think you are doing?" Ami questions.

"Nothing. Just standing here." I try and play it off.

"You know, eavesdropping isn't very nice," Eve scolds.

"Well then…" I start to answer, but turn it into a game, running from them and hoping they chase.

I bolt to the side of the house and duck around the corner. Not stopping, I look over my shoulder to see if they're pursuing. They took the bait, and are following. I speed past the stable and laugh. When I reach the next corner I catch a glimpse of Ami in pursuit. Eve has disappeared.

Eve doesn't ambush me from the living room door, which is surprising. Rather, her appearance from the other side of the house startles me, and I jump into the living room, nearly tripping on the way in. I stumble and scramble to exit through the kitchen.

"He's inside!" Eve yells loudly.

By the time she follows me in, I'm pushing through the swinging door into the kitchen. Emma joins the game and I'm cut off. I backtrack and run up the stairs, and to my room, narrowly evading Eve's grasp. The slamming of my door, and their footsteps coming up the stairs vibrates the house. My window is my only escape. It slides up, and I climb into the windowsill just as they push my door open. Our eyes meet. I grin before lunging out. I tuck and roll when I hit, avoiding falling into the garden. Emma sticks her head out of the window and I can hear the other girls yelling.

My time runs short as I regain my balance, Ami and Eve no doubt on my trail again. I run to the first place which jumps into my head, the stable. But the supply shed next to it is a little more enticing. Careful to be quiet about opening and closing the door, I move to the back and hide against the wall. Feet pass by, and I hear Eve calling.

"Rain. Oh, Rain! We're going to get you!" she taunts playfully.

I fight back a laugh.

How long can I actually hide here before they find me?

Not long it would seem, as I hear someone start poking around the stable. Trying to conceal myself with tools, I bump the shovel, and it makes a noise against the handle of another tool. Emma swings the door open, and she has a mischievous grin on her face. She climbs in and closes the door behind her. With the little bit of light seeping in from the cracks I put my finger to my lips. She nods.

"You're not going to give me up, are you?" I whisper.

"Would I do that?"

"I don't know. You might, just to keep the game going."

"Nah. Game's over. I won. Besides, I wouldn't let either of them put their grubby hands on you."

"You know I like Ami, right?"

"Yes. And I'm trying to save you from them *both*." She pokes me in the ribs.

"You don't have to. I can handle myself."

"I don't think you can. They're going to do whatever it takes to win your affection." She sighs and rests her back against me.

"I've told them that my focus is on stopping the vortex."

"Then let me do my job and protect you from them while you do."

I do need to talk to Evalyn about breaking the curse. I haven't seen or heard her in a while. Maybe when I'm done messing around I'll see if I can invoke her.

We become silent. After a few minutes, Emma stirs. She peeks out. When the coast is clear she jumps out, closing the door behind her. Only taking a few more minutes to compose myself, I exit the shed and squint as the sunlight blinds me.

Around the kitchen-side of the house, I come across Agatha doing laundry, and when she sees me she laughs.

"If they find you, you're in trouble," she warns.

"Yeah." I grin widely. "I have a question."

Agatha pauses what she's doing to direct her attention to me. "What is it dear?"

"Evalyn said she can control small things outside of you. Can I communicate with her that way?" I ask.

"I don't know. Evalyn rarely divulges her secrets to me, so you'll have to ask her."

"Perhaps if I enter her room?"

If anything will provoke a response when she's not in Agatha's body, intruding on her personal space will.

"I don't think it's a good idea, Rain," her tone and accompanying frown are serious.

"It'll be all right. She can be mad at me if she wants, but we need some answers." I place my hand on her shoulder briefly before entering the house.

I make my way upstairs and to the far back of the house, to the room on the left I know to be hers. The doorknob is unlocked. The room is dark. There's a light switch just to the right of the doorframe, and I flip it on. A single sized bed, with a heavy patchwork quilt draped across it is set against the wall near her window. At the far end of the room there are several bookshelves filled to the brim, and a large desk in the middle of them.

I step inside, and a chill runs down my back. The hair on my neck stands on end as a heavy presence falls over me. Closing the door quietly behind me, the heavy presence turns dark, and I can nearly feel Evalyn with the despair inside of me.

The pressure in the room builds, like when a thunderstorm is coming. I'm nervous, and aware Evalyn doesn't want me here, but I move forward to the desk. My eyes water at the intense feeling, and I can barely keep them open.

Something rattles on the desk. I stumble over to it while holding my palms against my temples. The pressure is becoming unbearable. I lean against the desk's chair, and watch a pencil jump around as if it were alive. Picking it up, I look it over only to have my hand thrust firmly against a blank piece of paper. My hand moves, and I begin to write something, but not of my own free will.

"What are you doing in my room?! I thought I made it clear this room was off limits!"

"Evalyn, I'm sorry, but I wanted to talk to you alone. I didn't know if you could communicate other than by inhabiting Agatha," I reply verbally.

"Fantastic. Well, I can. What do you want?"

"I wanted to know if you've come across anything which might help us cancel the time vortex."

"I've been researching it. Don't you think I'd have told you if I found something?"

"You've been silent for a while now. I wasn't sure. I wanted to know if there was anything I could do to help."

"You can stay out of my hair!"

I pause for a moment, trying to think of something disarming to say.

"Agatha's looking healthier since you haven't been possessing her. Thank you for taking her health into consideration. Could we keep it that way now since I know we can communicate through other means?"

"I've only been absent because I've been busy. I will need an outlet again."

"She's doing better. I really think we should just keep this as—" I'm cut off as my hand is lifted and slammed down.

She writes again. *"You can't tell me what to do!"*

"Evalyn, I thought we had a breakthrough. We were doing well together."

She slams my hand down again. *"If you just wanted to come here and aggravate me, you can leave!"*

"I understand your frustration, but it's time to let go of the past. You've shown you're remorseful about what happened. I want to help everyone in this house, including you."

"There's no helping me. I may feel some remorse, but I still resent her having the better life. James, her husband, was someone I loved from afar for a very long time. We all went to the same school. But because I was shy, and Agatha was more outgoing, he pursued her instead of me. They got married and had Ami. Ami is the daughter I didn't get to have!"

"But if you hadn't done what you did, you wouldn't know me. I would have died in the woods, and not met any of you. While you may still have an issue with what happened previously, you have to look at where we are now and realize people's lives are better because of it."

The physical pressure from the tension in the room begins to subside while Evalyn is silent on paper. I take it as a sign I'm getting through to her.

"We could make things even better if we break the curse and stop time traveling in a time we all like."

After another long silence Evalyn controls my hand once again, however, less forcefully.

"It scares me. I don't want to cease to exist, and I don't know what will happen if we succeed in reversing my power. My soul is encased in the house because of my power. If we break its bond, it might free me, and I don't know what lies beyond."

"Well, think of it this way. Remember the void. The souls who died in despair collected there at what I guess we could call 'the end of time'. That leads me to believe the souls not in despair would go somewhere else. If you were at peace when we broke the spell you might find yourself in a better place."

"How can I be at peace when what I wanted in life, I can't have? I died heartbroken and angry. How can that change after death?"

"It's something you're going to have to figure out Ev, but I'm willing to bet forgiveness is the first step. I am here for you when you need to talk."

There is silence from her again, but my hand remains pinned to the desk, and I know she's still there. After a few minutes she writes again.

"I've been doing some research through a number of texts for artifacts. Under normal circumstances, in normal hands they're simply relics. But in my hands, they could be the key to stopping my power."

"What kind of artifacts?"

"They can literally be anything someone has endowed with their power. They're how I discovered mine." She pauses for a moment. *"Because I put my power into the house, we might be able to break the cycle with it alone if I can muster the energy, but I'm searching for something which might amplify the power, or negate it."*

"What happens if we find what you're looking for?"

"I don't know. It would be trial and error, like when I put us in the void."

"Do you have any of these artifacts?"

"Only the one I used to heal you, twice. You didn't think you could survive such mortal wounds without intervention did you?"

"That could have been useful information previously."

"You don't want me using Agatha, so there was no reason to tell you."

"If I can learn what you discovered, maybe I can use it too."

"Maybe...Anyway, in my research through a number of historical records I found a tome from the library in Emma's time. I know who you are, but I know you well enough to know you won't like what I found. I will leave the decision in your hands, if you want to know."

Her ominous warning causes my heart to flutter. My breathing increases in speed. With what I've already recalled, and the accusation from Drake, I'm now even more hesitant to know my true self because of her cautionary words. However, despite my anxiety, that part of me which craves closure pushes me.

"I do." My voice is shaky. Beads of sweat form on my forehead.

"Then go over to the far right bookshelf, look on the third shelf down, find the book titled 'Astid Antiquity' and turn to page 952."

She releases my hand, and I set the pencil down. I move to the mentioned shelf and locate the book. When I reach up my hand quivers. My arm doesn't seem to want to grab the book. I force myself to take it and bring it back to the desk. Opening it, I flip through the pages until I reach nine hundred and fifty-two. For a moment I stare blankly straight ahead, rather than at the text. I build up my courage, look at the page, and begin to read. As I do, I am saddened.

The text is forthcoming with information about a kingdom which once flourished, but came under the control of a conniving, brutal young king. This king had conquered lands far and wide only to increase his name and wealth. Though he had never outright murdered anyone or invaded, he was feared by other kingdoms because of a dark assassin rumored to be under his control.

Drake.

Kings and dukes turned up dead, murdered, when they would not pledge allegiance to the king's cause. The clever king would step in after the deed was done, offering the people a ruler under the guise of keeping the peace. This king's name was Tiberius of the Kingdom of Astid. Tiberius was harsh to the people of his lands. He was a greedy ruler. People were taxed so heavily they had difficulty providing for themselves. Many starved to death all over his kingdom, including in the streets of his own city. He lived a lavish life off stockpiles of food and gold, but despite all of his depravity no one dared to question him for fear they might end up imprisoned or dead.

One fall day, Tiberius mysteriously vanished, and his older brother Drake succeeded him with an announcement the king had been slain. Rumors spread of Drake besting Tiberius in battle; however no body was ever recovered. The kingdom fell into disarray under Drake's inability to hold together what Tiberius had built. The people became rebellious, and war was waged for their freedom. Drake led his troops into battle against many of the rebellious cities, however their collective spirit was never broken.

The cities amassed against Asta, and the castle was overtaken. Drake was slain, and after his death the cities became independent again. The great city of Asta, of the Kingdom of Astid, was abandoned for a thousand years, left desolate for nature to reclaim. Overrun by the world reclaiming the land, the area became known as the 'Forest of Hunger' for its history of the two kings with greedy souls.

Finished with the dozen pages on my own life, I am distraught. I close the book and sit with my forehead rested on the edge of the desk, staring blankly at the floor.

After all this time of trying to help people, I was the cause of so much despair. My name is Tiberius, and I caused so much pain to so many people. How could I have been like that? I am a monster!

Standing up, I move away from the desk, leaving things as they are, and exit. The door squeaks shut behind me, and I shuffle heavily to my own room. Inside, I close the door and fall face first on my bed. Pulling my pillow over my head, I try to block everything out, but I am still here. My mind plagues me with destructive thoughts.

How can I live with myself, knowing who I really am? This is where my violent nature comes from. This is why I thrive in conflict. I am a bad person. I don't deserve to live. I don't deserve the second chance I was given, and I don't deserve this life.

I've already put these people through so much just because I lived. Maybe I should die.

I try to clear my mind, thinking of nothing but a black curtain within my mind, and avoiding the horrors I inflicted upon people. I focus on going to sleep and eventually, after struggling with a restless mind and body, I make it there.

But my rest is not peaceful. Instead I dream of horrific things. My memory floods back, and I remember it all. Visions of my evil conquests haunt me, only drawn out of them by knocks on my door.

Depression chokes me, and I ignore them to try and drown my sorrows with sleep. Grumbling, I toss and turn in my bed, finding it difficult to become comfortable as my skin crawls, disgusted with myself. The two sides of me rage against each other, and I am torn between who I am now, and who I was not so long ago. It angers me to be awake, and I find my way back to sleep.

~~~~~~

"Sire, a message," a herald speaks, holding a piece of folded parchment out to me. It's sealed with red wax, the letter D impressed into it.

On my seat of power, I look down over my throne room. I anticipate the message inside the parchment. I slide my finger underneath the seal and break it. Flipping it open slowly, the words 'It is done' are scrawled. I grin maliciously, pleased with myself.

It seems the city of Yaris will need a new king. I wonder how Drake accomplished it this time. A whole lineage must be difficult to kill off. Perhaps poison?

I will need to have a stagecoach prepared for my trip to save their city from anarchy.

I laugh to myself while the herald stands, waiting.

"What are you still standing there for?" I bark at him. "Leave me."

He runs away, nearly toppling my chef who is carrying my lunch platter. I scowl and stroke my chin.

Lucky for him he is not worth Drake's effort.

~~~~~~

Waking, I am deeply disturbed.

Each of the girls call outside my door, trying to coax me out, but I don't want to face them. I'm angry at myself, mortified by my past actions. My heart aches. I have no desire to move, or be more comfortable. The pillow lies on my face and my breath reflects off of it. My eyes water, and I cry silently.

Is it fair of me to not respond? They're worried. But I can't face them. They cling to me now, but when they find out, I'll lose them. Even Eve's previous actions aren't as cruel as mine. How can I go on living? How can I—

Stop your sniveling.

My mind is silenced for a moment in confusion. He is here. Tiberius. Not just who I was before I lost my memory, but a separate voice within. My psyche is fractured.

The girls are relentless at the door. I pull the pillow from my face. Hanging in my view nearby is my sword, the heirloom of Asta, and it's a visual reminder: I am evil. I war against myself.

The anger deepens, and I'm compelled by my urges. Acting on impulse, I snatch the sword from its hook and remove it from its scabbard. It gleams in the sunlight beaming in from the window.

Use it now! Claim this house as yours! Dominate them with your strength!

No! I won't. I'm not Tiberius! I'm not you!

Weak!

Infuriated, I move to the door and fling it open to find Ami, Eve, and Emma. Concern is apparent on their faces, but they have become silent.

"I need you to move…please," I mumble, nearly forgetting niceties.

Ami speaks up, "Rain, we're worried."

"I know. I'm sorry." I avoid eye contact, and my grip on the handle tightens. "I just need you to stand aside."

"Tell us what's wrong," Emma pleads.

Looking up, a rage builds in my soul, and I know it's Tiberius. He pushes for me to swing the sword into the doorframe to incite fear, but I fight his impulses back, and grit my teeth. I close my eyes, and turn my head to focus on fighting him, but his will pushes harder. I grab my head and scream.

"No! This is *my* body now. You can't have it back!"

I shove past the girls, my eyes watering. I nearly fall down the stairs taking them three at a time. Storming through the kitchen, I throw the door open to head outside. It slams against the wall, but I ignore it. In a sprint I head directly for the ledge of the plateau.

Do not do it! It is Asta's legacy! It was destined to be mine!

I don't want it! I don't want anything to do with you or Asta!

Swinging my arms behind me, both hands on the handle, I prepare to hurl the sword. The ledge comes up quick and, as I reach it, I swing my arms forward and release. I yell in rage as it spins and falls toward the ground. On the precipice of the plateau, I look out over the land below.

It will be better this way. I can't stay with them. I can't let them know I'm a murderer.

I lean forward, and the edge of the grass caves under my feet. I begin to fall. But I'm halted, hands and arms grabbing hold of me, gripping tightly to my chest. I'm pulled back from falling over. I struggle against them. I'm overpowered, the ability to end my life stripped from me.

I stare at it. Only feet away lies the answer to my problems, but I'm being pinned down. I succumb and sit in the grass. Bodies encase me.

"I don't want to be Tiberius! I'm Rain!" I push through hiccupping to plead.

"Shh," Ami consoles me and strokes my hair.

Can I go on living as Rain? Can I ignore everything I am as Tiberius? All this time trying to do some good in the world. All this time wanting to know who I am. It's clear that fate is making me atone for my evils.

It is who you are. I was struck down in my prime as king, but I can have it all again. I have power unimagined previously. The world can be mine now. Give me the body!

No! I don't want it! I just want to be who I have been for the past months. I want to be me.

You are nobody! Nothing! I am Tiberius!

I sob for what may be hours, until my body can't produce any more tears. We sit in the grass while the sun makes its way to the other side of the sky. My mind goes blank as Ami holds me, and Eve and Emma rub my arms and back.

"I don't deserve any of you. I don't deserve to be alive," I whisper, my voice hoarse from the physical exertion of sobbing.

"Rain, it's okay," Emma says.

Looking up and staring off into the sky, I avoid eye contact. "It's not okay. You don't know who I am, or the terrible things I've done."

"You've regained all of your memories?" Ami asks, and looks down.

"I have...and I wish I hadn't."

"It *will* be okay." Eve caresses my arm.

"With my memory returned, I am struggling to stay me – Rain. My real name is Tiberius, King of Asta. I've done evil things. I am evil."

They're silent for a few minutes while I watch cloud formations pass overhead.

"Rain," Ami speaks up soothingly. "When you lost your memory, you stopped being the person you were and became who you are now. Tiberius and Rain are not the same person, though the body is the same. Tiberius is dead."

She lies! You are more like me than you want to admit! Can you discount the similarities?

Silence!

Her words linger in the air and I want to believe there's truth in it despite Tiberius's intrusions. With his dark memories and feelings boiling to the surface, I'm certain my fight is only beginning to stay in control of this body, to stay who I am.

"We are here for you," Emma says while leaning over and kissing me on the forehead.

Ami smacks Emma lightly on the head. "Rules."

"They don't apply to me. I'm not in love with him."

Ami smiles, and Eve lets out a small laugh.

Desperate to get my mind away from Tiberius, and the past for a while, I focus on the women instead. "What rules? Is that what you've been so secretive about?"

They all look away from me quickly, and I know if I push, I might just make them slip up.

"I know I've heard something about rules. What are they?"

"We have no idea what you're talking about, Rain," Ami puts emphasis on my name, as if to reassure me.

"Emma will tell me." I sit up and face them.

My mood shifts. Tiberius is pushed further into the recesses of my mind, offering reprieve from the dark depression. Their comforting is beginning to work.

"It's not for me to say." Emma leaps up and stares away from me.

"I don't think so." I grab at Emma's hand. "I know there's something going on, and you want to tell me all about it."

"I can't keep anything from you, my beloved. If you really want to know…" Eve trails off while caressing my chest. She's immediately tackled, and silenced by Ami, her hand over Eve's mouth.

Eve shoves Ami over and tries to speak again. Before she can speak though, Emma leaps on her. Eve rolls, escaping her grasp and turns to face me.

"We established 'Rain rules' for how we're supposed to act around you. Like you can only kiss *me*." Eve laughs maniacally.

"Liar!" Ami yells.

Ami tackles her, and the three of them wrestle around in the grass. Their rivalry and horsing around causes me to chuckle. I can no longer hear Tiberius's voice in my head. Eve springs to her feet, and sprints toward the house. The other girls pursue her.

"I'll tell you all about it later, lover!" Eve yells at me while disappearing into the living room door.

I begin to stand up and follow, but Ami turns back and points at me to indicate I should stay here. She smiles sheepishly and disappears inside. There's playful screaming and stomping in the house.

With their antics, the weight on my heart and mind has been lifted a little, despite the memories still being present. I turn my attention to our slice of paradise up on the plateau, walking to the stable where the horse is lying. I make some clicking noises to gain his attention, and pat on the wooden structure.

"Up!" I coax while I retrieve his brush.

He climbs to his hooves, and I open the stable door to let him out. He moseys out in his own time, and I stop him with a soft pat on his cheek. I use the act of grooming him as a way of keeping my mind off the nightmares rattling around inside my head. Putting my full attention into taking care of him, I become lost in it. The work is satisfying.

When he is clean, I put his harness on and tie him up outside the stable. Moving trampled hay, dirt, and waste to the compost bin I am reminded that the bin needs earthworms in the near future to aid the composting process.

Finished with the horse's stall, I lay fresh hay down from the bales stacked against the house. I refresh his food bin, and checking, his water trough is still somewhat full. I remove the harness and lead him back in. Standing there I stare at him while he starts eating.

"We need to think of a name for you. Charles maybe?" I look at him for approval, but he offers none. "How about Valen? Does 'Valen the Horse' sound good?"

My steed's name was Buster. He was a great horse.

He's silent. Leaving him to eat in peace, I walk to the edge of the plateau nearest me and look out. Left to my memories, both mine and Tiberius's, I remember a number of things from my life before this one.

I vividly recall being a child. The chancellor came into my room to break the news that my parents had been killed, and Drake was gone. It was years later before I discovered Drake was responsible, trying to usurp the throne early. Instead, he was banished by my father's advisors.

Being indulged my entire life until I was of age to take charge of the kingdom, it's no wonder I became a narcissistic madman. I was thirteen! A teenager shouldn't be entrusted to rule! Even now I wouldn't want that responsibility back!

No, you were given the throne. It was my right to lead as I saw fit! Drake only helped accomplish that goal. To think, he had the nerve to attack me when I was about to make him Grand Chancellor. I deserve reverence!

Silence, Tiberius! I am in control of this body! This is mine now, and I won't let you have it back! Asta is no more!

He does as I command and is silent within me. I breathe a sigh of relief. I curse the day I was born, and it occurs to me that I know when that was now.

It doesn't matter. A celebration of the day I was born seems hollow knowing that for the first portion of my life I was spoiled and did terrible things. We may never see that date again, and I would be okay with that.

I head inside to the living room, and find Ami and Eve on the couch facing Emma, who is sitting on the table. They had been speaking before, but as I enter they fall silent. Before pushing through to the kitchen, I look over my shoulder to see them expectantly waiting for me to disappear.

The air is cool from the refrigerator when I open the door. I stand there staring at a number of different items I could eat, but leftover waffles entice me.

Despite our group having grown to five mouths to feed, there always seems to be leftovers.

I devour one, nearly choking myself. I guzzle a glass of water and recover. Even by the sink I can hear the girls' voices, just barely. Craning my neck, I try to make out what's being said, but I fail. Rather than eavesdropping and risking invoking their wrath, I join Agatha in the garden.

"Need any help?" I offer.

Smiling sympathetically, she nods. She hands me a half full watering can while she moves through and picks off dead leaves and bad food.

"I need some earthworms for the compost bin."

"We can search for some when we move the garden. This will be the last harvest. We're going to till the land back next to the apple tree for our next spot."

"Okay."

Agatha looks over at me with a playful gleam in her eyes. "It's a good thing I have a strong young man and a big horse residing at the house now. The tilling will be done in no time."

"I'll be happy to. I'm going to need everything I can to keep my mind away from…"

"It's okay. We will make sure you don't focus on the past. We'll keep you centered in the present." She reaches over to comfort me. Her hand rests on my shoulder.

"You know?" I'm struck with an epiphany the moment the words have escaped my lips. "Of course you know."

"I hope you're not too mad. She discovered it while possessing me. I wasn't sure you would want to know, and Evalyn was just as hesitant."

"No, I'm not mad at you or Evalyn. She warned me, and I looked in the book anyway. I already had an inkling I wasn't a saint."

There is a moment of silence between us, and the wind atop our plateau fills the gap. I blurt to break the silence.

"I'll go stir crazy if I'm not doing something. Do we have a tiller I could strap to the horse?"

"No, but I'm sure we could pick up some materials to make one, or perhaps purchase one in the next civilized time we stop in."

"When you harvest seeds, would you let me know? I'm interested in learning."

"Of course dear." Her regular, cheery smile returns.

After a couple trips to the spigot to refill the can, I manage to properly wet everything. Returning the watering canister to Agatha, I put my arm around her shoulder as she admires the garden. She leans into me. Our imitation mother-son bond leaves me feeling comfortable enough to ask a question bothering me.

"Am I a burden? I've brought a lot of baggage here. You have three more travelers than you used to, and I've put us all in danger."

Agatha looks at me and replies bluntly, "You aren't a burden. You've gotten us *out* of a few jams, and if it weren't for you our lives would be very boring."

"Thanks, Aggy." I kiss her on the side of the head.

"Please don't be so hard on yourself. You're a new man."

Releasing her, I snatch up a ripe, delicious looking tomato. Deep red, and firm to the touch, I pick it and wipe it off on my shirt. It sprays tomato juice and seeds when I bite in. Instinctively, I stick my neck out and jump back to narrowly avoid drenching my shirt. My face is another story. Agatha laughs. She pulls a napkin from the clothesline, wets it at the faucet, and comes back to wipe my face.

With a smirk she comments, "You remind me of my husband: strong, but in need of a little mothering now and then."

This makes me avert my eyes, and I feel sad she doesn't have him. "Did you ever find out what happened to him?"

Though a smile persists on her face, I can tell she's been drawn into sad memories. I realize I must have upset her.

"Never mind. It's okay. You don't have to answer." I try to backtrack.

"He was out when Evalyn died. I'm certain she held on just long enough to wait until he was gone. Of course, because he wasn't here, he didn't come with us when the vortex swallowed us." She sighs. "We landed back in Chas near our starting time once. It was about seven years for us, but only three for him. When I found him he had lost his grip on reality. He became scared, claimed I was a hallucination. He wouldn't come see Ami."

"I'm so sorry, Agatha." I hug her tightly and sense a well-hidden despair in her. "I shouldn't have asked."

"No, it's all right. I wept for many nights after, but it's only a sad memory now."

"Well, no matter how deep into crazy I fall, I'll always be here for you and Ami." I smile and try to bring a little light to the darkness.

I let her go, and we stand in silence, watching as the sun nears the edge of the sky. It has become a little chillier, both the air and because the conversation died. The apple tree catches my eye, and the branches look to be in need of trimming.

"Do we have anything to trim the tree?" I ask.

"Yeah, we have some branch clippers with the other tools in the basement. I'll show you where they are tomorrow," she says, her normal cheeriness returning.

"It's about time we go start dinner, isn't it?" I smile.

"You might be right." She nods, and I hear her stomach grumble.

We laugh and head inside.

~~~~~~

Finished with cleaning up after an uneventful dinner, I retire to my room. With too much time to think, my mind is brought back to who I used to be. While I don't want to revisit the memories, it is unavoidable as Tiberius's consciousness presses against mine.

"Tiberius, it is time," Ralig the Advisor speaks.

"Do I have to? I do not remember what to do."

"Young prince, we have been over the coronation procedures a dozen times now. Have confidence you will remember what to do when you are in front of your subjects."

I stand in front of a full-length mirror, adjusting my white gown and cloth pauldrons. My hair is a mess, but Ralig brushes it down.

"Just remember what we discussed…" Ralig reminds me.

Thinking of Ralig draws me into more of my past. With my light off, I sit at the head of my bed. I lean on the open window's sill and stare out as stars appear one by one in the sky.

Drake killed our parents and was exiled. I grew up under the care of several advisors to my parents, but Ralig was always there — he corrupted me. The coronation was smooth, and I was given the crown and scepter to rule the people.

But he had already been working, planting the idea in my head to 'liberate' the nearby city from its unworthy ruler. He persuaded me into giving up my innocence under the guise of his family being held unlawfully for a tax they didn't owe.

Lies. He manipulated me. He suggested sending a small band of warriors pretending to be bandits to kill the duke, and it was done. I came in after the duke's death: under the banner of 'peace and order', I took control.

He taught me everything he knew about deviously meddling in other kingdom's affairs. The second land I conquered was a small town, through subterfuge. I convinced the local mayor an attack from outlying lands was imminent and he would be safe under our banner. He swore allegiance to the Kingdom of Astid, and me. But I realized then it took too much effort to win people over.

Then word from Drake came, and I saw an opportunity to expedite the expansion of my kingdom. With Drake as my assassin, I was able to sweep away the old and offer 'new'.

Ralig corrupted me, and Drake furthered my darkness.

My mind turns away from rehashing my past.

I am no longer king, and Drake has no reach here.

Sleep creeps in and I take refuge in the covers.

~~~~~~

My night was filled with no dreams, no nightmares. I wake feeling a little refreshed.

After changing into clean clothes and putting on the crystal necklace, I stop for a moment to look out my window at a pre-dawn sky. The outdoors calls me. I bring my dirty clothes down with me, depositing them in the basket near the clotheslines.

The air is cold. I breathe deeply. Though I've had haunting thoughts, and my memories have come back, I refuse to let it cripple me right now. I return to the kitchen, and keep my mind busy cooking breakfast. Smells of sausage, potatoes, and onion brings in the first of the women, and I'm surprised which one.

Eve sits down, elbow on the table and presses her face into her palm. Her eyes are barely open, but I smile anyway.

"Food is your motivator today I see," I joke.

"Whatever it is you're cooking smells good, but it's not why I'm up. Had a nightmare about being caught in the firefight which killed my parents," she mumbles.

"Ah, I'm sorry." I bring her a plate of food. "Do you want to talk about it?"

"Thanks, babe. But no. I'm not in the mood."

The others wander in at different intervals. Agatha first, then Emma, and finally Ami. I serve them each when they come in, and when the last has been served I sit to eat.

"This time we're in is nice. Because of my personal 'issues', I'm glad I don't have to worry about others and the despair," I tell them.

"Rain, if you need to talk, we're here for you," Ami answers with a mouth full of food.

"I'll make sure to call on you all as needed while I dredge through my past."

Despite sitting down last, I am the first to stand up from the table. I clean up, and put a bowl of leftovers into the refrigerator. Keeping busy, I head downstairs to the tool room to search for the branch trimmers. It dawns on me that I don't know what they look like. Footsteps approach from behind. It's Agatha. She moves over to the far wall and pulls down what looks like a large pair of curved scissors with two long handles.

"Here you go. Don't hurt yourself." She hands them to me.

"Thanks, Aggy."

"If you need help, just let one of us know." She places her hand on my shoulder briefly before passing me on her way back upstairs.

A light mist covers the plateau when I step outside. Low clouds are moving past, covering things in a light fog. The tree is easy to navigate, and I work my way around it from the top down. Spiraling around, I finally reach the bottom an hour or so later.

I take a break on the edge of the cliff, my legs dangling over. The fog has burned off and dark spots flutter through the air in between other plateaus in the far distance.

This didn't take as long as I hoped it would. Maybe I could go spend some more time with Evalyn and figure out what we do when we gather some of these artifacts. What happens if we do?

I'm no longer a king. I have a new life here as a member of this household, with duties and responsibilities.

But we should be rightfully ruling. The heirloom was the proof. Our ancestor saw it, knew it! If Asta does not exist wherever we stop and rest permanently, then we breech the local government. We can take control once more!

Though Tiberius spouts mostly nonsense, he's right on the heirloom. It was proof. A reminder of what I used to be, and the kind of person I no longer am. It may have been useful to serve as a pledge to not becoming an evil man again.

When we shift through time, it will be lost forever. Can I get it back somehow?

I lie down. Ami exits the kitchen and heads my way. Her hips sway and draw my attention. I can't help but stare at her curvy figure, dressed in tight jeans and a red, V-neck, long sleeve shirt. She's biting her lower lip.

"Hey."

"Hi."

"How's it going out here?"

"I'm done with trimming. Just need to toss this all over the cliff there, and then I'll have nothing to do."

"It's weird, isn't it? Not having some adventure going on, I mean." She sits next to me.

"I am going stir crazy to the point I'm contemplating going to find my sword." I let out a sigh.

"You know that's insane, right? Even if you could climb down, how would you get back up?"

"I hadn't thought that far." I stand up and brush myself off. "How about we cut my hair instead?"

"Sounds like a better plan." She smirks.

Heading inside, she leads me to the bathroom and holds her finger up, indicating I should wait here. She returns with a chair, towel, and scissors. I sit, and she drapes the towel across my chest, tucking it into the neck of my shirt.

"Do you care how it's cut?" she asks.

"Not really. I just want it out of my face."

She begins cutting, and I watch locks fall. I close my eyes and relax, losing my sense of time while she cuts away. My head becomes lighter. I peek through my peripheral vision at the mirror, but I can't catch a clear view. Leaving for just a moment, she moves to the sink to wet a bar of soap, and grab a razor.

While she's busy away from me, I turn my head to see. She has cut my hair quite short. It's messy, but I can tell the sides are significantly shorter than the top. Returning, she uses the soap to lather up the back of my neck, and takes care to not cut me while bringing the hairline up. Wiping off my neck, she looks me over.

"Let's wet your hair and see how it looks," she says removing the towel from around my neck.

At the sink, I run my head under the running faucet while she sweeps up. When I run my fingers through it, it spikes up and looks interesting. It reminds me, though, of the way Drake liked to keep his hair.

"Shall we do your face next? You only look like half of a hobo now." She giggles.

"Sure, why not." I shrug.

In front of the mirror, she lathers up my face, and shaves with care. Slowly she runs the blade across my skin, and I watch her as she concentrates on not cutting me. Our eyes meet a few times, but she isn't distracted.

I have to be strong against Tiberius, against my past. For her. I can't let her down.

"There. Now take a shower, otherwise you'll itch. I'll get you a towel and fresh clothes, and leave them at the door." She reaches up and strokes my chin.

"Thanks, Ami." I grab her hand, and hold it on my face.

Our eyes lock, and I dive deep into her brilliant blue eyes. A few moments pass. I contemplate drawing her in for a kiss, but a noise in the hallway startles us both.

She drops her hand and leaves me to my shower. I take my time, letting the hot water soothe my body. It washes away both hair and tension. When I'm finished, I shake off a bit before stepping out, and retrieve the garments left for me. I dry off, and put on the clothes and shoes provided.

I deposit my dirty clothes in the washbasin in the yard, and walk around to admire the calm skies. Circling, I head for the tree to find Emma has taken over my job, throwing the branches off the edge of our plateau.

"Thanks." I smile at her. "I was actually coming back to finish."

"Wow! You're handsome!" she exclaims when she sees my new look. "I'm going to have to beat Ami and Eve away with a hoe."

"Thanks, I guess."

"Don't let them take advantage of you. I see how they both look at you. If they try, just yell for me and I'll come to your rescue."

I laugh, and we finish tossing the branches over the side. Watching the last branch fall, I estimate about how far my sword could have made it with my throw.

Get it back.

They aren't going to like it, but I have to have it back. It may be a reminder I used to be an evil person, maybe one day I can use it to redeem myself.

I caress the round gem hung from my neck.

But jumping from this height and using a shockwave, even with my crystal, I'd likely be hurt severely. I just can't anticipate how I'll be thrown upon the shockwave impact.

As a sign my thoughts of retrieving it might be valid, dark shadows appear, darting and swooping across the tops of nearby plateaus. Ear piercing screeches echo through canyons, and a flock of large, leathery winged creatures approach. Their bodies are minimal compared to their enormous wingspan, but they don't look like any sort of bird I've seen before.

Emma gasps, and lets out a scream as the creatures make their way around the plateaus toward ours. She makes a break for the house. When I look back, she's gained the attention of the other house members.

"Flying monsters!" Emma screams while running past them, and slams the door shut.

Do it!

"This is my chance," I mumble to myself.

Get it back!

Quiet, Tiberius.

Looking at the creatures, and then back at the women, I focus on Ami. She sees it in my eyes. She knows what I'm about to do. I grin. The flying reptiles approach closer to our plateau. I run back a dozen or so feet.

"Rain, no!" Ami runs at me and yells.

I ignore her. Timing it as the creatures near the side of our plateau, I begin running. Their flock begins a pass, and I leap with an extra push from a shockwave. Launching myself out, I soar through the air and find myself heading directly for them. A few hundred feet drop seems significant, but it passes quickly as I arc toward their pack. I near the creatures and connect with one.

It squawks and shrieks in protest. I slide along its leathery hide, trying to grip onto it. We spiral out of control, falling out of the sky together. It tries to snap at me with its beak, craning its neck around, while at the same time trying to regain flight.

I hear faint screaming, and look over my shoulder. Several hundred feet above, small figures peek over the edge. We tumble a few hundred feet more toward the ground before it finally spreads its wings out again, catching an upward air current.

Sliding from one wing toward the other, I catch its neck. It protests and tries to bite me, but I punch it in the snout and it leaves me alone.

I am empowered taking control, and it finally dawns on me: *This whole time I have been subconsciously seeking out conflict. It was Tiberius attempting to surface.*

It was me. I am what kept them out of danger. My prowess. My cunning.

I'm brought back to reality when the flying creature dives toward the ground at a significant speed. When another set of screeches comes from above, I fear for my life. Several of its flock are pursuing. One swoops down to try and grab me with a pair of mighty talons, but I slip underneath the creature's neck. The only thing keeping me from falling is my death-grip on its hide.

Coming up quickly on the ground, I assume it's going to attempt to dislodge me, or worse, smash me. We're coming in fast, approaching a tree, and I let go. The branch I hit is large. My head smacks against it. Dizzy, I do my best to hang on for dear life. The winged creature swings up, and swoops back around to grab me with its talons. I'm forced to let go of my branch to avoid it.

I tumble, hitting many branches on my way down, finally coming to rest on another thick branch. My body aches. There's a knot on my head, and I can feel a near future number of bruises across my body. The leather-winged beasts screech. I'm no longer in their sight. Their sounds recede, and it appears they've given up.

I guess that went better than it could have. I could be dead. Now, where am I? I'll need to find my bearings before I can start looking for the sword.

Sitting for a few moments, I gather my composure. That composure is lost when a long necked, scaly creature reaches its head into the tree, and begins to eat leaves right near me. My heart beats quickly, and I worry it might be omnivorous. I sit completely still as it takes little or no notice of me.

When it's gone, I breathe a sigh of relief and climb down the tree. A pool of water lies below, surrounding the tree. I drop into it with a splash. My clothes are soaked, but it's the least of my worries.

I'm in the middle of a number of the long necked creatures mingling about. I hug the tree closely. One misstep on their part would crush me. There is a break in the herd, and I push through the waist high pond to shore, toward the column of rock the house sits on.

Okay, focus. Even throwing it as hard as I could, it couldn't have gone far. It was about at the apple tree when it left my hands. I'm going to have to search in a pattern since I don't have the advantage of a bird's eye view.

Looking up, I try to figure out where the tree is, but it all looks the same from the bottom. I begin by starting at the base of my plateau and search for potentially familiar landmarks. Seeing a group of pools to my left, I think they could be ones I saw from above. Moving along toward my starting point, I keep my eyes peeled for any gleam of metal.

Hours pass as I search in a pattern starting at the base of the plateau, taking me out several hundred yards, and then doubling back a few feet away. The sun drags across the sky, and there's no sign of my heirloom.

Perhaps it dropped into a pool, and that's why I can't find it.

Coming to the edge of one near me, I look in and try to find a gleam, but the depths are obscured as it becomes dark in the valley. Looking up I expect to see a cloud, but instead a dark circle begins to envelop the sky. It's black on the underside, and I'm unable to see beyond it.

Despite its massive size, and the fact it's moving swiftly through the sky, not a sound is heard from it beyond the strong wind now coursing between the rocky columns towering above me.

While I'm entranced by the darkness, out of the corner of my eye I notice the enormous creatures have begun to scatter. A stronger gust of wind kicks up dirt and leaves. I throw my arm over my face to shield against the debris. The wind dies down. Able to open my eyes again, the sky is dark for several miles across, and the object is till high above. Only far away, past several towers of rock, can light be seen again.

Standing in near complete darkness I am reminded of the despair collective as it took over the white void.

Could this be the despair before the void?

But before I can think any further along those lines, a multitude of bright white lights beam down from the underbelly of darkness, and one falls directly on me.

Squinting and holding my hand over my eyes, I look up and try to understand what's happening. Long dark shadows descend within the beams of light. A whirring noise fills the air. I realize I'm in danger.

A shadow appears in the light column I'm in, causing it to look like an eclipse within an eclipse. I jump out of the way just in time to not be crushed. The ground is pummeled with a number of large objects. The ground quivers. Explosions of dirt, plants, and water fly up everywhere.

When I recover, I recognize the objects: numerous metallic cylinders with their foreign symbols. All around me as far as the dark circle covers, the cylinders collide with the ground.

Strangely though, the lights and cylinders are only being sent to the bottom of the valley; there are still a number of dark voids in the sky over the top of the plateaus.

That would make sense, I guess, based on what we had seen before. They were scattered strategically. So I'm witnessing their placement? But who is sending them?

The cylinders begin to light up as I had seen before, and their doorways open up. A familiar white light beams out, and I realize if they're open it means something is coming out. Running to a nearby tree I hide myself as best I can.

My curiosity takes hold, and I peer around the trunk to wait and watch for what comes out. The beams of light disappear from up above and the dark circle moves farther up into the sky. Light from the sun begins flooding back in as the dark mass becomes just a black disc as big as the sun.

I really hope the girls stay inside…Who am I kidding? They're outside looking down and watching. Maybe I don't always seek out trouble. There's no way I could have known this would happen only a short time after coming down here.

With my only defense currently being my shockwaves, I wait to see what emerges, and to assess any threat. Two different types of beings emerge, both bipedal.

The first type is tall, somewhat blocky and muscular, wearing a very strange type of gold colored armor that tightly hugs the being's body, and black gloves. Its oval, lengthwise-elongated head is covered with a helmet. A darkened pane masks its face entirely, but I assume they can see through it. They appear to have no weapons; but that doesn't say much. The palms of their hands appear to be about the size of my forearm. Being hit with a closed fist would likely result in broken bones.

The other humanoid creatures are much smaller, at least half the size of the obvious guard-beings, and wear no armor. They do, however, wear a strange band-like device which wraps around their head, with a large yellow lens covering one of its four large eyes. Their complexion is pale white; their bodies are skinny and appear frail; their heads are disproportionate and, like their larger counterpart, it elongates backward from their bodies. Only a few are dressed in very sharp, shiny, flowing attire that matches the color of their bald skin. In their hands they carry some sort of thin, white tablet which reminds me of Emma's PayPad.

More of the smaller beings appear than the larger ones. They begin to spread out, observing, and appearing to write on their tablets. The guards pace. The small ones take samples of foliage, water, and I presume air, in clear containers.

As a smaller one nears the tree I'm hugging, I duck behind a fern to avoid detection. I try to find a place I can escape to, but I'm surrounded. As I focus on not being identified by the one taking a sample of the tree I am hiding behind, I hear another one shout in a strange language. One of the smaller ones has discovered me from behind.

I guess it's adventure time.

A couple of the bigger ones bellow in their language, and start toward me, heavy arms swaying at their sides. I jump from the fern's, and walk backwards toward my column of rock. They start to circle me, the larger ones extending their right arms outward. Unsure of what I should do, I prepare to defend myself, arms out in front of me.

Annihilate them! They are threatening you!

No! I won't attack them first.

Several of the smaller ones converse, and seem to examine me from afar, appearing puzzled. They speak rapidly. One of the smaller ones tries to step toward me, but is stopped by one of the guards dropping his hand and holding it back. To the dismay of the guard, the smaller one pushes its hand aside, and steps toward me.

Do it! Kill the monsters!

Rather than sending a shockwave at them as Tiberius's consciousness suggests, I look behind me, throw my arm back, and unleash a small burst. Dust plumes upward from the shockwave impact. The guard pushes the small one back, and readies to attack me. I step back a few more steps, but run into the steep incline of rock. The smaller one reasserts itself, barking furiously at the guard.

Turning its attention to me, it nears again, putting both arms out to the side. I'm unsure if I should take it as a gesture to indicate it has no ill will. I keep one hand firmly raised, pointed at it. It moves its arms in a soft manner, and lowers them all the way to its sides. I'm not sure if it wants me to copy.

It turns back to one of its smaller companions, speaks rapidly, and then returns its gaze to me. Because of its four eyes, I don't know where to focus, and so my eyes dart from one to the next. The one it spoke to disappears while we stand there locked in a stalemate. When it returns it hands something small to the one addressing me.

Turning its head, it shows me a small black item stuck in its almost non-existent ear. It shows me what's grasped in its long fingers, and it's the same. A small, black sphere. It demonstrates by pointing to its ear and then to mine. With its hand open, palm up, it takes a few steps forward cautiously toward a rock in between us, and sets the black sphere down.

I wait for the being to retreat back to the group, and then slowly move to pick it up. The guards shuffle nervously, and stand at the ready with their meaty hands ready to grab me. Without taking my eyes off of them, or lowering my hand, I pick up the object and bring it into my vision. It's round and smooth like a polished pebble.

The one who set it down waves its hands at me, and points at its ear. I do as instructed, and slowly slip it in. It's soft, and puts no unnecessary pressure on the ridges. It squeals, causing me pain. My hand instinctively goes up to my ear, but before I can rip it out the noise dies down.

"*Prekoto vantose,*" it lets forth what sounds like a simple command while putting its hand to its throat, but I don't understand.

"What is this?"

It taps its throat. "This." I understand a word in my language in a masculine sounding voice, overlapping its original language.

"What just happened?" I ask.

He urges me to keep talking by keeping one hand on its skinny neck, and waving its other hand in a circle.

"All you did was copy one of my words."

"Copy. All. You. Words."

"Is that how you learn? You learn more just by me speaking?" I tilt my head a little.

"Speaking. More. More words."

"Should I just spout out a random assortment of words for you?"

He nods quickly, and I know he understands me.

"Yes. No. Dirt. Water. Air. Tree. Sky. What are you?"

"Wait, I think we have it now. Yes, yes, we do. Hello, can you understand me?" he replies with his original voice overlaid by the translation.

I'm astonished as it appears to now be able to fluently communicate. "I can. You're going to have to tell me how you did that."

"Simple. Through your speech patterns, sentence structure, and syntaxes, the *Trauna* in your ear accessed your brain activity. We were able to ascertain enough information. It seems we already have a version of your language on file and our system is now overlaying the translation."

"'Trauna' didn't translate. Is it the name of the device, or something we don't have a word for?"

"It is the device."

"What was 'prekoto vantose'?"

"Loosely translated; I need you to speak. What are you doing here? We were not aware your species had acquired the ability to travel the stars."

"I have no idea what you're talking about. Are you sure this trauna thing is working?"

"You are from *Earth* are you not?" He squints all four eyes, and the word 'Earth' comes out in my language with no translation needed.

"The word 'earth' is used in my language to describe the ground or dirt, but I've never heard of a place with that name. What are *you* doing here?" I shift my weight and lower my hand a little.

"No. I suppose not. Black eyes. Different from Earth." I start to interrupt him to explain my eyes, but he doesn't give me the opportunity. "This is supposed to be a wildlife refuge planet. It should not be inhabited by sentient beings. If you are not from Earth, where are you from?"

"This is the world in which I belong. What are you?"

"We are Vraditi. Or was that not what you meant? Let me restate. We are ecologists, transplanetary migration specialists."

My mind reels.

The idea of different bipedal, non-human creatures is still fairly new. But now encountering ones who can speak and have technology far beyond what my species has accomplished, I don't know what to think.

"I'm not sure what that means."

"We move species across planets to further their survivability and development."

I mumble to myself, "I thought I'd seen everything, but now I'm dealing with life beyond this planet too?" The being overhears me.

"You were unaware there is life beyond your planet?"

"Yes. Until now, I don't think anyone on the planet thought about it."

"There are more of you?" He tilts his head to the side.

Leery, I keep silent about my companions for the moment. "Let's just say, yes…and no."

"Scan shows four additional Human life forms nearby." It moves its finger on the pad it carries. Looking back at its brethren, then returning his stare to my direction, he shows no facial expression. "We are confused. Why is it yes, and no?"

"Stay away from them!" I threaten him with my open palm.

The guards starts to restrain me, but the one I've been speaking with yells out.

"Stay!" He looks around and they become still again. There is nothing in his facial expression to indicate malice toward me, but I'm angered at the thought of these beings confronting the women.

Eve could probably handle a few, but who knows how many of these things there are.

"Please. We intend no harm. We are just seeking knowledge. If there are four others, why would your answer be 'no'?"

I grind my teeth, unsure of just how much to divulge. Their demeanor is calm, and their guards' movements are calculated. They are threatening because they're not my species, technologically advanced, and far more intelligent. The harm in answering with little detail seems minimal.

"I had hoped to conceal the existence of my family, but it's not the reason I said no. There will be more of my kind, in the future."

"Explain." He cocks his head.

"The five of us are out of our original times. We've seen the future of this world which we call Salvoa."

"Log. Link planet name 'Salvoa' to '*reknos tavol* four'." He speaks out loud, but not to me. His attention is returned to me. "You have mastered time displacement?"

"No. We travel randomly."

"We must know more." He waves for me to come over. "Please, let us share information."

I hesitate. "How do I know I can trust you?"

"You do not. Consider, if we wanted we could extract all information you possess without consent. However, we are a peaceful species. We would ask that you share instead, and will not take more than you give," he states, and waves off the other members of his species.

For a moment they hesitate, but he commands them in their language, and it doesn't translate. They disperse, returning to their duties while I am left with the one I've been speaking with. My apprehension eases, if only slightly. I remain guarded, and hope they are as he says.

"Sharing? How about we start with introductions. My name is Rain."

"Rain? Named after the precipitation that falls from the sky. *Uokos.* Interesting. My name is Quva." He brings his hands up to shoulder height, elbows bent, palms toward his body.

I copy him. "Is this a form of greeting?"

"Negative." Quva puts his hands down. "Certain gestures are reserved for those with rank in our society. This particular position indicates 'Mission Second Command' as a rank, and is used in formal greeting. Outsiders to our culture are not assigned rank and therefore there is no need to salute."

"Understood." I drop my hands. "Standing here is awkward."

"Come, I shall prepare a better space for us to talk."

He turns and begins to walk swiftly away from me, only looking back for a moment to make sure I follow.

I fast-walk to keep up with his lengthy strides, but I walk a few feet off to his left. Quva looks at me expectantly, but even at this angle I can tell he's focusing on two locations at once when his head shifts a little back and forth. It's strange, and I don't know if he's truly paying attention to me.

"Please, tell me how you travel through time." He focuses all four eyes on me, yet still adeptly dodges obstacles.

"I will keep it short, for simplicity sake. A woman had an innate ability to travel through time at will. Something went wrong, and now a vortex takes us to a certain location at a random time—"

"What kind of 'innate ability'?" Quva interrupts me. "Is it the same as what you did to the rocks?"

"I've witnessed different types of abilities. Mine is not the same as Evalyn's. It's like channeling extra energy from within to make things happen around us."

"Do you mean *alkos*?"

"That word didn't translate."

"Strange." He seems genuinely perplexed, and we stop for a moment. "Can you move things with your mind, just by thinking about them?"

"No. And I haven't seen anyone that can."

"I would like another demonstration. I am interested in taking some readings." He lifts up his white pad and taps on it a few times.

Seeing no harm in demonstrating my ability to defend myself if he isn't being honest, I stop and turn to the rocks where none of his species are working. I hold a hand up, and build a shockwave so massive when it hits the ground a few hundred yards away, it sends an explosion of dirt and rock spraying outward from the impact point. Quva jumps back, startled. I turn back and smile.

No doubt the girls are watching and making wild assumptions right now. Eve is probably going insane, thinking I'm down here fighting.

"This is astounding! You would make a fascinating subject to study further, if you would be willing to undergo some stress tests."

"I'm not sure I like how that sounds." I scowl.

"I assure you, no harm will come to you. Under observation, we've never seen your species, or any cousins to it, manifest anything like this without the aid of technological advancements. If you are not from Earth, we must assume you have similar origins, and that is an extraordinary discovery and research opportunity we would like not to miss.

"We invite you to be a guest aboard our *tearikan*. Our star-ship. There we would ask you to exert your power while we take more accurate measurements and readings, as well as biological and neurological tests for our catalogue of species." Quva points to the black disc in the sky, but keeps his eyes focused on me.

"If I were to agree to something like that, there would be terms. My companions are off limits; do not involve them. If you try to kidnap or harm me, I won't hesitate to rip your ship in half." I'm firm when I speak, cautious to keep their interactions friendly.

"You are still hesitant. This is understandable. We can continue to talk down here to familiarize ourselves with one another until you are comfortable." Quva holds up a hand and turns away from me. "Allow me a few moments and then we can continue."

"Take your time."

Quva turns, and begins to order the others around with various tasks such as herding and preparation of the land for construction, making me question what they're doing. I wander around nearby, watching them work. As I do, I have an epiphany.

I bet they'll come across the sword.

You'll need it to defend yourselves against these creatures!

I will not kill them unprovoked. I am not a savage.

"Quva, I lost an…object…down here. It's a forged, sharpened piece of metal. If your team finds it, I would appreciate its return."

"Understood," he replies without looking back, moving to one of the cylinders.

His long fingers press on several of the strange symbols, and then issues a command to it which doesn't translate. The cylinder spurs to life and several beams of light from above converge on a clearing a few yards away.

In the blink of an eye, a structure has appeared out of nowhere where the beams had shone. It's short, white, and spirals into a gentle peak. It reminds me of a gift presented to me as Tiberius – a seashell from the beach of a faraway ocean. I'm startled.

Quva motions for me to follow, and when we arrive at the 'shell' he presses his whole palm on what looks to be a seamless wall. A door appears, sliding upward into the structure with a hum. He enters, and I follow behind into a single room with a shiny, white round table and a couple of white chairs. There are no lights inside, yet I can see perfectly because the walls give off a soft white light.

"How did this just appear?" I ask.

"One of our technological advancements is the ability to rearrange molecules to create different things. We developed a program to instantly change them from one thing to another in set patterns. In this case we used particles in the air to make this." He moves to one of the chairs and sits down, setting his pad down in front of him.

"This must be an extremely useful technology." I sit down directly across from him, and cross my arms while leaning on the table.

"Indeed it is. It allows us to be able to construct what we need, where we need, in order to facilitate whatever species we are currently transporting."

"So, are you preparing to stay here?"

"No, our stay is temporary, but the species we salvaged from a dying planet will be transplanted here."

Leaning back in my chair an alarm rings in my head. I stroke my chin thoughtfully.

The lizard-men. It makes perfect sense. The cylinders are planted by this alien race, the Vraditi, and they're constructing a habitat. I wonder, if I stop them, can I save all those tribal people? What would it do to the timeline?

"You seem deep in thought," Quva states.

"Indeed I am. So you're constructing a place for a species to live. I'm certain I already encountered them."

"You have?"

"A large, bipedal, scaled lizard creature."

"You are a fascinating specimen already. Time travel and knowledge of the species we carry. You must tell me more. Would you like something to eat while we talk?"

My stomach grumbles. Despite the hesitation urging me to be a little more cautious, I allow myself to have a little faith that they won't harm me. "Please."

"By the shape of your teeth, I would assume you are omnivorous." Quva squints two of his eyes in what I perceive is a questioning manner.

I nod, and Quva taps on his pad rapidly. Two beams of light shine down from the ceiling to directly in front of me. When the light disappears, a plate is left with bite size chunks of seared meat, and some brown paste next to it. Since there are no utensils, I assume he thinks I'll eat with my hands. I pick up a piece of meat and cautiously put it into my mouth. The meat is tender. The taste is exotic, and a little spicy. It's unfamiliar but delicious.

"With this technology," I start. "I wonder why you'd need to study my power. What you have is clearly superior."

"True, it is superior, but we rely on our machines to do it for us. No one of my race, or any other race we have encountered has a natural ability to make things happen simply by willing it." He nods. "Do many of your people have *alkos*?"

"Only a handful I know of. And their abilities differ. One had the ability to heal; another had the ability to move so fast he appeared invisible." I chew a few more meat-cubes vigorously, extracting the flavor.

"If any of your companions have an ability, it would be a terrible waste to miss an opportunity to observe."

"They don't, so put it out of your mind."

"Understood. How long have you been traveling through time?"

"Several months, but with everything I've seen, it feels much longer. How long have you been traveling the stars?"

"I have been traveling most of my life. This most recent trip has taken one hundred and twenty days, calculated at sixty hours per day. Since you have future knowledge, we would like to know what you know about the creatures you encountered, to compare." Quva finds an opening to return to the conversation of the lizard-men.

"The encounter happened during a primitive time. I'm not sure I should say much more than that. Tell me though, is this the only planet they can live on? There must be many other planets out there."

"We had several other habitats as candidate locations, however this was the closest and happened to suit the *Tarak* nicely. Your question indicates a negative encounter."

I become silent while I eat. Quva's four, bulbous eyes are trained on me, watching with extreme curiosity. He taps on his pad again, and two glasses appear with a clear liquid in them, one for me, and one for him. When I lift the glass up to my lips I expect water, but am pleasantly surprised when there is a sweet and fruity taste to it. Quva drinks his as well.

"How do you like the food?" he asks.

"The meat was good, but the paste looked unappealing. What kind of animal did the meat come from?"

"Technically, none. We simply created it based on one of the scans and patterns of a livestock creature. *Val.* The creature has a large scaly endoskeleton, features two long necks with separate heads and wanders about on all fours eating vegetation."

"I see. If I allow you to scan me, you aren't going to recreate my tissues and eat them are you?" I ask seriously.

Quva huffs, sounding offended. He speaks sharply, "We never eat the meat of sentient creatures or ones with the ability in their *erixet* to become sentient!"

"I didn't mean to offend, but I felt it was an important question for a species with your power." I pause to calm the tension. "*Erixet* didn't translate."

"Simply put, their building blocks."

Quva calms, and leans forward, resting his chin on an open palm while his elbow is on the table. He stares, as if trying to study me with his eyes. I know he wants to ask me again to willingly submit to their testing. I lean back and stretch.

"I'll allow you to observe me. But my terms are firm. Keep my warning in mind."

"Noted!" Quva's excitement can't be contained. "Your information will be a marvelous addition to our archive!"

"When we're done, I'd appreciate if you would transport me to a location of my choosing."

"Acceptable," Quva agrees and stands up, grabbing his pad. "Shall we go up to the ship then?"

Quva moves to the door and beckons me to follow. Upon exiting the building, the bright light from the sun blinds me momentarily. My eyes adjust, and my breath is stolen away by what I behold.

In the short time I ate, and we conversed, his team has changed the land in the canyons completely. None of the prehistoric creatures can be seen. All of the vegetation has been removed, and the land is now blanketed with a light purple substance. While Quva walks toward the closest cylinder, I notice it seems to be embedded further into the ground, the purple coating surrounding its base.

I catch up to him while he is already pressing on a few of the symbols. He turns, and waves for me to enter the white light inside the doorway.

If I hadn't done this before, I might be a little more hesitant. But I at least know this won't kill me.

A familiar sensation washes over when I enter, and my body rushes upward at a great speed. I halt abruptly, and my eyes adjust. I am standing on an enormous white platform centered inside a very large structure which reminds me of a honeycomb. Though the exterior of the ship hung in the sky is large and round, this enormous, oval area indicates I'm only seeing a fraction of the interior, despite this area spanning many stories up and down from where I am.

The walls reach high above and far below, glowing soft white like that of the structure Quva built below. Uncountable glass doors and walkways line them. Bridges cross over the great expanse in many locations, connecting one side to the other. Strange flying platforms buzz about, and thousands upon thousands of Quva's species move to and fro.

I'm astounded. *This is not just a ship, but a flying city! Incredible!*

Quva startles me when his hand touches my shoulder. "Be careful. We are up a very long ways, and if you fall you will surely die. Now come."

Quva moves along a bridge from our platform toward the left, curved wall. Following, I notice the staring eyes of many of his species, as if I were the strange one. They part down the middle so Quva and I can walk unimpeded along the walkway on this level of the ship.

Along the way to wherever he leads, I peer into the glass doors we pass to see what's going on inside of them. Without knowing anything about their culture or technology, I try to understand what is happening.

One room has a multitude of Vraditi wearing white coats which hang down to their feet, long protective gloves past their elbows, and strange dark face shields covering all four of their eyes mixing different colored solutions in slim glass tubes.

In another room there are Vraditi tinkering with machinery on a table filled with an assortment of metallic items, cogs and wires running to and from different panels.

I return my attention to Quva, but I've lost a lot of ground. He's several feet in front of me, and it takes a brisk walk to catch back up. He looks back, but says nothing about my lapse.

We reach a large platform with solid guardrails on either side. It levitates diagonally upward to the next floor, depositing several Vraditi before returning to this level. Quva waits for it to return to our level. When it arrives, the others move aside and allow us to step on and ascend to the next level alone.

The sensations of moving without actually moving makes me reach out and hold onto the railing. Before I become accustomed, we've arrived at the next floor, and exit the platform. Several room-lengths down Quva stops and turns to a room. Beyond the glass, there's nothing but white walls. He presses his hand on the exterior wall, and the pane of glass is drawn upward, disappearing completely.

He leads in, and begins furiously tapping on his pad once more. A small, closed off room materializes to the side, while at the back a number of different colored, floating panels have been pulled into existence from nothingness. Each of the panels seem to have different characteristics, ranging from wood-like to heavy metal.

"I would like to test the amount of energy you can exert. Start with the weakest of materials at the far end. I will monitor you from inside this safe room."

The enormous glass door shuts behind us, and Quva takes shelter. Nervous about being observed, I hesitate. Through a little window Quva watches and waves me on. Down at the farthest slab of material, I look again at Quva, and he nods. I put my hand up to unleash a shockwave. The sound echoes off of the walls, and nearly deafens me. My eyes shut automatically with a wince, and when I open my eyes again the wood is shattered, splinters covering the floor. There's a ringing in my ears, but Quva speaks, and I can hear him as if he's all around me.

"Interesting. Let me adjust the room's properties to cancel sound."

I attempt to speak, to ask him what he means, but when I try, nothing can be heard. My throat vibrates as I feel the words move up, but nothing happens. Quva waves me on from his room, and I shift to the next object.

A glass piece about as thick as the door waits for me to destroy it. With ease it's shattered. I shield myself from one of the shards as a chunk drops and sends a few pieces flying. Next is a slab of what looks to be marble, and I take out a sizeable chunk with only one hand. Not satisfied I put up my second hand and release a stronger, larger wave, cracking it to the core and severing it in half.

"Using multiple hands changes the amount of power put out?" Quva's voice comes again, and I'm confused at how I can hear him if he's making the room silent. I try to speak again, but nothing comes out, so I nod instead.

"Fascinating. Please continue."

Next is a metal slab, polished to near mirror qualities, and quite thick. One handed impacts the metal and leaves a small dent, and two bows the metal heavily. Due to its strength and thickness I am unable to destroy it. Displeased with my result I put one leg behind me to brace and I focus. I breathe in deeply and pool a large amount of my internal energy. On the exhale I throw both hands out, letting the energy flow freely from me. Arcing out, the room is rocked. The metal crumples and buckles on itself, and my force sends it into the wall behind it. Quva is startled when I look back to him.

"These readings are amazing. I must analyze the data and scans of your body to figure out how your body generates such an enormous amount of energy," he's excited.

I wave my arms at him and point to my throat.

"You are free to speak."

"One more. Make it strong." I grin while pulling my necklace off.

He looks at me, questioning my motives with just a look.

"And you should step outside for this." My grin grows wider, slightly deviant in nature.

Quva cocks his head to the side, squinting in what I take is a wary manner. The glass goes up, he exits, and it comes back down again. I watch him with his pad, and after a few taps a red flashing banner pops up. He taps again and the room's pressure compresses, as if I was under water. My ears feel clogged.

When I look back, a new material I'm unfamiliar with has appeared. It's completely black, solid, and a foot thick. I feel odd with it in the room, like it's trying to pull me gently toward it.

I keep my stance, and place the smooth round crystal in the palm of one hand while the other hand braces it. I focus on my target and channel everything I have through my palm.

He's forgotten to reactivate whatever nullified the sound before, and I'm deafened when my shockwave explodes outward arcing through the entire room. The side walls and Quva's safety room are thrashed as the shockwave rips through. The force sends me flying into the glass, nearly knocking me unconscious, but I keep enough sense to watch. In the blink of an eye the shockwave impacts the material and continues through, shattering it into fragments like a brittle dish being crushed under an immense weight. The back wall is next, and it decimates the paneling. All throughout, the innards of the ship are exposed.

I collapse, my energy nearly exhausted. The glass door opens up, and Quva is frantic.

"What was *that*?!" He's barely audible over the ringing in my ears.

Pushing myself up, I stumble to hold my footing, and dangle the necklace for him to see. "I found out by accident that this type of crystal amplifies my power significantly."

"Where did this come from?" He grabs it hastily, examining it.

"You know how I told you I encountered your creatures? Well these crystals were formed in their habitat."

"This type of crystal is from my home world. It is used in many applications including construction. The coating on the ground you saw on your planet below is this, just in a fine powder form." Quva releases it back to me and scrawls his alien language on his tablet. "But spontaneous growth is unheard of."

"They end up growing to pretty decent sizes, and they can withstand my power to a certain degree before they shatter."

"This is...astounding and unnerving at the same time," Quva is clearly shaken. "To think something of this magnitude becomes available to your species."

"Keep in mind we're dealing with different timelines here. What's done is done, and if you were to deviate from your plans based on your interactions with me, the repercussions might be catastrophic," I warn.

"Duly noted."

My head spins from the exertion. "Is there more testing?"

"Yes, but I need time to study this set of data." He looks up from the pad. "My readings show you are in need of rest. Would it be acceptable to ask for you to stay aboard so we may continue once you recover?"

"That should be fine."

"I will procure guest quarters for you."

He waves me out of the room, and walks along the honeycomb interior. A few more platforms up, we reach one of the enormous bridges which span the empty space. The railing provides me a sense of security, as we are even farther up than before.

When we're across, we walk a couple hundred yards more before stopping in front of another glass pane. Behind the glass is a white privacy wall with a doorway at the right side. Quva places his hand on the wall to open the glass door.

Inside the privacy wall, I'm surprised to find their living styles are not far from our own, though the lack of color leaves something to be desired. There is a large bed, with a couple pillows, and a sheet for covering. A plain desk sits against the wall with a simple chair. The only thing notable is a large black rectangle on the far wall.

"Please, make yourself comfortable, I will be back in a few moments." He disappears from the room.

Slowly moving about, I stop to run my hand across the top of the desk. It's smooth, with no imperfections. I sit in the chair, and though it's hard, it feels good to be off of my feet. I kick my wet shoes and socks off. The bed looks inviting, but I don't want to get it dirty with everything I picked up in the jungle. So I sit, waiting patiently for Quva to return.

A little time passes, and I don't know if it's been ten minutes or an hour, but finally he returns, and a new being enters the room. Its small, oblong, metallic body floats in mid-air. It has long arms hanging down its sides, but no legs. Rather than walking, it flies. It stops short of me, and Quva stands next to it.

"I requisitioned an attendant robot for you, as I may be a little while analyzing the data."

"Thank you? What does an attendant robot do?" I'm unsure if I should be grateful.

"It is programmed for 'level one' clearance and requisitioning. It can provide you with fresh clothes and food, nothing else."

"Okay. Before it gets me some new clothes though, do you have a shower? I need to clean myself up."

"I am unfamiliar with 'shower', but we have a purification system which will clean." Quva points to a door behind me at the back right of the room.

He pushes the door, and we enter a smaller room. There's no sink, shower, or toilet. The only object in the small room is a clear cylinder with several buttons on the inside and outside of it.

"This is our purification system. We use it to clean ourselves, and maintain good health. It cleans both the interior and exterior simultaneously." He presses a few buttons.

"Is it safe for me to use?"

"Our scan of your physiology shows while on the exterior we are different, internally we have much in common. You are compatible with this process." He pauses for a moment. "When it initiates you will have the urge to struggle and hold your breath. There is no need. It is better to simply relax, and breathe normally."

"That makes me nervous," I chuckle.

"You will be in no danger. Simply enter and press the green button to start a basic cycle."

Quva abruptly returns to the main room and I follow.

"How do I requisition things from this attendant?" I ask.

"Simply command it. If it is in the permissions of level one, it will have it created for you. I will demonstrate." Quva turns to the robot. "Attendant, fabricate a white robe to the dimensions of Rain's body."

The robot holds out its hands over the desk, palms facing down, and familiar beams of light appear from them. When the light dissipates, a fine white robe has appeared, neatly folded. Quva picks it up, and hands it to me. It has a silky-soft texture.

"This is amazing. Does the attendant have a name?"

"Negative. The attendant is not sentient and therefore does not have a name. It has a numerical designation. You may just call it 'Attendant'."

"You'll have to explain later how it can do what it does but not be sentient."

"We can share some information with you, however we cannot share all things. I will leave you to clean up and rest for now. I will be back later." Quva turns around and promptly leaves the room.

With the robe draped over my forearm, I turn to head to the other room, but am stopped by Quva returning hastily to the room.

"I forgot to mention. The attendant can be used to contact me in an emergency. Just say 'Attendant, connect to Quva'."

"Thank you."

He nods and leaves again, allowing me to enter the other room. Once inside I examine the tube again. It seems simple; a thick plastic tube which extends from the ceiling to the floor. There is no showerhead like at home, but both the ceiling and floor inside are perforated. The door is its own hinge, attached at an invisible seam, built into the rest of the plastic cylinder. When I pull it open it makes no sound. The robot hovers behind me, and I feel awkward with it being here so I drape the silky robe over it and proceed to remove my clothes, necklace, and the translator. I kick them off to the side.

I climb in, close the door, and press the green button. A soft locking noise can be heard, and I get nervous. The tube quickly begins to fill from the top holes, raining a clear gelatinous substance down over me. Before I know it, it's reached my shins, then my hips, and then my stomach. I begin to breathe heavily, nearly to the point of hyperventilating. When I push on the door to open it, it's stuck.

"What have I gotten myself into?!" Fear clenches my stomach as it reaches my chest.

I try to keep it together, remembering Quva's advice not to struggle, but when the gel reaches my chin I inhale deeply and hold my breath. The goo envelopes me, and reaches the top of the cylinder. A current starts flowing from top to bottom across my body. Suction from the bottom holes clasps my feet, but not to the point where I'm stuck in place.

My lungs begin to burn from holding my breath, and I struggle with the feeling they might burst. I give up and exhale and, while there is some relief of the burning, I now have no choice but to inhale. My mouth opens up, and I gasp like a fish would while floundering on land. The gelatinous substance fills my lungs, and the added weight on my chest brings me near panic. I cough and scratch at the door, but after a moment of my lungs pulling in and pushing out the goo with ease, I cease my panicking. My heart rate drops when it sinks in that I'm not drowning. While the feeling is still unnerving, I am able to relax some.

Why am I so trusting of Quva? This could have killed me.

Because you are a fool. You need to escape while you can.

They haven't done anything to indicate they're hostile. If anything, I've shown them that I'm unpredictable and dangerous.

I am dangerous! These things should be bowing.

Tiberius's thoughts grind against who I'm trying to be, and I'm thankful for the current massaging my muscles to keep me from becoming tense. I lean back against the plastic, and it becomes quite enjoyable, making me forget about *him*. It seems to run through a cycle. The pressure and flow change in various ways, and my muscles grow weak. My feet slip to the other side, and I'm propped up. I close my eyes, and for a moment I'm lost to the sensation and nearly fall asleep, until the speed of the flow increases quickly, and my body involuntarily expels my wastes. My eyes snap open, and I am mortified.

What? Oh! Gross!

The waste is gone before I can shatter the tube with a shockwave. I don't know what to think. After a minute of the quick flow, it returns to normal, then stops completely.

The cylinder begins to drain. When it reaches my mouth oxygen is reintroduced, and I cough to expel the mess from my lungs. By the time I've finished clearing my airways, the cylinder is drained, and warm air blows through the tube. Instinctively I put my arms out and let it dry me. The air stops and I search myself. I'm completely dry, my skin soft like a baby's.

That was…I don't even know.

The door unlocks and swings open with a hiss of pressure change. The robot attendant is still there, hovering in place with the robe draped over it. I chuckle. Feeling a little exposed, I pick up the robe and spin the robot around, despite it not being alive. Pulling the robe around my shoulders, I tie it off, and pick up the translator and necklace.

"Attendant—"

"Attendant at your service," it replies in a monotonous voice.

"Can you scan those clothes and replicate identical new ones?" I ask while turning it toward the clothing pile.

"Understood. Replicating." It sticks its hands out above the floor.

Within seconds it replicates my ensemble of clothing, down to Ami's embroidered orange chrysanthemum. I dress quickly with my back to the robot, the robe blocking its strange black gaze.

In the main room, I drop my dirty clothes and the robe on the desk in a heap.

"Attendant, replicate a copy of my shoes and socks, too."

It does as I ask and then follows and hovers near me, waiting for more commands. I have none to give now.

I lie on the bed. My whole body sinks into the soft, pillow-like surface. My eyes get heavy.

The girls would love this. But I'm glad they're not here. I don't know enough about the Vraditi to want them in this situation.

It's only a matter of moments before I drift off to sleep.

~~~~~~

The room is exactly as I left it when my eyes open, except for the robot now hovering in the back corner. My body feels heavy. My muscles are reluctant to follow my commands. I fight to push myself up. Dangling my legs over the side of the bed, I take a moment to adjust before standing and stretching.

As usual, I have no idea how long I've been asleep, but it feels like days.

Walking over to the robot, it's lifeless, its arms at its sides. Poking it causes it to come to life, but it only 'stares' at me. I shrug it off.

Though I am supposed to stay here, I am interested in seeing life aboard this starship. I head to the door. The glass pane opens automatically, giving me a start. It closes, and I step forward again causing it to pull up once more. Poking my head out, I see one of the large armored beings to my left. It doesn't seem to notice me, or maybe doesn't care I'm here.

The ship is a lot less busy than it had been before. There are still many Vraditi moving about on the different tiers, but it appears to be a quiet time. That doesn't stop the few walking by to stand and observe me for a moment before moving on. I wave, and they hurry off, making me wonder if I've just offended them with some sort of rude gesture.

I suppose I'll have to keep my hand movements to a minimum, just in case.

There is no sign of Quva though. I want to step out, but I feel the guard would stop me from doing so. I return to the interior of the guest room and find the robot hovering near the doorway.

"Attendant, can you create a light snack?"

"Unable to identify 'light snack'," it replies.

I have to think about it a moment, "How about bread with strawberry jam?"

"Permission to access your memory."

"Wait, what?"

"Permission to access your memory."

"Okay?"

It hovers up, reaching its arm out to grab my temple. I flinch and back away but it insists, chasing me around the room. When it succeeds in grabbing my head, there's a light vibration. It stops and moves to the table, creating an entire loaf of unsliced bread and a jar of preserves.

"Wow, that's some light snack." I laugh. "Can you create a knife?"

"Error. Unable to comply," it replies. "Request does not fall within granted permissions."

"Well, how am I supposed to put the jam on the bread?" I huff.

I rip a piece of the bread off, open the preserves, and try and scoop some out, however the bread is too soft and the jam is too stiff for it to work. I'm left to use my fingers to scoop some jam onto the bread in order to eat.

"Attendant, create a glass of water," I tell it before taking a bite.

A glass of water materializes on the table under its hand. While I am gorging myself a noise startles me in the room – the sound of many voices echo off the walls.

"Rain, please turn around." I recognize Quva's voice.

Wheeling about quickly to see where it's coming from, I notice the black rectangle has somehow come to life. I can see Quva through it like a window. He's in a room with many other rectangles with images on them. Moving over to it, I marvel at it, and wonder how it works.

"Are you all right?" Quva asks. "There were reports you had left your room."

"I'm fine. I didn't actually leave, just went to the door and it opened automatically, so I stuck my head out to have a quick look around." I run my hands along the large moving picture of Quva. "I had the Attendant create some food, but it wouldn't give me a knife to spread my jam."

"Understandably so. A knife could be used as a weapon, and does not fall under level one clearance," he replies matter-of-factly.

"Is this some sort of window?" I ask, stepping back from the rather large image of Quva.

"It is not. It is a screen which transmits images and sounds," Quva says diverting his attention to something out of my view for a few seconds, and then back to me.

I wave my hand.

"Yes, I can see you."

"Okay, I have to know. Do you usually host technologically underdeveloped species on board your ship? Because if my life hadn't been a strange ride of insane occurrences already, I might have lost my mind."

"We rarely bring a sentient being on board who is not up to our technological achievements, simply for fear of theft. However you have no means of theft, and would be easy to locate on the planet if you had."

He makes me laugh at his frank response, mainly because there's no malice behind it. "Interesting. What's next for me?"

"If you are rested, we can move forward with the next test. We are going to map and test the capacity of your brain while monitoring your response."

"Is it dangerous?"

"There is minimal risk associated with testing the limits of mental capacity."

"But there is a risk?" I hesitantly respond.

"It is minimal. I will be down in a few minutes. Please be prepared to depart."

The screen becomes black once more, and I'm left to twiddle my thumbs until Quva arrives. The glass door opens up, and Quva appears with another Vraditi.

"Rain, this is my colleague Xera. She will be assisting me in data collection, as it is her specialty."

Xera puts her hands up, facing outward and in front of her chest before nodding at me. As a female of her species, I can't discern any noticeable outward differences from Quva, except for a possible light ridge on her forehead which Quva doesn't have.

"It's a pleasure to meet you, Xera." I nod at her.

"Are you ready?" Quva asks.

"Yes."

Quva and Xera exit, and I follow. We walk a small portion of the length of the ship, reaching a floating platform stationary at our level just off of the walkway. Quva presses on his pad several times, and the platform doesn't just go up, but pulls away from the outer ring along this section of the ship.

I wonder what the capacity is of this ship. Will we ever reach a technologically advanced age like this?

As the platform ascends rapidly, I'm given a bird's eye view of the numerous levels. I grip the rail, fearing the fall. Though it's nice not having to walk, I become anxious. In the enormous expanse I am tiny. Several levels up, the platform stops ascending and moves horizontally. The rooms up here are larger than below, and I'm curious to why.

Still far out in the center of mostly empty space, I strain to see what's inside. There are a multitude of different colors inside many of the rooms; strange animals I don't recognize, exotic flowers, the lizard-men.

"They look so harmless behind glass." I point at the lizard-men.

He halts our advance and brings us near their enormous chamber.

"Do they thrive?"

"I don't know what repercussions telling you will have on the timeline of my world," I tell him candidly. "It might be detrimental to tell you anything pertinent."

"We are hopeful for their species to become self-aware. Is there no way to learn of their outcome?" he speaks with empathy for the creatures.

"I have some information, but if I were to tell you, it must stay between the three of us. You can't deviate in any way from what you intended to do. You must continue forward as if we had never met. Can you agree to this?"

He looks at me, then to Xera for a moment. She exchanges a glance with him and nods.

He introduced her as a colleague, but is she his superior? Or his significant other?

"Yes, this is agreeable."

"I encountered them recently – last month, in my timeline. I can't tell you how long that is from now though. There was a tribe of humans, mostly primitive, who were caught in a catastrophe where the earth opened up and swallowed many. I ended up below the surface in an intricate network of tunnels where I encountered the lizard-men.

"I hadn't seen anything like it before, and they were eating people, alive and dead. I had to fight to save them. We hid as long as we could before one of the tribal people cracked the code on one of your cylinders and activated it to send us topside. But I think she activated all of them in the area. The tribe and I had to kill a great number of the creatures, including one of immense size, for my people to survive."

Quva stands there absorbing the information, and then to my surprise, he smiles and returns us to our flight. "I must hear more, but for now we should continue with your testing."

"Wait. You aren't disappointed – or mad?" I am perplexed.

"Certainly not. To hear they survive long enough for your species to encounter them is still better than their fate on their home world." He doesn't look back as he guides the platform to our destination.

We reach a large room with a few chairs mounted on poles in the floor; one dead center in the room, and two off to the side behind a desk. There are seven of the black screens in the room. Four on the far wall and three attached to the desk. Quva opens the glass door and we step inside. Xera walks to the chair in the middle of the room and places her hands on the back.

"Please sit," she instructs.

I follow her command, and she joins Quva at the desk, behind the screens. They are there a moment before Quva stands back up and brings something over. A dome shaped like a helmet is placed over my head. I look up and see several cables attached to it, leading back to behind the desk. It startles me, and Quva notices my stare.

"Do not worry. It is simply a device to aide in imprinting and measuring," he reassures me. "I need you to keep your eyes directly forward and on the screens as much as possible."

Quva moves out of the way, and the screens flicker to life with white. Through the helmet I begin to hear white noise. It almost sounds like something, but scrambled. The noise begins to increase in volume, and new tones can be heard when random images appear on the screens. They change, and each time it does, the noises change. Beeps and tones, hums and vibrations, garbled language.

The frequency in which the image changes across the four screens to something new increases. They're never the same. It starts with scenery. Fields, trees, gardens, bodies of water, but quickly advances to civilizations, species, cities, technology, and the space in between worlds. The tones begin to harmonize, and soon it's like a ballad.

My eyes dart from one screen to another, only to catch a glimpse before it changes to a new picture. Before I know it, an entire musical piece is constantly being played. I'm entranced. My eyes begin to burn as I realize I haven't closed them to blink in a few minutes, and I am unable to do so. They are completely locked open.

As the images continue to flow, information about the Vraditi become imbedded in my mind. Their development as a species, their history, both cultural and technological. I am amazed when I learn the average Vraditi lifespan is three thousand of their own years and thus their advancement as a species has seen exponential growth.

Mathematics, star charts, spatial anomalies, and universal physics become engrained. I begin to understand a number of scientific facts and theories, including a bit more about temporal mechanics. They move me to their catalogue of encountered species, and their development as well. Humans comes up on the list but, before I can begin to understand how my species exists on another planet before it does on mine, everything begins to blur. I can no longer focus on the information coming in.

"Limit reached. Starting extraction process," Xera speaks.

Everything is fuzzy for a moment before my vision becomes white. My head begins to ache. I flail and cry out. I'm light-headed and dizzy. I am barely holding onto consciousness, and lose all feeling. The darkness I'm becoming too familiar with builds. It's come to take me despite no despair being felt.

"What is happening?" Quva asks.

"I do not know. Something is wrong. The extraction is causing pathways to collapse. There is a buildup of another energy within him. The information is...it is overwhelming him *and* our system!"

"Shut it down!"

"I am trying!"

I'm in the black world for only a moment when I jolt awake. My eyes open, and I see several Vraditi standing over me. I'm lying prostrate on the floor. They are talking, but everything is muffled, and I can't make out anything. My eyes roll back.

I'm thrust into the darkness within. Despair wells up around me, but it's blurry, and I'm not sure what I'm supposed to be looking at, or for. I sense nothing from the Vraditi.

Are they not a part of this collective consciousness?

I begin 'the walk' to move my time here along, and I see the women of my life. I'm confused because I've never had this reach before in sensing people's despairs.

Each one of them comes into view, and I sense they're upset. They feel they've lost me. In my mind's eye I see things through their eyes. They watched as I entered the cylinder, and fear I've been kidnapped. They worry and grieve over my assumed captivity, or death, and that they too will be abducted. They're hiding inside, in the basement. Agatha worries about me being inside the ship when the house shifts through time.

I suppose I'm going to have to tell Quva we need to cut the tests short. I can't keep them worrying. I just need to break out of the darkness.

Having addressed what needed to be seen, I wait for the exit light to appear, like normal. But it doesn't. Behind me, there is nothing, not even the remnant haziness of sensing the women. The imagery is gone.

Pushing to feel for the Vraditi leads to nothing. I am fully alone, and unnerved. Unable to escape the world of despair, my own begins to creep in. Between thoughts of being stuck in the despair forever, and dying away from my family, my heart speeds up. Dying with never having made restitution for my actions as Tiberius causes me anxiety.

I've never not been able to leave before. What's wrong?

I run, changing directions multiple times in hopes the warm light will appear, but there is no feeling of movement. I'm motionless.

"Help!" I yell out, hoping to reach the world of the living. *"HELP!"*

Without a firm grasp on how much time is passing, I switch back and forth between thinking it's only been a couple minutes to several hours.

"I don't want to be here anymore!"

Viewing and being overwhelmed by people's despairs leaves me with a deep scar on my soul; but the darkness by itself with no contact at all is much worse. I concentrate on the girls, thinking about being with them. I think about everything they've done for me, to me, with me. I try to imagine them here.

"There's too much left to do. I can't stay this way now. I have to come back to you. I have to atone for my past." I think of their faces.

My efforts are futile and I cease running. I collapse. My mind going blank for a bit while I lie there, waiting to vanish from existence, only to be reminded I am still alive by a barrage of thoughts.

Maybe I can't pull myself out. Every time I've been here, an external stimulus opened the doorway.

If I'm still here when they leave, I'll be crushed against the side of the starship, and Quva won't know what to do.

Death. My friend. My enemy.

Were it not for Drake's blade, I wouldn't have had these extra months. I would have died as Tiberius, and not as the man the women know. Funny how things work.

I regret not being able to say goodbye. I regret jumping off the plateau. I regret throwing the sword. I regret not loving them enough.

What is love? Is it the feeling you have when you miss someone after being apart even for a short time? A positive emotional attachment? Attraction?

Do I love any of them more than the other?

Ami. The answer has always been Ami. I love her, I miss her.

The questions in my mind plague me. I realize I've been weeping as I inhale heavily and let out a stuttered exhale. I roll around in nothingness, wallowing, and wishing my end would come soon.

~~~~~~

Curled in the fetal position for what could be hours or days I right myself to try again. Throwing my arms out to the side, I scream just to make myself known, and I put significant energy into it. I bellow, trying to break free to reality.

I have to leave. I have to keep my promise. I have to prove to myself I'm not Tiberius.

You will not escape me. You are me!

No, I'm not you, Tiberius – I am Rain, and you are dead. You are nothing more than memories!

I exist, and I will win over you.

Maybe I can reach out to them.

You won't succeed.

I can extend the darkness beyond my body. Can I control it? Can I use it to reach them?

Concentrating on the darkness, I sense the presence within me, latent. I think about the house. I think about reaching out to them as a sign that I need help. I visualize it happening, but as I envision the tentacle reaching for the house there's a sharp shock to my body causing me to lose focus. Another shock sends me to my knees, and I'm being electrified. A yelp escapes my lips.

It must be Quva!

"Help!"

I'm shocked several times, clearly under attack, but it stops and I try not to move again. I recover, second-guessing myself, and my decision-making abilities.

What was I thinking? What did I think might happen by agreeing to accompany Quva and let him examine me?

I would be at the house if I had just refused to look in the book. I should have taken heed of Evalyn's warning.

I sigh and begin to succumb to the darkness again. Before I can slink into self-loathing further, someone calling my name pierces the darkness around me.

"Rain!" it echoes.

Startled and overjoyed, I jump up and look around for the light. Having been in darkness, the voice is particularly loud as they call me again. It's feminine.

"Rain!"

"Keep trying! I'm here! Help me!" I yell. The only response I receive is my name again.

"Rain!"

Without the light to guide me to the exit, I'm stuck. I attempt to reach out with the darkness yet again to whoever is calling out to me. The electric shock hits me again. At this point I am convinced it's an attack to keep me from reaching out. I push harder to pass, only to be shocked harder. I finally break through, and can sense the helplessness of my family.

Instead of just one of the girls calling out for me, each of them has been, and I can sense them. They're near. To my relief the light finally appears in front of me. Despite feeling weak, I'm able to move toward the exit. Brighter and brighter, I approach the light, and when I reach it my eyes snap open to a bizarre sight.

I'm suspended weightlessly in the air within the room where I last was. Pitch-black tentacles are jutting outward in all directions from me. Ami, Eve, and Emma are there. Eve and Emma are outside the room, unable to reach me. Ami has dodged through though. My eyes meet hers. She grasps my hand firmly and I see the darkness in her skin, seeping through the veins in her arm. Seeing her in such a state scares me to full awareness. The darkness recedes, and I collapse to the floor with a thud.

In a rush of movement Ami is on top of me pounding her fists into my chest, and is crying.

"How could you?!"

Her skin has returned to normal. She's unhurt, but she's hysterical. I turn my head and attempt to shield myself with my forearms, but she throws them out of the way, and slaps me hard across the face before collapsing and bawling into my chest.

"I thought you were dead! First the chasm, then this!"

Emma shoves her hands in her coverall pockets and glares, a heavy frown on her face. Eve's eyes are red, burning with agony, jealousy, and anger. Beyond them Quva, Xera, and a group of Vraditi watch from beyond closed glass, clearly observing another experiment.

"What's going on? How...?" I try to comfort Ami by stroking her hair.

"You're a jerk!" She sits straight up and looks me dead in the eye, tears still rolling. She extends to hit me again, but Eve grabs ahold of her. She struggles to get free of Eve's grip. "Why would you do that? Didn't you think about me?"

Eve interprets, "We thought something terrible had happened to you. There were some shockwave explosions, and that led us to think the worst."

"We saw you go into the cylinder thing." Emma takes her turn.

"After you disappeared, we started throwing things down to draw their attention. Eve was ready to kill them. But Agatha said it was too dangerous. We hid in the basement."

I sit up and put my arms around Ami, hugging her close. Her sobbing slows, and the other girls finally break down and join me in comforting her. It's a few minutes before anyone speaks again.

"They began electrocuting you to keep the darkness contained. It was spreading everywhere. They said you had no vital signs, and I just wouldn't believe them," Ami chokes through her hiccups.

Quva and Xera enter the room, and I run my fingers through Ami's hair to calm her down a bit more. Quva has his pad and types furiously on it.

"Have you returned to a normal state, Rain?" Quva asks looking up at me briefly.

"Close enough. I was not expecting that response," I reply. "It's only happened before in a time of danger."

"What was it? Is this part of your *alkos*?" He looks at me in confusion.

"It's not. It's something else. If I thought the test would incite a negative reaction, I would have told you about my condition." I sigh.

"What *is* your condition?"

"A few months back we entered a void of nothingness. In this nothingness was a collective of what I can only call 'souls', who died in despair and hopelessness. Somehow it formed a consciousness, and threatened harm to my companions if I didn't let it inhabit my body." I half-chuckle: my story sounds insane.

"How is this possible? Are you saying there *is* something after death?" Quva stares at me in disbelief.

"In some form. We don't have many answers." I shrug.

"Your explanation explains the anomalous readings we received when we began to extract the implanted information. After a violent display, we were positive you had died. Then the black tendrils extended out.

"Are we in any danger? Your skin turned black and when this female touched you it began seeping into her. Can it infect others?"

"I don't…know."

Quva strokes his chin a bit. He taps around on his pad for a moment and appears to be deep in thought. "There are no reports of damage on the ship. No reports of illness or death. Still, if an outburst of this manner manifests again, we will take whatever action necessary to ensure the survival of this ship."

"I understand."

Xera speaks up, playing with a pad of her own. "We cannot risk another event by resuming the extraction procedure. Though it is dangerous to let you retain knowledge imparted, scans show your mind has already begun purging much of it."

Tapping Ami's leg, I tilt my head indicating I would like her to move. We both stand, but I brace myself against her. My head swims, and I'm nauseous. I look to Quva.

"I need to rest again."

"We will escort you to the guest quarters."

"Thank you." I close my eyes for a moment, trying to regain my balance.

When I'm ready, Quva waves for us to follow. We exit the room to the flying platform. We're there in just a few minutes, and when we enter there are four smaller beds lined up instead of the one there previously. Emma, excited, runs and jumps on the third one down and sprawls out.

"This one's mine!"

Ami and Eve race to the one first in the line. They both jump onto the bed at once, and collide. Wrestling around, they argue over whose it is. I turn back to Quva. He looks at me and squints all four eyes in question. I shake my head.

"Eat and rest. I need to conduct some work, and then I will take you up to the observation deck." His lips stretch into what I think is his version of smiling, but it looks more like a straight face.

They take their leave, and the women and I are left alone. While Ami and Eve continue their fight over the first bed, I lay down on the second with my arms behind my head. I kick off my shoes, and let out a heavy sigh.

Emma stands and begins jumping on her bed. Due to its springiness she is launched high into the room. She lets out a scream of delight, and catches the attention of Ami and Eve. When she comes back down she's launched up again and she giggles. Unknowingly she starts a game. Ami and Eve jump up and begin bouncing from one bed to another, continuing their battle. Emma joins in, and they wrestle around.

"Why don't we just push the beds together," I suggest.

"Oh, you'd like that, wouldn't you?" Ami stops for a moment, and gives me a smirk.

"Whoa there. Not what I meant and you know it. It'd just be easier for you to jump around."

"I think it's a good idea." Eve winks at me.

"You would!" Ami bats back.

Before I can get up, they are pushing the beds together and looking at each other with playful contempt. The floor vibrates and a hum sounds as the material slides across the floor.

Now with one large play area, they resume their jumping and roughhousing. Though they fight each other constantly, they appear to be getting along for the time being. Bounding through the air, they swing pillows at one another. I flinch as it looks like Emma is about to land on me, but she gracefully bounces in between my legs and throws her pillow at Eve.

"How did you get up here?" I ask, my voice raised a little to break through their ruckus.

"After the shadow reached from the ship to the house, they just showed up." Eve huffs while hovering over me and defending herself against a beating from Ami.

She leaves herself open for a brief moment and Ami smacks her in the face with her pillow, and then jumps across to the other side.

"We heard a noise outside, and we couldn't stop Eve from running out to check what it was. It was stupid." Ami sticks her tongue out to spite Eve.

"I took one of the big guys hostage and got us on the ship!" Eve puffs her chest proudly.

"They ended up giving us translators. They explained there was something wrong, and hoped we could help." Emma throws a couple pillows at Ami.

"I still don't think they can be trusted," Eve says, and then hits me in the face.

I flinch and throw my arms up to protect myself as they all begin to beat me. Grabbing my pillow, and shielding myself with one arm, I fight my way up. I swing it wildly to push them back. I bounce rapidly to offset their footing. When they've retreated, I launch my attack. I begin jumping up high, and diving on Eve, bringing the pillow down on to her, then swinging around and popping Emma in her side. Ami hits me from behind and I leap away.

After a long session of play we collapse on the bed. Emma laughs hysterically and, like a contagion, it causes us all to break into laughter with everyone fueling everyone else. It takes a while, but we quiet and relax.

"I'm sorry I've been such a burden to you all." I tell them. "I'm going to be better."

"Rain." Ami caresses me on the side. "We understand who you were isn't who you had hoped, but we still have faith in you."

"I know. But I mean with everything. I am going to try and be better about staying out of trouble. Like this."

I kiss her on the top of her head, and wrap an arm around her.

This is nice. It's a change from Tiberius's violent tendencies seeping through. Despite the mishap with the test today, nobody is dead. Maybe I can change. Maybe I can ignore the dark urges.

You will not escape me. You cannot. We are the same.

I ignore *him* and close my eyes. Lying in a state of rest for a long period of time, my stomach grumbles, and Emma looks up at me wide eyed as her ear was pressed to it. I snicker and sit up. Surveying the room for the robot, it's in the back corner as it had been before.

"Attendant," I call out and it springs to life, hovering over to the edge of the bed. "Can you create a larger table and four chairs?"

"Error. Unable to comply. Request does not fall within granted permissions."

"Attendant, contact Quva," I instruct.

In a few moments Quva appears on the screen.

"How can I assist you, Rain?" Quva asks.

"Can you have the Attendant create a larger table and four chairs?"

Without saying a word, Quva moves around on his end, tapping on his pad. The robot turns and replaces the current small table and single chair with a table large enough to seat all of us. The girls watch in awe while the light beams materialize items from nothing.

"Is that all?" Quva asks.

"Yes, thank you," I reply and stand from the beds as the screen goes dark.

"Attendant, create four meals." I dig into the information left over in my head from Quva's experiment, and recall what the meat was he first fed me. "Generate meat from the *Nuath*, cubed, seared and lightly seasoned. Then a salad on the side from the *Io* plant."

It moves around from one place to another, creating as requested on plain looking plates. When finished, it moves out of the way, and I sit to eat. The girls look at me with bewilderment, and I wave them over to the table. Surprisingly, they sit without fighting.

Picking up a piece of the meat, I put it in my mouth and chew to show them it's safe. They hesitantly do the same, and I can see the pleased looks on their faces when the exotic taste hits them.

"Attendant, four glasses of water," I command.

Four average size glasses materialize on the table and I take a drink. Picking up a leaf of the Io plant, I put it into my mouth and begin to chew. Having chosen the plant for its sweet properties I was unprepared to find it tastes like sweet chocolate. I shovel a few more leaves in to keep the taste going.

"Try the leaves!" I tell them excitedly.

They do and become animated while they chew. Emma lets out a squeal of delight. As we enjoy the meal I admire them for the strength they show to support me. It makes me happy knowing they are my family. We all finish our food and everyone is silent, until Emma decides to share too much.

"I have to pee."

"Well, that's unfortunate." I laugh, knowing the only option is the purification system.

"Why?" Ami asks with a quirked eyebrow.

I point to the door near the back of the room, and the three of them get up to look. When Ami opens the door they peer in, and collectively they dawn very confused faces.

"It's as fun as it looks, too," I add with a snicker.

"What are you supposed to do?" Emma asks.

"Get undressed, get in, press the green button and *don't panic.*" An ear-to-ear grin is plastered on my face as I know it will be just as disconcerting for them as it was me. "I did it."

"That's all I need to hear," Eve says pushing the others out of the way. "I can still do anything you can."

Ami and Emma return to the table, while Eve enters the room and slams the door. Because of the quiet, rustling can be heard. Just a moment later Eve pops the door open a little, and sticks her head out to show off her bare freckled shoulder and neckline.

"If you want to come join me, Rain, I'll let you." She winks and purses her lips in a kissing fashion. Ami runs over and shoves her back inside.

Ami slams the door. "He's better than that."

She returns to the table to finish her meal. The gentle hum of the purifier starts up, and only a moment passes before Eve's muffled screaming can be heard. It makes me laugh. Ami looks at me concerned, but I shake my head.

"She's fine."

"What is going on in there?" Ami asks.

"The tube fills up with *orakos,* a synthetic, gelatinous material which purifies the body. It cleans, moisturizes, expels waste, and bolsters the immune system." I'm surprised to pull up information left in my head from the experiment. "Though when I got in I just thought it was some sort of fancy shower. The hard part is breathing in the gel."

"It didn't choke you?" Emma looks concerned.

"I thought it was at first, but it's compatible with our lung structure. Our lungs simply pull the oxygen straight from the gel. When it's over you just cough it out and go back to breathing normally. Leaves you a bit light-headed though."

"Sounds scary." Emma shudders, shaking her arms off as if to rid herself of a bad feeling.

Eve's cycle ends. Fully clothed, she barrels out of the cleaning room, furious. She storms over to me, raising her hand to slap me, but I stand up and stop her, mid-swing. I smile, and we stand face-to-face, mere inches apart. She scowls at me. I grab a lock of her curly, bright red hair.

"Have you felt how soft it made your hair?" I curl it around my finger.

"You...I..." she stammers, trying to be mad. She smacks my hand away. "You should have warned me!"

"I thought you said you could do whatever I could." I look at Ami and Emma with a grin. "Isn't that what she said?"

They both nod with fervor.

"If I didn't like you I'd be beating you senseless right now. I can't believe you let me go in there!"

"You're a tough girl." I kiss her on the cheek, causing her to calm down a bit, while riling the other girls up. She backs away, sitting at her spot at the table to eat again.

Emma lets out an 'ugh!' and pulls me away by the hand. Ami scowls. Though she doesn't approve, she stays seated and quiet.

"I really have to pee...but I don't want to go in there."

"You'll be fine. I promise. It's a little scary, but most new things are."

Emma's big eyes make me want to give her a hug, but I smile and run my hand over the top of her head. She hesitates, so I gently nudge her. She goes over to the doorway and looks back once more. I nod and she enters.

Eve finishes her food, and moves to lie on the combined beds. Taking advantage of a moment when neither Emma nor Eve are paying attention, I move my chair and plate next to Ami. Placing my hand on her knee causes her to smile. She uses her foot to play with mine. I'm locked into her eyes, and there's that magnetism: the feeling of wanting to lean in and kiss her.

Can I imagine life without her? In that awful lonely darkness, she was who I wanted there the most. She is who my heart desires.

Though we had discussed not starting into anything too serious, that decision, that barrier has already been breaking down. I want to be with her. I want to make her happy.

But before I can say or do anything, Emma emerges with a terrified look on her face. She's shaking, and I get up.

"Shh. It's all right." I hug her and stroke her hair. "You're safe."

"I don't like that at all!" Emma hiccups, trying not to break into a sob.

"It's okay. Let's go lie down on the bed." I look back at Ami, and smile half-heartedly. She returns a full smile, and I can't tell if she's smiling because of my actions with her, or my caring for Emma.

Despite the negative reactions from Eve and Emma, Ami heads into the side room. I help Emma onto the bed, and sit next to her. She rests her head on my chest. I stroke her hair and it seems to calm her.

Dear, gentle Emma, how did you retain all of your innocence living in Chas?

Ami emerges with a triumphant smirk on her face, and I can tell she wants to taunt Eve, but her silence tells me she's thinking better of it because of Emma.

Together we huddle in a pile on top of the sheets, sinking into the soft bed. The urge to use the bathroom sets in before I can become comfortable, and though I squirm and reposition myself, I can't ignore it. Moving the girls off of me comes with quite a bit of protest, but they settle again.

In the purification room, I disrobe and step in. With the cycle started, I prop myself against the tubing. The gel reaches my mouth, and I'm still hesitant to let it in, but I don't hold my breath for as long this time. All too soon it's over. My muscles are relaxed, and I'm sleepy, though it seems like I had just been asleep not long ago. I dress and stumble back to the bed to find the girls unmoving.

"Attendant, lower the lighting in the room."

The walls dim, and I climb into the middle of the bed.

~~~~~~

Awoken by the screen flickering to life, and hearing Quva's voice, I slowly come back to reality. I also become aware my hand is in a place it shouldn't be; Eve's breast.

The girls also wake due to Quva's intrusion and I struggle to free myself. But with Ami practically on top of me I'm unable to pull away before they notice.

"What are you doing, Rain?!" Ami smacks my hand away, hard.

"I was asleep!" I protest.

"It's okay, lover. I didn't mind." Eve's words taunt Ami.

Emma and Ami try to wrench me away, but Eve's arms coil around like a deadly snake.

"Let go!" Emma yells.

"Stop!" I yell, half-strangled.

Ami grabs on Eve's ankles and pulls, while Emma yanks her arms from around my neck. They succeed and I'm free. Quva interrupts our debacle.

"Have I interrupted a mating ritual?" he asks, sounding a little flustered. "I can call back."

"No! Nothing of the sort, Quva. What's going on?"

"I wanted to check in on you and see if you were ready to head up to the observation deck."

"Yes, please. A distraction would be welcome." I distance myself from the three of them.

"I will be down shortly," he says, and the screen turns black.

I have the attendant raise the lighting while we wait. With a few minutes of awkward silence between the four of us, I'm relieved when Quva enters the room and waves for us to follow. Onto another flying platform banked just off the walkway, I hold on to the railing. Quva, never without his pad, types on it a few times, and we move out to about the middle of the ship. It shoots directly upward at an incredible speed. Nearing the top I look down over the railing, observing the city aboard the ship, and its bustling life.

Strange. Before this I would have never pictured a flying city full of life, traveling through space. But now armed with some Vraditi knowledge rattling around, it seems so commonplace. To journey through the stars. What an adventure that would be!

Directly above us on the ceiling, a hatch opens and the platform ascends into it. Inside we find ourselves hit with an amazing, fresh, and flowery fragrance. I inhale deeply and enjoy the calming smells.

We are surrounded by an enormous garden. Through the horticulture knowledge impregnated, I recognize many of the different plants, even in the dark. Patches of wild flowers grow everywhere, and they glow in many colors under a veil of darkness. Trees shimmer in the moonlight as if sprinkled with diamonds. Every type of plant has a unique quality to it, but they all luminesce to create a vibrant rainbow.

The girls gasp with awe and, though I know these plants, I have the same sense of wonder because I've never seen them in person. The ground not covered with flowers, bushes, or walkway is padded with a spongy, grass-like plant. I bend down to touch the lawn of alien grass and it's like silk.

Above us appears to be nothing but open sky, but it's darker than I've ever seen before. The moon hangs over us, full in its brightness, and it's so large I feel I could reach up and touch it.

"This is amazing!" Emma yells, and her voice echoes across the serene landscape. "Oops!"

"It is okay. I specially requisitioned the room. We are the only ones here," Quva tells us.

I remove my shoes and socks so I can feel the silky grass under my feet, and I motion for the girls to do the same. Quva stands on the platform while we venture out a bit.

While the girls wander around and observe, I turn back to him. "Thank you for this experience. I know it probably wasn't in your agenda to have me go into full meltdown."

"We offered a sharing opportunity. It was originally intended to allow you to see and experience a culture you had not previously, but it seems you may have obtained a little more because of the outburst."

"Despite that, we are grateful for the experience and information you have provided us. You, in relation to your species, are a wonderful specimen. But due to the outcome of the last test having such a catastrophic effect, we will not continue further.

"There is still the question of reconciliation between your species, and that of Earth, but perhaps another time."

I reach out and rest my hand on his small shoulder, and he reciprocates. "Another time indeed. I hope you're able to put the information to good use."

"On the chance your planet ever befalls a catastrophic event in which you might need to be moved, it is possible. Which reminds me, we are nearing the end of our construction."

"Will you be leaving the planet soon after the transplant?" I ask him, bringing my hand back to my side. "Wait. You normally take a few weeks to observe the transplanted species for acclimation, don't you?"

"This is correct, however we will stay longer to take readings of the temporal anomaly."

"Makes sense." I nod. "I have to warn you though, your ship can't be anywhere over our patch of land when it happens. The vortex will rip a chunk out of it."

"Understood." He nods back. "But please, do not feel you must stay and talk with me. Go enjoy the garden."

I turn back to see the girls already well ahead of me, running around the plants, stopping to look at new and different ones. Their delighted exclamations and laughter makes me smile.

Casually, I walk a carved stone path, looking up at the stars and moon. With the future uncertain, and my aptitude for putting myself into dangerous situations, I take the opportunity to live in this moment. I admire everything around me, brushing my hands against the fronds of a tree while I walk by, stopping to smell the flowers.

Following the stone path leads me to Eve with her arm against a tree, and her face against her arm. She's counting. When I look for Ami and Emma they're nowhere in sight. I whisper to Eve.

"What are you doing?"

"Shh! You're going to mess me up. We're playing 'Hunter'. Now go away!" she demands.

A child's game? I guess I'm not the only one taking the opportunity to enjoy small things. Her change from brutal tribe leader to a normal, carefree woman in just a few months is strange. Though no more strange than me going from murderous king to who I am now. We're better this way.

The stone path loops around the outside of the circular, domed room. My feet carry me toward the edge of the deck, but to reach it I have to veer off the path into the silky grass. I place my hand on the dome separating us from the cold, emptiness of space. The energy barrier is warm to the touch, and retracting my hand leaves a brief purple imprint. The marvels the Vraditi have engineered make me smile.

Below, the planet unfolds before me, showing me the world like I've never seen before. Though I can only see part of the planet, the illumination from the moon allows me to make out a landmass. It's a strange wonder to behold.

Returning my gaze skyward, I browse the stars and realize, with all of the information Quva implanted into my brain, there is still so much out there I couldn't possibly begin to fathom all of it.

I'm an ant. So many different worlds out there, and I'm stuck in the same place until we break the vortex.

I stargaze for a significant amount of time before being startled by Ami sneaking up on me. She grabs my arm and tugs.

"Come play with us," she whispers while looking over her shoulder nervously.

"I'll pass."

I brush my hand against her cheek to push a lock of her wavy brown hair out of the way, and admire her beauty in the moonlight. She pouts, sticking her bottom lip out and continuing to tug on my arm. I shake my head, and am ambushed by Eve too, as she rubs her cheek against mine from behind.

"C'mon Rain. It'll be fun."

Ami reaches over and lightly pops Eve on the forehead.

"Hey! This isn't how you play the game!" I hear Emma yell while running up on us. "You can't just leave me hiding and not try to find me!"

"I can't play with you. Eve would just follow and attack me in the darkness!"

Eve moves right up into my face. "Babe, I don't need a game to do that."

Emma leaps onto my back, reaching out and putting her palm against Eve's face to shove her away. Eve tries to close the gap by swatting Emma's hand, but Emma replaces her left hand for her right. Ami jumps in and pushes Eve out of the way. Eve just chuckles.

"It's all right – maybe later." Eve backs off.

"You just *let* her in your space." Ami taps me in the arm.

I playfully grab her, and pull her in close. "Would you have preferred it to be you?"

It catches her off guard, causing her to blush, smile, and turn her head away all at once. Emma smacks me in the head, and Eve sticks her hand in between our faces.

"No you don't," Eve protests. "You can't if I can't."

"I'm classier," Ami says smugly while pulling away. "A random kiss is meaningless. I'd rather he meant it, and not just to mess with you."

"Oh, but a single kiss is never meaningless. A missed kiss could be the last opportunity to kiss the one you love," Eve becomes serious and I blush.

Is she declaring her love for me, or talking from past experience?

Ami and Eve both cross their arms at the same time, and glare. Knowing the mood is turning serious, I attempt to alleviate the tension with a little redirection.

"Eve is sort of right. We need to just enjoy each other, and the time we have now, because we don't know where we're going to end up next, or the dangers we may face," I calmly tell them.

Emma shifting on my back nearly pulls me over, and I'm forced to set her down.

We watch the horizon of our world. Light from the sun begins to illuminate the edge, and it's breathtaking. The light pours over it, revealing a little at a time. We watch as the ocean, mountains, and landscape become completely illuminated.

"We should probably take our leave of the ship," I suggest. "Quva has permanently halted my testing. There's no sense in staying here any longer."

"Mother's probably worried sick."

They nod, and we begin the trek back to the platform, cutting directly through the garden, except to avoid obstacles. Quva is still there, sitting cross-legged, and typing on his tablet furiously.

"We're ready to go," I tell him. "We'd like to be taken home."

"We shall arrange your departure immediately." Quva pulls himself up.

The platform drops down, and we exit the observation deck back into the living quarters. As we begin a diagonal descent and move toward one side of the ship, Quva speaks.

"Before you depart, can you tell me if some of the Tarak survive?"

"I'm sorry. I killed a lot of them, and collapsed large portions of the network." I frown. "That being said, we don't know when Humans arise here. The Tarak likely have a very long time to flourish."

"It would be a shame if they never became sentient, but you make an excellent point."

"I think they did. They showed at least rudimentary battle strategies."

This lightens Quva's mood while we fly along. About mid-level of the ship it's apparent he's taking us back toward the main platform.

It takes a few minutes due to the sheer size of the interior, but when we arrive he doesn't stop as I anticipated. Instead we descend vertically, and nearing the bottom of the ship a large door opens up and we exit, high above the land.

I gasp for air. Being so far up, and only restricted from falling by the railing makes me nervous. Wind gushes by me and I inhale sharply.

I look down and the canyons are gone. The green areas which had been plateaus of rock pillars are now interconnected by solid, barren land.

"So this is how our land was shaped. What of the large creatures?"

"Herded away. They won't return to this area for some time. This matches up with your account of your time line, correct?"

"Yes, it does. The landscape changes over the years, but this puts Salvoa on the right path."

As we reach what used to be our plateau, Agatha emerges from the house with a relieved look on her face. Quva lands on the grass, and we exit onto familiar terrain. Ami runs to her mother, throwing her arms around her while I turn to Quva.

"We appreciate the information you have shared with us, Rain." Quva nods at me.

"I'm just glad my near death experience could be of assistance to your files." I laugh.

This strangely makes Quva laugh for the first time in our interactions, and it's weird. It comes out as several short bursts of vibrations from his throat. I laugh a little bit harder because of the odd nature of it.

"In what timeframe will the anomaly occur?" he asks after calming.

"Not sure, a couple weeks of this world's orbit. Just remember to move the ship completely away from this plot of land."

"I will have my Mission First Command reposition upon my return." He pauses for a moment, and then moves to a new topic. "Since we were not able to extract the knowledge, I must trust any bits of technological, archaeological, social, and agricultural information you retain will be kept safe. Such things could be devastating to your world if introduced before it is ready."

"The *Umarak*." I nod, citing a species who acquired information from another space fairing species, and met their demise by creating world destroying weapons with it. "I won't let their fate become ours. I will keep it safe to my grave."

"I am having something sent down." Quva types on his tablet. "We found your weapon while excavating."

Another platform descends, and is upon us in just a few moments. One of the Vraditi guards holds my sword in his massive hand, and it looks like a knife would in mine. The platform lands, and the guard steps off to hand it to me. I nod in thanks, noticing immediately there has been a change to it. Quva speaks up.

"The metal has been fused with lacings of the crystals from our home. Because of your ability to channel your power using the crystal, we thought as a defender of your planet, this would be a fitting gift."

"Defender…"

Am I?

No. You are its conqueror!

I'm not.

Away from the group, I keep my eyes on the sword.

"Your companions mentioned the noble goals you have set and tried to enact." Quva points to Ami, Eve, and Emma.

Instinctively, I know what to do, and put myself into a defensive stance, feet apart and braced for impact. I hold the sword up, and pointed out with one hand while placing my other hand on the pommel.

I force a shockwave out and through it. Rather than the unfocused wave which normally tears outward from my hands, a condensed shock-ring speeds toward the ground quickly. When it hits, it causes a crater, dirt and rock flying everywhere.

"Use just one hand," Quva instructs.

I pull the sword in, and thrust outward with one hand and push a shockwave through the sword. It comes out as a much smaller ring, and creates much less damage to the freshly laid dirt, but is still significant enough to be effective. Dirt splatters around, and I am pleased with the modification.

"This is amazing. I can finally focus it to avoid collateral damage," I grin. "Thank you Quva."

"Use this gift wisely."

This will help me protect the ones I love. I can reshape the world for the better.

Yes. We shall reshape the world for the better. That is our destiny.

No, Tiberius! This isn't about you. This is about protecting people. You had your chance and you destroyed it.

Turning back to Quva I propose an idea, "Quva, may we requisition an Attendant to create some provisions for the house? Simply some level one items."

"We can arrange this," he responds, and types on his pad.

One of the Attendants appears in a few moments, and I beckon it to follow. I lead it around through the basement, resupplying our stock of perishables. When I'm finished, I return the Attendant robot to Quva, and smile in appreciation.

The time comes to part ways, and I extend my hand out to Quva. He squints his four eyes in a questioning manner.

"It's our form of hello and goodbye," I tell him with a smile.

Quva extends his hand out, and I grip it firmly, giving it a quick shake and then release. He nods to me in understanding and turns back to his platform. I follow.

"Thanks for the experience," I tell him.

"It is we who should thank you. The data we have collected, and will collect, is invaluable to our species."

Quva holds out his hand. I take out the translator from my ear and hand it to him. The women follow suit, and we nod to each other. As he, the guard, and the Attendant return to the ship, I wave to him. Within moments they have disappeared into the dark mass. The starship begins shifting slowly away from the house, and stops dead again miles away.

Inside, we sit at the table. I sigh in relief at being home. Looking at the women in my life makes me realize how lucky I am to have a family who would do anything for me, including board a random starship to save me.

I put my arms behind my head and tilt back in my chair, staring up at the ceiling.

~~~~~~

The days pass slowly and we fail to do anything of any importance. Waiting for the time vortex to take us away, our lives continue as normally as possible. We each handle the chores about the house, and I care for the horse and the yard.

Taking a brief break from trimming the grass, I sit and stare up at the massive starship. Despite having some knowledge now of the universe, I am still in awe at the size of it, of the things I still don't know. But I want to.

If I weren't stuck here, I could see myself on a ship like that, traveling vast distances through the stars.

Agatha appears and hands me a glass of water which I promptly guzzle down.

"Thanks, Aggy."

"You're welcome, Rain." She smiles and returns to the house.

The water didn't satisfy. My stomach protests. In the kitchen, I'm met with an overwhelming smell of fish. When I look at the table, there is a full smoked fish on a plate surrounded by boiled potatoes and carrots. The table is set with fine dishes, nice silverware, and tall glasses of deep red wine. While I'm washing my hands, the others trickle in and sit at the table. When I approach they all look at me expectantly. Agatha beckons me to take my seat at the head of the table, and I move slowly to sit.

"What's going on?" I ask with hesitation.

Agatha grabs her glass and raises it up, and the others do the same.

Though I can't see my own face, I feel it redden; I'm embarrassed.

"It's thanks to you," Agatha starts, "that my daughter and I are safe when many bad things could, and probably would have, happened to us."

"Because of you, my days are no longer dull. I used to sit around and sew all day, but now I actually enjoy moving from time to time because of the adventures we have," Ami follows, and my face becomes hotter.

"If it wasn't for you, I'd be stuck in a dying city, married to Denis, and being miserable!" Emma tells me.

"While I didn't join you willingly…" Eve takes a moment to glare at me in jest. "I am glad I am here so that at some point, I can get a rematch against the only man who's ever bested me."

I laugh nervously. "Seriously, what is this all about?"

"We want you to know, who you are *now* matters to us, not who you used to be. You've brought meaning to people's lives," Agatha begins a speech. Tears form at the corners of my eyes. "We don't want you to worry about who you used to be, because you're Rain, and we love you."

My throat closes, and I'm forced to wipe my eyes. I choke back the hidden sadness, and smile to let them know I'm okay.

We dish up and eat. Though I may be looking at my plate, I can still feel their eyes on me. The smoked fish's robust flavor fills my mouth, and I savor every second. We enjoy the meal, and each other's company.

I finish and attempt to wash my dishes, but Emma stops me, pushing me back down into my seat. She smiles sweetly. I sip more wine, and feel my head swimming a bit. When my glass empties, Agatha refills it.

Apparently I'm just supposed to sit here and drink?

Being waited on is not new. Take it in.

They work together to clear the table off, all but for the bottle of wine and the glasses. There is a soft clatter of dishes as they clean everything up. I close my eyes and enjoy the soft, rhythmic sounds. Air moves about me, and I peek. They're preparing the table again. Ami places her hand on mine.

"You can't sleep yet," she says.

Agatha comes up from behind me and places down a single tier cake with a thin layer of white icing on the top. Eve sets down smaller plates while Emma lays down forks. Agatha cuts it up, and everyone receives a small piece. It's a moist, sweet chocolate cake, with vanilla icing.

After stuffing my face with dinner, dessert, and three and a half glasses of wine, I slouch in my chair. The bottle has been bled dry, and I have no doubt each of them are feeling just as dizzy as I am.

This time when I attempt to clean up my own spot, I am successful, but my feet are uncooperative, and I stumble around the kitchen trying to wash a small plate. Behind me I hear a thump, and Emma is face down near her plate, her eyes shut.

"Lightweight," Eve mumbles.

Trying desperately to wash my own dish, my motor skills have been thoroughly impaired when I pull the plate up and it's still dirty. It drops into the sink with a clank, and I shuffle outside without any real reason or direction. Slowly, I make my way to the edge of the grass, nearly toppling over a couple times as I do. Down in the grass, I stare up.

I guess one other thing I can appreciate about being in a time where there isn't a village or city, is there are no competing lights. The stars are so clear in the sky right now.

The noise of the door opening and closing grabs my attention for a moment, and I tilt my head back to see the house upside down. A figure is walking toward me, and it's not until she comes close I recognize it as Ami. She lies next to me.

"Have I ever told you about how my father and I used to look at the stars?" She intertwines her fingers with mine.

"No, you haven't."

"I was really little, but I remember him bringing me out at night and we would look at constellations," she reminisces. "He taught me a lot of them, but I don't see any of them in this sky. I guess because this is so far behind in time from where I came from."

My eyes become heavy from the effects of the alcohol, but I attempt to keep the conversation going, "Did you ever imagine there was life on some other world out there?"

"Not really, but it's probably because I've been too involved with this one." She rolls closer.

I wrap my arm around her and pull her in. She rests her head on my shoulder, and we become silent. The comforting warmth of her body pressed against mine outmatches the cool breeze drifting past the house.

~~~~~~

The morning sun wakes me. Three bodies, instead of one, smother me. Ami is in the same position, while Emma is curled up in my other arm, and Eve is sprawled across my legs backward and snoring. Closing my eyes again, I stay there until they begin to stir. Ami is the first to say something.

"Where did you all come from? This was a private deal," she huffs.

"Private? Out in the open?" Eve mouths off. "He was out here, and that's as public as it gets."

"Well, you weren't invited," Ami sneers.

Emma says nothing, but I feel her move. Ami and Eve bicker back and forth, and I tune it out.

The ground begins to tremor in a familiar manner, and I stay put on the ground. The dark circle of the starship sits in the sky, observing, as the majestic blue vortex begins to swirl up around our property line. The world beyond our barrier blurs, and as a last farewell to Quva I wave heartily in hopes he sees me. All too quickly the sky changes, and Quva and his ship are gone.

I sit up. It appears to be late summer by the heat from the sun, as well as the surrounding vegetation being full and green. In front of us lies a city under construction in an arc around the house, behind us is the forest. We have landed somewhere between Emma's time, and the Forest of Hunger's rule of the land. Far off to the left is a crew of workers tearing into the forest with large machinery, cutting down, and moving it off.

"Mother!" Ami screams at the top of her lungs – my heart skips a beat. "Mother come out here!"

We all climb to our feet and Agatha appears. She covers her mouth in shock.

"What's wrong?" I ask. "What's going on?"

"I think we're home. I think this is close to our original time!" Ami squeals.

"More importantly," Evalyn takes over Agatha without hesitation. "I bet we can find the imbued artifacts I know of. Maybe we can stop the vortex here."

"We can find my father!" Ami squeals again. "We can bring him home!"

"Then," I start, and place my hand in hers, "we have a lot of work to do before this month is over."

~~~~~~

~~~~~~~~~To conclude in REcoil!~~~~~~~~~

ABOUT THE AUTHOR

Thomas W. Everson loves spending time with his wife, Brandi, whom he adores, and their amazing son, Thomas (Bubby). They indulge in the fantastic and stretch their imaginations with books, shows, movies, LEGOs, and video games. Thomas is inspired by much, and loves to test the boundaries of fiction.

Like what you read? A review on Amazon would be appreciated!

www.ingramcontent.com/pod-product-compliance
Lightning Source LLC
Chambersburg PA
CBHW070054120726
47909CB00002B/391